MISS FANNY'S VOICE

Dorit Peleg won the Tel Aviv Foundation Grant and the
Haim Kugel Prize for *Miss Fanny's Voice*. Following the
novel's publication, she was awarded the Israeli Prime
Minister's Grant for Literature. Born in 1953, she is the
author of another novel, *Una*, and several collections of
stories.

ALSO BY DORIT PELEG

White Lines
Una
A Chinese Drawing
Two Fairytales (with Maya Cohen Levy)

Dorit Peleg

MISS FANNY'S VOICE

TRANSLATED FROM THE HEBREW BY
Michal Sapir
in collaboration with the author

VINTAGE

Published by Vintage 2002

2 4 6 8 10 9 7 5 3 1

Copyright © Dorit Peleg 1992
Translation © Dorit Peleg 2000

Doris Peleg has asserted her right under the Copyright,
Designs and Patents Act, 1988 to be identified as the author
of this work

First published in Great Britain by
Jonathan Cape 2001

Vintage
Random House, 20 Vauxhall Bridge Road,
London SW1V 2SA

Random House Australia (Pty) Limited
20 Alfred Street, Milsons Point, Sydney
New South Wales 2061, Australia

Random House New Zealand Limited
18 Poland Road, Glenfield,
Auckland 10, New Zealand

Random House (Pty) Limited
Endulini, 5A Jubilee Road, Parktown 2193,
South Africa

The Random House Group Limited Reg. No. 954009
www.randomhouse.co.uk

A CIP catalogue record for this book
is available from the British Library

ISBN 0 09 927353 5

Papers used by Random House are natural, recyclable
products made from wood grown in sustainable forests.
The manufacturing processes conform to the environ-
mental regulations of the country of origin

Printed and bound in Great Britain by
Bookmarque Ltd, Croydon, Surrey

The English version of this book is dedicated to Edith Piaf, Janis Joplin and Marianne Faithfull.

I

The evening fell grey on the playground. Miss Fanny sat on the bench at the far end of the park and looked at the mothers gathering up their children and dragging them home behind them. The young girl was the last one left. She looked around her uncertainly; the parents had engaged her for three hours at one and a half lira per hour and she wanted the money. She also felt uncomfortable about taking the child back early. But the playground had emptied and there wasn't a soul to be seen except for the woman who sat at the edge of the park and looked at her as if she were made of broken glass, and she was always there. The girl decided there was no choice but to leave and she called to the child in her charge in a high clear voice, which broke against the painted metal poles of the slides and the seesaw planks, 'Uri!'

Uri ignored her cries. He was absorbed in the sandpit in a game unintelligible to anyone but himself, and for that purpose he had dug many deep canals with high towers besides them. Now that he was the sole ruler of the sandpit there was no reason for him to leave. The twilight descending on the park did not bother him and the girl was too young and unsure of herself to impose her authority. He went on playing, digging his fingers deep into the sand that had hardened at the bottom of the pit, and it was only when the girl, having called three or four times, rose from her seat on a tree stump near the swings and advanced on him with a threatening step, that he raised his head and answered her: 'I'm busy.'

'What a pain,' the girl said to herself as if he weren't there within hearing. 'If I didn't need the money . . .' She didn't complete the sentence and said to the child again, this time firmly, 'We have to go.'

'Why?' asked the child.

'Because it's going to rain soon. Can't you see there's no one here any more?'

'So what?' said the child. The reason obviously did not seem convincing enough and he went back to his digging.

Before the girl had time to reply, he raised his head again and added, 'Besides, there're still people here. *She's* here.' And he pointed his chin at the woman sitting up very straight, as though nailed to the plank, on the peeling red bench at the edge of the park.

'That one? She doesn't count,' said the girl contemptuously. 'She's always here.' And in a more decisive tone she added, 'That's it. You'd better stop. Otherwise it'll be like last time.'

The child apparently remembered what had happened last time. He reflected for another minute and decided to capitulate. 'But first I have to finish this hole,' he said stating his terms.

'What's not finished about it? It looks completely finished to me,' the girl said, but it was evident she didn't feel like getting into a real confrontation, or whatever it was that had taken place last time, and she sat down on the concrete rim of the sandpit and watched him.

'It isn't finished,' the child said and without looking again in her direction settled down to his digging. He raked up handfuls of damp sand from the bottom of the pit and transferred them to the top of the tower at his side.

For the first time the girl showed an interest in what he was doing.

'D'you want to reach the bottom?' she asked.

The child made no answer. Perhaps he thought that the question did not deserve one.

'Or is the wet sand better for the tower?' Rather than addressing him, the girl was thinking aloud. She hadn't brought a book with her. She might have forgotten, or it

2

might have been part of her agreement with the child's parents.

'You wouldn't understand,' the child said unemotionally, as if stating a self-evident fact.

He finished transferring what was apparently the last fistful of sand, patted the top of the tower with both hands to make it firm, then jumped into the hole he had dug. From there, unexpectedly, he stuck out his tongue at her, stretching it as far as it would go.

'Phooey! Shame on you,' said the girl. 'If I'd known this is what you were going to do, I wouldn't have waited for you one single minute longer. That's it, we're going.' And she took hold of his shirt and dragged him out of the sandpit and on to the balding lawn. The child let her drag him without protest. Now that he had carried out his plan, whatever it had been, there was no resistance left in him. The girl stood him between her knees so that he couldn't wriggle and forced him into his sky-blue down jacket.

Miss Fanny did not believe that the child had done all that complicated work of digging and building just so that he could jump into the hole and stick out his tongue. It was rather, she reflected, the essential concluding gesture, the icing on the cake, or the cherry on the icing. She looked on as the girl laboriously thrust the little boy's arms into the sleeves of his jacket. The girl pulled the zipper up with a final movement.

Afterwards she watched them as they walked away, their backs to her, the girl tall and somewhat clumsy in her padded jacket and the child tiny, cublike, wrapped in exactly the same kind of jacket. The girl's jacket was red and white. Soon they became two distant specks of colour, red and blue, and finally these too dissolved into the darkness, which grew deeper and deeper, swallowing them both up, and the swings and the big merry-go-round and the whole playground, and the asphalt road and the nearby blocks of flats, and only Miss Fanny remained on her bench, a solitary ship drifting in a sea of mist.

2

By the time Miss Fanny got home paths of rain were already traced on the window. The wind, still gathering strength, was whipping up dead leaves and sweet wrappings, and in the fitful gusts, in the dancing leaves and pieces of paper, she had recognized the harbingers of the true, powerful wind which would soon break out, the heavy showers of rain. She smelled them in the air and hurried to fasten the belt of her coat and tighten her collar and leave, longing for home and a cup of hot tea. The moment she turned the key in the door she heard the wind slamming at the wall of the building with all its force. The large raindrops burst through the netting on the stairwell window and Miss Fanny was glad to get into her apartment. First she took off her coat and hung it in the entrance, where it could dry without getting in the way, and then she sat down to rest for a moment before making tea, but as soon as she sat down in the armchair her hand strayed absent-mindedly to the table next to her and lingered there. She was particularly fond of this table; it was Viennese and she had bought it in an antique shop in the days when one could still buy such things; not the heavy, too massive kind, she would hasten to add whenever she described it, but light, slender and upright, enough for one or two teacups at the most, but with wonderfully sculpted legs. Her hand wandered over the table as if searching for something, and when it encountered the coral necklace she picked it up, as she usually did in moments of distraction, for her thoughts were already elswhere.

The colour of Miss Fanny's coral necklace was somewhere between red and orange, the colour of flame. Often, when she sat in her big, comfortable, shabby armchair, gazing at the fire

4

which did not burn in the artificial fireplace, she moved it through her fingers as though counting the days that had gone by. Miss Fanny had received the red coral necklace on her twelfth birthday, and her father, whose birthday it was too, laughed and said that Fanny's necklace was the most beautiful present of all. They had promised to add a coral every year until she came of age, but only two had been added, one before she left Berlin, and another which had been sent to her in Switzerland, before the letters stopped coming. There was Aunt Leda, of course, but she wasn't the kind of person you felt like reminding about birthday presents, and anyway without her parents there was no longer any point to the whole thing. On Fanny's twelfth birthday they said on the radio that the economic situation was grave and expected to get even worse. Then Fanny's mother whispered to her father to turn off the radio, it was the girl's birthday, after all, and Fanny's father turned the knob until some dance music came on, but Fanny didn't care what they said on the radio. She fell in love at once with her new coral necklace, and the fact that her birthday fell on the same day as her father's caused a secret tremor of excitement to go through her anew every year. Her three best friends, Vera, Lily and Martina, came to visit her in the evening and the four of them tried on the necklace in turns, stretching their necks from side to side in front of the mirror like four young swans, and even Aunt Leda said that they all looked like the swan maidens in Tchaikovsky's ballet. Afterwards they had ice cream and *apfelstrudel*.

The pictures flicker before Fanny's eyes as she slips the necklace through her fingers, their colours slightly faded, though, like a flock of weary swans, their necks drooping. Soon they'll blur and disappear altogether, she muses, and her fingers slowly smooth the beads, each of which has a shape of its own, until they tire and their motion slows and ceases and the coral necklace drops from her fingers on to her lap.

On the day she received the necklace Miss Fanny had a halo of brown curls, golden at the ends. Her curls were wild and sprang mischievously in all directions when she tossed her head and laughed, which she did often. The corals, on the other hand, had not changed. They remained exactly as they had been on her twelfth birthday, orange-red and burning with the same flame, their fire undimmed.

Miss Fanny roused herself and stood up to put the kettle on to boil. She had been partial to tea ever since her childhood, when it had been the pretext for the most pleasant ceremony of the day, lavish with cakes and moist kisses and teasing. Her father, who had been a merchant and travelled all over the world, brought this custom back with him from England, and Fanny's friends loved coming to her house at teatime. Gleeful cries flew from chair to chair, little sallies with no malice in them, and even Aunt Leda's barbs lacked venom, or had she been too young to notice? But even Aunt Leda – and why, she sometimes wondered, did it have to be Aunt Leda of all of them who alone remained? – even Aunt Leda could not spoil the charm of the hour, the sweet smell of yeast dough and poppyseed and still-warm cheese, the fragrance of the tea. Now she tried to hold this ceremony alone; it wasn't the same, but nevertheless she sometimes succeeded. In capturing something of the warmth, of the island of tranquillity floating in the turmoil of the day. And although she could not talk to herself because if Mrs Nussbaum didn't hear her, Mr Rosen certainly would, she was free to think.

She didn't always think of the past. The days went by, umbilically attached to one another, whether she thought about them or not. Sometimes she thought about the firm and wondered whether her pension fund was as good as Aunt Leda's savings scheme or not. In any event, this was the pension fund offered by Bruck & Sons, Import-Export Ltd, and she had no possibility of changing it. She never said this to Aunt Leda, of course. Sometimes she wondered what they would talk about if this important subject no longer came up for discussion during the hour and a half they spent together on Tuesday afternoons. At least once, she thought, she would have liked to surprise Aunt Leda with some amazing remark, cruel as lightning or at least as stunning, which would leave her dumbfounded. But she never did. Or at any rate, she'd never done so up till now.

Bruck & Sons' business was the import of umbrellas. What lay behind the 'Export' in the name of the company Fanny did not know, even though she had been with the firm for over thirteen years now. The umbrellas were splendid affairs, with heavy carved handles, the kind of umbrella sported by gentlemen in Prague or Budapest or Vienna for the past hundred and fifty years at least. It was only about a year ago that Mr Bruck had deigned to make a concession to modern technological progress and begun to import simpler umbrellas as well, with less ornate knobs, but which on the other hand boasted the innovation of opening up at the press of a button.

Mr Bruck had deliberated much before consenting to this compromise, not to say surrender, to the grab-and-run ideology of modern times, and it was only the steep drop in sales over the previous decade which had finally persuaded him to take this step. But then the decline in sales became even more pronounced and even the aforesaid forced entry into the world of modern umbrellas did not do much to improve matters, and in fact Miss Fanny, together with the rest of the staff at Bruck & Sons, did not know whether Mr Bruck alone was unaware of the fact that his firm nowadays also imported articles made of the cheapest and most common plastic, or did know and lived with his knowledge in silence in the old-fashioned office behind the heavy oak desk and mountains of papers.

When Mr Bruck's clientele began dying out, sometime in the late fifties, the part of the firm designated as 'Sons' took the reins. 'Sons' was Mr Egon Bruck's only son, then a young man with a protruding Adam's apple and the vestiges of a certain insecurity in his manner, who saw clearly what his father perhaps also saw but refused to acknowledge, and this was that the old Russian aristocracy, the elderly *yekkes*, the Czechs and the Hungarians, the last surviving remnants of the Austro-Hungarian empire in Israel, were fast diminishing, and were no longer capable of sustaining anything but a small workshop for the upkeep of the kind of umbrellas to which they were accustomed and which they never lost, but certainly not a firm the size of Bruck & Sons, and one morning, sitting before the dark oak desk that Bruck Senior had brought with him from the house in Berlin, an immense piece of furniture which three beefy Thessalonian porters were unable to lift, he informed his silent father in a slightly shaking voice of his wish to add a new branch to the business: the import of a completely different type of product. When he began to describe his plans in detail Bruck Senior stopped him with a weary gesture, and told him in a few simple words which sounded as though he had had them ready for a long while, even though Bruck Junior had not hinted at his plans – which had indeed been brewing in his mind for a number of years – by so much as a word, that he would allow him to try out this new direction on condition that he himself remained completely uninvolved, whatever the difficulties proved to be, and that Bruck Junior never came to him for help or even advice. Bruck Junior listened in silence. His Adam's apple quivered. When his father had concluded his short speech he rose from his seat and in a fit of enthusiasm caught his father's hand and shook it and promised him, his eyes bright with a suspicion of tears, that the line of business he had in mind was not only safe, but sure to succeed and to flourish, and that he, Bruck Senior, would yet have reason to be proud of him one day, and without noticing the expression on the old man's face he turned and ran out of the office, slamming the door behind him for the first time in twenty years.

Behind the door the old man's face remained sealed. He displayed no emotion at his son's burst of enthusiasm just as he had offered no opposition when he described his plans, and it only seemed, in the morning light which was perpetually dim in the old office behind the storerooms, that his features, especially the jaw, had lost a little of their hardness and sunk just a little further, drooping heavily like the jowls of a bulldog.

The very next day Bruck Junior began to organize the new branch of the business: the import of special gadgets from the Far East, mechanical and otherwise, a collection of various objects impossible to group under a common heading, unless this were the term he had employed whem presenting his plan to his father, at which the only expression of the interview had crossed the old man's face, an involuntary twitch of the mouth, and perhaps this was why even Bruck Junior, from that day onwards, refrained from describing them as 'gimmicks', and stuck to the official name emblazoned on the office paper he had printed for himself, 'Unusual Gadgets of an Ornamental and Entertaining Nature'.

Among these articles were sunglasses made in Taiwan whose arms were two naked Thai dancers, and in the Japanese version, a woman on the right-hand side and a man on the left; little figurines, from the strangest imitations of Dresden china shepherdesses (despite everything, Bruck Junior still bore the deep indelible stamp of his ancestral heritage) in flexible rubber, which made it possible, for example, to push the shepherdess's petticoats in or pull them out according to the purchaser's whim, to replicas of Brigitte Bardot, the Beatles and even Elvis Presley, all of them with their mouths wide open and their necks thrown back; reptiles, cockroaches and toads that leaped out of elegant gift boxes; stink bombs in musical boxes, which sneezed after the mushroom of smoke had petered out and cried shrilly 'Bless you!' in Japanese, English, German and, to Fanny's amazement, even in Swedish; and Japanese calendars with pictures of cranes, long-stemmed flowers or geishas. Bruck Junior distributed these calendars in vast quantities among the customers of insurance companies, electronics firms and especially garages and spare-parts agencies, and they were a great success — perhaps the greatest success of the year, as he announced with satisfaction at the party celebrating the first anniversary of the new branch, after his father had left following the short speech he traditionally made to the office workers on such occasions. Mr Bruck Junior presented every employee, in addition to a modest bonus, with a calendar from the surplus stock with a red-haired geisha painted on it in bright colours. The surpluses were mainly of the geisha calendars, but not, as young Mr Bruck complacently pointed out, because this line had not succeeded; on the contrary, the demand for them had been greater than for all the rest, so it was only natural that a few of them should be left over for the office. There were also squares of brown plastic with little pegs, the kind one places on one's desk to clip memos to, but with the innovation that at the press of a finger the device opened up to display a photograph of the desk owner's wife, or his children, or the original picture provided by the manufacturers, that of Mount Fuji capped with snow, or of the naked upper half of the geisha who appeared on the calendars dressed in a brightly coloured kimono. Miss Fanny believed it was the same geisha because of the identical expression in her eyes, a veiled, enticing look slanted at the viewer as if to seal some unspoken agreement. Among the mechanical toys there was also a sweet little dog, Fanny's favourite, which barked and barked endlessly on a high, rather plaintive note when you wound the key on its back, and at the same time wagged its tail up and down amusingly. The dog was an excellent gift for acquaintances with small children or grandchildren, and Fanny had indeed given it to Mrs Nussbaum, her third-floor neighbour, for her granddaughter. A less endearing toy was a pair of mechanical dolls attached to a single rod: when the spring was wound, one of the dolls, the male one, would approach the female with a series of peculiar jerks, and as soon as he had reached a particular point, the latter would suddenly open her legs. The brand name of this toy was Amor Amor. To Fanny's relief it did not do well, and after a short while its order was cancelled and it was no longer kept in stock, perhaps because it was not as sophisticated as other, far more lifelike models, which came on to the market at about the same time. The sunglasses, on the other hand, were a tremendous success, and not a single year had passed since the inauguration of the new branch without the order for this product being renewed. The Japanese also supplied little pictures from the mythologies of all major religions, with or without neon frames. In addition to the above, the firm imported tiny naked dolls made of soft pink rubber, which yielded to the touch of a finger, posters in the spirit of the times in phosphorescent orange or green, and marker pens redolent of jasmine or mint.

Fanny felt somewhat uncomfortable about the new branch of Bruck & Sons, especially at the beginning when the new products had just begun to arrive, but she attributed this to a certain conservative strain in her nature she could not get rid of, and tended to reproach herself about it. She wished she could relate to the strange gadgets in the same matter-of-fact way as the young typists, Batya and Raya, to get a bit of simple fun out of them and nothing more. After all, she reflected, it was not possible that the firm should remain exactly as it had been thirty years ago, when Egon Bruck had founded it. Nothing remained the same. And in her mind's eye there appeared the face of the clerk from the mortgage bank she had visited that morning. There was a measure of solemnity in this visit: she had come to make the last payment on her apartment, and from that moment on, she said to herself as she sat and looked at the thinning hair of the bank clerk whose head was bowed over the forms, the flat was hers, undeniably hers. The clerk wrote down the details with his customary slowness. 'Fanny Fischer,' he wrote, his lips shaping the words, 'ID Number . . .' Miss Fanny wondered whether all those details weren't already noted down on her card. 'December third, nineteen-sixty-five,' he finally recorded the date, and stamped the paper. He gave the little photo on her identity card a cursory glance and mechanically handed it to her over the counter, then stayed his hand and looked at the photograph again. 'Nice picture,' he remarked. He raised his eyes from the photo to Miss Fanny with a hint of criticism. 'When was it taken?' Fanny's neck burned as she replied, fumbling in her purse for no reason, that if she wasn't mistaken it had been about two years after she arrived in Israel. 'Long time ago,' observed the clerk. 'Yes,' said Fanny, 'I really should replace it.' But in her heart she felt a slight stab of surprise, as she always did whenever she encountered the difference between the way she perceived herself and the way the world perceived her. Her twenty-eight-year-old face stared at her from the photograph with a reproving expression. And indeed it was high time, thought Fanny, that she accepted the uncompromising working of arithmetic: fourteen years of mortgage payments separated her from the picture. She had to recognize the change in her and replace the photo with a new one, just as she had to accept the change in Bruck & Sons and stop worrying about it, except she couldn't. And so she contented herself with suppressing any resistance she might have felt and did her job even more neatly and efficiently, if that were possible.

The teacup was already cold. Miss Fanny sat up in her chair. Again, she realized, the old sepia pictures had slipped through her fingers and given way to reflections on more recent times, whose shades were body pink and phosphorescent green. These reflections, which concerned her job at Bruck & Sons, had once been dark brown, but now they too were suffused with the flamboyant dawn of the Empire of the Rising Sun.

3

Aunt Leda refused to change the nameplate on her door even though the fashion which had shaped it had died out over a decade ago. Consequently, the old rectangle of hand-carved olivewood remained on Aunt Leda's new French-polished door, a memorial to times with a stronger attachment to local folklore. Gustav's name had neither been erased nor changed, as negligible in death as it had been in life.

'I'm sorry to say this, Fanny, but you look terrible.'

'I'm glad I can still provide you with a little happiness, Aunt Leda,' smiles Fanny. The old lady pours them each a little more hot tea. They scrutinize each other closely, two wary lionesses experienced in battle.

'And what about that man of yours, Fanny?' asks Aunt Leda. This too is an inevitable question, regularly repeated, the stab of a blunted claw. 'The one with a slight squint in his left eye.'

'He's very well, Aunt Leda,' Fanny answers coolly. 'Head of the foreign accounts department in the Swiss National Bank.'

'*Ach*, so?' Aunt Leda opens her eyes wide, as if she hadn't known the answer to begin with. 'How did you let an opportunity like that slip through your fingers?'

'Temporary paralysis, Aunt Leda,' says Fanny. She takes another of Aunt Leda's excellent butter biscuits and nibbles at it daintily. She's only allowed three: if she exceeds her quota, she knows, she will be severely reprimanded. She wonders if Aunt Leda is as strict with the friends who come to play rummy with her on Monday afternoons.

'Women should not behave like pigs, Fanny,' Aunt Leda would say sternly. And once she even slapped her fingers. But that was when Fanny was still in her early thirties, and in the presence of the banker, then just a clerk at the beginning of his career.

Only once had Fanny asked her, sweetly: 'Do you mean men, Aunt Leda?'

Aunt Leda gave her a piercing look.

'Even if you do grasp my meaning for once, Fanny, it doesn't mean you have to shout it from the rooftops. After all, you're no longer fifteen.'

Ever since then the rules of ceremony have been strictly observed.

'You're not a child any more, Fanny,' Aunt Leda would take the trouble of reminding her. 'How about that savings scheme I advised you to look into? Cost-of-living index only. Forget about the dollar. Have you done anything about it?'

'I haven't got around to it yet, Aunt Leda. Sometime soon.'

'It's your future,' Aunt Leda shrugs her shoulders and takes a praline. 'And it's not that far off.'

'As a matter of fact, Aunt Leda,' says Fanny this time, as she takes her coat from the tall stand, 'the future is already behind me. I reached this conclusion a few days ago.'

This was perhaps the first time she had succeeded in rendering Aunt Leda speechless. She looked at her in silence as she put on her coat.

'And so', she went on, 'it seems I can stop worrying about it.' She leaned over and kissed Aunt Leda on the cheek. 'On the other hand,' she added, bracing herself for the blast of cold wind outside, a dark, hostile winter wind, 'I treat myself every day to a piece of cake at the Ritz Café. They have wonderful cheesecake.

'Perhaps you'll join me some day,' she concluded and slammed the door quickly. Bent double, she abandoned herself to the mercies of the winter storm, striving to get as fast as possible to the nearby bus stop.

Miss Fanny never went into the main branch of the Mashbir department store of her own free will. Or into any other giant department store, for that matter. She was very much afraid of them and tried to avoid having to go into them, even though she never admitted it, even to herself. She was ashamed of this weakness of hers.

To Mr Aviad, the deputy manager of the store and the person in charge of Winter, who had been summoned from his office to attend to her, she seemed a big blurred face floating in the space of his store. This illusion might have been created in part by by the steamy breath of the people crowding the shop floor, mingled with the vapour rising from their wet woollen coats in the heated air and with a general, stifling sense of winter, back pressed to back, red noses gradually thawing to their natural colour. Mr Aviad sometimes tended to see things not quite where they were, and certainly not where they were supposed to be. Mr Pinkas, the head manager, once said of him in a moment of annoyance that he should have been a poet, but when he saw Mr Aviad's pale face and his wounded eyes he was immediately sorry and said that he was joking, of course, and that Mr Aviad should not take things so seriously. It was however, precisely this seriousness which he valued most highly in Mr Aviad, and which was responsible for his promotion to the post of deputy manager.

When Mr Aviad realized his eyes had been playing tricks on him again, he quickly shook his head and approached the woman with the same brisk, wrathful stride that had carried him out of his office, before her face suddenly appeared before him and had him all confused. Mr Aviad was angry at having been summoned from his office – him, that is to say the deputy manager of the store, the highest executive level – right in the middle of the feverish preparations for the transition, always so difficult, from the winter to the spring season, a transition which he wanted to complete as quickly as possible in order to take the responsibility for the contents of the store off his own shoulders and transfer it to those of Mr Kitov, who was in charge of Spring. But this woman, what's her name, something with an F, insisted on seeing him and him only. Mrs Zelnick had said, surprisingly, that she didn't actually seem like a pest, and that she had asked her to say she hadn't come on her own account, but on behalf of someone or other whose name Mr Aviad could not for the life of him remember, even though Mrs Zelnick had all the details off pat, confound the woman, she had a memory like a computer, but as soon as he stood up to circumnavigate his memo-laden desk the problem of reductions on imported fashions popped into his head and the blasted names flew out of it. Something with a B.

The moment the woman opened her mouth he understood Mrs Zelnick's reaction because there was really something very pleasant about her, quite unlike the shrill tones of complaint he was used to hearing from customers who demanded to see the manager. Apologetically she said that her name was Fanny F., the name immediately escaped his overloaded memory again, but people called her Miss Fanny, and that she was here on behalf of Mr Bruck. At the sight of Mr Aviad's blank face she hastened to explain, lest any misunderstanding should arise, that she was referring to Bruck & Sons, Import-Export, and when this too failed to produce any sign of recognition on the deputy manager's part she went on to explain that it was a big import company (and export, she added quickly, but she was unfamiliar with that side of the business), dealing in umbrellas. 'And unusual gadgets of an ornamental and entertaining nature,' she concluded almost despairingly. Only than did the light finally dawn on Mr Aviad. Bruck & Sons, Import-Export! Yes, yes, he knew them well.

Miss Fanny's face lit up. In that case, she could go straight to the heart of the matter, that is to say, the matter for which she was here. Mr Bruck – Mr Bruck Senior, she meant – was very concerned about the decline in the sales of his umbrellas in their department store. For some years now sales had remained fixed at an exceedingly small number, and she had been sent, to tell the truth (here she blushed hotly and red spots blossomed on her cheeks and neck), to find out whether the quality products of Bruck & Sons were being properly displayed, in a manner that would attract the notice of the customers. What Mr Bruck had actually said, in his gruffest voice, was that he was sure those scoundrels were hiding his superior products in some obscure corner where nobody could see them, so as not to harm the sales of the cheap rubbish which yielded them a far higher profit. But when she had reached the store, and searched all over, and she could assure Mr Aviad that she had searched thoroughly, she had found no trace of Mr Bruck's elegant umbrellas with their sculpted handles, and as the deputy manager knew for himself – here she permitted herself a faint smile – the products in question were of a very substantial nature. Here she stopped and took a deep breath.

Mr Aviad became aware of the ticklish sensation in his stomach of incipient nausea, which always preceded moments of extreme unpleasantness. He cursed, not for the first time, the principle which made him insist on dealing with every irregularity in person, rather than passing it on to his assistant, as he could and in fact should have done. First he cleared his throat to gain some time, but Miss Fanny's eyes, fixed on him with confident expectation through what was quickly turning into a dense smokescreen, would not allow him to prevaricate, and he had no choice but to dive, head first, into the facts.

'. . . so the truth is, Miss Fanny, that for at least three years now we have not been marketing Bruck & Sons' umbrellas, and it's only due to this special arrangement we have with Bruck Junior, or, to be more precise, due to this personal

17

favour we're doing him, that we go on acquiring a certain number of umbrellas every winter, in return for an equivalent amount of ornamental articles from your other branch, because I don't need to tell you, Miss Fanny, that we can't be expected to purchase products that are a total loss, or we would have gone out of business long ago, ha –'

Miss Fanny's eyes, huge and wide open in astonishment, unintentionally cut short Mr Aviad's nervous laughter, a smoke-strangled bark. She appeared not only to take a step backwards, but to shrink and withdraw into herself. Mr Aviad closed his eyes, so as not to see the stunned face hovering in front of him, and with the cruelty of desperation went on to say what he should have already said a year before.

'And I must tell you, Miss Fanny, that next year we won't be able to continue with this ... hmmm ... arrangement, even if Mr Bruck did study at the same gymnasium as Hoffstatter from the Board of Directors, because we can't keep in our warehouses goods for which we have no use. The warehouses are getting fuller every year, there are always lines we have difficulty in selling, and soon they'll be full to the brim, and then, ha –'. And in the eye of Mr Aviad's mind there rose a new, apocalyptic image, that of the warehouses exploding under the pressure of unsold goods and with a mighty bang sending them flying in all directions, armchairs upholstered in modern fabrics, bottles of body lotion, leather belts, an entire army of articles, too many to count, all soaring in a great arc towards the expectant crowds, who fall upon them with cries of joy.

Miss Fanny, her face pale, retreated with the little bird-like steps of a woman from another generation, when girls were drilled in the manner of walking becoming to a lady as if these were dance steps, until there was no need to think of them any more. Her eyes were fixed on Mr Aviad with the gaze of a mesmerized bird, but she evidently did not see him, since she never responded to his pleas that she come into his office and have a glass of water, at least, or of grapefruit or orange juice, or to the almost desperate calls with which he tried to bring her back, even though he himself had no idea what he would say to her if she actually turned around and came back to him from her hurried, stumbling flight between the rows of elegant Marks & Spencer petticoats; entreaties that did not become a department manager in the least, as he realized later in his office, his ears burning, and in the presence of customers, too.

In the cosmetics department Miss Fanny had to stop for a minute to recover her breath. How she was going to repeat the things she had just heard to old Mr Bruck, she did not know and did not want to think about. For a moment it crossed her mind not to go back to the office at all, but this was not a practical proposition after thirteen years. The only way out she could think of was to tell Mr Bruck that she had looked for the umbrellas and found them, as he had suspected, badly placed, but that all her efforts to persuade the manager to move them elsewhere had been to no avail. But then Mr Bruck would emerge from his dark office over the yard, like a bear from its lair, and for the first time appear in person in the Mashbir – which he detested from the bottom of his heart, just as he detested all other department stores – to demand his rights. No. She would say that she had found them well placed. But then why weren't they selling? The best products on the market, sir, nothing to touch them, for thirty-six years. No: now she had found the right solution. They had in fact been pushed into a corner, but she had appealed to the sales manager, and before her very eyes he had them moved to a prominent spot, to the best place in the whole store for the display of umbrellas.

Fanny breathed deeply. She felt as though she had just reached the end of a long race. Now, in order to compose herself, she forced herself to remain standing next to the pillar against which she had been leaning and to look around.

The place was full of women. Women, women and more women filled the aisles between the counters, talking to each other in a mysterious birdlike code which for one moment of panic was completely incomprehensible to Miss Fanny, as though she had lost her command of language. After a short stab of alarm, however, the words took on meaning again, and Miss Fanny understood with relief that the two women next to her were discussing the advantages of woollen over synthetic, or partly synthetic socks, which last they dismissed with contempt. A few of the women dragged along a male escort, a son or a husband, but it was clear from the way in which he trailed behind them, an appendage of secondary or no importance, that his presence was of no more significance than that of a peg on which to hang the articles collected from the shelves, or a dummy against which to measure the shoulders of a flannel shirt. Fanny suddenly longed for the comforting presence of a man, any man who would be hers like the touch of a warm shoulder in winter, no more than that, and just the thought of it filled her with a warm, comfortable feeling. She took another deep breath and expelled it with a sigh. The two women next to the cash register paid and picked up two bags holding four pairs of Orlon socks each.

Fanny trudged along the wintry street, only half-heartedly struggling against the cold wind and letting it delay her on her way. Today more than ever the street, which had only a few shops and was mainly firms and offices like hers and one restaurant for businessmen, seemed bleak and unwelcoming. The street was a kind of preparation for the peeling entrance to the building which housed the office, for the gloomy stairwell, and for Mr Bruck's face when she told him the tidings she had invented. She lingered for a moment outside the wholesale coffee establishment and watched the old mill grinding the beans, but even the smell of fresh coffee brought her no comfort. In the end, for lack of any alternative, she began going up. She knocked on the old man's door and went in. At the sight of his face she was struck dumb and could not bring herself to utter even one word, but there was no need for it. Mr Bruck gave her a long, penetrating look and dismissed her with a wave of his hand. She beat a hasty retreat, stumbling over the high threshold, which always tripped her up when she was nervous. For some time, rustling the papers on her desk to no avail, she tried to convince herself that Mr Bruck could not possibly have guessed all that she had heard that day, but her thoughts had a hollow ring to them and she did not really believe them. Mr Bruck had no illusions about business concerns like the Mashbir. He knew that they wouldn't acquire for no good reason merchandise they could not sell. No, Mr Bruck was now fully aware of the true state of affairs and Fanny never wanted to see his tired face again.

5

From the window of Mrs Nussbaum, the upstairs neighbour, came the sounds of hesitant, untrained singing. A sequence of clear-cut piano notes followed in rapid succession, and Miss Fanny could hear Vera Nussbaum saying, her voice faint in the violet–grey twilight air, 'G, Netta. That wasn't G.'

The childish voice hesitated for a moment, as if vacillating between the countless possibilities offered by the evening, and began singing again: '*Seit – ich – ihn – ge – se – hen . . .*' Netta's heart was clearly not in the Schumann *lied*. Miss Fanny's heart contracted with longing.

'That's better,' said Mrs Nussbaum's disembodied voice, 'but you haven't grasped the intonation yet: "*Seit – ich – ihn – ge – SE – hen . . .*" Not "tse" but *se*, zei. Von Chamisso did not write in Chinese.'

Netta's voice did not join in Mrs Nussbaum's deep laughter. When the laughter died down, she began the passage anew: '*Seit – ich – ihn – gesehen, glaub – ich – blind – su – sein –*'

'G again,' said Vera Nussbaum. 'You have to hold the G.'

Miss Fanny went into the house. The sounds of singing were cut off as soon as she began climbing the stairs: Mrs Nussbaum's door was soundproof. These were the terms laid down by the neighbours when she came to live in the building, once they learnt that she gave singing lessons. Fanny knew it was no longer fashionable to call them by this name, but she couldn't bring herself to call them anything else. Fräulein Neuerbach would have never dreamed of calling her lessons 'Voice Lessons'. They were singing lessons.

When Fanny reached the door of her apartment, a particularly loud piano note managed to break through the soundproofing and reach her ears. It was a G major chord. The injustice inflicted on the Gs must have exasperated Mrs Nussbaum until her patience snapped. 'G – G,' Fanny heard her say and in her mind's eye she saw Netta standing before her, her hands folded on her stomach, her downcast eyes staring fixedly at the floor as she repeated the note in rebellious obedience, a rebellion which broke down when Mrs Nussbaum wondered aloud how, for God's sake, she imagined she could produce any sound at all with her chin pointed down at the floor and the passage blocked, child, completely blocked. Before Miss Fanny's eyes rose with absolute clarity, as if it were happening at this very minute, the picture of her own singing lessons with Fräulein Neuerbach.

'No, Fanny,' said Fräulein Neuerbach with acquired patience, 'you're singing a B flat. And this song is written in D major.'

Fräulein Neuerbach sighed.

'It's really a strange way you have, Fanny, of singing all your notes flat!' she said in an aggrieved tone, as if this were some extraordinary perversion, a grave transgressing of the laws of nature, the casting off of all restraint.

She once heard her say to her mother: 'Everything would be all right if it weren't for this obstinacy of hers. Once she decides to be pigheaded about something, you can't budge her an inch!' And her mother nodded her head as if she understood exactly what she meant, although with Fanny's mother you couldn't tell if this was out of absent-mindedness, because she wasn't really listening, or whether she was indeed familiar with this obstinacy of Fanny's that Fräulein Neuerbach was complaining about. But Fanny was not being obstinate at all, on the contrary, her great and burning ambition was to learn to sing in the purest possible way, the one truest to feeling, and then to conquer the concert platform like her idol, Elisabeth Schumann. But she heard the world flat and this must have been the reason why she had never succeeded in finding her place in it the way most people she knew had. Somehow she always lagged at a distance from the right note. Something was out of tune.

Miss Fanny suddenly realized that she had forgotten to buy cottage cheese. And without cottage cheese to spread on her bread there was no point in the whole salad. She sighed, took her purse out of the handbag that lay on the chair and put her coat on again.

As she left the building she heard Mrs Nussbaum's voice humming the beginning of the next line of the *lied*. Her voice was not in the least musical, in the sense of being pleasant to listen to; it was stiff and limited in range, but it conveyed the notes with absolute accuracy: *tum-tum*. 'Repeat after me,' she said.

Netta's hesitant, slightly broken voice tum-tummed after her obediently. She's a little too high, thought Fanny, and indeed Mrs Nussbaum wasn't long in pointing that out. Fanny wondered if Netta, with her broken voice, had any chance of ever becoming a real singer and immediately suppressed the thought which followed, that perhaps it would have been more fair on Mrs Nussbaum's part to dismiss Netta; and reminded herself that today singing was taught not only to make the pupil into a famous opera singer, but also to correct speech defects, in enunciation for example, or to bolster a faulty self-confidence, and that as far as Netta was concerned it would probably be of more use to her if she knew how to accompany herself on the guitar, than if she were to become another Elisabeth Schumann.

In the grocery store, once she was there, she bought not only cottage cheese but also a little piece of smoked fish, which she liked but considered a luxury and so rarely bought, and six eggs, so that she wouldn't have to carry them home with her on her next big shopping trip. Perhaps they would even tempt her to bake a cake. She asked for some baking margarine too, just in case.

'Baking a cake, Miss Fanny?' Avram asked.

She smiled at him. 'I might.' She liked this familiarity,

which allowed the grocer to take an interest in the use that was made of his merchandise, this closeness between people, which was sometimes too stifling and chafed her, but in which she usually found some encouragement, or at least consolation, and it prevented her from feeling lonely.

'You should put on your hood, Miss Fanny,' she heard him call after her. 'They said on the radio it was going to rain.'

She nodded and smiled even though he couldn't see her, transferred the eggs to her other hand and with her freed hand raised the hood of her coat so that it covered her head. The air had indeed turned sharper and colder, heralding the approaching rain, and it pinched her nostrils. She breathed it in deeply. There was almost nothing in this country she loved more than the air before it rained, and the smell of the earth afterwards. Perhaps, she reflected with a sudden pain, because it reminded her for a moment of her native land.

But surely it was possible to love something just for its own sake? She quickened her step, her enjoyment of the tranquil evening somewhat spoilt, but as soon as she turned into her own street her thoughts cleared and she lifted her face upwards, taking in the sky. The evening was growing darker. The sky was now a deep blue-grey, with streaks of a darker purple, and in contrast to the azure summer sky, which because of its transparency always seemed far away, it seemed to lie right on the street, enveloping the houses on either side and the children on their skateboards and the few cars and Fanny herself, as though they were all swimming in a palpable substance, liquid and hazy, which was the evening.

On the third floor the lesson was about to end. She heard Mrs Nussbaum say: 'That wasn't bad, Netta. Let's hear the first verse one more time.'

'Up to the end?' asked Netta.

'Up to wherever we get,' said Mrs Nussbaum and embarked on her deep laugh. After a while Fanny heard Netta's laughter joining her, more cautious, fainter, a little halting. She hasn't yet learnt how to breathe properly, she thought.

Again the wonderful strains of the song filled the street: '*Seit – ich – ihn – ge – se – hen . . .*' and Fanny put the basket with the eggs and the smoked fish and the cottage cheese on the low wall in front of the building and sat down next to it, listening. This time Mrs Nussbaum did not correct Netta's singing and let her continue to the end of the passage, even though this time as well she hit the G too high. The purple had all seeped away and the sky turned a true, piercing blue. You couldn't put your finger on anything, and Miss Fanny did not bake a cake that evening.

6

The next day it rained hard all afternoon. Fanny sat at home, looking at the rain trickling down the window in long snail-like streaks, and thought about the child Uri and what he might be doing now. She wondered what the girl who looked after him would say if she went up to her one day and offered to take her place, and whether she would look at her suspiciously if she said there was no need to pay her. The girl's face looked out at her from the window, the streaks of rain tracing on it a puzzled expression. Finally she decided to go to the cinema.

At six o'clock the street was already dark and the lights of the restaurants and cafés glittered like promises not made to her. She walked quickly, tightening her coat around her body, until Dizengoff Street ended and with it the people who sat there behind glass like rare delicacies inside a showcase, warm and protected.

The cinema's box office shone out from the dark, igniting sparks of rain in the faces of the people standing in the queue. They shielded their heads with the raised collars of their overcoats and a few of them with rolled-up newspapers, which became soaked and wilted as the waiting wore on. Miss Fanny looked at the glass pane behind which glowed the heroine of the film, a beautiful woman with long hair and very red lips, bent backwards at an impossible angle. For a moment she wondered whether her choice of film had been the right one, but it was already too late to look for another cinema and she was carried along in the rush of bodies until she reached the box office and bought herself a ticket.

In the entrance she was met by the damp smell of wet hair

mixed with the hot breath of popcorn from the machine on the counter. She found herself a corner to stand in and looked at the faded green carpet, which had tiny flakes of dirt and brown popcorn kernels stuck on to it, and breathed in the familiar smell. All at once she was assailed by all the evenings she had spent with Nathan in this cinema, in other cinemas, but always on the same carpet, and for a moment she tried to feel as if she was really standing there beside him, but very quickly this picture shattered against the incontrovertible presence of a man and a woman who were standing right next to her, drawing fistfuls of popcorn in a mock, giggly squabble from the large cone the man held in his hand. The cuffs of their coats were still dripping small drops of rain on to the carpet.

A distant bell sounded and everybody began streaming towards the door of the theatre. Fanny waited for a moment and then mingled with the crowd and was swept inside. The usher showed where her seat was and she hurried to her row and sat down with a sense of relief. In a minute the lights went out and the newsreel came on. The flickering circles made way for a tall crane mining minerals in the Dead Sea and Fanny heard a voice on her right say with breathy impatience, 'I'm sick of these newsreels, I've seen this one already three times this week,' and after her eyes grew used to the darkness she recognized the couple who had stood next to her earlier in the foyer. The man was still holding the cone of popcorn, but now they both drew out of it unhurriedly, at long intervals, and only a few kernels at a time. Their heads were pressed together, forehead to forehead, and they looked into each other's eyes even while they were munching the popcorn.

After a few minutes the screen turned white again and the lights in the theatre came on. The faces of the audience were cut out sharply in the strong light and Fanny shrank in her seat and tried to look down the front of her coat. The man and the woman next to her whispered again and immediately fell silent, and she felt their eyes on her intensely although she didn't know whether this sensation was true. She shoved her hands deep into her coat pockets and closed her eyes. She'd have done better to stay at home.

Through her closed eyelids she felt the darkness thicken and opened her eyes. The film's opening credits began scrolling on the screen, each letter in a different colour and slightly skewed from its neighbour, so that the lines went up and down in a gay, florid zigzag. Fanny smiled and sat up in her chair, intending to forget the theatre and especially herself for the next two hours, but the couple again crowded into the corner of her eye and now their profiles had almost merged into one, for they were kissing passionately, their arms moving up and down each other's body, travelling tiny, unmeasurable distances on the damp coat, up and down, sinking into the soft body of the loved one and again emerging, up and down, a ship dipping and rising, and Fanny had no choice but to follow these movements with the precision of a lab instrument, bobbing up and down with them, her lips moving, trying to recover in herself, with the desperation of a landlocked sailor, the lost rhythm of the waves.

7

It was a cold, cloudy day. Every fifteen minutes or so a weak drizzle would come down unenthusiastically and immediately cease. There were few passers-by in the street, their faces hidden under their umbrellas or inside the collars of their coats, and a warm feeling of relief pervaded Fanny as she pushed the glass door open and entered the Ritz Café.

She liked this café and went there at least once a week and sometimes more, if she had the time. There she never felt peculiar or out of place. The habitués of the Ritz were almost all of them more peculiar than she was. And all the magazines from home were there, *Stern* and *Die Welt* and sometimes even *Frau und Heim*, no more than three weeks old. Had Batya and Raya known of her fondness for these magazines she would no doubt have sunk in their estimation and immediately become just another middle-aged *yekke*, but at least in the Ritz, where she was in no danger of meeting anyone from the office, she allowed herself the luxury of reading them.

Another reason she liked the Ritz was that although it was very different from the noisy, crowded cafés of Berlin, it somehow reminded her of home. It had something of the cafés of Charlottenburg about it, at any rate as she remembered them from the few occasions she went there escorted by her mother, or, more precisely, as her mother's escort. Perhaps it was, in addition to the newspapers, the presence of so many people from home: whenever she went into the café her ears immediately caught snatches of familiar speech. Certainly the elderly owner of the place, who was also the waitress, contributed to this feeling with the frilly white apron securely tied around her waist and broad hips, with the silence in which she approached you, patiently waiting for your order. And perhaps it was the simple fact that she could go into this café and sit there alone without her loneliness becoming so painful. Here in Israel, it seemed, people were not in the habit of going to cafés by themselves, but in couples or in large, noisy groups, so that after a few minutes of sitting by herself her loneliness would grow so intense that she wouldn't be able to take it any more and she'd get up and leave. To the Ritz people mostly came by themselves. She liked the way they sat down at their tables and relaxed, especially the men, stretching their legs out in front of them, pulling their hats down on their foreheads, their cup of coffee or beer at their elbows, the newspaper spread out on the table. No one bothered their neighbour once they saw him slump into this position. And yet at the same time, if you wanted to talk, there was almost always someone to talk to.

The man stood up and negotiated the two tables separating them. 'The Fräulein has a light, perhaps?'

There, she said to herself as she rummaged in her bag, which was too full as usual, only a minute ago I glanced at him and thought that he looked interesting, and all by himself, and that it might be nice to talk to him for a while. And here he is.

'Although I'm a very light smoker,' she said and handed him the box.

'Whereas I'm a heavy smoker, and I almost never have any matches on me,' he said with a deprecatory half-smile.

'Perhaps that's why,' laughed Fanny.

'You have a point there,' he agreed and lit the match and raised it to the cigarette in his mouth. His lips were thin, slightly curving at the corners, and his nose was a little arched. His brown hair was already beginning to recede at the temples and at the top of his forehead, but nevertheless, Fanny concluded to herself, he was definitely an attractive man.

'May I sit next to you?' he asked, as if she had already given

31

her consent, and indeed she had. 'It's more fun than sitting alone.'

'That's true,' Miss Fanny laughed, and felt that she was all radiant and sparkling, like one of the stars in the films she used to see in her childhood. Somehow she felt carefree and light, as if whatever she tried to do now would come to her easily.

His name was Ritzi, or more precisely his nickname, short for Ferenz, and they joked about this for a long while. What better place to meet Ritzi than at the Ritz, or: At the Ritz with Ritzi. He was Hungarian and Miss Fanny claimed that she had guessed this at once because there was something about Hungarian men . . . she said and did not complete the sentence, surprising herself too, or mainly herself, since he did not know her and could not have guessed, therefore, that a remark of this sort, and indeed her behaviour today altogether, were quite unlike her. He urged her to tell him what it was about Hungarian men that made them different, and she laughed and blushed and protested, and said finally: a certain chivalry. This he agreed to immediately.

Suddenly they saw that three hours had passed. They also found out that they were both very hungry. And then Fanny discovered, to her surprise, that one could also order light meals at the café, cheese or mushroom omelettes, for example, or blintzes, and various similiar dishes. It had never occurred to her to ask, but to tell the truth even had she known she would not have eaten there. There was nothing drearier than eating alone in a restaurant. The food would have stuck in her throat, she would have felt on display with every forkful she brought to her mouth. Whereas now she ate cheerfully and chattered to Ritzi without taking any notice of the people around them, and they took no notice of her. Ritzi had already eaten there before, by himself as well, but for him it was different: he was a man.

And they even managed to make it to the cinema in time for the second show. It was an adventure movie, Fanny didn't remember its name because they had run to the cinema so as not to be late and were past the billboard in a flash, and even though she had managed to read the name she immediately forgot it as they hurried down the stairs to the theatre, and it was only two days afterwards that she saw in the paper it was called *The Thief of El Dorado*. It was both funny and scary. Whenever a new danger loomed out in the night, or the hero fell into the trap set by his enemies, she gripped Ritzi's arm tightly, she felt so at ease with him, as if he'd always been there.

As soon as they got home she put the kettle on to boil. Ritzi sat on the sofa and read the newspaper while she arranged the pretty blue tray with the fine china cups and the teaspoons, humming to herself an old childhood tune because there was something so right about it, she making coffee in the kitchen and the man, her man, sitting on the living-room sofa and reading the paper. Suddenly her home seemed to become more of a home, or at least to gain in importance, as if it had been stamped with an invisible seal: right. She hadn't felt this way since Nathan left. She measured out the coffee carefully and opened the tin of biscuits she kept especially for this sort of occasion, which never came about. That is to say, her former pupils from the days she gave singing lessons still sometimes came to see her, but the truth was that she kept the tin of fresh biscuits, which she replaced every week, for an occasion exactly like this one, but this was the first time it had actually happened. Since Nathan. Miss Fanny suddenly felt very excited, and for a moment her knees felt weak and she almost had to sit down on one of the kitchen chairs, but then the kettle boiled, and she scolded herself and straightened her back as she had been taught and poured the coffee into the yellow filter jug which the girls in the office had given her for her thirty-eighth birthday, breathing in the pleasant smell of coffee, and carried the tray into the living room.

And then, after they had drunk the coffee and she had replenished the dish of biscuits, the unpleasantness began.

Ritzi slid down on the sofa and looked at her from under

33

lowered lids. Suddenly he asked, 'Haven't you got anything to drink in the house?'

Fanny said, confused, 'I thought you didn't want any more coffee. Ah,' she suddenly understood, 'something cold. I can make lemonade,' she offered, embarrassed, because Ritzi didn't answer immediately but went on looking at her from his semi-recumbent position on the sofa, his back slightly hunched and his head at an angle, watching her with the same sidelong, distant look. For a long moment he didn't answer and then he said, 'No. I meant a *drink*. Something a bit more serious.'

'Oh, you mean alcohol,' said Fanny. She was still embarrassed and she didn't understand the way Ritzi was looking at her, his being so remote all of a sudden, a stranger.

'Yes,' said Ritzi. The corners of his lips curled up, not quite in a smile.

'I'm afraid there's only some quince liqueur,' said Fanny. For some reason she felt miserable all of a sudden, so much so that she couldn't even give her voice the proper apologetic note.

'Quince liqueur?' asked Ritzi. It was obvious from his tone that not only was the beverage in question unacceptable as a real drink, but even as a liqueur it was extremely peculiar. Fanny felt, despairingly, that merely keeping such a drink in the house put her beyond the pale.

'My aunt gets a bottle every year from a friend who comes here from Romania. She comes to take mud baths in the Dead Sea. The friend, that is.'

'Aha,' said Ritzi. All at once the distance melted away from his face. He sat up straight on the sofa and rubbed his hands together vigorously, like someone who is all eager anticipation. 'In that case, let us drink a toast to the lady from Romania. We are neighbours, after all.'

Fanny giggled, still on the verge of hysteria, and hurried to the little glass-fronted sideboard where she kept the liqueur. She herself seldom drank it, even though it was very good. Most of the time she simply forgot it existed. She wasn't in the habit of drinking alcohol and drinking alone at home seemed to her even drearier than eating alone in a restaurant.

Ritzi had recovered his good mood completely. He raised his glass: 'To us!' And Fanny, blushing, responded with a nod and took a bigger sip than she had intended. Tears welled up in her eyes and stung them and she felt her face burning. Ritzi emptied the glass as if it were full of milk. Then he smacked his lips. 'Good for Romania! An excellent drink. I admit I was inclined to look down on it at first, but I take that back – an excellent drink!' And ignoring the rules of etiquette he leaned forward and seized the bottle by the neck and filled his glass again to the brim.

In the darkness of the room Fanny's voice rose, muffled with an anxiety for which she could not account: 'Ritzi? . . .'

Ritzi was lying on his back. A thin plume of smoke rose from his mouth and spiralled towards the ceiling, and now that she had grown accustomed to the darkness and the room seemed to lighten up she could follow it with her eyes.

'Ritzi,' she said again, more urgently.

'Mmmm,' said Ritzi.

'Do you think . . .' and suddenly, unable to check herself, she asked the stupid question: '. . . do you think it could work out? The two of us, I mean.'

'Given the limitations,' said Ritzi after a moment's silence.

Fanny was silent too. 'Aha,' she said at last, although she had no idea what he meant.

Ritzi stretched, then put out his cigarette in the empty glass of milk which Fanny had left the night before on the bedside table. He sat up, shook his head, muttered 'Damn', and got up.

From behind the back of the darkness and the sheets Fanny looked at him. He picked up his trousers from the chair and stepped into them, muttering again, 'Damn, it's cold.' They had not taken the trouble earlier to move the heater into the bedroom. Fanny wanted to avert her eyes but went on looking at him. He pulled up the zipper of his trousers and there was something about this movement that was final, and with complete inconsequence, because she recognized in it the movement with which the girl had zipped up the little boy's coat in the playground, Fanny knew that she would never see this man again. It was one of those glimmerings which are completely unfounded, but nevertheless, or precisely because of this, their truth is irrefutable.

The man – she could no longer call him Ritzi, he was a man she did not know – looked down at her. She felt his eyes resting on her and on the pillows and sheets, the whole mess he had left behind him and that he no longer belonged to. The man looked at her as he buttoned the top button of his shirt, and finally he said again, 'Yes, perhaps. You never know. Given the limitations.' His hair was rumpled from lying in bed and now it looked thinner than it had before. Somehow, although he had put his clothes on properly, something about his appearance remained slovenly, not quite finished. Absurdly, she felt ashamed for him. Perhaps he sensed it because he smoothed his hair down with his hands, trying to pat it into place. His haste, which had not been noticeable when he dressed, was evident now in the fact that he did not ask for leave to use the comb lying on the chest of drawers. He was apparently in a great hurry to get somewhere, although he tried not to show it. Now Fanny understood what the limitations were that he had referred to. She waited to feel disgust, but did not feel anything. She wasn't even particularly eager for him to leave, as if this moment and herself with it, the darkness in the room, her body between the sheets, her head on the pillow, the man looking down at her and waiting for the perfunctory time to pass before he could go, the poinciana outlined against the moon in the window-frame, the heavy air, all were suspended outside the realm of time, and so they would remain, time without end.

'Well, I'll be going,' said the man. 'It's late.'

'Yes,' said Fanny. 'It's certainly late.'

'Your telephone number's written on the phone, I expect,' said the man.

'Yes,' said Fanny. 'I expect so. I never checked.'

'I'll write it down on the way out,' said the man.

'Yes,' said Fanny.

'Well, goodbye for now,' the man said. For the first time that night he seemed uneasy, out of place.

'Goodbye,' said Fanny. 'Be careful not to bump into the coat rack in the hall. It sticks out a little.'

'Don't worry,' the man said. He turned around rather clumsily, as if acting according to a willed decision in which his body did not fully participate, and walked out. From the other room his voice reached her, swathed in darkness: 'I'll be in touch.'

'Yes,' said Fanny. She heard him pause for a moment in the living room, heard a match strike, then the rustle of fabric, and the door opening and closing. 'Yes,' she said again.

8

The sky flamed red and then darkened, as if someone had sprinkled it with sand. Miss Fanny stood on her balcony and watched the sun set, crimson and wild, beyond the houses which separated her from the sea. After the sun had gone down behind the tall building on Hayarkon Street, the air turned grey and all of a sudden it grew cold. A shiver went through Miss Fanny and she went into the bedroom and took her Spanish woollen shawl out of the closet and wrapped it well around her shoulders and returned to the balcony. She leaned against the railing again. It was a beautiful time of day and she didn't want to lose it, to sever the thread it wove between her and all other things, which were at once very remote and yet connected to her in a special way.

On the roof of the house opposite hers to the left, the lowest house on the street, two floors only, people were also standing: a man and a woman. They were young, though not very young, somewhere in their twenties. At first they stood with their backs to her, at the far end of the roof, watching the same sunset. The man stood beside the girl, a little behind her, encircling her waist with his arm. When the sun had completely disappeared they must have felt cold too, at least the girl did, for she turned to the man and said something and the man immediately flung out his arm and pulled her close to him, hugging her in a strong, tight embrace. They stood like this for a long while. Then the man lowered his head and buried it in the hollow of the girl's neck, and so they remained, she with her head erect looking straight ahead towards the sea, which perhaps they were able to see from there, and he nestled in her shoulder. The girl had a full figure and was wrapped in an orange sweater which glowed in the last rays of the setting sun in a fierce, lion-like, golden light. The man was thin and dressed in simple dark colours, dark blue or brown or black, it was hard to tell in this light which blurred and unified everything. There was something in the total abandonment with which he buried his head in her neck, as though yielding all of himself to her, which touched Miss Fanny deep in her soul. She looked at them standing there on the roof, slowly being gathered by the evening and absorbed into it, turning gradually into a silhouette traced on the evening with Chinese ink only a shade darker than it was, but in Miss Fanny's eyes they were already imprinted as they had stood in the faint dusky light, the etching of an embrace, and so they were not lost to her, and despite the fast-falling darkness she went on seeing him sinking into her, seeing her staring, erect, straight ahead into the evening.

Miss Fanny hummed to herself a snatch of a song which had been a favourite of hers as a child:

> To the well a knight shall come to drink
> White his horse shall be, black his eyes
> And in the setting sun his cape will shine
> Orange and gold.

She didn't know why this song came to her mind, perhaps it was because of the colour of the girl's sweater. A great calm came over her, one of those moments of grace when the heart ceases to contract and demand something it cannot be given, and seems rather to expand and slowly, softly, sink to rest on a bed of rose petals. Fanny remembered her mother, whom she had not thought of for a long time, and how she used to sing this song to her little niece. She must have sung this same song to her, Fanny, as well, but she was then too young to remember.

On the roof of the house across the street a light suddenly went on. It was a powerful light, yellow and cruel, and it tore through the darkness like a knife. The couple broke apart as if the light had cut right between them.

Mrs Shelly, the first-floor neighbour, pushed the roof's iron door open with a strident creak and came out, carrying a plastic tub full of laundry. The roof did not belong to any of the families who lived in the house. It was common property.

Moths immediately appeared from somewhere and started circling around the bulb. From where Miss Fanny stood they seemed like dark flutterings against the light, as if the bulb was flickering.

'Good evening,' Mrs Shelly said, pleasantly sociable.

'Good evening,' the couple answered together. They stood hand in hand and seemed uprooted, vague and insubstantial, holding each other's hand as if afraid that if they didn't do so they would fly away. Their voices were lost in the night beyond the railing.

Mrs Shelly laid down the laundry tub next to the railing. She bent and took off the top of the pile a bag of pegs and hung it around her neck. This was a special contraption she'd invented. 'I've been meaning to tell you,' she said.

'Yes,' the young man said. His voice was flat and toneless.

'Somebody's been messing up the roof,' said Mrs Shelly. 'I don't mean to say it's you, but' – she took a peg out of the bag on her neck and fastened it with a click on to the edge of a towel – 'I'm asking anyway. Empty cans of paint and newspapers and even pieces of old sandwiches I've found here. You've been painting something, maybe?'

'No,' the man said. His voice sounded even fainter, as if some hope had been taken away from him.

'I'm not saying it's you, don't get me wrong,' said Mrs Shelly and secured the other end of the towel to a sheet, 'but I'd like to know who's been making a mess up here. It's the second time I've come up and found all kinds of rubbish.'

The couple kept silent. In the yellow artificial light they seemed even more ethereal than before, a momentary, flimsy presence. The sheet flapped wetly against Mrs Shelly's face, like the wing of an enormous bird.

'I've been telling everyone,' continued Mrs Shelly, straightening the sheet on the clothes line, 'It simply isn't possible that people could come up here and leave a mess on the roof just because it isn't theirs. *Skandal*,' she said in an Ashkenazy accent and stretched against the fast-obscuring sky a pair of large white drawers.

For the first time the girl opened her mouth. 'We told you it wasn't us,' she said. There was a suppressed anger in her words. Her voice was lower than that of the boy, more solid, and it immediately became clear to Miss Fanny who the two sides in this confrontation were.

'I'm not saying it's you,' Mrs Shelly said affably. 'I'm just telling everybody so they'll know. After all, it's your roof too.'

'We heard you,' the girl said.

'All right,' said Mrs Shelly. She went on hanging her laundry, from now on mostly underwear, along the clothes line. The terms of the battle were unequal: the two had nothing to occupy themselves with. They stood there for a few more minutes watching their neighbour, who did not address another word to them. Mrs Shelly was hanging out her laundry at an even, precise pace in which there was no superfluous movement. The pieces of underwear were well stretched before being caught with a peg, and undershirts with long sleeves were pegged exactly at the armpits so as not to leave pinch marks. Miss Fanny saw the man gesture to his companion, as if wishing to leave, but the girl refused. She turned her back on her neighbour and again faced the sky beyond the railing, now completely black, studying it as though she could read some message in it. For lack of an alternative the man too turned around and stood beside her like before, but now his hands hung slackly at his sides. Mrs Shelly went on working with the rhythmical, effortless movements of an athlete.

Once finished, she looked over the rows of her laundry,

smoothed here and there a garment which had gone astray and stepped out of line, and in the end, apparently satisfied, bent and picked up her plastic tub and put it under her arm. Before leaving she asked, agreeably, 'Shall I turn off the light for you?'

The couple kept silent, their backs to her, though one could see in the man's back that the situation was not natural to him and that he was keeping himself from turning around and answering her. Clearly he was trying to present a united front with his girl, but it was costing him a great deal.

Mrs Shelly shrugged and left, without turning off the light. The iron door creaked to a close behind her. In the ensuing silence you could hear her clogs clopping down the stairs: clip-clop, clip-clop, clop. The girl turned sharply to the man and said in a low voice, 'I hate her.' She flung it at his face as if it was him she hated and Miss Fanny could see the man shrink back, beaten. The girl broke away from him and went over to the door and put out the light. Darkness flooded the roof at once.

9

After that evening a sort of vague disquiet took hold of Miss Fanny. She felt that something had to happen, or rather change, but she didn't know what or how. She also did not quite understand what this incident between two neighbours in the house across the street had to do with her. At any rate she stopped nodding to Mrs Shelly when she passed her on the street. She strongly hoped this did not mean she had to move because she loved her apartment, and the neighbourhood too.

It could be, though, that at the bottom of this disquiet lay the events which were developing rapidly at work. After that visit to the Mashbir, a change came over old Mr Bruck. He left his office less and less, and when he did everybody commented on how his face had fallen. This comment was literally true, for the muscles, old Mr Bruck's jaw muscles, having up till now heroically struggled to support the flabby flesh of old age, had finally given up the fight, and large parts of the face seemed to sag and become loose, pendulous bags of skin. Old Mr Bruck, as Batya and Raya told each other, had grown old overnight.

Nobody knew what had happened between him and his son on that fateful day when he'd summoned Bruck Junior to his office. Father and son had sat there alone, and any stormy feelings which might have flown from this side of the large oak table to the other had sunk into the dark wood and by the next morning had disappeared without a trace. Only Fanny, who, at Mr Bruck's request, had been detained in the office late that night in order to complete a special inventory, saw young Mr Bruck emerge from his father's room, his face all aflame and looking like a child who had just received a good spanking, but underneath the embarrassment which reddened his ears

43

there lurked something else, which he himself seemed reluctant to expose – almost, so it seemed to Fanny, a certain complacency.

At the end of December old Mr Bruck notified the office workers (ladies, actually; all the men employed by Bruck & Sons worked outside the office, at deliveries and so forth) of his retirement. And even though this was expected and had been in the air for the past few months, the announcement had fallen upon them like news of the death of an acquaintance long ill with an incurable disease. The actual occurrence of the event, its actual coming about, strikes the listener, despite the long period of preparation, with dumb astonishment, a refusal to believe, almost with shock. Such was the impact of old Mr Bruck's announcement; and the office girls watched with hospital visitors' eyes the stricken old lion slowly descending from his throne, his big body with the old-age spots, a body which had lost its resilience, making its way down paw after paw.

The administrative arrangements to do with the retirement were few. The remaining stock of umbrellas was sold at a considerable loss to a business house in Germany, and for the first time the 'Export' in the company's name had some corroboration in reality, but since this business house was associated with the firm which manufactured the umbrellas, this corroboration was a bit dubious. On the first of January Bruck Senior did not come to work. A grey, depressing cloud hung over the office until twelve o'clock when the movers came. The heavy old furniture was taken out of the room piece by piece, from the gigantic writing desk to the bookshelves made of the same solid dark-brown wood, whose contents were the only thing old Mr Bruck took home with him; all the rest were sold to an antique shop. They didn't bring in much, since they weren't what are known as period pieces but simply old furniture, heavy and functional, but they covered part of the cost of the new, modern furniture, the latest thing on the market, as Bruck Junior proudly declared,

44

made in Sweden, chrome and glass. On the wall was affixed a monstrously enlarged version of the calendar geisha (the clothed one), his first success, like a giant talisman.

After old Mr Bruck's retirement the atmosphere at the office of Bruck & Sons, Import-Export underwent a change everybody felt, though it was difficult to define. This feeling, quite disturbing in itself, did not originate in the business side of things: business-wise their situation was better than ever before. The stock had grown richer by a few dozen items, the number of firms associated with Bruck & Sons had increased and spread over all the big cities. The difference was in the atmosphere, in the way young Bruck spoke to his employees, in the way they spoke among themselves. A certain old-world courtesy had disappeared. The office operated now in a way which reminded Miss Fanny of the mouth of Suzy from the office next door when she talked on the phone – chewing-gummy, slack, the lipstick smeared beyond the outline of the lips. *Disziplin*, she said to herself: that's what was lacking in the new era. Discipline. Young Bruck tried, in a way which was transparent to everyone but himself, to flirt with Raya, the prettier of the two clerks, but Raya stood firm, and delivered detailed reports which inspired giggles and cries of 'You don't say!' and snorts of contempt in her audience. This included Batya and their friend Miriam from Suzy's office, Abrahamov Ceramics and Quality Tiles, and sometimes Fanny as well. Throughout the years the office employees had developed towards Bruck Junior the sort of attitude which is usually directed towards those who are of second rank. The father may have had a hand in this, or it may be that the shadow cast by his massive presence had been enough to render the son pale and even a little ridiculous; his Adam's apple quivered as he spoke, and Batya claimed that his ears did too, although this was pure slander. After the initial shock caused by the retirement they suddenly realized the gap that existed between their casual, almost patronizing attitude towards Bruck Junior, and the fact that he had been the one who'd managed in

45

practice most of the office business over the last few years. The truth was that they simply weren't very fond of him. Indeed, nobody claimed that they had to be consumed by a great, passionate love for their employer (except for Raya maybe), but it was hard for them to feel even a simple liking for him, and without that it is hard to properly identify with the interests of the firm.

Nevertheless no change of staff seemed to loom on the horizon. As far as the office staff or its furnishings were concerned, apart from his own room, Bruck Junior did not change a thing. Perhaps he did not even feel the winds which were blowing at him from the secretarial benches. He was not a man of outstanding sensitivity. Perhaps he did not mind the distance at which the workers kept him, except for Raya, and she excelled at keeping their relationship on the thin borderline between refusal and surrender. In secret she told Batya that she meant to drag things out until she and Itamar could be married, that is to say until about September, October at the latest. Beyond the end of the year, anyway, she was not prepared to wait.

Towards the end of the month it grew very cold and Batya and Raya started up the old heating system, which crackled and roared like a herd of elephants, as Raya said loudly when Mr Bruck passed through the room. But young Mr Bruck refused to take the hint, even from Raya. Any investment in the firm in the near future, so he declared, would be made only for the purpose of expanding and consolidating the business itself. During their lunch hours they usually stayed in the office because the days were too rainy to sit in the sooty little garden at the corner and none of them could afford to eat at a proper restaurant. And for some crummy hummus, as Batya said, it wasn't worth dragging themselves up the dripping alleys to the cheap steak house on the corner of Herzl Street. So they all brought sandwiches from home, and salads they'd prepared beforehand, and ate their lunch together, exchanging stories about the events of the night before. Fanny would listen. Sometimes Bruck Junior would call for Raya under the pretext of having an urgent letter to dictate, and Batya and Fanny would exchange glances.

Thus Fanny had no suspicion of the events which were about to take place that late winter evening in young Mr Bruck's renovated office.

They were alone in the office. Batya and Raya had already gone home, but Fanny, who was in charge of the inventory, had stayed behind to tie up some loose ends so that she could have a full report ready for Aryeh, the company's auditor, who was to come the next morning. She always tried to do everything in the days prior to the meeting, but somehow there was always something left over till the last minute and she had to stay late in order to get it done.

Bruck Junior was sitting on his minimalistic executive armchair, chrome with green and white upholstery, behind the transparent executive desk. There was something embarrassing about the fact that when the table was not littered with papers Fanny could see the director's feet underneath the glass surface, tapping on the floor with perpetual impatience. His shoes were very small for a man's, and Fanny's eyes were always drawn to them as if by magic, till it was only with difficulty that she could tear them away and return her look to its proper place, somewhere between Mr Bruck's eyes and his chin.

Mr Bruck cleared his throat briefly and said, 'Have a seat, Miss Fanny, it won't cost you anything,' or something of the sort, which was intended to sound amiable but was in fact quite loathsome. Somehow Mr Bruck never succeeded in carrying out his good intentions, whether because of some basic clumsiness in the way he tackled the matter, something elephantine and almost brutal, or simply, as Batya said, because he was a stinking son of a bitch. Fanny gave her thoughts a good shake, and, by the look young Bruck gave her, she must have shaken her head as well.

'Are you with me, Miss Fanny?'

'Yes, of course,' Miss Fanny said and blushed. Ever since she was a child she had this detestable tendency to blush every time she did not speak or act exactly as she felt.

'Ah. You seemed a bit preoccupied,' said young Mr Bruck, who, unlike his father, did not know when to let go.

'It's the electric typewriter,' Fanny said. 'I still haven't quite got used to it.'

'Ah,' said Bruck Junior and nodded his head several times. 'The IBM. I understand you, Miss Fanny. It isn't easy to get used to modern equipment after working with machines which were up to date some twenty years ago.' Young Bruck leaned forward on the table and for the first time Miss Fanny noticed a small bald spot hidden underneath the carefully combed hair, and wondered whether it would constitute a disloyalty if she were to tell the girls about it tomorrow morning, for she too wanted for once to be the storyteller and not just the audience. With a mute sigh she decided she couldn't do any such thing. 'But I promise you', young Mr Bruck continued devoutly, 'that once you get used to it you won't want to so much as look again at a manual machine, not to mention pen and paper. Unless they're mint-scented, of course,' he added and laughed, too loudly.

Fanny, who was angered by the allusion to old Mr Bruck's era, did not join in his laughter and contented herself with just a smile. She could afford to do this because she was held at the office to have no sense of humour. And indeed she found it difficult to participate in the bantering exchanges which daily flew over her head at the office, mainly because her command of the language was not flexible enough, but also because apparently this kind of humour, which the girls called 'bashing', she no longer had any hope of developing at her age. All the same, even Batya admitted that Fanny sometimes had the most incredible 'flashes', for the most part quite unintentionally.

'Or jasmine,' she added, because all the same she did have a developed sense of duty.

But Bruck Junior had already finished laughing and now did not even bother to smile at Fanny's modest contribution. On the contrary, his face grew serious, his look focused, and he turned it on Fanny above the lenses of his glasses, which he wore whenever he wished to impress upon his interlocutor the importance of the subject he was addressing. 'I called you in today, Miss Fanny,' he said, as though Fanny had been summoned to his office by a battery of senior secretaries rather than by his sticking his head out the door and calling her to come in, 'regarding a matter of essence.'

A stab of alarm went through Miss Fanny. Perhaps Bruck Junior did after all think that she, Fanny, was too old for the young, dynamic office Bruck & Sons was to be from now on, as he had declared on the very first day of the new era, when the movers had gone and left his office gleaming with chrome and glass. Perhaps she was about to be dismissed after all.

But this wasn't what stood at the top of the matters-to-be-taken-care-of list, which was kept, well ordered and marked with checks and minuses, in young Mr Bruck's head. 'I have called you', he continued, his voice deepening with a self-importance greater than usual, 'to ask your advice about a new item I am considering adding to our stock.'

Miss Fanny's eyes widened and she nodded silently, as befitting the great honour Bruck Junior was bestowing upon her, all the while wondering for what reason she was found to deserve it.

'I have chosen to consult with you of all people', he went on in this tone which always gave Batya a powerful urge to stick a pin into him, 'because I rely on your . . . ahem . . . *judicious* judgement. I cannot see you being carried away by *fun*. The girls at the office may see the items we're importing as objects of amusement, but *we*, Miss Fanny,' and again Fanny wondered helplessly what made her worthy of being included in this elect company, '*we* know that they are not toys at all. They may be so for our clients, Miss Fanny, I'm not denying it, on the contrary, whatever's good for them, this is what they're paying us *money* for.' And here Mr Bruck interrupted his speech and gave Miss Fanny a piercing look, as if to make sure she was following his train of thought properly. 'Good money. And for that money to *keep* flowing in, Miss Fanny,' stressed Mr Bruck, and Miss Fanny saw before her dazzled eyes rivers of money of all shapes and kinds, tiny five-agorot coins that roll and get lost in corners, torn one-lira notes which bus drivers hand out and which then the grocer won't accept, shiny new hundred-lira notes the likes of which she had held in her hands only very rarely, well-worn tenners wriggling slowly towards her, like good-natured carp, and behind them dollars, yen, francs, roubles – an utterly groundless vision, since their clients never paid in anything other than Israeli currency, and that in business cheques – all streaming towards her in a swelling river, which was fast becoming a huge delta, a sea, threatening to devour her.

'This item', said Mr Bruck, and terrified she realized that she had missed a part, perhaps an essential part, of the speech, 'is especially important because if we do add it to our list of merchandise, and if this experiment *does* go well, it might mark the beginning of a new era for Bruck & Sons. That important.' Again he paused, to heighten the effect, and this time Fanny took care not to lag behind and nodded her head emphatically up and down to show that she was following him with the utmost attention. This emphatic acquiescence evidently found favour with young Mr Bruck, who softened a little the hitherto severe tone of his speech.

'Miss Fanny,' he said, 'I want to hear your impartial opinion. Tell me plainly and frankly: do you think this item suitable for Bruck & Sons, or not?'

Fanny felt a feeble urge to protest, to argue that she was not qualified to lay down an opinion on such a fateful subject, but the words betrayed her as usual and she saw Mr Bruck reach out to the top drawer of the filing cabinet beside him, the only piece of furniture in the room which wasn't transparent, and take out a package wrapped in shiny blue paper. The wrapping paper was meticulously folded along the original lines, but wasn't taped closed: it looked as if Mr Bruck had already opened the package but had taken the trouble of wrapping it again. Now he unfolded the paper with deliberate, precise, almost ceremonial motions, and bit by bit Miss Fanny saw a medium-sized cardboard box emerge, with a design which, from where she was sitting, she saw upside down, and a text of some kind. Miss Fanny tried to read the words, but to no avail, and reflected that she might be in need of reading glasses. At last the peeling process came to an end. Before Miss Fanny's eyes stood two different boxes, one on top of the other.

Mr Bruck took the topmost, larger box and held it for a moment. For one impressive moment the fate of the firm of Bruck & Sons remained sealed in its box. Then Mr Bruck laid the undisclosed object on the table. He opened the cardboard flap which closed the box and drew out a hard plastic surface on which, in hollows especially suited to their shapes, lay three shiny white objects.

It took Miss Fanny a minute to realize that these were a toothbrush, a razor, and a shaving brush, all made of white plastic.

It took her another minute to realize that the long handle of each of these three accessories was in fact the nude body of a woman.

She blinked, trying to conceal from young Mr Bruck the instinctive revulsion she felt at the sight of this unholy trinity. To avoid looking at his face, she looked again at the accessories his hand was still exhibiting to her. The naked woman who was the toothbrush was standing with her profile to her. The naked woman who was supporting the razor faced the spectator directly. And the naked woman of the shaving brush was kneeling down. This woman was legless, that is to say, ceased to exist from the knees down. All three women were, of course, headless.

All these amputated members had something extremely oppressive about them.

Silently, thus intensifying the effect a hundredfold, Mr Bruck laid the box on the table, face up, and picked up the other box. Miss Fanny swallowed and hoped for the best.

Mr Bruck opened the lid of the box and very carefully took out its contents. He pressed his palms together at their roots and spread out his hands. The object lay between them like a delicate lotus flower.

The first thing Miss Fanny noticed was that the shape of this object was an almost identical copy of young Mr Bruck's hands, in which it rested: two gilded hands joined at the roots and spread open. Between them lay another object.

Only at second glance did Miss Fanny see that this object, which at first she took to be a tiny statuette, was also a razor. The handle of this one too was a naked woman. But this time the woman was sculpted not only on one side, profile or front, but on all sides, and when she hesitantly reached out and took her, upon a commanding nod of Mr Bruck's, and looked at her closely, she saw that the woman's body was strained as taut as a bow, like the body of a discus thrower, and above it her arms too were stretched to their utmost, supporting, Atlas-like, her precious burden. But soon Miss Fanny's eyes abandoned the woman's body, and even her hands stretching out towards a sharp-edged sky, and were riveted to her face, a face you couldn't tear yourself away from, petrified in the grimace of one last great desperate effort in which she was doomed to freeze for ever, never to shed her burden.

Miss Fanny released the deep breath she had been holding in her breast.

'Amazing, huh?' asked young Bruck with satisfaction. 'You've no idea what a battle I fought in order to come in first in the race for the rights. It was a tough, bitter contest,' he said proudly, 'but we won.'

His voice altered as he looked back at the product. 'Do you get the idea, Miss Fanny? Some men like to shave straight downwards, no nonsense about it, others must hold the razor diagonally and shave with small motions sideways, but whichever way they hold it this woman, whose only aim and desire is to shave them right, will be looking at them, and what gentleness this concern brings to your shave, you tell me, Miss Fanny, with what warmth it fills a man's heart first thing in the morning, with what tenderness. It's all over with nicks, Miss Fanny. What man could injure himself with the gaze of such a beautiful woman beseeching him to take care? From the daily torture shaving turns into a pleasure, a treat, a real *luxury*.' Mr Bruck had used up all the air in his lungs and now took a deep breath. Miss Fanny looked at him, marvelling: the small object nestled in his palm had turned young Mr Bruck into a poet.

'And this other set, Miss Fanny,' Mr Bruck's voice was gaining in strength, 'what you're looking at here is the simplest version, pure plastic, although of excellent quality and in all hues, red, black, green, white. All colours. But you can also order the same set in the most expensive materials. African ebony, Miss Fanny. Crystal. Ivory, Miss Fanny – can you imagine this set in soft cream-coloured carved ivory, the very best, no nonsense about it, real ivory? Miss Fanny!' Mr Bruck's voice soared to hitherto unimagined heights. 'Real ivory! There won't be one man in this country who thinks anything of himself, not one man worth anything, who could afford to invite a lady friend to stay the night without possessing a Bruck & Sons pure ivory shaving set. Think of it, Miss Fanny. Try to picture it to yourself.' Miss Fanny closed her eyes and tried to think of something else. 'There are five hundred thousand men old enough to shave in this country. Out of these at least fifty thousand consider themselves to be Somebody. Such a man, Miss Fanny, will not allow himself to lag behind the times. A man who owns a Cartier watch couldn't live without a Bruck & Sons shaving set made of ivory. Or at least crystal. Or jade, Miss Fanny!' Mr Bruck's voice rose threateningly. 'Original jade! There's nothing that a man who's above the common herd could not permit himself. Men cannot permit themselves earrings, Miss Fanny. Not men who go out in the morning to board meetings. They cannot permit themselves necklaces, bracelets, anklets, medallions. But they can, they must, have at least one shaving set worth something. A twenty-two carat gold-plated razor. A shaving set and a toothbrush of black ebony. Or of jade. Or both of ebony and of jade. Do you get it, Miss Fanny? Do you understand what I'm driving at?' droned Mr Bruck's relentless voice, driving her forcibly towards towards the nightmarish vision of hundreds and thousands and millions of men getting up in the morning, dabbing at their swollen eyes with a damp cloth, glancing at the mirror, contorting their mouth this way and that, thrusting out their lower lip, blinking their eyes, picking up an elegant velvet case with the inscription Bruck & Sons embossed on it in golden gothic letters, extracting from it a naked woman made of crystal and wetting her hair, rubbing her headless stump against their stubbly chin, whipping up the foam, putting this woman down and taking out of an ivory-inlaid ebony box a second woman and starting to scrape their chin with her with leisured motions from right to left, pulling their mouth sideways, passing the knife at her head over the other corner, shaking her well, rinsing her leg stumps with water, laying her down on the Italian sink and taking out of the jade case the third woman – God, what a terrible sight, she too is headless – and vigorously beginning to brush their teeth with her, her breasts stick in the incisors for the umpteenth time and in a fit of fury they smash her against the sink and break her in two, how horrible, tomorrow morning they'll have to acquire a new trio at the agency. Blubeard rinses off the last traces of foam with warm water, dabs at his face with the towel, does not rub, as the beautician ordered, and tells himself for the umpteenth time that he should have selected the other, gold-plated model, guaranteed absolutely durable.

'Well, Miss Fanny, what do you say? What do you think of Bruck & Sons breaking into a new line – men's accessories? And don't think, Miss Fanny, we shall stop here. Oh no, not at all. We shall break into the market with a great fanfare: not only shaving sets for men but also cufflinks, tiepins, gilded shoehorns, toilet sets for men . . . and all this is just the first part of the operation. But about what comes later I still can't say anything. The matter is too delicate . . . hmm . . . yes, too delicate.' Mr Bruck's throat-clearing shook Miss Fanny out of her apocalyptic vision and brought her back to the solid ground of reality. She looked at him speechless. Nothing in the world could have induced her to utter even one word.

'Yes, Miss Fanny. The vision is a great one. And exactly for that reason it is so important to tread cautiously. Without hesitating, but with careful consideration. And I ask you again – tell me your opinion, and no gilding the lily. If we go for this series, Miss Fanny, it means an initial investment of thousands, maybe tens of thousands of dollars. I must have the additional opinion of someone who has known the company for a long time, the opinion of someone who's mature, intelligent, judicious.'

Miss Fanny's threatened opinion scurried like a frightened crab into the depths of her brain. She could not draw from there even one coherent thought. With broken, stammered words, which for the most part did not add up to one complete sentence, she began to explain to Mr Bruck that her lack of experience in these matters, etcetera, why, surely he can understand, particularly a woman like herself, Mr Bruck, who is unfamiliar with the routine of married life, of course these accessories have an aesthetic of their own, but perhaps a man, it would seem to her, could better appreciate their worth than her, since she had never had this experience of the morning shave, at least not . . . Her voice died away into the wonder of total despair when she realized to what depths she had sunk. All at once her mind cleared and her thoughts crystallized. She collected the papers stacked on the table in front of her, that she had brought because she thought she was summmoned to discuss the coming inventory check, stood up and in a few plain words explained to Mr Bruck that she was not properly qualified to assist him in his difficult decision, apologized and said goodbye.

It was only on her way home from the bus stop, hurrying along Ibn Gevirol Street in the pouring rain, that the shame finally rose and burned in her cheeks. At night she woke up every few hours soaked with sweat. Legion upon legion of naked women came up to her, headless, legless, stretching their arms out to her in mute, desperate supplication, wailing to her, to Fanny, to save them from their awful fate. But she only looked at them in horror for one short minute and immediately turned away and fled, fled away from them, as far away as possible, leaving them to their abject servitude.

It rained steadily all the next day and kept on raining after she returned home from work. The restlessness which had taken hold of Miss Fanny increased until she could no longer bear being pent up in the apartment and in the evening, when the rain had abated, she put on her woollen coat and went out. On the street everything was wet and drops of water trickled down from the branches of the tamarisks glistening in the lamplight. An after-the-rain smell came up from the street, a sharp scent of wet plants mixed with the faint stench of the garbage which had not been collected because of the city workers' strike. She recalled that yesterday at the office Batya had said angrily, 'This town is full of shit.' The 'sh' came out sibilant and harsh and Fanny's face had twitched in an involuntary grimace, but now she thought there was something in what Batya said. She decided not to think about it any more.

A drop fell and shattered on the tip of Miss Fanny's nose and she brought it to her lips, enjoying the taste of clean rain and the bitter aroma of woodbark. She walked quickly, almost briskly. It was an odd way Miss Fanny had, always to walk faster whenever she wasn't going anywhere; that is, she always walked at a more vigorous pace whenever she went on one of her nightly rambles, which proceeded along a more or less set course until she returned home, than when she was heading towards some definite destination, even if she was in a hurry. The very thought of having to walk fast in order to get there would tire her in advance. Whereas when she was merely out for a stroll she would inadvertently quicken her step: the fast walk invigorated her. She almost felt younger.

From the houses drifted the voice of a singer in a well-known Hebrew song. She knew the singer, and the song too; that is to say, she recognized the voice and the tune, but she couldn't remember the names. They sounded familiar to her, she supposed, from the transistor radio which was playing all day long in the office. When she heard songs she particularly liked she would sometimes ask for their names, and the name of the singer, and try to remember; but usually she forgot them, and after telling her two or three times Batya and Raya would get cross with her, for what kind of a question is this anyway, Fanny, everyone knows this is Geula Gil, what's wrong with you? Until at last she stopped asking. There was something strange but in some way also soothing about the fact that the same song was heard from all the houses she passed. It gave a wave-like quality to her walk, wave after wave of snatches of song which joined together to form one chain, and she toyed with the illusion that it was she who was stringing these beads together into the complete necklace.

But once she left Horkanus Street, which stood at a right angle to her own street, she slowed down. This time the walk through the nocturnal streets was slow to have its usual effect and failed to bring about the elucidation of thought, the focusing, which usually enabled her to solve the problem that was troubling her, or at least to clarify it. The episode at the office had left her cocooned in a sort of dim numbness, and she still felt too strong a reluctance to think about what had happened there, or even to evoke in her mind the picture of the office as it had looked last night under the electric lights, as one would feel a physical aversion to touching something sticky and loathsome. She looked up at the lit drawing rooms, at the settings in which the lives of the people who dwelled there took place. In many of the rooms, surprisingly many, there were tall phylodendron plants with large leaves reaching almost to the ceiling. Many of the ceilings had been lowered and were made of wood. Miss Fanny wondered why people wanted wooden ceilings in a country as hot as this, but could not decide which of her conjectures was the right one. The familiar singer was replaced by an oriental-sounding group and the music became faster and more strident.

When she reached the small streets near the sea the musical programme had apparently ended and the announcer's voice emerged from the houses. The streets grew quieter, and in a few minutes she arrived at the little park near Yehezkel Street. Walking towards her were a man and a woman who seemed in their late thirties. The woman was fair-haired and wore a pink angora sweater which filled out her figure and made her look plumper, but also endowed her with softness. To Miss Fanny they looked at first like an old married couple on their evening stroll. But when they drew nearer she changed her mind: the woman was listening to her companion with an expression of intent interest, too declared an interest for him to be the man she'd been married to for many years. Neither was the tone of the man's speech that of someone speaking to a woman he was long familiar with. As always happens when people pass each other by on the street, she clearly heard a fragment of what the man was saying at that moment: '*No, my brother is a millionaire in his own right.*' This was a totally unexpected sentence, certainly not the kind of sentence you would expect to hear at random on Yehezkel Street at a quarter past eight in the evening, and Fanny wondered if he had said it in order to impress his companion, or because he really considered it his duty to clear up some mistaken notion she had about his family, such as his brother's having inherited all his money from their father.

This issue occupied her as far as the Pe'er cinema. But still at the back of her mind there hung a foggy cloud inside which was the thing that had happened the day before at the office, and this cloud refused to disperse. She started to walk back up Shimon Hatarsy Street. The garbage lay sprawled on the streets in piles. Apparently people were taking advantage of the situation to get rid of cumbersome old articles which ordinarily they would have been ashamed to dump in front of the neighbours. An especially substantial pile rose beneath the house next to the school, perhaps because the school had added its trash to that of the neighbours, and next to it stood an old-fashioned armchair, made in the old style from green raffia straps. The entire left-hand side of the armchair had sunk in, and this made it look a bit crooked and wobbly, and for some reason delightful. There was about this old lopsided armchair something of the air of a chair in a fairytale, a slightly magical air, and Fanny was suddenly seized with an overpowering desire to sit in it, in this very armchair right there in the middle of the street. And quite uncharacteristically she could not resist the temptation and indeed went up to the armchair and sat in it, crossing her feet daintily no more than a few inches away from the heap of garbage. She lifted her nose at the trash pile. 'A cup of tea perhaps, my dear?' she asked out loud. Now that she was seated she felt the pressure of her right shoe – her right foot was larger than her left one, and this always caused her trouble when she was buying shoes – and she took it off and started swinging it up and down on the tip of her toe. Suddenly the shoe was torn free from her foot, like the cork from a champagne bottle, and flew straight on to the heap of garbage. An irate mew came from the heap. A large bristling black cat emerged from it, licked its underarm majestically and, its head held high, made for the nearby lawn. There it flattened itself and suddenly vanished from view, a clandestine shadow stretched out on the ground. Fanny burst out laughing. Now that she had conquered the street all for herself she sat back carefully in her armchair and looked down the hill. The moon shone out of the small puddles and the street sparkled at her, roguish and playful too.

If Nathan was here, a dangerous thought came to her, a thought opposed to all the contracts she'd signed with herself, he would call her One-Shoe-Fanny, like he did then. And in the inevitable way in which one event stems out of another, once we've let the first one happen, she saw him standing at the entrance to the house across the street, opening his arms to her and laughing – come, One-Foot-Fanny, come to me – and she was already gripping the arms of the chair so as to stand up and walk to him, when the light came on in the stairway and she saw his absence, framed in the straight white lines of the entrance.

In a cloud of talk a couple came out of the building, a boy and a girl. The boy was rattling a large bunch of keys, as young boys do who are not yet used to being entrusted with a car. They came out too quickly and Miss Fanny had no time to retreat. When they saw her they gave a little start, surprised, but immediately pulled themselves together and continued walking without giving her another glance. The girl brought her head close to that of the boy's and they whispered to each other something Miss Fanny could not hear. Afterwards they both burst out laughing, the boy's laughter rough, slightly coarse, and the girl's the crystalline laughter of a seventeen-year-old, uninhibited, free.

Miss Fanny sank into her armchair. All at once the lightweight feeling she had while sitting there watching the gleaming street deserted her. She felt heavy and useless in the shabby armchair she'd found for herself. She felt old. And at that moment she was flooded by the knowledge that she was forty-two, and by the absurdity, no, the grotesqueness, of this spectacle of her, an adult woman, sitting on the pavement on the green raffia straps, swinging her feet at the garbage.

She stood up slowly and picked up her shoe and cleaned it of a piece of dirt that had clung to it. As she made her way up the hill again towards Hill Square she reflected that the couple must have thought her one of those old ladies who rummage in garbage cans. Bag ladies. And perhaps I shall end up like that, she thought, and immediately reproved herself for this piece of nonsense. Miss Fanny could not stand such thoughts, childish, defeatist, full of self-pity. This was not the upringing she had received. The word 'upbringing' reminded her of Aunt Leda, and it immediately grew clear to her that she had to see her, but one couldn't visit Aunt Leda without prior notice and so she decided to call her up the minute she got home and arrange to meet her the next day after work.

This decision braced her a little and her step again grew brisk, so much so that the illuminated picture, as she walked past it, was at first no more than a brief flash, the fraction of a blink before the eyelid closes, but its impression was so powerful that Fanny slowed down unawares and then started retracing her steps, walking backwards, facing the same way so that the picture would be revealed to her from the same angle as before, until she stopped in front of the lit window. The window was on the ground floor of a small house, two storeys only, and the room was probably the drawing room or perhaps the study. The imprint on Fanny's eye was almost that of a sacred picture, but one with a distinctly Jewish stamp, and she remembered light surrounding a man's head like an aura, and within the glow the head swaying back and forth, its lips moving, as though in prayer.

Once back at the same spot the picture proved true. A lamp was hanging low in the middle of the room, just above the head of the person who was sitting there, encircling him in a halo of light. Now he was sitting motionless. When she looked closely, she saw that it was a young man, almost a boy, or perhaps a young woman, she couldn't tell, but she didn't want to cross the street and come any closer lest he should see her peeping into his room. A moment later the boy began swaying again and she could see his hand reaching forward and his lips moving, but this time he seemed to be eating something, grapes maybe, or sunflower seeds, and she understood that she'd been standing there for too long and moved away.

By the time she got home the picture's influence had faded and she felt the old restlessness, which had subsided a little, stirring in her again. She lit up the kerosene stove and left it outside for a few minutes, to let the smell wear off, and then brought it in and stood it in the middle of the drawing room. The stove burned with a blue flame which still had red flickers dancing in it, and gave off a pleasant warmth and the remains of the kerosene smell, but even when she had moved the armchair nearer and sat down in front of it, reaching out to the heat which flowed from it in waves, she could not quell this restlessness in her which identified itself, as the time went by, as a kind of dull pain which the closest name she could give to was, perhaps, longing. With a sense of impatience, almost of anger, she recognized once more the throbbing of the old scar.

That she would never be Elisabeth Schumann, nor even a good second-rate opera singer, she had realized definitively by the time she was twenty-four; and even at that age she had been honest enough to know that the war had nothing to do with it. The pain, a sharp pain of rejection – for she didn't feel that she had failed in her love of music, but that music had rejected her – made her want to draw as far away from it as possible; she refused to become a music teacher, or an accompanying pianist at school ceremonies or at public events, just as she would have refused, if her beloved had sent her away, to become a servant in the house of the new mistress. This, more than the low pay, was why she had also stopped the singing lessons she gave shortly after arriving in Israel. But once she had completely blocked this possibility in herself, and had forbidden herself to practise, or even to sing in the shower, the notes began to bubble in her like noodles in a pot, phrases from works she once knew by heart, the 'A-D-D-F-sharp' at the beginning of Schubert's 'An die Musik', or 'Près des ramparts de Séville' from *Carmen*. 'You, Fanny, Carmen you'll never be,' she heard old Herr Fried sigh, smiling. 'We'd better get back to Gluck.' And absent-mindedly she started humming 'Che farò senza Euridice'. Sometimes it was just notes, pure notes, which floated into her mind as if an invisible finger had tapped on a xylophone key, soaring from somewhere in the chest and whizzing through her head before she could stop them. Sometimes she felt that all the things which flowed through her in the course of her working day, or on her evening strolls, the halo of light around the boy's head in the illuminated room, or the armchair standing alone in the street beneath the stars, and even the couple who had passed her by with the strange remark about the millionaire, all of these were crowding inside her like a myriad bubbles in all colours, brown and phosphorus green and dark blue like the nocturnal street, and if they did not find a way out they would turn into a jet of steam and tear a great hole in her so that they could forcibly break out, to the open space.

Miss Fanny sighed. She went to the small cabinet at the corner of the room which housed her phonograph and inside which, in two compartments, stood her records. But having opened the doors of the cabinet, she hesitated. She felt that she had better not listen now to Pergolesi's 'Stabat Mater', which she had originally intended to play. The crystalline boyish voices were too pure, too perfect, they would only sharpen the feeling of lack in her. She knelt down and began going through the records, rejecting them one by one. Nothing seemed to fit the strange mood she was in. Finally her finger encountered a thick, square casing, and stopped there. She had no need to look: she only had one such box. It was a special edition album, three records with all the songs Edith Piaf had recorded. This album was one of Fanny's most precious treasures. She guarded it jealously because it couldn't be bought here in Israel, and had one of the records been broken or damaged she couldn't have replaced it. Edith Piaf was the singer she loved most in the realm of popular music. In a strange way she felt a great closeness to this singer with the clear voice and the ruined face, who looked at you (Fanny once saw a short film which had been made just before her death) with a gaze which was cracked but as steadfast as steel, a gaze which did not let you go – as opposed to most people she knew, whose gaze wanted her to go, regardless of what they said, because they couldn't take her presence. It was uncomfortable for them, demanded from them something they did not want to give or couldn't. Fanny felt that if she had somehow happened to be around Madame Piaf, she would have looked at her with her tough steadfast gaze and invited her to sit down. She would have opened a bottle of whisky and stood it on the table between them (Fanny never drank. But she would have with Piaf). And then.

As far as I care, the sky can fall, Piaf sang, and Fanny, quite out of character, went over to the sideboard and took out the bottle of quince liqueur she had offered Ritzi and poured herself a glass, to drink with Edith. Then she poured herself a second glass. The phonograph plate went round and round. The earth can collapse too, sang Piaf, for all I care, as long as you love me. Fanny slammed the glass down on the table, forgetting that she might leave a damp circle on the antique wooden surface. Her head whirled with the two glassfuls. She felt that she had better stop because soon she would start thinking about that which she didn't want to think about, she would start thinking about Nathan. And this she absolutely did not want. What do I care, as long as we love each other, sang Piaf, and Fanny with an iron will lifted herself from her seat and went to the phonograph and picked up its arm. The voice ceased immediately. But now she couldn't be without this voice, alone in the empty space of the room, and she replaced the arm and Piaf's voice rose, clear and true, from the black vinyl. Still, it was better to be left with the longing than with nothing at all.

She listened to the songs all evening until she went to bed. Slowly the pain eased and the spirit of the street girl, determined to rescue her piece of sky from the garbage, seeped into her, and she decided not to let everything that had happened yesterday get her down. Tomorrow she'd speak to Aunt Leda and then she'd see. Meanwhile she sat and listened to the songs, turning the glass in her hands until the drink grew warm, and as the hours went by a feeling of complete calm spread in her, and within it, like being under a warm, muffling blanket, she did not feel the need for anything. Perhaps this was happiness.

'This time', Aunt Leda said with satisfaction as she hung Fanny's wet coat on the special hanger in the bathroom, 'I've settled my score with her.'

'With whom, Aunt Leda?'

'With Bentov, that's whom.'

Bentov was the upstairs neighbour, from the second floor. The picture of Mrs Shelly hanging her white drawers on the roof surfaced in Fanny's memory and she wondered if over the years she had begun to resemble Aunt Leda, clinging to eternal vendettas about carpet shaking or the spilling of a pail of water, and was relieved to remember that this hadn't actually been her quarrel, but that of the young couple from across the street.

'How?' she asked.

'I pulled at the edge of her carpet and it fell on the footpath. At least twenty people stepped on it before she noticed. As if it belonged to a carpet store on Dizengoff Street,' said Aunt Leda with tremendous enjoyment.

'It doesn't suit you, Aunt Leda,' Fanny said helplessly.

'This whole country doesn't suit me,' said Aunt Leda, 'but if I have to live in it, it'll learn to behave itself.

'Changing her name from Ben-Lulu to Bentov still doesn't make her into a human being,' she concluded, and carefully shut the door to the bathroom, which faced the building's central ventilation shaft.

Fanny shrugged, giving up. The old enmity was a part of Aunt Leda, just like reading *Yediot Hayom* every morning at eight. 'As long as you don't put arsenic into her floorwash,' she said rashly.

'If you're suggesting she drinks it, I wouldn't be surprised,' retorted Aunt Leda venomously. 'And I'd be grateful if you didn't credit me with Borgian tendencies.' Suddenly she was once more the *grande dame*, frail and offended.

I'm simply tired, it's the fatigue, Fanny thought. And aloud she said, 'I was only joking, Aunt Leda.'

'Balkan humour,' said Aunt Leda, but with that she had apparently exhausted the offence. 'Will you have tea?' she asked as usual, even though they'd been drinking tea at her house every week for the last twenty years. Fanny wondered what would happen if one day she upped and asked for coffee. You've been doing too much useless wondering lately, she said to herself.

'Yes, please,' she said out loud.

'I'll put the kettle on,' Aunt Leda said and disappeared into the kitchen. Fanny sank into one of the purple velvet armchairs, remembering too late that it wasn't the kind of armchair you could sink into. The massive carved-wood backrest slammed painfully into her back. She hoped that her spine wasn't damaged.

'At your age one would expect you'd at least know how to sit properly,' Aunt Leda said from the kitchen door, where she suddenly appeared holding the biscuit jar. 'What would your mother have said?'

'Nothing,' said Fanny.

'That's true,' Aunt Leda agreed, surprisingly. In their mutual gaze Fanny's mother materialized for a moment, vague even when alive, errant and capricious, easily swayed by any breeze, never interfering in anything she didn't have to interfere in, or rather in anything she wasn't forced to interfere in.

'I've come to you for advice, Aunt Leda,' said Fanny, and immediately felt silly, like the heroine of some novel.

'Wait a minute, the water's boiling,' said Aunt Leda.

Aunt Leda's answers certainly didn't sound as though they were taken from a novel, thought Fanny with mixed feelings. She waited for Aunt Leda to return with her Chinese teapot decorated with blue jasmine flowers – she had never heard of blue jasmine, but did not dare say so to Aunt Leda – then said with the adamance of despair: 'It's about work.'

Aunt Leda laid the teapot down on the thick crocheted napkin. In her eyes work was a topic whose importance justified one's full attention. Work ranked highly, maybe highest, in Aunt Leda's value system, not because she was a socialist, God forbid, but because work meant stability, continuity and especially money, that is to say the ability to live in a proper, i.e. solid, manner.

'You're not thinking of leaving Bruck & Sons,' she said. 'An excellent, solid place. I hope you're not crazy enough to give up thirteen years of service. I know Egon Bruck from back home, a perfectly decent family, they used to live on Wendelstrasse. You don't find a job like that every day.'

'I haven't said anything yet, Aunt Leda. And Egon Bruck is not there any more. He's retired. I already told you that two months ago.

'That's actually part of the problem,' she added, reflectively.

Aunt Leda looked at her with a pair of wide-open blue eyes, faded but carefully made up in black. 'You don't mean to say that young Bruck tried . . .?'

'No. That's not it at all,' said Fanny impatiently.

'It did surprise me,' said Aunt Leda and sat back in her chair. 'Well then, will you finally tell me what it is?'

That's what I've been trying to do, Fanny wanted to say, but restrained herself and said instead, 'The firm is changing.'

'That makes sense,' said Aunt Leda. 'A new broom.'

'But in a way that . . .' Fanny struggled to find the right words, 'I find difficult.'

'What do you mean?'

And Fanny told her briefly what had happened two days earlier at the office.

When she had finished describing the new item on Bruck & Sons' list of merchandise, and the firm's far-reaching plans for the future, Aunt Leda took a deep breath and straightened up. Her eyes were lit with the cunning blue fire of victory.

'Well,' she said slowly, in a strange intonation.

'Well what, Aunt Leda?' said Fanny impatiently.

'Well, why do you think Mr Bruck went to the trouble of asking for little Fanny's advice, of all people, on such an important matter as the firm's policy?'

'I really don't know,' said Fanny, 'but whatever the reason, I would gladly forgo the honour.'

'Fool!' whistled Aunt Leda. 'You little fool!' She leaned towards Fanny and said, stressing each word separately, 'Either he's thinking of promoting you to the rank of partner, or else he's thinking of promoting you' – here she paused dramatically – 'to the rank of wife!'

'He has a fiancée,' Fanny said despairingly. 'This is pure nonsense, Aunt Leda.'

'Six years,' said Aunt Leda with emphasis. 'He's had her for six years.'

'And suppose it were eight, Aunt Leda. What does it matter? And even if he did want to leave her, I can assure you he'd look for someone a little more . . .' She fell silent. She couldn't make herself say the words which were to follow, and Aunt Leda understood her meaning well enough without them: Young and Pretty.

'Well, then, it's the other reason,' said Aunt Leda, but without conviction this time.

'Believe me, Aunt Leda, he can find a better business partner than me. As you very well know.'

Aunt Leda kept silent. The bitterness in Fanny's last words had pierced the wall of obstinacy she had wanted to raise around herself, and shattered it.

'I guess he simply wanted to talk to someone so it'd be as if he were talking to himself. As if he were talking to the wall, or to a mirror,' Fanny said pensively. 'That he actually wanted someone who wouldn't answer him back, who wouldn't give him the advice he pretended to ask for, who would reflect his own opinion. Like a mirror,' she repeated, her voice fading. 'Someone who doesn't really exist. A piece of furniture.'

Aunt Leda's big blue eyes gazed at her from between the black exclamation marks of her mascara, and all of a sudden she leaned forward and took her hand.

'Don't look at it that way,' she said urgently. 'Why don't you just see it as if someone appreciated your opinion enough to ask for it?'

'Because I know it isn't so,' said Fanny.

After that they sat silently for a long time.

'He wasn't . . . offensive,' Fanny said finally. 'It's just that the whole business . . . this whole *thing* makes me sick.'

'It's a job,' said Aunt Leda decisively. Once on the firm ground of everyday facts, she regained her usual peremptoriness.

'It's not the same job,' said Fanny.

'It's a job,' said Aunt Leda.

'It's going to be very difficult for me,' said Fanny.

'You'll get over it,' decreed Aunt Leda. Now that she had made up her mind, she seemed to have lost interest in the matter. 'We'd better drink our tea at long last. It must be completely cold by now,' she said, and by inclining the spout of the teapot forced Fanny to lean forward and hold out her cup.

As she went out to the street, into the stormy gusts of wind which flung stinging little drops of rain at her face, Fanny recalled the beginning of their conversation and shook her head. For the first time in her life it occurred to her that Aunt Leda was an old woman, seventy-two years old, and that it might well be that for her – for Aunt Leda! – this was the beginning of the end. The thought resounded in her head menacingly, woven into the sounds of thunder like a low bass motif accompanying a melody, and she realized that even if she did not always like Aunt Leda, and perhaps did not even like her most of the time, nevertheless this possibility frightened her beyond all measure.

12

The next day, when she came back from work, the phone rang and she was surprised to hear Aunt Leda's voice at the other end of the line. Aunt Leda did not mention their meeting the day before, but after informing Fanny of Bentov's latest outrage, trash bags left all night outside her door, she asked if she wanted to join her on a visit to Myra's village in the Sharon. Fanny felt a sudden surge of warmth. Aunt Leda hardly ever took her along on her visits to the *moshav*, perhaps because she didn't go there that often and she preferred to keep Myra to herself. Clearly she hadn't intended to invite her in the first place, and her pedantic voice suddenly inspired in Fanny an unexpected rush of gratitude and affection.

Myra was a childhood friend of Aunt Leda's and the only one for whose sake she was willing to go to the trouble of leaving the city limits of Tel Aviv. To any other acquaintance who dared suggest such a possibility she would retort drily that even if she did have to spend her days in this sweltering godforsaken town, it certainly would not cross her mind to drag herself to places which were even more forsaken and even less interesting. But Myra suffered from rheumatism and worked herself to the bone on the farm, and even Aunt Leda recognized that she could not be expected to make the trip to Tel Aviv at the end of a working day. Fanny loved the rare visits she'd made to Myra's farm, and even more than that she loved Myra herself. She was Aunt Leda's complete opposite and yet astonishingly like her, like the negative exposure of a person standing against the sun: where the latter was a dark opaque mass which blocked the eye, Myra was a pool of transluscent water you could see through right down to the bottom.

Myra's husband came especially to pick up Aunt Leda in his car, an almost brand-new Peugeot 404 loaned to him by his brother, a successful building contractor, and Fanny and Aunt Leda stood on the street for a long while admiring its gleaming white paint while Jacob explained its virtues to them with great enthusiasm. Then Aunt Leda remembered that she'd forgotten her shawl and Fanny ran up to fetch it for her. Finally Jacob asked for leave to use Aunt Leda's bathroom before they left, and Aunt Leda said he wouldn't know how to unlock the door and went up with him. In fact she didn't like people to go into her house without her being there to keep an eye on them.

When they finally left Tel Aviv, twilight had already descended and a silvery greyish-blue light enveloped the road and the cypresses planted along its sides. Fields of alfalfa stretched on both sides of the road across the valley, and Fanny watched the blue dissolving into the green and permeating it until they both became a deep blue like that of Van Gogh, and she thought with longing how little she had seen lately of landscapes and open skies and greenery, but then they entered the region of the orchards and the intoxicating scent of citrus blossoms, with which no other scent can compare, vanquished all else around her, and her thoughts as well.

In the back seat with her were crowded two other passengers, *moshav* people who had taken the opportunity to spend a day running errands in town with the ride back guaranteed. One of them was a tall thin man wearing a well-cut old-fashioned wool jacket, probably his city jacket, who sat hunched in his corner and kept silent for the whole trip. The wool gave off a good smell of tobacco, pipe tobacco, not cigarettes, but he didn't smoke during the ride. Fanny wondered if he refrained out of consideration for the others, or for fear of Aunt Leda. The second man was short, thickset and springy, made of graduated hues of brown like one of those dolls you assemble in rings, one ring on top of the other. At first he leaned forward and talked very earnestly with the driver about village affairs, particularly about some new farming equipment he wanted to persuade the cooperative to acquire. Then, perhaps because he had despaired of the measured 'Yes' and 'No's meted out by Jacob, who concentrated on his driving and also apparently did not want to commit himself to his passenger's scheme, he leaned back in his seat and finally fell silent. The evening gradually blackened and the trees with their dark green foliage were only barely visible, a large sombre mass at the side of the road, dissected by deep narrow channels of twilit sky. But inside the car the heavy scent was palpable and intoxicating like a powerful physical presence, more powerful than that of the passengers who, as the trip went on, lost their reality and themselves became dark masses devoid of any identity, huddled inside the car as the trees outside huddled on the black soil. The man sitting next to Fanny looked at her for a while with his head tilted sideways, as if wanting to strike up a conversation but not knowing how. Finally he said, 'I remember you. You came over last year, didn't you?' 'No,' Fanny said, 'two years ago.' Her words seemed to her to be rising from the bottom of a deep well, slowly making their way up through the sweet, viscous liquid of the citrus bloom.

The smell became more and more palpable, almost solid, and you could discern in it areas in which it was lighter, and slightly acid, and others where it had condensed into one dark consistency of sweetness. 'It's a shame you don't come more often,' the man said. His brown rings dissolved into each other in the darkness of the car. 'It's pretty where we live this time of year. In fact it's always pretty,' he hastened to correct himself, as if afraid he'd been caught belittling his village. 'And next year we'll have a swimming pool. Then it'll really be worth while coming,' he added with a laugh, in a proprietary tone. He peered towards Fanny through the obscurity which was fast thickening. This was the moment when the slow, gradual

73

darkening of dusk comes to an end, to become the precipi-
tated, almost instantaneous falling of night. 'We're always glad
to see someone from the outside.'

Fanny smiled and nodded at him. The smell of citrus grew
more powerful as the darkness deepened until it almost made
breathing difficult, like an acute pain in the chest, a pure
weight concentrated around the heart. The man next to her
looked at her through the darkness. The solid mass of his body
was very close to her, and it smelled of metal and leather and
fertilizer, but surprisingly this blend was agreeable to her and
she breathed it in deeply. This smell, laced with the almost
intolerable scent of the citrus, drew her closer and closer to
him. As if drunk, all she wanted was to lay her heavy head on
the brown ring of his shoulder and inhale that smell, from as
close to as possible. She wanted to bury her face in the thick
winter coat and feel the rough brown cloth against her face.
'I'm sure you have a bathing suit,' her neighbour said and his
voice grew a little husky. In the cramped space of the car his
voice sounded very loud, even though the words were said in
a low voice, almost in a whisper. He touched Fanny's knee,
covered by the woollen cloth of the skirt, with the tip of his
finger. 'You can afford to.' The memory of his finger lingered
on her knee like an actual, scalding touch, long after it had
fluttered and gone.

The car slowed down and turned into the narrow road
leading to the village. Now they were travelling through open
fields, and the air from the window next to the driver streamed
in clear and cold. The scent of citrus had disappeared. Fanny
did not have a bathing suit, but she said, 'I'll come. In the
summer,' and then the lights of the first houses glimmered in
front of them and everybody started to move in their seats and
prepare their bags and packages for the approaching arrival.
The road was riddled with potholes and the jolting of the car
bumped the travellers against each other, but there was no
thrill in this contact. When the car stopped the sounds of the
village started up, the chirping of crickets, the even ticking of

an engine, the voices of children at play, and they flooded the night, which was now very near and immediate, close at hand, rapidly propelling towards her illuminated rooms, objects, the smell of poppyseed cake.

Myra's hug was her old familiar hug, brief and strong, and her heavy brown eyes were glowing. 'It's been almost a year, Ledchen,' she said and linked her arms in theirs, urging them to come inside, but Fanny stayed behind to look for one of the nylon bags which had gone astray. She was glad of the chance to be alone for a few minutes. Her thoughts were scattered, and she found it hard to gather them. After Myra and Aunt Leda had walked a little further and the echo of their voices had died away, the sounds of the village made themselves heard again and rippled clearly in the night. Fanny leaned her head against the side of the car, letting the nocturnal sounds flow through her in a slow, quiet stream. Finally it wasn't possible to delay any longer and she took Aunt Leda's bag from where it had slipped between the seat and the door of the car and walked into the brightly lit house.

Jacob apologized and vanished to put his working clothes back on, and Aunt Leda immediately took out the contents of the bag, which held as always, despite Myra's repeated protests, some article of clothing she had bought for her, this time a blouse.

'Come on, Leda,' Myra protested again in her low, slightly broken voice, 'as if there weren't any blouses in the cooperative store.'

'Yes. Pure sandpaper,' said Aunt Leda, and Myra burst out laughing and waved her hand, giving up. She hastened to put the bag and the wrapping paper on the chair in the corner – Fanny was sure she never wore any of those clothes except when Aunt Leda was visiting – and urged them to sit at the table, which was laid, as always, with home-made sour cream, thick plum jam and the wonderful crisp yeast cakes which were her special pride.

'Have another piece of cake,' she told Fanny. 'You haven't tasted the poppyseed one yet.' Her kind, penetrating gaze rested on Fanny's face and she turned to her friend: 'Our Fanny's quiet tonight.'

Aunt Leda glanced at Fanny. Her mouth twisted a little and it was evident that the rare outburst of feelings for her niece was already behind her. But she said only, 'As you make your bed, so you lie in it.'

Myra looked at Fanny again. 'Ah,' she exclaimed suddenly, 'I almost forgot. I have something for you.' She went over to the table in the patio and lifted a knitted napkin from the little basket which was standing there.

'Here, open your hand,' she said to Fanny. Fanny spread open the palm of her hand. At first she felt a slight scratching, and then a completely different sensation, soft and fluttering: it was a chick, a tiny yellow chick. She cupped her palm a little, and the chick snuggled in it like in a nest. She smiled at Myra.

'Take it home,' Myra said.

'Maybe I will take it,' said Fanny, ignoring Aunt Leda's scorching look. 'I'll raise it in the bathroom. I'll call it Emil,' she told Myra, laughing. This was the name of the banker with the squint. But she did not enjoy provoking Aunt Leda. The truth was that she couldn't find her place in the warm, well-lit room, in the crisp taste of the pastries, not even in the familiar murmur of Myra's voice. A part of her remained outside. It was this detachment which allowed her to defy Aunt Leda, but the rebellion tasted flat.

'Yes,' said Aunt Leda. 'That's exactly what Fanny is missing at home. A rooster.'

'Leda,' Myra said gently.

'Don't you Leda me,' retorted Aunt Leda. 'I know what I'm saying.'

Myra shook her head. 'Your tongue always ran away with you,' she said. 'I remember what Herr Professor Braun used to say: Leda, Leda, one day you'll fall on your tongue and stab yourself to death.' And soon they were immersed in their

76

childhood, in incidents which had taken place some fifty years ago and more, in that first day at school when the two of them had stood on either side of the classroom, their backs to the wall and inspected each other with a piercing childish eye. Fanny had already heard every one of those stories several times. She liked hearing them, but today her heart wasn't in them. Quietly she left the table and went to the open door and stood there looking out, feeling the slight tickling imprisoned inside her fingers and the chick's heart beating its gentle fluffy throbs into her palm. The night air was wet and imbued with the smell of trees and the odours of the henhouse in the yard and the neighbours' cowshed, beating, it too, with the invisible heartbeat of people she couldn't see, and she looked into it, trying to decipher it so as to find in it something she could not name.

'Stand up straight, Fanny,' said Aunt Leda. Then came the low murmur of Myra's voice, hushing her.

13

The paper decorations hung limply, damp to the point of dissolving, and the cheesecake Fanny had brought was the only one in the row of cakes on the counter which looked like a cake. The hall was half empty. The people in it stood, the men that is, looking at the others over the rims of white plastic cups filled with Carmel Hock wine, and the women sat, their legs crossed and their handbags clutched to their stomachs, on straight-backed chairs lined against the wall. Margie seemed to sense Fanny's restlessness and laid a reassuring hand on her shoulder: 'Don't worry. We've just come early, most of the people aren't here yet. It'll be all right,' she promised her, the way one makes a promise to a little girl, and Fanny looked up at her with an apologizing, only half-consoled smile, for Margie was taller than she was by at least a head.

'It'll be all right,' Margie repeated, but her eyes were already searching for Yosef among the sparse gathering. Having failed to find him she relaxed, for such was Margie's nature – what can't be helped, can't be helped, was her favourite maxim; she took hold of Fanny's arm and said, 'Come on, let's get ourselves something to drink. If there're no men, at least we'll get drunk,' and dragged her over to the refreshment counter. At that moment a deep bass voice called 'Margie, Margie,' and when they both turned their eyes to the door they saw Yosef there. The glance was unnecessary because no one else could have owned such a voice, which seemed to emanate from the very depths of Bluebeard's belly, but in fact belonged to the gentlest and most sweet-tempered of men. Even Margie admitted that, adding, 'Hell.' And she explained to Fanny, 'There's no fun in cheating on him. If you don't tell him, he'll never know, and if you do, he'll just look at you with those hangdog eyes. So what's the use?' Seeing that this was the case, she had forsaken her bad old habits to the surprise of friends and enemies alike. Sidelong glances at handsome strangers in restaurants, or conversations with men sitting next to her on the bus, did not count in Margie's eyes – these were part of a basic training routine, essential for keeping out the rust, a habit that had become second nature.

Yosef seemed to be in a festive mood. He brandished the bottle in his hand and his teeth shone behind the tangled beard which refused to own to any particular style or fashion. Margie hated that beard, but she confessed to Fanny that she was afraid of what might be revealed once he shaved it off and so she only tormented Yosef about it but did not really insist that he get rid of it.

'I see you've managed to drag Fanny here,' he called even before he reached them. 'That's what I call an achievement! Write me down for the first waltz, Fanny,' he joked. Fanny smiled at him. She liked him very much and somewhere deep inside her she envied Margie a little for having him, and for being able to treat this fact lightly and take it for granted, even as a nuisance at times; but she knew that she herself had no chance of ever being in Margie's shoes because she and Yosef were too much alike, birds of a feather, and so perforce Yosef was attracted to blonde, high-breasted Margie with the loud throaty voice, and towards Fanny he could only feel the same camaraderie which unites the infantry soldiers, in those moments when they are not too miserable.

'I'm afraid my card is full, Yosef,' she answered good-naturedly, 'but I might be able to cancel the colonel.'

'Don't do that. The colonel is an excellent shot,' said Yosef and they both laughed. Margie said impatiently, 'What are you two babbling about again? You'd better talk to Philo and find out when they're finally going to start this lousy party. Academics' night! Just the name makes me sick. Let's get out of here.' And Margie was quite capable, even though the party had been her idea and even though she had been the one to drag Fanny and Yosef there, of getting up and taking off like a comet, carried on the tail of her wrath, but at that moment the door opened, a group of people whose faces were red and shining from the cold burst into the room laughing and chattering, rubbing their hands together, the music suddenly reached an ear-pounding volume and Margie swept Yosef off in a wild samba with the same enthusiasm with which she had just insisted that they leave.

In an instant Fanny was left alone. She felt rather stupid, staring at the wall as if she were about to enter into conversation with it, and she decided to walk over to the bar and pour herself a glass of wine. She knew that she would not be able even to touch the cake, even though frosted cheesecake was one of her favourites.

Having poured herself some wine, she returned to her corner and stood with her back to the wall, sipping from the cup at long intervals so that it wouldn't empty too fast. She refused to sit; at least not that. Margie had, of course, forgotten all about the promises she'd made to her back home in order to get her to come, that she wouldn't desert her for even one minute, that she would stand by her as if she were stuck to her with Superglue. Come on, Fanny, you can't sit around at home all day like Hansel and Gretel, damn it. But since Fanny had not expected her to keep her promises in the first place, she wasn't angry with her. In any case it was impossible to be angry with Margie. She had no solid centre around which to focus your anger. Margie was a volatile chemical element. Fanny took another tiny sip from her cup and looked around. She hated white plastic cups, first because she hated all disposable tableware, and second because she couldn't help biting into the soft plastic, small bites all around which turned its rim into a volcanic zone of depressions and protuberances which afterwards she couldn't stand to touch her lips to, and finally because the lipstick marks could be seen on the white plastic for miles.

In the middle of her fifth or twentieth sip she began having that strange feeling we always get at the hollow of our throat when someone is staring at us. At that point she was already resigned to the idea that she would have to go through the evening as it was until the moment when she could, without offence, pick up the bag she had left on arrival in the corner of the hall, being firmly determined not to clutch it to her stomach all night, and leave. But now she raised her eyes in sudden hope to the direction the glance had come from, with that miraculous intuition which always directs us to the person looking at us, as if their gaze were a thin wire touching our shoulder. But the man, for indeed it was a man, was Ritzi.

Fanny immediately withdrew her look, as though she'd struck an exposed electrical wire. Her heartbeat intensified, reverberating in her chest, and for one terrible moment she thought she was going to collapse of a heart attack right there in the Academic Staff Residence Hall. But she gritted her teeth and refused to die. Under no circumstances was she prepared to die in the Technion's single staff dorms, in the whole world there was not a more abhorrent place to die in and she was determined to hold on at least as far as home. A moment later her heartbeat slowed and she felt a blessed relief spreading through her limbs and sapping them of strength, but she would not admit herself defeated and sit down, not for the world. She searched her mind for something to do, and for the thousandth time regretted that she was not a smoker because it seemed to her that nothing retrieved your composure better or gave you a more vital respite than extracting a cigarette, tapping it against the pack with a skilled hand, thrusting it between your lips and lighting it with a match, or, even better, with a well-designed lighter. Absurdly she was reminded of Mrs Shelly and her clothes line and she angrily chased this persistent memory out of her head. Lately all kinds of trivial memories, flashes of utterly insignificant moments, had begun pushing their way into her mind at times when they were not only useless but also confused her thoughts and diverted them from the issue at hand, and she was quite fed up with this phenomenon, which seemed to have become a permanent bad habit.

When she raised her eyes again she saw Ritzi approaching her from the other end of the hall and was struck by panic. Stop it, she ordered herself, stop it right now. This man is not Andrey and you are not Natasha and let's get that straight. From the corner of her eye she saw him crossing the room and exchanging greetings and banter with acquaintances on the way; obviously he was a regular in this place (in this place too?), and suddenly it became overwhelmingly clear to her: she was not going to meet this man, come what may. With the miraculous courage sparked by desperation she turned to the man next to her, whom she'd only noticed that very minute, and said, holding on to the narrow margin of airiness left to her by necessity, 'Shall we dance?'

The man gave her a surprised look but answered politely, having apparently been trained into obedience years ago, the manners so instilled in him that he couldn't oppose them, like a kind of built-in Pavlovian response: 'With pleasure, of course. *Bitte*,' and offered her his elbow on the way to the dancing floor.

Fanny, her cheeks burning, let him lead her to the middle of the hall. On the way she crossed Ritzi's astonished gaze and ignored it, cruising away on the arm of her forced knight towards the sagging belly of the paper chains, now near collapse.

At that moment the lights dimmed. The hall sank into semi-darkness and from the invisible phonograph there rose the voices of the perennial Bolivian trio in 'Besa Me Mucho'. For some reason Miss Fanny could never hear this tune without her heart being wrung a little, a brief, painful pull, perhaps because of all the warm Latin nights steeped in jasmine scent which she had never had, perhaps because of the great promise that was imbued in this tune, she didn't know why this tune especially, and which had never come true for her. 'Como si fué esta noche la ultima vez . . .' The stranger tightened his hold on the small of her back. It was a habitual response, quite mechanical, set in motion by the intimate deepening of the South American voices in this section, and Fanny, her eyes closed, wished for a brief and hopeless moment for arms that would be tightened for her, just her, perhaps to remind her of something that was hers and the man's she was dancing with, perhaps this was their song, perhaps they had once danced to it, in a past already become nostalgia, in a garden restaurant in Seville, and she pressed her hand to his, I haven't forgotten, and at that instant she realized, with a start of alarm, that she was mistakenly pressing the hand of the strange man, and saw the startled look he gave her, and she lifted her hand to smooth back her hair, beads of sweat breaking out on her forehead.

When finally the lights went on at the end of the dance, which had become a long slow torture, she broke away from him with a small bow of thanks, and again intercepted the same surprised look. No doubt she seemed to him utterly bizarre. Ritzi was still circling, his eyes half-closed and his cheek pressed against his partner's, as though floating on the melody's dissolving train. The woman he was dancing with was a very plump blonde who seemed to have been poured into her dress and welded to the glittering material. But Fanny refused to think even one contemptuous thought about Ritzi's bad taste. It was more degrading than she could bear at the moment. In a burst of courage she knew she had to hold on to, otherwise her determination would fail her and she would remain all evening standing listlessly in her corner between the wall and the refreshment counter, she quickly walked to the entrance and picked up her bag and went out, without saying goodbye to Margie and Yosef.

The cold night air blew in her face, fresh and invigorating, and she breathed it in gratefully. A few car headlights were making their way up an invisible road on the mountain, and before she left she stopped and looked at them for a while, leaning her head back against the wall.

14

In April Raya left the firm. Itamar had unexpectedly obtained an excellent post as an electronics technician at the Elron factory, and he and Raya were to be married half a year earlier than they had hoped. Fanny was invited to the wedding. The ceremony took place at the Felicity wedding halls in Haifa because the groom's parents lived there. The parents of the bride had no money to spend on the wedding, and certainly none that could buy the young couple a two-room flat in Ramat Shaul, and therefore had no say in the matter of where the ceremony was to be held. They only paid for the special bus which had been hired to drive the guests on the bride's side to Haifa, to enable them to get there on time.

Fanny also took the bus. The day of the wedding she left the office earlier than usual, and the feeling of freedom inspired by the early departure was combined with the joy of travelling and that of breaking her routine in general. It was still daylight when they left Tel Aviv, the faint elusive light of dusk, the most beautiful light of all, thought Fanny, and she took care to sit on the left-hand side of the bus so that she could look at the sea when they approached Haifa, and was proud of herself for remembering. The golden-grey light sank softly, like twilit feathers, on the black asphalt of the road and on the gas station at the exit and on the dunes and the water. The sea was especially calm, smooth and endless, and little waves rippled on it gently, taking their time, in no hurry to get anywhere. Fanny wore her beautiful blue dress, the only dress she owned which had a décolleté to it, and over it she wore her black Spanish shawl, for the nights were still cool.

At the entrance they were greeted by the parents with broad

smiles stretched across their cheekbones, and Fanny handed to Raya's mother the cheerful red kettle in its festive wrapping. She couldn't help hoping that Raya would not look like her mother in twenty-five years' time, for there was some faded and depressing resemblance between the two, but she immediately drove this unworthy thought out of her mind.

As she entered the hall she looked around her uncertainly. Batya hadn't taken the bus because she had promised Raya to spend the day before the wedding with her. Raya had reserved for the day a room in the Dan Carmel hotel so that she could be all alone and loll about in a perfumed bath for as long as she wanted, she told Fanny half-defensively, half-defiantly, and so that her mum wouldn't be on her case the whole day before the wedding. In the afternoon she had her hair done at the hotel's hairdressing salon, and even had her hands manicured, and in the morning she simply slept – it was wonderful, she told Fanny later when she came to the office for a visit after the honeymoon in Eilat. Fanny could not help but admire her determination. Raya did not knuckle under the joint offensive of both her mother and the groom's parents, all of whom, though for different reasons, endeavoured to prevent her from realizing this plan, and all of whom were united in thinking that this was nothing but sheer luxury and outrageous waste. But Raya said that that she refused to arrive at her wedding a nervous wreck. If they won't have it, she said to her mum when her patience gave out, fine, let them call off the wedding. This final threat did the job, as she had known it would. Raya's mother panicked – her daughter had always been a wilful child, given to caprices, and the last thing they needed was for one of her whims to pop up now and ruin everything. Raya's capable of it, she said to her husband in secret, she's capable of calling off the whole wedding just because of this trifle, and even if she took it back later, think what kind of an impression it would make on Itamar's parents. I too would think twice before taking in such a temperamental daughter-in-law. And so the matter was settled.

To Fanny's mind too the room at the Dan Hotel smacked of almost forbidden luxuries, the sort of things which aroused in her a mixture of reluctance and yearning. The thought of true luxury always gave her goose flesh. Fanny was brought up to buy only what was really necessary, only practical, useful things. In her home no one ever economized on school fees, or on warm clothes, but anything which was considered a luxury (and there were some items for which this definition was debatable) they treated with a certain suspicion which had more than a drop of contempt in it. This is fine for shopgirls, Fanny's grandmother used to say in a tone which perfectly wedded the most refined way of looking down one's nose with the acceptance of the inevitable. The only one to violate this rule was Fanny's mother, who in her vague and charming way took whatever she fancied at the moment she fancied it, and never paused to think about it. But Fanny's mother had a special, exceptional licence which nobody ever contested.

'Fanny!' Miss Fanny heard Batya's voice calling above the guests' ceremonious hum – What a beautiful bride . . . I've heard that the bride's parents didn't . . . D'you think I could have just a roll for now . . . Absolutely not, Marcus . . . With a sense of relief she hurried to where she saw Batya waving at her, hemmed in between two people dressed in their old-fashioned holiday best and a few elderly aunts. The man and the woman next to Batya turned out to be her parents, and they shook Fanny's hand with the vigour of a different generation and told her they were glad to meet her at last, after having heard so much about her, and so forth. Fanny said that she was glad to meet them too and she was being sincere because a moment earlier she had almost despaired of finding Batya and felt lost, wandering among the medley of guests, each of whom knew at least a familiar soul or two.

'They usually reserve an entire table for friends from work, but our office is so small we can't even fill a table,' Batya said and looked longingly at the table next to them, at which were seated young men joking among themselves with the cheerful rowdiness of weddings, probably Itamar's collegues. Batya's father intercepted his daughter's look and said in a low voice, fingering the white tablecloth, 'It's a pity you wouldn't go by yourself, Batya. You could have sat at the young people's table,' and Batya blushed all the way up to her hair roots, a violent red which could be observed climbing up her face – something which surprised Fanny no less than her mother's remark, '*Nu*, what can you do, our Batya's such a shy one.' At any other time Fanny would have looked upon this description as a total misrepresentation of the facts, but this little scene, and the colour now fading in Batya's face, forced her to accept it at face value. How little we know about the people we spend most of our time with, she thought. And aloud she said, 'Actually it's good that we're sitting here together. I'm sure I wouldn't have felt comfortable over there,' and she smiled at Batya's parents. The mother said at once, 'Nonsense. A young girl like you,' and Batya said, 'That's Fanny. Always making an old woman of herself. Doesn't she look great?' 'Absolutely,' said both her parents in unison. At that moment everyone turned their heads in the same direction and a buzz of excitement went through the room. The bride had entered the hall, at exactly the right moment for Fanny, who had begun to feel considerably embarrassed. Batya immediately sprang up, crying, 'Here's Raya. I swore to her I wouldn't let them all rush her,' and rushed to be the first to fall on her friend's neck. Batya's mother lowered her eyes to the table. Her fingers drummed nervously on the white tablecloth. 'It'll be hard for her there without Raya,' she said to her husband in a half-whisper, and he nodded silently, understanding her hidden meaning as well as her overt one.

Fanny also got up to congratulate the bride, but there were so many people milling around her, and their determination to reach her was so much greater than hers, that she finally gave up and decided to congratulate her when she visited their table on the usual round of greetings after the ceremony. In the meantime the sound of the gong was heard and the Rabbi called, in an Ashkenazy accent, 'Four men are needed to hold the canopy, four men for *Mitzvah*,' and the clamour intensi- fied. The ceremony was about to begin. This time Fanny hastened to rise, so as to obtain a good place to see from. For some reason the *huppa* had always attracted her, perhaps because then she could observe the people from close by, the expression on the faces of the bride and groom, the Rabbi's gestures, the tears shed by the mother of the bride, the glass shattering under the groom's foot and the moment she especially loved, that of lifting the veil from the bride's face. After the crowd had settled she found herself standing next to Batya.

On her other side stood Raya's mother, who every few minutes gave a loud sniffle, and when she wasn't wiping her nose with a large white handkerchief stained with lipstick, she would stretch out her hand to adjust her husband's collar as he stood beside her under the canopy, or straighten his yarmulke, which had slipped sideways, or smooth down his tie. Raya's father jerked his head like a horse who was being overly fiddled with, and you could see that he was trying to accept it all with good grace. Raya refused to look at her mother; her gaze was raised the whole while to Itamar's face. At last the Rabbi had completed the rapid stream of Aramaic words, the *ktubba* was handed over, the glass was shattered, and everyone fell on each other's neck in an outburst of emotion and sobbing, the more intense the more closely related they were to the newly weds. After a few moments Raya contrived to extract herself from the tangle of kissers and huggers, her face flushed, her eyes bright and her hair slightly wild. The expression on her face vacillated between great excitement and impatience. She glanced around as if looking for someone, and when she located Batya she called out hoarsely, 'Here, Batya! Good luck!' But Batya was busy crying into her handkerchief and didn't hear her. The bouquet flew towards her in a long arc and Fanny saw that she wouldn't come to her senses fast enough to catch it. She couldn't stand the thought of the bouquet, the beautiful wedding bouquet, falling on the floor, which was already littered with paper ornaments and with the napkins the children had thrown around, and on an instinctive impulse she flung out her hand and caught it at the very last moment before it hit the floor. Immediately continuing this motion she offered it to Batya, who took it, still sobbing into her handkerchief, too confused to understand what had happened, and then Raya reached them and fell on Batya's neck and they both burst into tears and kissed each other on both cheeks and Raya said to Batya between sobs: You'll see, it'll be all right, I promise you, don't cry, and Batya answered her between sobs: I know, I know, what a pig I am to make you cry at your own wedding, and Fanny wanted to say: What bride doesn't cry at her wedding, but didn't say it, and they all got extremely emotional until Raya's mother came and led her away to kiss Aunt Irene, who was quite offended that you didn't come to receive her *Mazel Tov*.

Only then were Batya and Fanny left alone, alone, that is, in the crowd dispersing among the tables, and the spring of Batya's tears ran dry and she stared with uncomprehending detachment at the bouquet in her hand, and then at Fanny, and for the first time she realized what had happened, and Fanny too looked at her with similar embarrassment, and the colour flooded Batya's cheeks again but immediately left them as she said determinedly, 'Well, we'd better go back, they're beginning to hand out the drumsticks,' and Fanny smiled and agreed and they both returned to the table, but in Fanny's heart a small excitement still flickered which refused to die, reviving every few minutes, and the touch of the small bouquet of violets, the bride's bouquet, still scorched the palms of her hands.

At the table Batya's parents smiled at her tearfully and her mother could not restrain herself and even kissed her, several moist kisses on both cheeks, till Batya said in her everyday voice, 'What's all the fuss about, I'm not the one who got married,' and threw the bouquet down by her plate. Batya's mother opened her mouth to remonstrate with her and immediately closed it. And again it was Fanny who broke the tense silence when she asked Batya, 'Mr Bruck hasn't come?'

'What d'you expect?' said Batya. 'If she hadn't quit, he wouldn't have had any choice. But as it is, why should he come and see what a fool he's made of himself all this year?'

'Why, do you mean to say that Mr Bruck was after Raya?' asked Batya's mother interestedly, leaning forward, and from that moment on the conversation flowed fluently until the meal was served.

After they had distributed the little cups of black coffee and cakes in their frilly paper cups, an invisible band – probably a tape recorder concealed in some corner – struck up the 'Tango Jalousie'. The bride and groom danced first, according to custom, and Fanny thought how pretty Raya's fair head looked lying on her husband's shoulder. At that point in the evening her face had shed its tension and her gaze rested on Itamar's face, tranquil and confident. Little by little the first few daring guests joined the young couple, and soon the small dance floor was crowded with couples whirling to the rhythm of the waltz which followed the opening dance. There were some really old couples among them, people well beyond their sixties, who moved with surprisingly nimble familiarity to the sound of the well-known, predictable melodies. Romantic melodies for couples. Fanny's glance strayed. Batya was sitting between her parents watching the dancing couples and her face was frozen in the same artificial smile which her own face probably displayed. The rose-coloured bubbling lightness she had felt for a moment, even if vicariously, effervescent like a sip of champagne, evaporated at once.

With a sudden, jarring shift of gears the waltz and tango tunes changed into loud pop music. Fanny supposed that this was what the young people wanted and it was their celebration and it was only right, but she found it hard to get used to this music, which seemed to claw at the sensitive spots in her ears.

At the nearby table the commotion grew and at precisely the same moment, as if by tacit agreement, they all rose as one and dispersed around the room. One of them, a tall, sturdy young man with a black mane of hair falling on his forehead, approached Fanny's table. He stopped in front of Batya, who was sitting with her back to the wall, and asked, leaning both his hands on the white tablecloth, 'May I ask you to dance?' His voice was a typical *Sabra* voice, a bit rough but pleasant. Fanny held her breath and it seemed that the entire table was doing the same. Surprisingly, or perhaps not so surprisingly, Batya's parents held their tongues. They did not say anything and did not urge their daughter to get up and dance, and after a brief hesitation Batya said, 'Yes. Why not?' and rose and flung herself whole-heartedly into a wild dance, which Fanny wasn't familiar with but thought that Batya moved her arms and legs to it with great expertise. The mother and father glanced at each other briefly and looked back at their plates. Fanny crumpled her paper napkin and looked at Batya and her partner, who had moved in the course of the dance to the further end of the room, and were now swallowed among the other dancers. She felt uncomfortable, now that she was left alone with Batya's parents. This was the moment when people usually felt themselves obliged to turn to her and express their interest. But Batya's mother was absorbed in conversation with one of Itamar's old aunts, who, it turned out, had emigrated to Israel from the same small town in Lithuania she herself had come from. Batya's father offered the woman's husband a cigarette, and his face too lit up with a new vitality as they talked about bathing in the old river and about the smell of goose fat frying in a hot pan in winter. The whole table was immersed in waves of quiet conversation, rising and falling, and Fanny sat forgotten in her chair, flooded by the ebb and flow of a hushed sea of words. She was glad that everyone had forgotten their obligation to be kind to her and to keep her from feeling alone. She wanted to be alone, to secretly touch the tiny ember which still flickered there and to feel its warmth spread through her slowly. She, Fanny, had caught the bridal bouquet.

15

The longing, this longing she was unable to name, grew in
Fanny side by side with the unease she had begun to feel at the
office. After Raya left them a kind of desolation descended on
the place. Batya continued to work with the same teeth-gritted
determination as before, but her heart wasn't in it. Fanny too
felt Raya's absence. Something of the office's former lighthearted spirit was lost, apparently for good. Raya's jokes had
never cut as deep as Batya's mockery, and her nature, which
had something very harmonious and pleasant about it, had
kept her friend's thornier one in check. Now that Raya was
gone Batya went around with a clenched face and an irritated,
daunting look. The girl sent by the employment agency to fill
in temporarily for Raya was miserable; every mistake she made
won her a venomous, well-sharpened arrow from Batya's
brimming quiver. The large room in which the three of them
worked began to take on, in Fanny's eyes, the shape of an
aquarium gradually sinking into disrepair, in which the
electricity is slowly dimming, the walls accumulate a thick
layer of dirt and the light streaming in grows murkier and
murkier. The world enclosed between the glass walls turns
darker, the water loses its mysterious emerald hue and becomes
grey and finally black, and the fish, the fish swim with rigid
monotony back and forth, back and forth towards their
impending doom.

When young Mr Bruck asked Miss Fanny to stay behind in the
office that evening after hours, there grew in her, along with
the surprise and the anticipatory sense of grievance, a
presentiment of disaster. She didn't know what sort of a

disaster it was that this feeling alluded to, but the remaining hours until five were totally ruined. From that moment onwards she could no longer concentrate.

At five o'clock precisely Batya and the new girl collected their things, took their coats off the hanger and left, waving goodbye to Fanny at the door. After Raya left, Batya adamantly refused to remain in the office even one minute beyond working hours. While they had only the temp from the employment agency, who wasn't familiar with the work, a large amount of matters accumulated which they didn't have the time to attend to and Mr Bruck asked Fanny and Batya, at a special meeting he'd called ('A meeting!' sneered Batya. 'He'd call three monkeys sitting on their arse in the Biblical Zoo a meeting'), to stay and work overtime until someone more permanent came in. '*Force majeure*, you understand.' Fanny nodded in silence, but Batya said unhesitatingly, in fact quite brazenly, 'Sorry. My mother's ill and I have to get home early to cook.' Mr Bruck knew no less than Fanny that there wasn't a word of truth in this, but of course he couldn't say so. He couldn't fire Batya either because then he would be lacking two skilled and experienced workers instead of only one. He therefore contented himself with the chilly comment, his Adam's apple quivering as always when his emotions were involved, 'I'm sorry to see that you are unable to give your work the same attention and wholemindedness that Miss Fanny dedicates to hers,' and sent them both away. Back in their ofice, with the door to Mr Bruck's room closed, Batya said to her harshly, 'And you too. Incapable of saying no. This jerk would tell you to sleep here if he could.'

Fanny said nothing and collected the inventory update forms scattered on her desk into one neat pile. But deep down she thought that Batya was right. She was incapable of standing up for herself, ready to give in on anything out of sheer cowardice. But she didn't know what to do about it.

That was why she decided now that if Mr Bruck started on his usual speech, about her being his oldest and most experienced employee, and how she was the only one he could count on, etc., etc., and how therefore he was asking her to stay behind every day after the others had gone in order to go over the day-to-day transactions with him, she would refuse no matter what. During all the hours which remained before the meeting she encouraged herself to stick to this decision, and took a great deal of trouble over the wording of her refusal speech, but the effort turned out to have been unnecessary. This was not at all the motive for Mr Bruck's request.

With particular courtesy Mr Bruck asked her to sit down, and even went to the trouble of dragging over for her the armchair which stood by the wall and which was reserved for meetings with important customers. He offered her a cigarette, and, when she declined, a piece of chewing gum. When she declined that too (being resolved to maintain a firm attitude and avoid situations which might make her feel uncomfortable later, at the hour of the Great Refusal) he leaned back in his seat, hemmed and hawed, then cleared his throat and finally apologized, surprisingly, for imposing on her for the second time. (Second to what? wondered Miss Fanny, confused, but quickly abandoned this enigma so as not to miss the rest of his speech.) He realized, Mr Bruck went on, that he was burdening her with a heavy load of responsibility, which she, precisely because she was a truly responsible person, must find difficult to shoulder; but it was exactly because of that, because of the great and commendable responsibility with which she treated every detail of her work for the firm of Bruck & Sons, that he allowed himself to impose on her again, and already at this point he wished to say without delay that the opinion she had given him last time, reserved though it may have been, had been of great help to him, and it was important to him that Miss Fanny should know this. It's not necessarily a categorical opinion which helps a person make up his mind. Sometimes merely raising different aspects of the matter can be of far greater value. For example, the important and interesting comment she made at the time, regarding the special aesthetics of the shaving sets made of rare materials, had suddenly shed a new light on this issue and made it clear to him why he was so attracted to these items when there was an abundance of other, much cheaper accessories for which the profit rate was much higher. He had suddenly grasped that something of his father's aesthetic values had stuck to him after all, something of his high ideals, though with a far more developed business sense, he hoped, and it became clear to him beyond the shadow of a doubt that he was indeed interested in establishing one branch in the firm which would be of high quality, maybe less quickly profitable but undoubtedly more stable and deeply rooted, and were it not for Miss Fanny, it was probable that this important realization would not have occurred to him at all. In fact, she had been the one to tip the scales and give him the necessary confidence to clinch this deal, and it was only thanks to her, you might say, that Bruck & Sons could dedicate itself with such tremendous momentum to lifting the new initiative off the ground; and perhaps it would be possible, already in the not-so-distant future, to credit her with raising the standards in the entire branch of men's accessories in Israel, so that no longer would the Israeli man lag behind, but would be on a par with the American and the European both, if not actually ahead of them.

And therefore, Mr Bruck continued in a lower voice, he was asking Miss Fanny to bear with him and help him out once more, for it was extremely important, with each breakthrough into new territory, to retain the balance in the all-round activities of the company. It went without saying that Bruck & Sons could not survive on a range of quality products alone, and balance, he must say at the risk of repeating himself, was the key word in such situations. It was his duty, as the person in charge of the interests of the firm as a whole, and with them, of course, the interests of the entire staff, to expand at the same time in the opposite direction as well, into products whose nature might be a bit on the common side, but then so was their circulation, and their high profit margin would balance the large investment needed for the high-quality products. The first initiative was a long-term one, whereas the one he wished to consult Miss Fanny about now was an investment which would bear fruit in the near future, even, you might say, the immediate future. And Mr Bruck opened the bottom drawer of the metallic filing cabinet once again and took out a package, this time wrapped in green. Once opened, the wrapping revealed a reel of film, and Mr Bruck installed it in the office's brand-new projection machine, the object of Batya's admiration. He then pulled up a gleaming white scrolling screen and turned on the machine. The rattle of the projector filled the room.

The yellow light flickered, blinked rapidly a few times and focused. Black circles widened quickly like pond water struck by a stone. On the screen appeared a young woman with Asian features, wearing a raincoat, who was hurrying briskly down a street. She stopped by a fruit stand and bought a large bunch of grapes, which the vendor wrapped for her with un-Israeli care. After that she continued walking and on her way purchased also a baguette, a few carrots and a jar of honey, and then she reached the building where she seemed to live and started climbing the stairs. From about the grapes stage onwards the spectator could sense that a certain man, moustachioed and correctly dressed in a white shirt, suit and tie, was following her.

The girl rummaged in her handbag and took out a large set of keys and opened the door. First she unlocked a heavy lock in the centre of the door and then an ordinary lock next to the door handle and finally a Yale lock, and then the door opened. Unfortunately, she did not take the same care locking the door on the inside, and after she went in the moustachioed man, who had appeared in the stairwell the minute the door was closed, produced a Yale key and opened the door too and slipped inside.

For a few minutes you could see him following her with his eyes while she put the kettle on and poured herself a cup of coffee, took the pins out of her hair and let it hang loose over her shoulders, and finally took off her clothes and stepped into the bath with a lighthearted whistle.

What followed next was a long and complicated series of close-up exposures of certain parts of the body which were better left unexposed, and some ringing slaps, and after that some very brutal blows indeed. The surprising part was when Fanny found out that the girl actually knew the man and even knew that he would be coming and for exactly that reason did not lock the door. The grapes were put to extensive and comprehensive use and so no doubt were the rest of the products, but at this stage Fanny closed her eyes and did not open them again until the end of the film. But she could not close her ears, however desperately she wanted to clamp her hands on them and leave them there, and so she could not prevent the loathsome sounds from penetrating. She barely made it to the end of the reel. Her face was red and swollen as if she had been holding her breath throughout the fifteen minutes of the screening.

'Of course,' remarked Mr Bruck with some hesitation, 'there might be a slight problem as to the distribution of this, uh, product. There's a certain amount of supervision, quite justifiably of course, the thing mustn't fall into the hands of irresponsible elements, and so some sort of, uh, *combination* of this initiative, well meant as it may be on our side, may be called for.' Mr Bruck's hand toyed somewhat nervously with the reel's cardboard packaging. 'We might market these items only as part of another set, that is to say, the film would be a kind of bonus attached to a different product, like the toys they put inside large boxes of cereal and so forth. I had thought, Miss Fanny, that it might be most fitting to couple it with our plastic shaving set, the keystone of our prestige sets, and point out on the package that the set can also be purchased in other quality materials such as wood, ivory and so on, and this way we'd be obtaining free publicity as well.' He paused for a moment and took a deep breath. 'Well, Miss Fanny, what do you think? Obviously,' he hastened to add, 'our customers cannot expect to get two fine products for the price of one. The set will be sold at full price, no compromise. We have a good product here, Miss Fanny, an excellent product, and respectably packaged, I've no doubt our customers will be able to appreciate it. And this is our chance to take over the market, Miss Fanny. The market will fall into our hands like a ripe fruit,' Mr Bruck repeated and stared at Fanny with two expectant eyes, but these words brought back to Fanny a certain scene in which the moustachioed man, the girl in the raincoat and the grapes had taken part and she leaped up and ran to the office toilet, reaching the sink in the nick of time.

To Mr Bruck's expressions of solicitude, to his worried enquiries whether she was ill and why didn't she say she was feeling unwell, he would never have permitted himself to keep her in the office under such circumstances, and so on and so forth, she responded with a faint wave of her hand, and she also rejected his generous offer to drive her home. She would do perfectly well on the bus.

That evening, as she sat in the front seat of the no. 5 bus behind the driver, Fanny knew that despite her thirteen years' tenure in the firm she had to leave Bruck & Sons without delay, and find herself another job.

16

In those days Miss Fanny felt as though she was spinning down from a great height, whirling and whirling like a long reel of paper which had become undone, and each winding coil of paper dragged behind it another coil, and another coil, and another one. The days were long and yet very short when she looked back at them. The nights had a white quality, not only because summer was drawing near, but that quality nights have when you sit and look for hours through the window without turning on the light, until the darkness lightens up. The sky turns blue and then pales. The night becomes a sort of day, only quieter and more isolated. Fanny liked the isolation of the night, which protected her from the need to find something to occupy herself with, as the day demanded. She began staying up until late at night and sometimes until the early hours of the morning. First she used to read or knit and later she listened to music and at last she only looked out. The flow of her thoughts in those hours was easy and free of the compulsion to arrive at some purpose, some practical solution, which hung heavily on her during the daytime till she became a trapped animal, breathless, hysterical. Of course, in all this running about to and fro she couldn't arrive at anything. Neither did the night thoughts get her anywhere, but at least they did not weigh on her and did not make her hate herself for them. There was no more rain. The nights were white and long and the days were dazzlingly bright and even longer, much too long. The best time was the evening, when she almost always went to the playground.

In the playground it was always evening and the calls of the children mingled with the twilight haze, distant and diffused. Fanny always sat on the same peeling red bench at the edge of the park and watched them play. In the dusky light their movements had a somewhat detached quality and their play seemed cut off from any purpose, whole unto itself. The child Uri would sometimes come with the girl who looked after him, probably the neighbours' daughter, but he never played with the other children, only on his own. He would find himself an empty corner of the sandpit and not budge, so that after a few minutes the other children would stop treading there, as though he had drawn around it clearly defined boundaries which allotted it to him alone. Every once in a while, not often, he would raise his head and look around, as if to make sure that the sky was still there and the apartment houses and the swings, and somehow his gaze would almost always encounter Miss Fanny's, pause on her for a moment, and return to the sand. Even though he had never spoken to her Miss Fanny believed that her presence was important to him, like a landmark you could always rely on to be there, something you could always touch, like you'd touch an old teddy bear, to be reassured by its familiar feel, and that was why she took care to come to the park every evening she could, which was almost always. She didn't have all that many other things to do since she'd left work, and this feeling that her presence was significant to someone, that it mattered to someone whether she was there or not, helped her go through the day without losing herself in its constant flow. She felt some kind of an alliance with this child she'd never exchanged a word with, alliance in a conspiracy, perhaps, or at least an alliance of presence. This moment was something to hold on to, a moment for giving assurance and receiving it in silence, and then she could go home calmer and lighter. On those days when Uri did not come to the park she would go back home with a load unlightened, a lack unfilled. On those days she would turn on the radio and listen to all the programmes until transmissions ended.

Once she lingered in the park too long, after evening had already fallen and the shadows had deepened to almost complete darkness, and a pair of lovers came and sat on the bench opposite hers. They did not notice her. Immediately after they sat down they turned to each other, and each of them put his arms around the other, the girl in an upward motion and the boy contrariwise. Miss Fanny remained trapped on her bench, torn between the wish to rise and flee and the embarrassment of being revealed to them now, a moment too late. She looked at them for another minute, hesitating, and all at once she felt the contact of Nathan's body, not as a memory but as a real, painful physical presence. The evening grew still darker and the fragrance of honeycomb deepened, as if it had been raining. It was a fresh, wonderful smell, and within it her dilemma seemed petty and out of place. The boy moved his hand down and lifted the hem of the girl's skirt, and the exposed stretch of thigh gleamed in the obscurity of the park like a lost coin.

Later she understood that even if she stood up and left they wouldn't notice her, so immersed were they in their own world that there was no room left in it for anything but themselves, and when they started toppling sideways on the bench in a kind of unstable pyramid, she got up and quietly walked away up the lane towards the exit.

At the beginning of May the weather turned unexpectedly and the world again became grey and liquid. Through the milky grey distance everything looked blurred as if seen through the glass of an aquarium. The women on the bench next to hers would take out the last Valencia oranges of the season from rustling plastic bags and peel them. The sharp odour of the oranges would spread in the air and pinch Fanny's nostrils, and remind her how her biology teacher, Herr Ebenreich, used to show them the etherial oil in the citrus rind by pressing the fruit against thin brown paper, and how the stains would remain, cluster upon cluster of tiny droplets. Later on the oranges disappeared and big juicy Grand Alexander apples took their place, but the apples did not have a strong fragrance and Fanny did not enjoy them like she did the Valencias.

On rainy days the children rarely showed up in the park and only Uri continued to come, indefatigably, with his young nanny and sometimes with his mother. This was a new arrangement. The mother would come on Wednesdays and at weekends, and Fanny guessed that she worked in a bank. On the days when his mother was there Uri was much more lively. He kept jumping up from the sandpit and calling her over to see what he had built or dug or to tell her a thought he'd had. Sometimes the mother sat on the edge of the pit and watched him while he played, and then he was happiest. He talked less because he had no need to attract her attention, but from time to time he would raise his head and look at her and his face would be taken over by a smile of complete happiness. On those days he did not look in Fanny's direction. Occasionally Fanny would feel sad, deserted, peeping from outside into the closed circle which surrounded the child and his mother, but there were days when she managed to feel as if she belonged to them, if only by a little, as if she had some right of precedence, so to speak, and then she would go home hugging this feeling close to her so as not to lose it.

All in all Fanny wasn't, in this first period, really worried or sad, but she wasn't happy either. The days went by and she went along with them. She dutifully applied for all the jobs advertised in the paper whose requirements she seemed to meet, but somehow nothing came of them. In most places, it seemed, they felt that at forty-two one was a bit too old to start on a new job, or looked for someone with experience in computer-card punching.

Sometimes Fanny wondered at the fact that she had no close girlfriend, no one she could turn to for advice or even just to complain to that she was having a hard time. She supposed this had to do with her having arrived in Israel already grown up, past those periods when people go through all the experiences which tie them together, studying in the same class, long trips, the army. The friendships formed in those periods, which are the deepest and the most enduring, she had missed. And still it was strange that she hadn't succeeded in having even one friend. Everyone has a friend. True, at the office she was on friendly terms with Batya and Raya, and she knew that they liked her, but this friendship almost never went beyond the office limits; and even if she sometimes went with them to the cinema, and even though she'd often heard them — always as a third party — pouring their hearts out on one subject or another, she never felt that any response was expected of her, and she never felt free to pour out her own heart. Margie was a friend, but the sort you went out with to events you felt uncomfortable going to on your own, not the sort that you talked to. Not really. With a strange and not a little ambivalent feeling, Fanny acknowledged that the person who was closest to her of all the people she could think of was Aunt Leda.

As she reflected on this, she recalled a conversation she'd had with Aunt Leda one *Sukot* eve, years ago, or rather an argument. Aunt Leda had claimed at the time that the circumstances of a person's birth and upbringing, their parents, the environment in which they had spent their childhood and perhaps their adolescence, determined their nature in such a way that it could no longer be changed. The person himself, his main essence, was determined in those years and it could never be shed or altered, nor would he ever be free of it. Fanny fought against this claim tooth and nail. In blatant violation of all the rules of prudence she usually adopted on her visits to Aunt Leda, and even of the most basic rules of behaviour, she spoke her mind in the most blunt and direct manner. You think so, Aunt Leda, she flung at her, because you arrived in this country already too set in your ways, too old to give up your five-o'clock *Kaffee-Klatsch*, your *Berliner Tageblatt*, your deep conviction that Berlin is the shattered spine of Western civilization, now and forever irreplaceable.

And it's not true. It's not true, Aunt Leda, and I, who came here at the age of twenty-six, still came resilient enough to change, to be able to adapt myself to the culture which exists here even though you look right through it as if it were dirty glass, I can see the beauty which doesn't exist for you, I shall turn into part of it, you'll see. And with a turmoil of emotion in which only now, looking back, Fanny could recognize the pain of the knife being thrust exactly at our most sensitive spot, at the very centre of this fluid, uncertain yearning which our huge wish to believe will come true is only equalled by our huge fear that it won't, and with a scorching feeling of failure, looking back from this distance of her forty-two years, she wondered whether this closeness suddenly forced upon her was not positive proof of the justice of Aunt Leda's old claim. Aunt Leda, by the way, was not at all upset by Fanny's passionate outburst of emotion and only shook her head and tut-tutted once or twice, and then, clearly losing her patience at Fanny's refusal to take the hint, asked her if she wanted another cup of tea, for who could tell if the stock of excellent Ceylon tea, which had suddenly turned up in the wholesale store near her house, would last until Fanny came to visit her again next week.

But despite, or perhaps because of, this closeness between them, which was clear to her now and which she no longer tried to deny or to resist, she couldn't go to Aunt Leda and ask for her advice, any more than she could bring herself to tell her, a month earlier, of her decision to leave work. She had put off telling Aunt Leda until the very last day. Each time she thought of going over something would surface from the edges of her mind, something nagging and unpleasant she didn't want to face, and she would recoil and put off the inevitable conversation until tomorrow, till Tuesday's visit, till next week. Only on her last day at Bruck & Sons, after she had collected her few personal belongings and with a small pang of surprise suddenly seen how few they were – a clothbound notebook in which she wrote her memos, the silver-plated pen old Mr Bruck had given her on her tenth anniversary with the firm, a raincoat she kept on a hanger behind the door for unexpectedly rainy days – as she deposited them, a pitifully meagre parcel, on the armchair at home, she knew that there was no way out and that she had to go and see Aunt Leda that very night, before the weekly Tuesday visit, because she knew that she wouldn't be able to lie when Aunt Leda asked her her usual question, so routine that it no longer held the expectation of a real answer, and neither did she want it to look as if Aunt Leda had extorted this admission from her through lack of an alternative, with her back forced, so to speak, against the wall separating truth and falsehood.

Back then it was still winter, and she wrapped herself in her woollen shawl and went out right away, without dawdling, for she knew that if she lingered for so much as a cup of tea she would no longer be able to make herself leave. Outside it was already dark. There was in the early obscurity which descended on the streets something piercing and sad, some- thing which, if you were in the right mood, and if you let it, would turn into a heaviness within you, and Fanny hurried along the dripping streets huddled in her shawl, trying not to think and not to let this early gloom seep inside her. She hadn't phoned before she left, that was more than she could handle. It was also wrong from a tactical point of view because it would have given Aunt Leda the necessary respite to get her heaviest guns ready. And so without prior warning of her arrival – an unprecedented act – and trying not to think about that either, she crossed Ibn Gevirol Street and turned into Professor Schor and at last knocked on Aunt Leda's door, wet and red-nosed from the cold.

Aunt Leda's voice behind the door sounded surprised. It also shook a little, or so it seemed to Fanny while she was standing bundled up in her shawl in the stairwell, waves of warmth throbbing in her face from the fast walk and perhaps from faint-heartedness, as ridiculous as that would have been, as though this step, which she had decided upon already weeks ago, had become real only now, the moment she came to announce it to Aunt Leda. But Aunt Leda's voice shook and again she was struck all of a sudden by the realization that Aunt Leda was an old woman, really old, in a way which couldn't be denied, and immediately there surged in her a desperate childish need to be given back that steadfast rock, steadfast even if not particularly welcoming (and could you expect that of a rock) which Aunt Leda had been for her ever since she could remember, since her earliest childhood.

'It's me, Aunt Leda,' she said once more, reminding herself again how right and important it was to ask who was there before opening the door, particularly with everything that was going on nowadays, but still she couldn't drive away that other thought, stubborn and nagging as a fly, that these words, uttered in a slightly shaking voice behind a locked door, straining to disguise their apprehension, old age was uttering them. Like Mrs Shliakoff from the ground floor, whom it took a quarter of an hour to open the door in order to lend Fanny her tall wooden ladder.

'Wait a minute, don't come in with those shoes on, you'll ruin my floor,' said Aunt Leda and disappeared into the bedroom. Fanny was left in the doorway like a person standing on a hanging bridge over an abyss, able neither to advance nor to retreat. Aunt Leda returned with a pair of pink plush slippers, which must have been taken out of her second-best shoe cabinet, designated for those pairs no longer considered worthy of regular use, and therefore honourably transferred to the wooden chest in the corner, just in case. Fanny always wondered whether the case in point referred to guests, or to the possibility that burglars might break in and rob Aunt Leda of her best slippers or of the new pair of winter shoes she bought every two years at Mykolinsky's, according to the principle that it was more worthwhile to invest in really good shoes once every two years, than to throw your money away on rubbish.

'Here,' said Aunt Leda and dropped the plushy pair at

Fanny's feet. Fanny leaned back against the wall and took off one shoe, but before she could complete the process she lost her balance and her foot, half garbed in pink plush, landed on the floor with a thud. She then changed her other shoe. Aunt Leda picked up the two wet shoes and took them out to the veranda, carrying them ahead of her at arm's length with the look of a person holding their nose.

When Fanny was finally allowed to sit on the sofa, after she had been examined from head to toe and it had been established that no drop of moisture had penetrated through her raincoat, she sank with relief into the velvet upholstery, but this relief immediately evaporated when she remembered why she had come there that evening. There was something about the house which felt different, and after she had looked around the room she realized it was the sofa she was sitting on. Always in winter, when she came for her usual Tuesday visit, the sofa was covered by a thick cloth cover with a machine-embroidered floral design. In fact, in summer too the sofa was covered because of the dust and grime, and it was only during that remote period when she used to visit Aunt Leda once a month with the banker-to-be that the flowery cover would be removed and the beige velvet revealed. Now it turned out that on the safe days of winter, when there was no danger of either dust or wet nieces, Aunt Leda sat in full majesty on her beige velvet. Interesting, thought Fanny absent-mindedly, one would think she'd leave the flowery cover on even when she was alone in the house. Though actually why should she? How many years has she got left to enjoy her beige velvet, she thought further and immediately turned her eyes away.

'You'll have tea,' stated Aunt Leda unquestioningly and again disappeared in the kitchen, leaving Fanny stranded on the sofa. Fanny would have been grateful had she stopped vanishing all the time, after all she wasn't Houdini, but it seemed Aunt Leda had chosen that particular way to express her dissatisfaction with this unexpected and unscheduled visit, and meant to let Fanny wait.

Finally, after five well-emphasized minutes, Aunt Leda reappeared carrying her black lacquer tray with the thin porcelain cups and Tuesday's biscuits. Fanny was glad of the familiar tray as of an old acquaintance. Its appearance, like on any ordinary Tuesday, made her feel a little more at ease; but after she had finished her first cup of tea she saw that it hadn't made what she had to say any easier, nothing would make it any easier, and that she had no choice but to dive, head first, into the story.

But already after the first sentence she stopped, for as soon as she said, 'I've left Bruck & Sons, Aunt Leda,' she saw herself, like in a movie, diving head on into an empty pool, straight on to the concrete floor with a dry, echoing thud, and that thing which had been hovering with folded wings at the edge of her consciousness spread its huge pinions and its great shadow enfolded everything. Most terrible of all was that Aunt Leda did not say a word. She kept silent and more silent still, and the air in the shuttered living room became more and more dense, and the tea in the cup gradually lost its amber colour and grew colder until there was no more of it, although Fanny could not remember having drunk at all; and when she finally spoke, she raised towards Fanny a face which seemed to have sagged all at once, the face of a really old woman, and she asked helplessly, almost tenderly, 'Fannylien. Why all this?'

Fanny felt as though a hand had closed around her heart and suddenly clenched. Never, not since she could remember herself, not even when she was a very small child, had Aunt Leda called her by a pet name. All at once a terrible, dispiriting weariness descended on her, the closest thing to utter despair she had ever felt in her life, and she closed her eyes but could only see black with bright circles in it. Finally, when she could no longer bear the silence, she said quietly, almost in whisper, 'I couldn't do otherwise, Aunt Leda. Honestly I couldn't.' Aunt Leda just kept looking at her with that flaccid gaze, so unlike her, waiting without any real hope for the next sentence, a word, something that would resolve what had just been said or at least explain it, but when the explanation failed to come her blue eyes within their thorny mascara wreath lost all expression. They seemed to sink backwards, into the bone, fading away, until Fanny could no longer remember what they had looked like on that day which she'd always remembered with such special clarity, thirty-odd years ago it had been, she suddenly realized, at the window of the train bound for Paris. The train had spun its wheels, spraying the gravel between the iron tracks, and blown thick white columns of steam, obscuring Aunt Leda's white handkerchief and the gleam in her eye, severe, malicious and beautiful. Back then her eyes had held all this, Fanny thought, and then only the severity was left and the gleam would appear only occasionally, usually at times of great anger, and now even the severity seemed to have been extinguished and only a faded blue remained, and a few sagging folds at the hollow of the eye.

Abruptly Aunt Leda leaned forward and a stream of words burst forth from her mouth. The creases on her face stood out all of a sudden, as if this face was now redefined in terms of creases, of dwindling, of old age. Her mouth moved quickly, urgently, shaping the words. She leaned over the table, not noticing that she was splashing tea all over the tray. 'It's not too late yet. Go to Mr Bruck, explain it all to him, tell him it was madness, a moment's folly, tell him that you've changed your mind, that you want to come back, that you'd just lost your head for a couple of weeks and now you realize it's all been a mistake, a simple mistake . . .' Her voice died out at the sight of Fanny's face. Fanny did not know what it was that she had seen in it, whether the helplessness, or the evidence that it was of no use, or the great anger that was swelling up in her, side by side with the pain which didn't stop gnawing, tearing inside her as if she were filled with shards of broken glass. She tried to be sensible, to ignore the tangle of bad feelings, to remain decisive and calm.

'It wasn't a mistake, Aunt Leda. It's what I wanted. I couldn't stay there any longer.'

'I wanted, I decided, that was my decision,' mimicked Aunt Leda furiously, her words lashing out in an sudden, astonishing outburst of energy. 'I decided, I wanted, and who's to want a pension for you when you're sixty? Do you think I could have held out for even one moment without the retribution money from Germany, and I didn't even get anything for the house, nothing. Not Entitled to Inheritance, they dared write in there, compensated only for the Loss of Opportunity for Higher Education. They had no idea what they were talking about, loss of opportunity, Paris, thirty-two rue Miramar, second floor, Paris, thirty-two rue Miramar . . .' And Aunt Leda suddenly started to cry, a loud, grating sound, almost a wail, the crying of someone who's not used to crying, and Fanny sat straight-backed and watched her and the horror crept inside her from the feet upwards and right into her heart, but she couldn't stop looking, even though she knew she was watching a private, absolutely confidential image of Aunt Leda which wasn't intended for anybody's eyes, certainly not for hers, Fanny's, but some pole had been stuck in her back and would not let her turn aside or close her eyes, Aunt Leda and this contorted face, Aunt Leda and the stifled sobbing, the whimpers which dropped one by one on the beige velvet, crying had nothing to do with Aunt Leda. And the icy feeling in her heart knew that Aunt Leda was right, that she shouldn't have left her job, the monthly transfusion into her bank account, the desk in the corner by the window which had been hers, hers alone, and now was not hers any more, nothing was hers any more except for the apartment bought with the Jewish Agency money and with the remainder of the sum her father had stuffed into her pocket before sending her to Switzerland, to tide her over until they arrived.

'They've already got someone else, Aunt Leda,' she said helplessly, hating herself for this capitulation, for the shameful need to clutch at the facts.

'Not as good as you.'

'Better than me, Aunt Leda,' she said wearily. The weariness washed over her, a vast weariness she was glad to abandon herself to, because it submerged and muffled the cold horror, and shut out Aunt Leda's voice and her crying, her short, faint, puzzled sobs which were now subsiding.

Forever, she knew, she would retain in her memory Aunt Leda's hand, still shaking a little, pouring the tea into the porcelain cups, and her newly wrinkled mouth asking her, with that same strange, shocking tenderness, 'And what will you do now, Fannylein? What will you do?'

'I don't know, Aunt Leda,' she said finally. 'I really don't know.'

17

Little by little Miss Fanny was overtaken by worry. It would waylay her in odd corners of the house, by the south-facing window in the kitchen, for example, where she so loved to sit on sunny mornings; it would rear its ugly head when she watered the potted plant in the corridor, or when she was arranging the few groceries she'd bought on the refrigerator shelf, and when she opened the bottom drawer of her wardrobe all the shoes seemed to wear out right in front of her eyes. When she examined the monthly report from the bank the withdrawals column seemed to go on infinitely, and when she leafed through the newspaper for Advertisements panic had already blurred her eyesight and she had difficulty in reading the small print. By the end of four months she had gone through all her reserves of ready cash (Mr Bruck had been generous enough to grant her partial compensation, even though she had resigned), and she faced the choice of either cutting short her pension fund's savings plan — breaking up a pension plan! An idea her whole being revolted against — or selling her jewellery, a gold chain with a medallion, a gold bracelet she had received from Aunt Leda on her eighteenth birthday, and an old-fashioned sapphire ring; or finding work immediately. Fanny chose the third option. She cast aside all scruples and answered every possible advertisement, from Deputy Domestic Manager in a Large Public Institution to Saleswoman in a Delicatessen. And indeed, when she had overcome her last compunction and answered a call for enterprising and dynamic women to lend themselves to the distribution of beauty products, she was instructed over the phone to present herself that very day at five o'clock in the

afternoon at a certain address in the city, to receive guidance
and a portfolio of sample products.

The advertisement went thus:

SELECT BEAUTY COUNSELLORS
If you meet the following requirements:
- Well-Groomed, Mature Appearance
- Enterprising and Dynamic
- Working Knowledge of English, French or Yiddish
- Innate Talent for Salesmanship and the Attributes of a
  Born Agent
WE HAVE JUST THE JOB FOR YOU!
Call Yaffa at———on Monday
Training and Instruction Will Be Given Only to Those
Found Suitable

Fanny reflected that if the word 'mature' meant what she
thought it meant, she finally had a chance of landing the job
despite the heavy load of her forty-two years. The word
'select' made her think more than anything of a box of
chocolates, but at this stage she was beyond insult at the
possibility of being taken for a select sweet.

At four she put on her beige suit with the narrow skirt,
which was classified in her wardrobe as her business suit,
combed her hair carefully and even powdered her nose so it
wouldn't shine. After all, that's what being a beauty counsellor
was all about. As she left the house she glanced at her image in
the long mirror at the entrance, and even though it was an old
mirror, and because of some flaw it always made the legs seem
shorter than they actually were and the face longer, she was
pleased with her appearance. The image mirrored back to her
exactly the kind of woman according to whose advice she
would buy beauty products without hesitating. She radiated
maturity, experience, and even – that's the way Fanny felt at
that fleeting moment she looked at herself in the mirror –
elegance.

But to her disappointment there was nobody to even so much as glance at her impressive appearance. At the address mentioned in the newspaper, which turned out to be a small two-room flat cursorily turned into an office, were crowded about thirty women of all ages and one flushed and perspiring instructress who tried to raise her voice above the din. She was waving a wrinkled brochure with her right hand as she endeavoured to address the women huddled in the small room: 'Girls, girls! Can we have some quiet, please!' Fanny reflected that she hadn't expected ever again to be included under this collective denomination. There was something ludicrous about the whole spectacle, and she was wondering what in fact she was doing there when the red-faced woman finally succeeded in hushing her flock.

'Girls! I'm not sure how many of you know exactly what it means to be a beauty consultant. Whoever does know, would she please raise her hand? Is there anyone?'

Three women with a tired look and one girl who'd been steadily chewing on a piece of gum ever since Fanny came into the room raised their hands. Fanny noticed the transition from the advertisement's 'counsellors' to the perspiring instructress's 'consultants', and wondered what view she should take of this new professional description. 'Consultants' did have some international flavour, but on the other hand 'counsellors' seemed to her more dignified, richer both in experience and in remuneration. Privy Councillor Johann Wolfgang von Goethe. She shook her head to drive away this untimely semantic debate and hurriedly tried to catch hold again of the thread of the lecture.

'Girls! The woman does not exist who doesn't want to improve her looks. Even those who look like Ava Gardner. And you show me one woman who does her Passover cleaning and rushes to the market and cooks the Seder meal for her own and her husband's family and who looks like Ava Gardner. I'm prepared to put one thousand lira right here on the table if you find me one such woman in the whole of Tel

Aviv *and* the suburbs.' Giggles in the audience. The present company was obviously pleased that there was no Ava Gardner to be found in all of central Israel. It was a sort of collective acquittal. Fanny too felt somewhat relieved, although she could not help noticing that except for a pile of brochures and sample portfolios the instructress had brought nothing with her.

'And this, girls, is what you should work on. The inalienable right of every woman to look better.' To life, liberty and the pursuit of happiness meditated Fanny lazily. A last ray of sun frisked around the gilded frame of the speaker's spectacles and darted back from it in blinding flashes as she shook her head emphatically. 'Never tell a woman that this or that product would make her look good. Always say that it would make her look *better*. See? Otherwise it's as though you were saying that without it she looks bad, and then you've aroused her antagonism. Never arouse antagonism. Always be pleasant, smiling and eager to help. The customer is always right.'

The flushed speaker's voice rose in a crescendo which broke like a wave over the small audience assembled before her: 'The customer is *always* right! If you think that Peach no. 22 would look best on the customer but she thinks Cherry is her colour, the customer is right. Everyone knows best what suits her. If you argue with her you might end up convincing her, but she'll always be left with the feeling she should have bought what *she* wanted. And why should you argue with her? Will *you* have to live with this lipstick? Her *husband* will have to live with this lipstick! And if he doesn't like it, then next time his wife will remember she should have listened to you. And then you'll have acquired a good customer.

'Girls! I'm telling you for your own good. Do not argue, do not force. Try to listen to what the customer is hinting at, try to see what it is that *she's* set her heart on. The moment you've grasped that – the customer is yours. And don't forget: if you persuade her not to take what she wanted, what are you left with? A little satisfaction. If you agree with her choice, she's sure to buy something else. What are you left with? An additional ten per cent. Ten per cent, girls! Get that number into your heads. Never forget what you're there for. Your goal is – ten per cent.

'Girls, we all know how difficult the situation of the working woman is. We all know what it means to keep house, raise a family, send the children off to kindergarten in the morning, make meatballs for lunch and on top of it all try and make some money to help with the family income. Today a bright new prospect opens up before you. A job you can do at the hours convenient to you, on the days convenient to you – in short, that'll save you precisely those problems which make the difficult situation of the working woman even more difficult.'

The speaker's tone became hurried, almost urgent, as though she wished to jump some hurdle in an unnoticeable manner. 'In this brochure you'll find all the details about Fruit Charm's range of products. Our line this year is based on the theme of Fruit of the Season, orange tones for winter and watermelon for summer, and they're brilliant, simply brilliant. I shall give each of you a portfolio containing products for sales and for demonstration, and each one of you must sign to confirm that you have received the portfolio. If –' The speaker's voice became desperate, anticipating the pandemonium which indeed broke out at this point, 'If any of you finds out that she is not suitable for the distribution of Fruit Charm products and renounces her original intention of working as one of our employees, she must return the portfolio to us without delay. I shall note down the name, address and telephone number of each one of you . . . Girls!' she implored, 'one by one, form a queue. I'm begging you, it won't work out this way, lady! I'm not allowed to give anyone a portfolio without her signature and address, we'll never be finished today if you go on like this –' The crimson instructress tried to perform simultaneously several actions the conjunction of which was plainly impossible, such as writing down the address one stocky woman was dictating to her, adding a brochure to a portfolio with her other hand, and shielding with her writing hand one of the portfolios in the pile from the masticating girl, who was trying to divest her of it prematurely. 'Lady! If you don't stop this I'm taking you off the list. You wait in line like everybody else, we won't get anywhere without patience . . . ' The girl increased the tempo of her chewing and demanded, with glutinous derision, 'How're you going to take me off the list when I'm not even on it? This whole company is crackers. "Peach Lipstick"', crushingly she imitated the instructress's intimate tone, revealing an unexpected talent for mimickry, 'Banana mascara. Why, you'd have to be nuts to buy this sort of garbage. Make way, make way, gi-rls, I'm goin' home.' And the crowd gave way, or rather split asunder, like the Red Sea in its heyday, before the majestic sway of her exit.

Fanny did not quite understand everything the chewing-gummy girl had said, but she had a heavy feeling that she agreed with the general gist of it. Still, she waited patiently until she had reached the table, almost the last one, and received the cardboard portfolio from the instructress's clammy hands, and then she wrote down her address in neat, shapely letters, and went home.

18

This was the third building she'd been to, but she seemed to be standing in exactly the same stairwell – the same murky cream colour, the marble panelling in urgent need of the bi-weekly maintenance cleaning, and a faint smell of stew, the same stew, it seemed. Cabbage, Miss Fanny decided, and pressed the buzzer firmly. After all, she couldn't just stand there all day staring at the walls. Still, it was strange, she had time to reflect as the steps drew nearer and the door opened to a narrow crack, why this neighbourhood, which wasn't all that far from her own, was considered perfectly respectable, one of the best. In Berlin there was never room for doubt, she had time to think before the door opened wide and the woman who had opened it stepped forward and stood opposite her on the doorstep.

'Yes?' said the woman.

Her voice was neither cold nor friendly. It was as neutral as a voice could be, utterly colourless, not in the sense of its tonal richness but in the sense of any tendency towards affirmation or negation, attraction or rejection. Enough of your superflous musical analyses, Miss Fanny scolded herself and looked at the woman. The woman's eyes looked out at her with the same toneless neutrality. No, you definitely could not call this look chilly, Fanny said to herself; it reflected no wish to put her in her place, no intention of pouring cold water over her. It reflected nothing. Nothing at all. And for some reason this nothing depressed her more than anything else she might have found there.

The woman's eyes still rested on her face with the same non-committal, and perhaps therefore untiring, detachment.

She's capable of standing here for hours just looking at me, thought Fanny, suddenly alarmed. She could easily stand here in the stairwell till nightfall. She knew that she was propelling herself into a hysterical spin but was unable to stop. The woman's eyes looked at her as if she were something that had been standing on the second-floor landing ever since the house was built, with no particular interest but with no impatience either, the way you'd look at a flower pot. Furniture again, thought Fanny with mounting panic, and at that moment she felt that if she let her anxiety swell any further it would devour her and take over completely and there was no telling where it would all end, and this realization cleared up her thoughts and helped her look the woman full in the face and launch into the speech she had so thoroughly and resolutely prepared the night before in front of the mirror.

'So we have products for every season and for every skin type,' she concluded somewhat breathlessly. 'And they're also especially suited for the Israeli climate,' she remembered to add at the last minute, with a haste she immediately felt was unnecessary and damaging. The flush-faced instructress had admonished them not to forget this detail, which is especially important, girls, it gives them the impression that this is not just made-in-Israel, you know, cheesy, but deliberately so, something unique.

The uniqueness of Fruit Charm's products did not, it seemed, make any particular impression on the woman standing in front of her, framed by the mirror and and by the gilded pattern of the wallpaper behind her. Only now did Fanny notice her features. They seemed to have been carefully chosen so as not to create in the spectator any definite impression, any deep-reaching imprint which might incline him this way or that. She had thin, dry, brown hair, gathered in a bun at the back of her head, a nose of average proportions and thin lips. It was as if out of the inventory of all possible features, only those devoid of any special qualities had been sifted out for her.

This prolonged waiting in the stairwell opposite the silent woman became, as it drew on, harder and harder for Fanny. She felt like an actress in a travelling troupe, desperately trying to generate some sympathy in her audience, while they – the providers of her next meal – remained utterly indifferent to her.

'So . . . do you think you might be interested in trying one of our products?' she asked finally, stammering slightly, but with a firm resolve not to let this situation go on any longer. 'I have some demonstration samples here with me. It won't cost you anything.'

As she ceased talking and the silence again grew between them, she became afraid they might really remain like that all night long. Perhaps, she thought with a new pang of alarm, she was dealing here with a deaf-mute, or worse. And then the woman finally opened her mouth. 'I never use make-up,' she said.

It was as if she were a doll, responding only to direct approaches, the pushing of a button, thought Fanny, and then the absurdity of the answer caught up with her and she asked – on the verge on anger, for no real emotion could be aroused by that presence, monotonous almost to the point of non-existence – 'So why didn't you stop me? Why did you let me talk for so long?'

'It's always worth listening,' said the woman.

It might have been the look on Fanny's face which revived in her some brief, feeble spark and made her add, 'You never know.'

Fanny looked at her again, and she didn't know what it was that made her stay her look on the face of the woman opposite her, but in a different way, more closely and attentively, nor what it was that made her say quietly, in a way which surprised even her, almost gently, 'No. You never know.' She picked up her portfolio of samples and turned to go, giving the woman a small, experimental smile which she tried to make as non-binding as possible, but the woman just went on watching her expressionlessly from her doorway, doubly illuminated by the bulb in the hall and by the mirror, all the way down the stairs.

The next few apartment buildings Fanny also left with scant success, but with a far better acquaintance with the character and substance of Israeli shared living. Before this, she reflected, she'd enter a building with the sole purpose of reaching a certain flat on a certain floor, and would therefore be quite impervious to whatever else the building had to offer. Now that she didn't aim for any apartment in particular the entire building called out to her, all its floors and corridors and stairwells and entrances, and she found herself sniffing the smells which drifted from the door cracks, listening to the voices rising from the flats, to the arguments, to the music on the radios, to the life which pulsated in the house and made it vibrate, like a body vibrating with the beating of many hearts.

Her only success, in fact, came in the fifth building, where the door was opened by a girl of about seventeen who immediately cried out when Fanny introduced herself, 'How lucky!' She'd just discovered that her mascara had run out, she explained, and tonight she had a party, and all the stores were already closed. Without checking the quality of Fruit Charm's Aubergine mascara she took one and paid for it, but when Fanny, very much heartened by this unexpected success, tried to sell her some other products following the instructress's system, the girl flatly refused. She only bought Revlon products, she explained to her, Made in America, some girl she knew brought them over from abroad.

'And it's no use trying the other flats either,' she added. 'She lives here in number ten and she sells to all the neighbours.'

'Thanks,' said Fanny, hesitantly. She started collecting the scattered products and returning them to her bag, wondering if she should try her luck anyway, but the girl remained standing there, watching her, until she was done, and she felt awkward knocking on another door under her watchful eye, as though she wouldn't take her word for it.

The next day Fanny set out again, armed with her samples portfolio and the bag of products for sale and with renewed hopes, but already after the first building her hopes waned and after the second one they spluttered out. Strange, she said to herself, after all, the people here aren't without means, I'd expect feminine curiosity at least . . . But feminine curiosity was not aroused, or at least she wasn't able to arouse it. In the end she came to the conclusion that the blame lay with her and her alone. You're nothing but a great big glorious failure, Fanny Fischer, she told herself, and there's nothing else to be said about it.

Nevertheless she made one last desperate attempt in another building, but that too was cut off almost at once. The first flat was empty, which was perhaps what drove her to knock on the door of the next flat twice, even though the first time she was answered by nothing but silence. They can't all be out in this building, she said to herself and rang the bell. After another moment of stillness she shrugged and picked up her bags and was just about to go, when she heard old, tottering steps shuffling woollen slippers on their way to the door, and a voice, just as old and tottering, shouted at her, 'There's nobody home.'

After this the steps shuffled back inside. Fanny stood stunned in front of the locked door. The only thing she could think of was how sorry she was not to be a schoolgirl, one of those who went around collecting donations in pairs, because they at least would have had someone to share this bizarre joke with, whereas she had no one. But after a while the words didn't sound that funny any more, and for some reason a great black sadness settled over her and all she wanted was to go back to her own home and lean back on her sofa with a cup of tea and listen to the radio, as did all the people to whose flats she'd been that evening, and all the people in the other flats whose lights were visible from the street.

In the morning, on the bus on her way to return the demonstration portfolio to another perspiring woman, she thought that somehow there had been not just absurdity in those words, but something beyond that, and even beyond the sadness they had aroused in her, something which in some undefinable way was connected in her mind to this country as a whole. She immediately took that back, however, shrinking at the very idea that she allowed herself to think such philosophical and generalizing thoughts, and tried to concentrate on drawing some lesson from this latest crushing failure, and on attempting to understand what that flaw was in her that prevented her from ever becoming a good saleswoman.

19

Miss Fanny went into the bathroom and closed the door behind her. She always closed the door behind her, not for fear of a sudden draught but because of some need imprinted in her in her childhood to shield herself whenever her body was exposed, even though she lived in the flat all by herself, even though it was impossible to see into the bathroom once she drew the living-room curtains. And it was a pity, for hers was a handsome body.

Miss Fanny's body, perhaps because it hadn't been worn by giving birth to children and breast-feeding them and carrying them around, was unmarked by the years and remained almost as it had been when she was a girl of twenty, fair and smooth and uncreased. All that had happened was that it had grown a bit broader, as though more generous, more abundant, readier to give of itself. Miss Fanny would have preferred it to wear out, as did any woman's body that was used for its true, original purposes, and at times she viewed her body in the mirror — indeed, she seldom looked at it especially at all — with disfavour, the way you would look at any useless tool. Miss Fanny would have preferred her breasts to be heavier, as were breasts that have suckled more than one baby, and her belly to be fuller and even to sag a little, if that was the price she had to pay for bringing a child into the world, and she was willing to pay with the lines of worry that are etched into your forehead when your child is late home, or rebels against you in the difficult years at the end of childhood and before adulthood; with all these and more she was willing to pay, but it was not granted her.

Sometimes she wondered how this had happened. That is to

say, how had it happened that she, Fanny, had reached the age of forty-two without a man or a child of her own. This puzzling was merely theoretical, a bit like going over an account sheet with the well-known deficit at the bottom line, for Fanny knew all the stations on the road which had led her hither, but did not know, and knew that she could not know, the hidden reason at the root of things which made her road pass through these particular stations and not others. Perhaps, she sometimes thought, it was simply a matter of luck.

Even Aunt Leda did not know that at a certain point in her life Fanny had come much closer to marriage than met the eye, certainly closer than the novice banker with the squint. She once had, Fanny did, a man of her own, or whom she thought her own, and she used to laugh at him with daring impudence and go to the cinema and the promenade with him and hang on his arm when they went for a walk in the evenings. His name was Nathan, like Lessing's Nathan the Wise with whom she used to tease him, and he was indeed wise and handsome and the most wonderful of men, at least in Fanny's eyes. Fanny kept him jealously to herself and never brought him over to Aunt Leda's for afternoon tea, or to her erstwhile job at Tnuva, perhaps out of some deep, unformulated foreboding that warned her not to flaunt this prize of hers before the world, nor to make much of it, but to keep it as unobtrusive as possible and thus appease the wrath of the Fates, but even in this she was unsuccessful. Despite her caution, despite all her efforts to keep him within the small realm that was theirs and theirs alone — and perhaps because of this? — her Nathan met another woman, and fell for her, or perhaps it was she who'd fallen for him, and left her. But the heartbreak, and the terrible nights alone in bed on her wet pillow, and the days at work, when right in the middle of typing a letter or filling out an order form she would be seized by uncontrollable weeping and be forced to run and lock herself up in the narrow toilet cubicle and cry her heart out, all the while hating herself for this sobbing, so full of self-pity — all of this did not make her regret what had been or wish that it could be undone, or make her sorry for having been with him, even if for such a short while, for there was no period in her life when she was so aware of herself, not only of her physical self but also of her emotions and desires and sudden, violent urges, as she had been in her days with Nathan.

Miss Fanny took off her light sweater and the blouse she had on underneath it and undid the hooks of her bra. Half-naked she stood and looked at the mirror, which returned her reflection till half-way down between her chest and her belly. Thin lines were incised just above her bosom, between the slope of her breasts and her neck, and as always Miss Fanny put her clenched fist on this place and rubbed hard, but the creases did not disappear. They had been there for years, and it wasn't age which had made them; she had inherited them from her mother. She too, Fanny remembered, had had such thin furrows when Fanny was still a child. Fanny's mother, who had been a beautiful woman and was vain about her beauty, hated these flaws and would go at them with a fury, scrubbing them with special brushes and trying to soak into them creams and lotions she had brought over especially from Paris, but all in vain. It wasn't a question of age but of heredity, and Fanny, who had been present at some of those battles of her mother's, did not even try to fight them. All in all, excepting these creases, she had a good-looking body, and she knew it, but what good was it to her if nobody saw it but herself, or some occasional man, an overnight visitor, some Ritzi?

Miss Fanny took off her skirt and underwear and adjusted the taps so that the water wouldn't be too cold or too hot, and stepped into the bath. She took her showers sitting down and Nathan used to tease her about it, but it had been her habit ever since childhood and she couldn't change it, or perhaps did not want to, for sitting thus in an almost foetal position, with the warm water streaming over her body, was so pleasant to her that she didn't want to give it up. This bathing, free even of the effort of standing up, relieved her of the toil and tensions of the day, and it gave her her few moments of solace after Nathan had left. There was in this sojourn in the warm water, half-lying, half-floating in the white bathtub, something of the return to the womb. So Miss Fanny felt as she sat on the gleaming enamel bottom of her bathtub and reflected how odd it was that you could, even after such a long time and even for a brief moment, find consolation in so physical and irrelevant a thing as bathing in warm water, and how much, exactly at this point, our physical existence was revealed, an existence which was probably common to us and to all other creatures and perhaps even to plants, whatever the vegetal equivalent was of a hot bath, and to what extent we were still children who had not yet fully grown, and might not even have left yet, perhaps would never leave, our first, original home, the place where we had come into being.

Always at this time, as she sat curled up on the steamy white enamel bottom, she would choose one event, or rather a brief interval, or something even more limited, one circumscribed moment of happiness, from her time with Nathan. Strange, that almost always the same two or three moments would float up in her memory, again and again, while she had after all almost a whole year to choose from. Whatever the reason, these moments of all others had been chosen to be etched into her memory, and they were stamped there the way possession is branded into the living flesh, with letters of white-hot iron, impossible to remove or to efface, and that was why they beat all the other moments in the race to reach the blank projection screen of her consciousness and unfold there. At first, especially in the first period after Nathan had left, Miss Fanny tried to stop them. With all her might she tried to block their way to this smooth white surface which was her consciousness, or so she saw it, to seal all the cracks, to surround it with tall dense fences of prickly wire, but all her work was in vain. The great white surfaces were too wide open, exposed to any wind, and any amount of wire in the world would not have been enough to fence out those memories and prevent them from returning and screening themselves before her. So that finally she gave in, and with time she even began to look forward to these moments at the end of the day, these short intervals of respite she allowed herself, when, she knew, she could sit, her muscles relaxing under the hot flow, and all the weariness and the small humiliations and the constant hurt melting in it, together with the scrutiny and the self-laceration and the reproach, just sit there flooded by the hot steam and watch over and over again, with the sweet scabbing of time, those beloved moments brought back to life before her with the precise, astonishing sharpness of memory. For she found out that such was the marvellous power of the imagination that it allowed her, for those few brief moments, if she watched herself carefully and never tried to stretch them beyond their allotted limits, to relive her moments of happiness as though they were taking place at the very moment she was sitting there, huddled against her knees in her foetal position, as though they themselves were the only present, and everything that had happened later, his going away, and the rend that was riven in her from end to end, and the dull pain that followed, all these had never been.

The first time they went out together, the first time he invited her out right after they met, they went to see a movie at the Ophir cinema. The film was a simple comedy, a comedy of lovers and errors, and however much Fanny tortured herself over it and however much she racked her brains she couldn't remember its name, even though almost any other detail of the film or of the cinema, the chairs, the air-conditioning, each one of the most trivial details was engraved in her memory, except for the name; and when the lover in the film jumped on his bike and started pedalling frantically down the forest lane in pursuit of his beloved, crashing into tree trunks and falling and again setting out and getting his hair caught in an oak branch, Nathan's hand slipped down and folded itself around her hand, and a small tremor went through her body from head to toes, a thrill which is almost a shudder, for it contains as yet the sweet fear of what is to come, because it is not known, and because it is known.

That was the first happiness.

And once, in bed, leaning on his elbow beside her, his face bent above her and looking at her from very close by, he told her that he loved her.

And that was the second happiness.

One day in winter they drove in Nathan's car to the sea, only they didn't go down to the beach at the end of the drive. They stayed up high, and parked the car in the fallow fields bordering the cliff, and walked to the edge. The field was all aflower with early winter blooms, bluebells and yellow-weeds and daisies and she even saw a cyclamen there, and they walked among the flowers, feeling the soft grass and the pebbles under their feet, until they reached the rocks at the very edge of the cliff. There a sort of hollow in the ground was revealed to them, a cradle made of soil and cushioned with rocks, and Nathan sprawled at its edge, leaning against its rim, and she lay inside the cradle and rested her head on his stomach, looking up, up into the blue sky which was so clear that it kept disappearing and every once in a while she had to blink in order to get it back, and his hands stroked her face with the absent-mindedness of a beautiful day while he looked far away into the sea, which spread around them blue and round like an endless barrel, and every now and then she glanced beyond the sky, backwards, into his face.

And that was perfect happiness.

20

At the end of the month Margie called unexpectedly. The familiar voice with the strong guttural accent seemed to release something in Fanny, and the scrambling of the breathless impatient words, so much in haste to reach their destination that they collided with each other and tripped each other up, aroused in her an immediate desire to unburden her troubles on a sympathetic shoulder, an attraction to the possibility of relief suddenly open before her, but also a recoiling from that very same need, a repugnance which had taken root in her during those past weeks from meeting people in general and familiar people in particular. Finally, of course, the first impulse prevailed, and she made a date with Margie for the next day at five in the afternoon at the Ritz.

At least there was some focus to the day, once she had before her a definite point to arrive at rather than a huge shapeless mush, extending on and on without limits and without a hold and with no rhyme or reason; for reason operates only from one point to another, and it evaporated into the monotonous stretch of her days. There was one hour every day, though, in the late afternoon, which she used to spend at the playground, and she was sorry to miss it, but Margie had no other free time and she yielded. At three o'clock she took a shower and dressed carefully for the first time in a long while. She ironed her dress, even though there were almost no creases in it, and even changed her underwear. As she dressed she thought of the child Uri and wondered if he would notice her absence from the park. If he did, would he miss her, would her absence even cause him some anxiety, like the anxiety caused us by the sudden disappearance of something which is an inseparable part of our surroundings, like an old picture on the wall? She felt a brief qualm and almost regretted having agreed to this date, but immediately scolded herself for indulging in such imaginary fancies and told herself she'd better start making more such plans, because she seemed to be losing her grasp on the pragmatic, everyday realities, which she had always held in high respect. She had a stable and unchanging faith in the importance of everyday minutiae — work, shopping for groceries — that unenchanted ground of reality without which you couldn't stand firm, in which your feet were planted.

At four o'clock the heat was still standing in the streets like a vast, echoing presence. White shades of light flickered in the air. Fanny turned the corner of the street carefully, feeling her way in the unknown hour as if in a foreign territory. The houses began to cast short, compact shadows which didn't yet reach the the pavement. The tapping of Fanny's shoes reverberated in the street like the pulse along the length of the body: there were almost no people outside at this hour, and the few she encountered were mainly straggling schoolchildren on their way home, flushed, their hair dishevelled, walking quickly with a resilient tennis-shoes step, or rather, reflected Fanny, with the step of the very young. Strange, she thought, and her hand went up mechanically to fix her hair, weighed down by the sun, that to this day, at the age of forty-two, she hadn't managed to get used to the fact that she was wearing high heels, and every click they made sounded to her exaggeratedly sharp and loud. And yet she knew she couldn't afford to wear tennis shoes. She had seen young girls wearing such shoes with their summer dresses, but she knew that on her they would look ridiculous. And besides, the very idea of sports shoes and socks in this heat seemed to her unbearably hot and stifling.

The bus went through the empty streets with rattling speed, like a metal ball in the grooves of a pinball machine. The driver sat impervious and totally concentrated on some point straight ahead, and Fanny wondered what it was that he was seeing there, for there seemed to be no connection between this staring of his and the road, or the few pedestrians who were crossing it, sometimes almost beneath the bus's wheels. On the bus itself there were only a few people scattered among the seats, and Fanny sat and watched the houses go by, hazy and faded, in the dusty windows, until her stop came up and she rose hurriedly because the driver hadn't shown patience towards those who lingered, and stepped off the bus with a feeling of relief. The door closed behind her with the choking sound of compressed air and for a moment she remained standing on the street near the pavement, still travel struck, looking around her without knowing where she was, or in what direction to turn.

In a minute she collected herself. Again she ran her hand through her hair to try and infuse some life into it, straightened the strap of her handbag and walked towards the Ritz, whose name she could see a little further down the street. She hoped Margie would be there on time. She had the deplorable habit of arriving twenty minutes or more late to a meeting she herself had scheduled, and Fanny did not want to sit there those twenty dreary minutes on her own, despatching expectant looks to the door each time it opened, her neighbours turning mechanically to look at the door and then back at her, catching the disappointed expression on her face, the little unavoidable grimace at the corner of the mouth once it turned out that, this time as well, it wasn't your man.

As she pushed the door open she was hit by a blast of cold air, and she felt its touch on her burning face with gratitude. She looked around her hesitantly, and to her surprise saw Margie waving at her from one of the tables at the back of the café, and remembered that the insurance company she worked for was just a few buildings away. She sat down across from her and Margie immediately said, as she always did, 'You look great, Fanny. Wait a second, I have to run to the toilet,' and disappeared. She probably hadn't wanted to leave her bag unattended, thought Fanny and looked around her. This was the first time she had visited the place since the evening with Ritzi. Somehow she found it difficult to go back there afterwards, although it was her favourite café. But yesterday, when Margie suggested the Ritz, she told herself categorically that it was time to stop all this nonsense. She was merely cosseting herself, indulging in preciousness of the worst kind. The thing was over and that was that. You can't attach an emotional value to each place according to an event which happened to occur there, and silly whims should be overcome through reason. Reason and matter-of-factness, Fanny felt, were now her most useful allies. And in any case the place looked exactly as it had before. Her encounter with Ritzi, she made sure with cruel punctiliousness, had left no mark on it. The same tables, the same Viennese prints, the same *Stern* and *Die Welt* in the newspaper holder on the wall. The proprietress in her white apron approached her with the same measured gait and asked her the same question, and she gave the same answer she had always given: coffee and *apfelstrudel*, please. The proprietress confirmed the order with a nod and shoved the notebook into her apron pocket. And then, surprisingly, her face cracked into a smile and she said, 'We haven't seen you here for a while.' Fanny nodded, too stunned to reply. It was as if one of the stolid tables had opened its mouth to speak. This sentence, which suddenly stood out in the desert of her long empty days like a strip of green colour, touched her so deeply that her throat contracted and she could only smile at her, and nod back emphatically. The woman acknowledged this with a motion of her head and went back behind the large counter, swallowed in the espresso machine's cloud of white steam.

Margie came back from the toilets, smoothing down her skirt, and sat down. Immediately she took out of her purse a little flat powder compact and attentively examined her face. 'Mmmm,' she said, pursing her mouth in the mirror, 'I have to lay off those cakes. But not today,' she added with her gleaming smile – her teeth were all perfect crowns, the handiwork of their joint dentist – and Fanny smiled back at her. The tension she had felt earlier was dispelled. The proprietress came back and placed before her a cup of coffee and a plate with a slice of apple cake, and the good coffee smell struck her nostrils. She stirred the sugar and Margie put away the powder compact, corrected her hair with two or three practised pats and asked, 'Well?'

'I left my job,' said Fanny.

Margie's mouth fell open. 'What?'

At last, Fanny thought, she had managed to say something that surprised Margie. A double surprise, for Margie, like Aunt Leda, did not expect Fanny ever to say anything astonishing. Perhaps, she went on thinking, some change in her was finally taking place.

'I've left Bruck & Sons,' she said. For some reason she found it difficult to start on her story. In the depths of Margie's mouth she could see the only gold tooth left there, probably because it was a rear tooth you couldn't ordinarily see, the last souvenir from Bratislava. When she first met Margie, on the wooden bench in the corridor of the second floor of the Jewish Agency, Central Europe, she had three of those.

'You're completely out of your mind,' said Margie.

'I had no choice,' Fanny said.

'Ah,' said Margie, suddenly enlightened, 'they went bankrupt. You poor thing.'

'No,' said Fanny. 'I quit.'

'So what are you talking about, what choice?' demanded Margie. She had no patience for guessing games.

Fanny tried to explain briefly the chain of events that had led to her resignation, but the more she explained the more she felt she was becoming incomprehensible, even to herself, and when she got to the reel of film she stopped, with a strong feeling of incompetence, and ended with the stammered words, 'And then I felt I couldn't work there any more.' The moment of unburdening, of relief, she had so looked forward to had slipped between her fingers, turned into a great unnecessary embarrassment.

'Couldn't? What are you talking about?' retorted Margie with unexpected passion. 'D'you have any idea what *I* have to go through at the office every single day with that odious Frankfurter?' Fanny nodded. Frankfurter's name had come up innumerable times in her conversations with Margie. So far Margie had managed, with the sense of balance of an experienced acrobat, to repel his assaults without his feeling injured and seeking revenge, as had already happened in a considerable number of cases which she would enumerate to Fanny in a breathless cascade. Dahlia Negris, for example, whom he'd fired without compensation because she didn't have tenure. 'With me he wouldn't have got away with it so easily,' Margie had said at the time, gritting her teeth, 'but why get that far?'

'This was completely different,' Fanny said with an effort. 'It wasn't even . . . *personal.*'

'Then I really don't see what your problem is,' Margie shot back at her. Her curious anger, which Fanny wasn't able to fathom, still hadn't subsided. 'What's it to you? Let him show you fifty pornographic movies and buy three hundred kinds of plastic naked women, if that's what makes him happy. If he didn't even make a pass at you . . .'

'I couldn't take it,' said Fanny. She felt as if she was sitting opposite a wall, an ample blonde wall, redolent of expensive scent, which soaked up her words and stifled them. She felt invalidated. Slowly, anger began gathering in her too, cold, white anger. If Margie says one more word, she decided, I'll tell her she's incapable of understanding and that's that. But at that very moment Margie, in her abrupt fashion, underwent a complete change. Her anger vanished and a barely suppressed excitement took its place. She leaned forward, towards Fanny, unconsiously patting her hair again.

'But the main thing,' she whispered to Fanny as if she had

been cut off in the middle of telling a spellbinding story, 'I haven't told you the main thing yet.'

'Anything good?' Fanny asked gratefully. She felt a welcome relief at this unexpected turn in the conversation, which had weighed on her, she now understood, precisely because it touched that disturbing point of uncertainty, that small bubble of doubt that was constantly hovering at the back of her mind even though she refused to look at it, standing in the leaves of the plants as she watered them, in the stains of sun on the kitchen's south window sill, in the car lights which travelled, white and transitory, across her bedroom ceiling at night.

'Yosef and I are getting married next month,' said Margie. With her acute sense of the dramatic she didn't add anything to this, just looked straight at Fanny, waiting for her reaction. Only her hand, irrepressible, again strayed to her hair and patted it with her habitual nervous gesture.

Fanny knew she mustn't disappoint her and she didn't, despite the stab of pain which cut, swift and sharp, through her heart. After clapping her hand to her mouth with the exclamation of excitement and wonder that such an announcement deserved, and after kissing Margie, leaning somewhat ludicrously across the table, on both cheeks, it was possible to go into details. Which Margie did, with graphic enthusiasm, right down to the last town in Italy which they intended to visit on their honeymoon. Yosef had initially thought of a hotel in Safed, but after all they were no longer eighteen.

'And of course we'll live in my apartment', she concluded, 'until we find a bigger place. Yosef tried to convince me to live with him, but really, a room-and-a-half on the ground floor! . . . And with a parking lot right in front!'

Fanny laughed. There was something about Margie's uncompromising tyranny, something so wonderful and refreshing that it made you relinquish in advance any wish to oppose her, and all you wanted was to creep up close and lay your head on its comforting shoulder. Even the banality of some of her sayings was soothing, by virtue of being so free of doubt. 'I'm sure you'll make Yosef a wonderful wife,' she said sincerely. 'All his problems will be solved the moment he moves in with you. You won't allow him to have any.'

Margie laughed with her. 'That's for sure,' she said, and for a moment they were together again, like in the good old days – and were they ever good? – the old days, at least, when they'd just arrived in Israel and met on the wooden bench opposite Bar-Giora's room at the Agency. And then her eyes grew sharp as she looked at Fanny, and she said, 'The trouble with you, Fanny, is that you're too fond of looking.'

Fanny's laughter was cut short, as if she had just been dealt a powerful blow in the stomach. Among all the many things that Margie said, which you were used to not taking too seriously, she would suddenly formulate something in so precise, so true a manner, that it left behind it only an empty, resounding void.

'You're right, I think,' she said. And thank you for not saying the rest: so fond of looking that you never get down to living. For a moment she felt, despite the pain, closer to Margie than she had ever been throughout their long acquaintance, so close that she might really have fallen on her neck and had a big, relieving cry, but once again, with her dazzling speed, Margie was no longer there.

'Well,' she said, examining her face anew in the tiny mirror, 'I've got to run. We have tickets for *Traviata* tonight and Yosef will go beserk if I'm late by so much as a minute. He's decided to make a civilized human being of me even if it kills him,' she added with a grin, and Fanny grinned back at her, liking her despite the nagging pain, despite the hole she had left in her, empty and gaping, and she nodded when Margie said she'd let her know, of course, when they had the final date. 'It's all rushed, as usual, you know me, everything at the last minute and this time Yosef's also running around. Afraid I'll change my mind,' she added and laughed a last laugh, wholesome and liberating, and a few elderly readers of the *Berliner Tageblatt* lifted their heads for a moment. 'He doesn't know I had it all planned by April last year.' And Fanny laughed too, her envy stingless, since its very yearning was imbued with the knowledge that there was no chance in the world she, Fanny, would ever be like that, and she could only watch her from afar the way one watches an unpromised land, with an envy which wasn't poisoned because it had no real hope, the sort of envy which is found, ultimately, to be rather like affection.

She left the café with Margie and waved goodbye to her as she walked away up the street. Then someone bumped into her shoulder and she realized she was still standing there on the pavement in front of the café, obstructing the way for anyone wanting to go in or out. The light had turned grey, the light of dusk, but it was still strong. She looked at her watch. It was six; there was no point in going to the park any more and she still had time, always more time, and she decided to go and finally give the signature they'd asked her for at the pension fund after she'd left work.

The offices of the fund were at the centre of the commercial area downtown and when she got there the clerks were already noisily locking their filing cabinets and desks and only barely agreed to attend to her. Because of you I won't get home until after the kids have gone to bed, said the clerk's eye, fixed on her balefully, and Fanny almost gave in, but the thought that she'd have to go back there once more stiffened her resolve and she kept silent and let him open the metal filing cabinet and rummage back and forth in the drawer, muttering to himself, until he found her file and gave it to her to sign and slammed the drawer shut, and already she was out in the steamy evening air and the exhaust fumes of the cars, but when she looked up she saw the evening vault shimmering with a pale blue light.

The bus lurched slowly through the crowded streets near the Shalom department store, until it got to the wider section of the road next to the store itself. Fanny looked at the enormous base of the building. Then she tried to tilt her head so she could see the top, but since she had the seat furthest from the window she only managed to see a few more storeys up. This town's changing beyond recognition, she reflected absent-mindedly while the bus advanced in halts, jolting and swaying back and forth the people who were standing in the aisles. When they finally reached Allenby Street and the ride became smoother, she returned to her thoughts. It was true: the city was constantly changing, every day there were new buildings, public institutions, maternity clinics, cafés, new roads, new neighbourhoods across the Yarkon, but she, Fanny, did not manage to keep up with its amazing speed. She was forever lagging behind the city, which advanced in giant leaps, shedding its past and leaving it far behind, while she struggled uselessly to catch up with it. The city always outpaced her and adapted itself far more quickly to any innovation, and while her eye still collided with the Hilton Hotel or the Shalom department store with a shock of surprise, the city had already adjusted itself to them and conducted its life and bustling traffic around them as though they had always been there. Only she, Fanny, couldn't leave the past behind her. She was forever dragging it along, always looking around and searching for it, perhaps because inside her it kept leading some kind of independent life. Even in her own home there were moments when she felt as if she'd just moved in, and she had been living there since 1952. For the first time, looking at the people who were sitting at the sidewalk cafés on Ben Yehuda Street putting their glasses to their lips, it occurred to her that perhaps the city itself had something to do with her feeling of foreignness. Because everything changed so quickly, and by the time you climbed one of the dunes by the sea long enough to know it, so that even with your eyes closed you could see its pale slope in the sun, feel the grainy drizzle of sand between your fingers, it was already gone, already a hotel had been built on it, or it had been paved over with large coloured concrete slabs to facilitate access to the beach, or it had been turned into a promenade. Nothing stayed in its place long enough for you to get used to it, long enough for it to become a part of you. And perhaps that's why it really didn't.

The bus stopped at the station. A sudden gust of wind came from the sea and the dress of a woman standing at the lights spun into a red whirl. Then the light changed, the bus moved forward and Fanny turned around, trying to see her for another moment, but the wind had meanwhile subsided and the woman was already across the street.

21

The following day, seized with longing, she left for the park early. That day too was very hot. The crests of the cypresses had turned from deep green to a greyish, almost silvery hue, like that of olive trees, and Fanny thought that summer had undoubtedly arrived. At first she could not see Uri and immediately felt a twinge of disappointment, but then she saw that she had been mistaken. He was there, but was not playing in his usual corner of the sandpit but running around, quite uncharacteristically, on the gravelly part of the playground and on the footpaths which led to the remote benches at the edge of the park. The girl who usually watched him was not to be seen.

The child ran hither and hither with great purposefulness, swinging his leg as if kicking something from place to place, but the tip of his shoe struck only thin air. This did not bother him at all. He ran quickly, his face absorbed and serious, and you could see he was putting a lot of effort into observing the rules of the game, although their exact nature escaped Fanny. Suddenly, at the peak of a slide which had brought him, spurting streams of dust under his shoes, almost to the edge of the park, he halted abruptly in front of Fanny's bench, and stood there motionless for a moment, digging the toe of his shoe into the dusty ground. He looked at her from under his hair, which was dishevelled and stuck to his forehead, and immediately lowered his eyes again. Finally he lifted his head and looked straight at her. Fanny looked at him too. Her first impulse had been to smile at him, as seems to be required when a small child suddenly stands there and looks at you, but a different feeling, which followed in the wake of the first one, restrained her. She felt that this would diminish the value of the encounter, take away its significance and turn it into just a chance encounter in a public park, and therefore she refrained from smiling and just looked at him. He wasn't a handsome child or even what people would call a nice child, but he had this quality of almost total concentration which set him apart from other children, and that must have been the reason, she said to herself as she sat there looking at him, why she had been attracted to him in the first place, of all the children in the park. And then the child broke his silence.

'Do you know why elephants and nightmoths die standing up?' he demanded, looking at her directly, straight in the eye, the way children don't normally.

Fanny was embarrassed. She found the observation interesting, not to say astounding, although she was not altogether sure of its correctness. In any case she didn't know the answer. 'Because of the "t"?' she tried her luck.

The child's face changed at once, and took on an expression of disappointment mixed with scorn. Fanny was immediately sorry. You're just like everyone else, she told herself remorsefully, saying things just to please, trying to second-guess the other instead of finding out what you really think. At most, she told herself, you could have said you didn't know.

'That's nonsense,' the child said.

'You're right,' said Fanny humbly.

Her unconditional surrender apparently placated the child and he explained, 'Nightmoths, I mean those big ones. The black ones,' he added, so as to leave no room for doubt.

'Oh,' said Fanny. 'I thought at first you meant those tiny ones that fly around bulbs.'

'No,' the child said.

After a short pause he added, 'Just the opposite of cockroaches.'

'That's right,' said Fanny. 'Cockroaches immediately turn on their backs.'

'That's why I don't like them so much,' the child said.

'Me neither,' Fanny said, and unable to repress herself she suddenly smiled and unexpectedly the child smiled back at her, a very brief smile, though, rather the glimmer of a smile than an actual smile, and immediately his features rearranged themselves in their usual severe expression.

Fanny pondered the question again. Elephants and night-moths, she could find no common thread between them. 'Do *you* know why?' she asked hesitantly.

'No,' the child said. 'I only thought about it yesterday. I haven't found an answer yet.'

'How do you know they die standing up?' asked Fanny, still hesitantly because she didn't know whether this question as well might not seem to him one of those · clever adult questions, and how do you know that, smarty-pants. She tried to put the question as simply and straightforwardly as possible.

'Moths I've seen. About elephants it was in the book my dad read to me yesterday,' the child said. He kicked at the ground again. 'Well, I have to go. Orly'll be here soon.'

'Orly's the girl who always comes here with you?' asked Fanny.

'Yes. And she's not a girl, she's grown-up,' the boy said and broke into a run. The dust cloud he left behind him took several minutes to settle.

22

When Fanny entered Maskit's, the store seemed to her at first empty of customers. It was only a moment later that she noticed, at the foot of the stairs to the right, Aunt Leda standing there with one of the shop assistants, and she was filled with wonder to see how small she was. Only now she realized that for many years she had been seeing Aunt Leda only at her apartment, and almost always just the two of them; at the most they were joined by the Monday afternoon *Kaffee-Klatsch* Frauen, who were all more or less Aunt Leda's height, or the banker, who was a man, and therefore expected to be taller. Now she saw that despite her erectness Aunt Leda was really very small, smaller than the saleswoman even, who wasn't that young herself any more though she dyed her hair black, and with this new and somewhat unsettling awareness Fanny descended the stairs to the lower floor.

This whole business of an early birthday gift was a bit odd and certainly irregular. Usually for her birthday she received from Aunt Leda something small and meticulously wrapped, a quartet of lace handkerchiefs in a flat box with a transparent lid, or a fine doily to be placed under a fruit bowl. Full decades were marked by a large tablecloth. Sometimes Fanny suspected that Aunt Leda had bought them all at once at the liquidation sale of the linen store on her street, which had been closed down at the end of the fifties, because she seemed to have at her disposal an inexhaustible supply of such linen, cloth dinner napkins, slightly larger pieces to spread on the living-room table, endless varieties of cloth squares in all shades of white which would be produced and distributed carefully according to the event and the recipient. In fact, Aunt Leda had brought them over from home: they were a part of what she had taken with her to Paris. Either way, Fanny had accumulated a large stock of dainty handkerchiefs which were too nice to wipe your nose with. Aunt Leda did not believe in excess, and therefore Fanny was surprised when she announced to her over the phone that she wished to meet her at Maskit's the following Tuesday, so she could choose a vase or a ceramic bowl for her birthday. 'Something nice,' she said, and Fanny was amazed. The more so since she knew that Aunt Leda, who had difficulty walking, though of course she adamantly refused to admit it, left her apartment as seldom as possible, and even her fruit and vegetables were delivered to her. At first she thought she had run out of handkerchiefs, but immediately dismissed this idea, which was definitely unworthy, for there was no lack of stores of the old sort along Ben Yehuda or Bugrashov Street which were still in business. No, Aunt Leda's announcement reflected some profound change which was taking place in her, and Fanny found herself afraid to get to the bottom of it.

'So far I haven't seen anything,' Aunt Leda said. Without bothering to lower her voice, and completely ignoring the shop assistant, she added, 'I can't see why Rosie told me to come here.'

The display was indeed disappointing. The shelves were crammed full with vases and bowls, but the earthenware, most of which had for some reason been shaped and dyed to resemble bronze, was heavy and cumbersome. There wasn't one article of pottery which had been allowed to be itself, a simple container for flowers or fruit. Most of the jars were bulky, overladen with ornamentation and handles. There was much pretentiousness in them and little of the true beauty of a ceramic pot, the beauty which is hidden in the curves of the vessel, in the clay itself.

'Let's have a look at the other shelves,' said Fanny. 'There are some more bowls further down.'

'Maybe something like that would suit you,' suggested the

shop assistant, pointing at a curious rectangular vase of a greyish-brown hue.

'Thank you,' said Aunt Leda and looked her straight in the eye. 'We'll manage on our own.'

'I don't understand why Rosie told me they have beautiful things here,' she said again in a loud voice to Fanny, or mainly to herself, with a perplexity that verged on anger. 'Perhaps they had other things and they ran out.'

'Let's look further down,' Fanny said. They approached a shelf laden with fabrics. Those were actually pretty, woven in the folkloristic design which was the store's trademark, and Aunt Leda fingered one of them. 'This might do for a new cover for my sofa,' she said. She gave Fanny one end of the cloth and unfolded it. An expression of disgust spread over her face. 'Not big enough,' she said.

'This fabric would be wonderful for a bed cover.' They heard the voice of the shop assistant, who, in an unexpected burst of courage, had cropped up beside them again. 'We also have them with fringes.'

'It's not big enough for a bed cover,' Aunt Leda said and the tone of her voice left no room for argument. 'It's not big enough for anything.' The woman melted away, utterly crushed. 'This might do for the sideboard in the hall,' said Aunt Leda, somewhat appeased. She pulled at the cloth expertly until the price tag appeared, but when she examined the printed digits her expression changed. 'So much money,' she said, and her voice remained hanging in the air like a trail of distant wonder.

Nevertheless she carefully folded the cloth exactly along its previous creases and returned it to the pile. Order there must be. Then they walked on, and once they saw that along that wall there was only jewellery and embroidered blouses, they proceeded to the display of glass vases on the opposite shelves.

But the colours were very loud and ill-matched, and the combinations were jarring. Even beautiful colours like blue and green they'd managed to spoil, thought Fanny. Aunt Leda halted in front of the glassware and stood motionless for a few moments looking at it. 'I can't understand why Rosie told me there are beautiful things here,' she muttered for the third time. Suddenly she said in a loud voice, loud enough for it to be a declaration, '*Nothing* here is beautiful!' Her voice rang out in the empty store sharp and challenging and Fanny anxiously awaited retaliation, but the shop assistants chose to keep their silence.

All the same Aunt Leda reached out and took one of the vases, the same blue-green vase Fanny had been looking at before, and turned it around until the price tag was revealed. 'So much money,' she murmured again. 'And for what, for what?'

She tapped her fingernail against the glass. The glass made a dull sound. 'How come they make such ugly things?' Aunt Leda said. 'Even the glass doesn't ring.'

'I believe it's too thick, Aunt Leda,' said Fanny timidly.

'Nonsense,' barked Aunt Leda. 'It's just worthless. And so expensive,' she repeated and her voice had that same note of distant wonder, as though she was faced here with a phenomenon which, however hard she tried, she couldn't make out.

Fanny looked at Aunt Leda's strained, baffled face, and then at the new glass vases whose price tags glittered with silver and gold. Again she looked at Aunt Leda's face examining them, angry and uncomprehending, and suddenly these two were arrayed before her in two distinct warring camps, Aunt Leda on the one side and the glass vases with their loud colours on the other, and she understood that Aunt Leda's defiance stemmed from her belief that she was entitled to full value for her money, something which was completely at odds with the rules of the game in the new world in which she lived. Aunt Leda was prepared to pay a lot for what she considered quality, but she would pay almost nothing for anything which wasn't made of really good materials and crafted in the best possible way. She still didn't know, with her supply of linen so carefully arranged on the shelves of her cupboard and with Bidermann from the hardware store selling to her at wholesale prices without her knowledge, she couldn't have known that the world where you paid pennies for a dress simply because it was made of cotton and not of silk, or because the underskirt didn't have real Bruges lace on it, did not exist any more.

Aunt Leda's finger fell from the glass rim. She stood for another moment looking at the shining vases. Her face in the artificial light looked pale and more tired than usual. Then she turned away and started walking towards the stairs, but in the middle of the store she suddenly stopped and turned to Fanny. Her arms spread out but she arrested them and they dropped at her sides.

'Why are there no beautiful things?' she asked quietly, almost supplicatingly, and there was a note in her voice which pained Fanny because she had never heard it before, a faint note of despair.

Fanny didn't know who the question was addressed to, whether to the shop assistants, or to her, or whether it wasn't addressed to any of them because she knew they couldn't answer it. 'Let's go have coffee and cheesecake at Mersand's,' Fanny said. 'Let's go, Aunt Leda.' But she had to touch her arm twice, and the second time even to urge her on a little, to get her to move away.

23

As she walked home in the twilight, which lay thick over the street like a purple blanket, she heard the sound of Netta's voice from the third-floor window and realized that she had once again returned in time for her weekly lesson. She paused, undecided. Only in special moments, moments of grace, was she able to listen to those lessons of Netta's. When she had heard, at the homeowners' meeting ten years ago, that a singing teacher would be moving into the building, her heart had contracted with sudden anxiety. Although she did not oppose Mrs Nussbaum's moving in, and in fact she had been the one to suggest the possibility of soundproofing which had convinced the rest of the neighbours, she tried as best she could to avoid being at home during those hours when Mrs Nussbaum was giving her lessons. From the west window of her living room, which opened on the front of the house, you could clearly hear the voices and the sounds of the piano, and even though she had never openly admitted it to herself, she tried not to be near it during those hours. Most of the lessons took place in the mornings or early afternoons, when Fanny was working, so she was almost never at home. Only Netta's lessons were for some reason given at a later hour, in the evening, and then Fanny would sit in the kitchen, which faced the backyard.

Netta's voice still did not flow freely. She had not yet overcome her tendency to breathe in the wrong places, but had already succeeded, so it seemed, in breaking through the barrier of the G in the lower octave, since now Mrs Nussbaum's remarks were directed elsewhere. 'You're using your throat, Netta,' Miss Fanny heard her say in her deep voice, which had old traces of laughter in it like smudges of ash on the bottom of an ashtray, 'although I've told you a thousand times: sing from your belly, only from your belly.' Here came a slight pause, and in her mind's eye Fanny saw Netta standing in front of Mrs Nussbaum, her blank face stubbornly lowered to the floor. 'If you go on singing from the throat you'll ruin your vocal cords,' concluded Mrs Nussbaum. 'Now let's move on to the next line.'

In her mind's eye Fanny saw Netta straightening up and taking a deep breath. And indeed, after a minute her voice could be heard again through the open window: 'Und immer – fragt – der – Seuf – zer . . .' This time they were working on Schubert's 'The Wanderer'. Today, surprisingly, Netta's voice was free of superfluous breathing and flowed, clear and confident, in the darkening twilight air. She's made pretty good progress, thought Fanny and felt an absurd stab of envy. When Netta started taking her singing lessons, about a year ago, she hadn't believed she would reach that level. Suddenly she could hear again old Herr Fried, her singing teacher in Lucerne: 'Don't stop,' he had told her. 'Don't give up.' But by that time she had known she had nothing to give up. 'It's not true,' Herr Fried said. 'The important thing is not to be Elisabeth Schumann. The important thing is to sing,' but she knew that what he said wasn't true, that she had to sing as she wanted to sing or not at all. The trouble was that little by little, and especially of late, this not at all was becoming too much for her.

It was such a final, comprehensive, all-embracing not at all that she had forced on herself – not to participate in the municipal philharmonic choir, as she'd been invited to do when she arrived in Israel, not to go to Maureen Forrester's recital at the City Culture Hall, not to sing even to herself, even when she was all alone and no one could hear her. Sometimes she felt as if a great, massive silence was growing in her, sealing her against the sounds which came from the outside and even against those which came from the inside.

The memory of a trip she had once made in Switzerland suddenly came back to her. She had gone hiking in a valley near Lucerne and by evening had reached the village where she'd intended to stay the night. But the inn was closed, and she stood before the door not knowing whether to continue on her way or to wait. At first the neighbours were very kind to her, and took the trouble of explaining that the innkeeper had gone to visit his relatives in the nearby town and would soon be back, but as night began to fall she stood by the locked door of the inn and saw the tall, heavy shutters closing one by one until even the echo of the clangs had died down and no sound was heard in the night air.

'No, Netta,' Mrs Nussbaum's voice tore through the gloom like a knife. 'You're singing all wrong again. It must be on your mind all the time: work from your diaphragm, always from your diaphragm. Don't forget.'

Don't quit, old Herr Fried had said. He smelled of tobacco. Don't quit, quitting is cowardice. But Fanny had thought that quitting required real courage. Now, listening to Netta's voice struggling with the second verse, she wondered whether he had not been right after all. But this thought was so frightening she immediately thrust it back deep inside, to hide it from sight, and hastened to think of something else. Aunt Leda. What had come over her all of a sudden? Perhaps she had guessed her crochet napkins were practically never used, she thought ruefully, nor her white hand-woven tablecloths. She could at least have placed the napkins under a vase, or under the knick-knacks on the dresser. I cant't stand crochet, she told herself out loud to silence the whispering underneath, but to no avail. For the first time she understood, and this understanding sent a strange chill down her back, that she had not wanted Aunt Leda's gifts; that she had preferred to see in them the embodiment of an old woman's niggardliness, whereas Aunt Leda, and this was suddenly very clear, had sought in this way to bestow upon her, piece by piece, her past. Napkin after napkin she handed over that past to her, the only thing she could give her, and she, Fanny, refused to accept it. She, who had always accused Aunt Leda of intractability and lack of feelings, was not able to accept even a doily.

The sounds of Netta's voice again pierced through the darkness, now very thick, with the first verse of the song. She sang it from beginning to end without interruption, as Mrs Nussbaum always let her do at the end of the lesson. From the distance of time her old excuse suddenly seemed to Fanny so cheap, shabby, almost petty; this was something she didn't often remind herself of, and in fact, she realized now, she had done her best to erase it from her memory. Her singing lessons had been paid for in half by Aunt Leda. The other half she had paid for herself, mainly from the money her father had sent with her to Switzerland, and a little from the allowance the Grunwalds had given her. When she had realized what she finally had no choice but to realize, that a great singer of the kind she had aspired to become she would never be, she decided that she no longer had the right to go biting into Aunt Leda's salary, which was small enough as it was, and that instead of wasting the rest of her money on a lost cause she had better save it for the move to Israel. And indeed that sum constituted the first payment on her present flat.

Suddenly, for no reason, the old lack raised its head again, and far more powerfully than she had felt it twenty years ago, when she had performed that surgery upon herself. Today, she thought with a sudden, frightening surge of anger, she would give without hesitation the flat itself, with all it contained, for the right to take back that decision. She wiped her hand on her forehead, amazed by that thought which had more than a touch of insanity in it. She needed a cup of tea urgently.

'All right, Netta, I'll see you next week. And remember about that lower fifth: you have to reach it from above and then downwards, not from below. I think you've made some progress after all,' said Mrs Nussbaum's deep voice with the traces of laughter at its bottom, and sure enough Netta burst into a high, slightly broken laugh, and Mrs Nussbaum's deep voice joined her. Fanny went into the dark stairwell and climbed the stairs quickly, so as not to run into Netta on her way down.

24

Because this country always conveyed itself to her in terms of light, and even of white, dazzling brightness, Miss Fanny found it difficult to accept the early nightfalls in winter, when by four o'clock you were already hesitating about the whereabouts of things, and a building might be a few steps away from where you thought it stood. She always felt robbed; especially on those days when she had to work late and complete darkness had already fallen by the time she left the office. Now that she wasn't working she regretted the lengthening summer days. The days clamoured for something to fill them up and she started roaming the streets in the mornings. Each day she would pick out a different neighbourhood, so as not to repeat herself, first in her vicinity and then further out.

One morning, in the area between Ben Yehuda Street and the sea, she passed a school building standing next to the road. It was a two-storey edifice and its large windows opened on to the street. From one of the windows came the voice of a teacher giving her lesson. 'Quite right, Orit,' she said in a crêpe-paper-flower voice, the voice that is unique to nursery-school teachers, stressing the words distinctly syllable by syllable. 'And now, children, who can tell me: Who do we thank?'

A child's piercing voice hastened to answer, rattling the words out with enormous speed: 'I know, Miss: Work!' 'Good, Itamar,' said the voice of the teacher, 'but you should have raised your hand first. Who else can answer this?' – 'Itamar's answer doesn't count?' enquired a girl's clear soprano. 'No,' answered the teacher's voice decisively, 'because he didn't raise his hand.' 'Then I want to, Miss,' rose a new voice, an alto, whether a boy's or a girl's Fanny couldn't decide. 'But I asked first, Miss,' protested the girl of the soprano voice. 'OK. You answer it, Tamar,' decreed the teacher. 'Work and Craft, Miss!' 'Good. A correct answer and a full one,' said the teacher. 'And you, Itamar, must learn to raise your hand,' she admonished the invisible Itamar.

'Now, children, I want to hear all of you together in chorus. When I've said One, Two, Three. No one starts before that. Is that clear, Itamar?' demanded the teacher. 'To Work and Craft. And you, Idit, don't forget you sing second voice and not first.' – 'But I want to be with the girls,' complained Idit, whose voice was indeed lower than usual for a girl her age, ten at most, Fanny estimated. 'You can keep on wanting,' declared the teacher. She had no sympathy, apparently, for vain whims. 'You can't always get what you want. All together, now: One Two and Three –'. A chorus of childish voices broke into song: 'Who will save us from our nee-eed? And who will our hunger fee-eed? And who will give us precious mi-i-lk –'. – 'Stop, stop,' shouted the teacher, really angry this time. 'Itamar! Get out.' 'But what have I done?' asked Itamar's voice, which Fanny now clearly recognized. 'You know very well what you've done. You should be ashamed of yourself. Your father works very hard to put bread in your lunchbox –'. 'It's sandwiches you mean, Miss,' interposed a new clear voice. – 'It doesn't matter. What matters is that Itamar is insulting his father by –'. 'I'm not insulting my dad!' yelled Itamar. Signs of hysteria could be discerned in the childish voice. 'Don't you say I'm insulting my dad!'

'I *will* say so, Itamar,' said the teacher's voice with false composure, 'because anyone who throws his tangerine at the back of someone sitting in the first row puts to shame both the song "To Work and Craft" and his father, who's worked hard to buy the –'. 'Stop it, stop it,' screamed the childish voice, choking with tears. 'You're just – it's not true! You're a liar! My dad –', but now, near suffocating, he was unable to complete his sentence and just sobbed bitterly. 'You see,

Itamar,' said the teacher's voice soberly, 'where unruly behaviour gets us.' The sobbing continued, hiccuppy, uncontrollable, then all at once stopped. Itamar's voice, hoarse, unrecognizable, yelled, 'I hate you!' and the noise of a chair being dragged across the floor could be heard audibly. The teacher, briefly visible at the window, must have dragged the unfortunate Itamar by his collar to the door as he screamed and kicked at the legs of the other children's desks, the noise reverberating like a train passing through the pillars of a station.

'And now, children,' said the teacher, again out of sight, her voice slightly husky, 'let's get back to our song. One, Two, Three –'. And the children, as though nothing had happened, started again on the first line: 'Who will *sa*ve us f-rom our ne-eed, who will our *hun*-ger fe-eed, and who will *gi*-ve us precious mi-i-lk –'. Their bright, crystalline voices soared through the classroom windows to the blue morning sky, and for a moment Fanny lost the meaning of the words and just stood there bathing in the stream of pure, monotonous voices which hovered in the air, dispersing among the branches of the great fig tree in the yard.

All at once, like a ball from a cannon's muzzle, a small, chubby boy shot out from the building straight towards the fig tree. His nose was running and his face was red and swollen. He flew to the tree and flung his arms around the trunk, shuddering with sobs. He looked so heartbroken that Fanny forgot herself and her fear of unfamiliar people, even if they were children, and hurried to him, but when she reached him her courage failed her and she didn't hug him as she had intended to do, just touched his shoulder timidly. The child started and turned a terrified face towards her. 'Don't – please don't be frightened,' said Fanny, who didn't know what to say. With new-found determination she added, 'You were right and the teacher wasn't.'

The child kept on looking at her, the terror in his face easing gradually into simple wonder. Finally he sniffled and

158

wiped his nose on his sleeve. He held Fanny with a steady gaze, and kept silent.

Again Fanny didn't know what to say. His silence embarrassed her, yet she felt that he was expecting her to say something more, and she tried to find the right words.

'Don't despair,' she said with sudden inspiration. 'You'll have a different teacher next year.'

The child scribbled with his sandal on the sandy ground. 'She's our form teacher until fourth grade,' he said flatly.

'And what grade are you in?' asked Fanny.

'Second,' said the boy.

'Maybe you could ask your mother to transfer you to another school,' suggested Fanny, with the dim feeling she was being uneducational.

'I have,' the child said.

'And what did she say?' asked Fanny.

'That it's not up to her, it's up to the council.'

There followed a short silence. The child sniffled once more, but this time it was an after-the-fact sniffle, more a reminder of past crying, so that it shouldn't be forgotten too quickly. Fanny felt that this was the right moment to change the subject. She racked her brains but couldn't find anything special to say.

'Itamar's a nice name,' she said rather lamely.

Itamar shrugged, keeping silent. He seemed well acquainted with this sort of remark. All the same, he apparently did not want the conversation to end, for he kept looking at her.

'What's your boy called?' he asked.

Fanny tried to answer, but couldn't. The child looked at her expectantly.

A bird suddenly flew up from the top of the fig tree, flapping its wings with a loud, rather startling sound. They both started and raised their heads to look at it. The bird quickly circled above the tree and then turned and flew away, a black dot diminishing in the sky in the direction of the sea.

After the bird could no longer be seen, Fanny said, her face still turned upwards to the dazzling light, 'Uri.'

25

This tendency she discovered in herself, to see herself as furniture, or to be afraid that other people saw her that way, worried Miss Fanny. She knew that the more this feeling, which she herself could not but view as some sort of an aberration, intensified in her, the more it would strike root in those around her, and she tried her hardest to get rid of it, but could not shake off the oppressive feeling that most, if not all of the people she came across – the conductor on the bus, the clerk at the employment agency, the assistant at the bakery shop – did not see her at all, or saw her less and less, and in her place their eyes encountered some presence which was not her, Fanny, at all, but some kind of a neutral presence which, although it did admittedly take up room for a moment in time and space, had no existence beyond that moment, and would soon expire and vanish. They felt obliged to react in some way, however limited, to this presence; but if Fanny lingered, or if it seemed from her mode of address, from her unnecessary stammered words, that she was trying to ask them for something beyond that, they became impatient, and their response, which grew briefer and briefer, turning from forced politeness into explicit coolness and sometimes into actual rudeness, made it obvious there was nothing they expected of her except that she clear out already, and cease this farce she was acting out before them, an inanimate object trying to present itself as a significant human being.

She wondered why she had never felt this way when she had a job and an office of her own to sit in. The fact that she too had a place of her own, a thread which was hers in the web of life, must have allowed her to occupy a more substantial and solid volume when she came to ask for the help of others. Without it she felt herself floating about in the space of the world, a nomad, anchorless.

This feeling may have been the reason why she didn't slam the door in Ritzi's face when he appeared there one evening all of a sudden, without so much as a by-your-leave and with no previous warning, and rang the bell. Instead, after a slight hesitation, she asked him to come in and silently served him the whisky she had bought the day after his last visit, in direct opposition to what her heart told her and against all common sense, out of the muddled, dim and senseless thought that maybe, all the same.

Since she kept silent, Ritzi had to carry the burden of the conversation, and with a certain feeling of revenge she enjoyed watching him struggle to produce a forced stream of words in order to cover for the absence of the real thing. Her vengefulness did not go so far as not to cooperate with him; she responded appropriately, answered what was expected of her, but refused to make an effort. She refused to manufacture in an artificial manner what had flowed out of her at the time so naturally, to fake the innocent joy of that evening. Neither did she have any wish to restage what had happened then. What had happened had died that very evening, when the strange man stood above her and looked at her lying between the rumpled sheets while zipping up his trousers – suddenly she realized that it was then, at precisely that moment in time, that the strange feeling had risen in her for the first time, as if she were a piece of furniture, one more sheet, a blanket, a flower pot. That's where it all began. And suddenly there flared up in her a pure flame of hatred for this man, whom for that brief moment she held responsible for her misfortune; but as quickly as it flared it also waned and died, for Fanny wasn't twenty any more and knew that one milestone was as good as another to mark the road, but that no single one of them could delineate it, in the phrasing of that Greek whose name she'd forgotten.

'So what do you say?' asked Ritzi. His voice was budding with the impatience of one who is about to despair of his interlocutor, of his own initiative.

'Say about what?'

'About the nightclub, *nu*. What I've been talking about all this time.'

Fanny stalled for a moment and tried to consider the offer, but her thoughts were like wisps of cloud swept in the wind. She simply couldn't stop the clouds and gather them into a coherent picture.

'Let's go. Why not?' she said.

Ritzi was left open-mouthed by her sudden compliance. The truth was that Fanny hadn't even heard what he had said before, but guessed that he had arrived at this idea as a last desperate measure. In a nightclub there'll be no need to talk so much, she thought, surprised at her total lucidity, that's what the show is for. And afterwards they can return to her flat. And maybe then it would be possible to move on to the bedroom.

And what did she care, she told herself in a voice she didn't recognize, an irresponsible voice with shadows of carelessness rippling through it, the light shadows of cirrus clouds. Return home with him – that she wouldn't. But why shouldn't she go with him to a nightclub. Why the heck not.

'I'll just get dressed,' she said.

Ritzi nodded enthusiastically, with gentlemanly understanding. A woman must dress up, certainly. A real woman at least.

As she left the room she was glad to get away for a moment from this man who was sitting on her living-room sofa and probably taking advantage of her absence to pour himself another drink. She remembered how she had felt at the end of that evening, her absolute certainty that she would not see this man ever again. Reality, she reflected, cannot live up to such absolute criteria as those of the inner intuitions of the soul. Though in fact, she suddenly understood, in fact her feeling had been right: that other Ritzi, the Ritzi of that evening, she would never see again.

In front of the wardrobe's closed door she paused briefly, hesitating. From the moment she left the living room she had been seized, perversely, by a strong reluctance to get all dressed up for this outing, this caricature of an evening out. For a moment she thought to turn back and go as she was, in the everyday dress she had worn for her afternoon job hunting. But then she decided not to. She made herself take off the dress, which smelled faintly of sweat, and the nylon stockings – even now, after almost twenty years in this country, she couldn't bring herself to go to a formal interview without stockings; and she even took a brief shower. Let him wait. Leisurely she put on some make-up, drew a light shade on her eyelids, and from among the dresses in her closet she chose the beautiful blue dress, her most beautiful one, the one she had worn to Raya's wedding. This event, a parody though it might be, shall be experienced to the full.

When she entered the living room Ritzi gave a genuine whistle of admiration.

'You look smashing,' he mumbled, and the old-fashioned compliment made Fanny smile, which he took as an encouraging sign.

'I'll have to make sure they don't snatch you right out of my hands,' he went on, but now the falseness had crept back into his words, no longer a spontaneous reaction but aimed at a purpose, calculated, and again he aroused in Fanny the slight revulsion she had felt towards him from the moment he showed up. He might have sensed it, for he immediately fell silent and stared at the floor, and Fanny looked at his closely shaven chin and at the tiny drops of perspiration which dotted his upper lip, and subdued the urge to ask him if he owned a shaving set by Bruck & Sons. Suddenly she wondered, with a sinking feeling, whether this whole business was not one big mistake. What did she have to do with this man? What did she have to do with nightclubs? But she hastened to push away the familiar, flaccid voice of passivity, of staying-in-one-place. No, this evening she'll go out no matter what. She, Fanny Fischer, will go to a nightclub.

Ritzi's car, a dark lump in the faint light of the streetlamps, was parked in front of the house, and he hurried around it and opened the door for Fanny with a gallant gesture. He waited until she got in and sat down, gathering the edges of her dress, then slammed the door with a powerful bang, and Fanny gave an involuntary start. Inside the car there was the unpleasant smell of something rotten, perhaps leftover fruit thrown into the small waste-basket on the floor, and she rolled the window all the way down, even though the wind which blew in as they began to drive mussed up her hair.

Although the nights were still cool, there were lots of people sitting in the cafés on the pavements. Enclosed under arched covers of transparent plastic, illuminated by the strong light which framed them in the night, they looked – eating and talking and gesturing with their hands without it being possible to hear them – like passengers in a spaceship. One of the cafés had spread above the pavement an awning with glowing pink and white stripes, which made it look like a giant ice-cream cone. Loud music came from its entrance, and Fanny hummed the tune, which she recognized. Through the window she could see men and women standing (or sitting? she wondered with the lazy detachment of the traveller who passes by the sights but is never a part of them) and licking ice cream. And then there were no more lights at the side of the road and no reason to look there any more. There was a segment of road steeped in darkness and then Fanny noticed lights flickering ahead, and she watched them as they grew bigger and bigger before her. It's hard to believe, she said to herself suddenly with real anger, that I've been living in this town for almost sixteen years now and I can't remember the last time I took a trip to Jaffa. The last time she had taken a trip at all. Only now she realized to what extent she was woven into the starched white sheets on her bed, the smell of fresh coffee in the morning, the small bedside table with the glass of milk and the biscuits, how deeply she had settled into her flat, deep into the comfortable armchairs, into the sofa, the carpets, into the familiar walls themselves, so much so that she had almost become one of them, part of the pattern on the upholstery, and had she had wallpaper she would probably would have merged into it as well. How lucky that she hated wallpaper and always had, she thought with a sigh of relief, then saw the absurdity in the thought and told herself firmly to stop thinking backwards and only forwards from now on, forwards. The lights grew sharper and clearer until they became a resplendent, fabulous tiara glinting on the walls, the churches, the mosques of Jaffa. Jaffa, she said to herself and something fluttered in her for an instant. Jaffa. The city's skyline glowed with a faint, weird, violet radiance, like a city seen from afar in a dream. The familiar pain gripped Fanny's chest, as always when she stood before something that was too beautiful, too beautiful to take hold of, to contain, to turn into a part of herself.

'Dammit, always these traffic jams on Thursday nights,' mumbled Ritzi angrily and she shook off her daydream and looked at him as if she'd just realized that he was there too. You wouldn't be here if it weren't for him, she reminded herself, meaning to hurt, and tried to feel grateful to him but couldn't. Ritzi honked his horn long and angrily at an elongated, new-looking car which had overtaken him on the right. 'Bastards,' he muttered. 'Bought a '66 model and act like they own the road.'

Fanny murmured something in a conciliatory tone and tried to concentrate again on the lights, but couldn't assemble them any more into the luminous mosaic they had been before, and soon they were on the outskirts of the city and the proximity made them invisible to her, as always.

Yefet Street was full of car honks and the sweet smell of

baklava. People shouted at each other across the street, asking what kind of pitta they wanted and how many to buy. Men in trousers flaring out like bells crossed at red lights in front of the row of crawling cars, pulling behind them young women in high heels who stumbled on the pavement, their little handbags flailing wildly at their sides. Miss Fanny tried to preserve the lights before her eyes, but they kept fading and finally she could no longer hold on to them and the exhaust fumes and the vivid colours of the windows of Jaffa's clock tower concealed them completely. The faces of the people in the queues in front of the pitta bakeries were illuminated by the pale light of the lamps which hung above the counters, and every now and then, when the fire in the depths of the bakery flared up, flashes of red played over them as in an Inferno by Bosch. Couples paused in front of the shoe stores' windows, assessed them and went on. The night became hot and crowded, full of dense humanity. Not the night of the far shimmering lights on the cliff, which had woven, Fanny understood now, another city, drawn with the clear precise lines of illusion, sparkling from afar with deceiving radiance, beautiful, leading you astray.

Ritzi, with a dextrous motion, turned the car into a side alley and pulled over. The car gasped once or twice, gave a last jolt and was still. 'Here we are,' said Ritzi, switching off the lights and turning to her in the darkness. For a brief moment they sat in this way, across from each other, profile to profile in the semi-darkness which filled the space of the car, but there wasn't a shred of truth in this scene and Fanny couldn't stand it for even one moment longer. She opened the door and got out.

The sea breeze hit her face, a great cool blow which brought her relief. She turned to Ritzi, who had already climbed out on his side and was busy locking the door, turning to her a half-offended, half-accusing back. They walked in silence down the alley towards the main street. But in the realm of the lights another, brighter world was opened to them, where everybody walked along in pairs, holding hands and arm in arm and embracing each other, like in Noah's ark, thought Fanny, no one's alone here, and a similar thought must have gone through Ritzi's mind as well, for he linked his arm in hers and now they, too, looked in the eyes of the passers-by like any other couple. And perhaps, Fanny thought and a wave of deep dejection swept over her for a moment, perhaps the other couples were like them.

26

More than anything she was surprised by the utter blandness of the place. The vestibule wasn't really shabby, or mean-looking, but it was altogether lacking in character, and had she entered there by chance she wouldn't have been able to tell if this was the entrance to a community centre in Petah-Tikva, or to some second-rate theatre, or to a kibbutz culture hall on lecture night. The walls were covered by the standard stucco and the room was empty, save for a low table at the entrance around which sat three middle-aged men in windcheaters. The walls too were bare.

The minute he entered the club Ritzi seemed to put on a different personality, or rather a different manner. With an abrupt gesture, so unexpected and so out of place that she had no time to resist him or even to protest, he wrapped his arm around her shoulders and swept her straight over to the table. 'Chaimkeh!' he said. 'Haven't seen you for ages. What's the matter, they stopped using napkins at your place?' The man at the end of the table flicked the ash from the tip of his cigarette without looking at it and without looking at Ritzi, as if he knew what he'd see there and it wasn't worth the effort. 'They'd eat the napkins if we let them,' he rumbled in a deep bass voice and the man in the middle burst into a high staccato laughter which ended as abruptly as it had begun. The first man growled, 'I told you to cut it,' and his voice reminded Fanny of gipsies and a bear dancing heavily in the moonlight. The man next to the wall, at whom, so it seemed to Fanny, Ritzi's words were principally directed, said, 'OK, y'allah, go in. We don't need any napkins right now. Maybe for the restaurant, I'll come by next week.' His face was large and sunk in the folds of fat which surrounded it, the face of a fat man who had once been fatter. Hidden in this face, he had small eyes which had already seen everything. 'Great,' said Ritzi. 'Wonderful.' He pushed Fanny in front of him, forcing her into quick little dance steps, towards the other end of the room.

'Forty lira,' said the heavy man behind them and Fanny automatically turned around. Next to the table stood a pale couple dressed in the uninspired fastidiousness of the suburbs. The man in the couple pulled out his wallet.

Maybe the root of the trouble lay with the words, thought Fanny. The combination 'night club' conjured up in her mind a scene of smoky intimacy, throbbing with the beat of soft sensual drums, perhaps the sharp cry of a jazz singer immediately sinking into the muffled, cradling mumble of a soul song, tiny crowded tables, and smoke, smoke, smoke, the smell of alcohol, the murmur of guttural voices, the clink of glasses, all this a carpet spread at the feet of the singer's slightly hoarse voice; whereas here there was this large space, so large that all the people sitting in it couldn't dissipate the feel it had of something very spacious and very empty, the tables, square matchboxes placed at fixed intervals, the people dancing with mechanical, disjointed motions on the stage – all this struck Fanny with a shock of complete surprise. Ritzi's cajoling, forcing hand grasped her wrist again and navigated her to one of the side tables, next to a plaster pillar. 'Over there, that's fine,' said his voice in her ear and she didn't try to resist him, just let herself be swept along.

The waitress started moving towards them before they had the time to sit down. 'A drink, right?' said Ritzi and rubbed his hands together with an extravagant enthusiasm which made the waitresses chuckle. He'd apparently regained his self-confidence in this place he seemed familiar with. 'Quince liqueur?' He turned to Fanny teasingly, and Fanny, in complete contradiction to the cutting reply she had intended to make, in complete contradiction to herself, burst into loud, almost wild laughter.

'Gin and tonic,' she said firmly. That was the drink which the protagonist in the Hemingway novel she'd been reading that week imbibed every few pages, and if it was strong enough for a man like Hemingway, she decided, it would certainly do for her.

'Whisky for me,' said Ritzi and peered at her with surprise mingled with apprehension. He couldn't understand the nature of the transformation that was taking place in her, and if the truth were to be told, neither could she, but even if she did know what was happening to her, she wouldn't have dreamed of giving him an explanation.

'No good mixing one's drinks, eh? Black & White, please,' he told the waitress with emphasis and she nodded, shoved her notebook into her skirt pocket and took off. 'You have to keep an eye on these people, otherwise they stick you with the local stuff and charge you for Chivas Regal. You have to show them you know exactly what you're having, and no tricks. Black & White isn't Chivas Regal, but it's good whisky.'

'No pinching pennies in such matters,' said Fanny. Her voice sounded to her thicker than usual and flowed by her ears with viscous slowness, as if she'd already had a few glasses. The air flowed around her heavy and viscous too, sliding slowly like a treacly syrup. Inside it glittered, like penny coins, the piano notes of Mantovani's band. Oh Paolo, Paolo, if only you had never learned how to play. If only you had never been born.

Fanny was alarmed by her own thoughts. She didn't recognize the subtle venom which hissed and sizzled in her veins. She had never had such wicked thoughts before. She tried to return them to their dark birthplace and Mantovani to the world of the living, but it didn't work, and finally she gave up and leaned back against the pillar, enjoying its cool, rugged support and the soothing evil of her thoughts.

This delightful new pastime was cut short by Ritzi's voice.

On the strength of her wicked new character she almost told him to his face right then and there what she thought of all his twisting and turning, and in fact what she thought of him altogether, but the last remnants of ancient inhibitions held her back.

'They have a great show here, you'll see. Real quality stuff.'

What are you talking for, she wanted to ask him, why are you making such an effort? We have nothing to say to each other anyway, at least be quiet. But she didn't say anything. The delicious sense of evil was dissipating little by little and she tried to hold on to it with real regret, this was the Fanny she'd have liked to spend the rest of her days with, but in vain. The new, marvellous feeling was fading away and soon there would be no trace left of it, as probably happened with the influence of narcotic drugs, thought Fanny and made up her mind to addict herself to opium that very week, or at least to gin and tonic.

'When's the show going to start, then?' she demanded in her new, thick voice.

Ritzi glanced at her with the same wonder, mixed with something of the awe we always feel towards what is unknown and amazing, and therefore harbouring a possible danger, a threat which might be realized.

'Usually the show doesn't start before eleven, midnight even on weekends. We're a bit early,' he said.

'Early! Half past ten at night, early,' jeered the new Fanny. 'Don't these people go to work in the morning?'

'I don't know,' said Ritzi.

The waitress saved him from further embarrassment. She suddenly appeared at their table and placed on the damp Formica surface one glass that was thin and bubbly and another that was large and amber-coloured. Fanny's glass had a slice of lemon stuck on its rim like a territorial marker. Ritzi delayed the waitress with a gesture of his hand, lifted the glass to his lips and took a small sip, and only then let her go, satisfied. You're vile, Fanny said to him in her heart, and immediately there came an echo which returned: And what are you, if you're with him knowing that? She silenced both voices at once and fixed her eyes on the stage.

The couples on stage kept on moving with inexhaustible energy. Fanny wondered whether the joyousness they exhibited was genuine or forced, and recognized with bitter honesty her wish to find it false, so that her own exception wouldn't sting so badly. There was nothing left to hold on to except the glass in front of her and she brought it to her lips and took a big sip. The drink was very bitter and she thought hostilely of Hemingway, but at the next sip the taste began to appeal to her and by the third she felt as if she'd been drinking gin and tonic all her life.

'So what've you been doing with yourself since we met?' she heard Ritzi ask, as though her entire life had been nothing but a straight line stretched between the two bright spots of their meeting. There was something patronizing, almost belittling, about the way he asked the question, as if he assumed in advance that there couldn't have been any event of importance in her life, certainly not one as important as their meeting. He leaned back in his seat, took out a pack of cigarettes and chose one, tapped it against the table and put it in his mouth and lit it. Then he remembered, straightened up and gallantly offered her the open pack. When she refused he sprawled back again, stretching his legs under the table. Fanny drew back her legs. 'So what's new?' he asked again. The obtuseness of the question was so complete that it seemed intended, although Fanny knew it was nothing but plain insensibility, but it was precisely that which she couldn't bear.

'I have to go to the bathroom,' she said and stood up at once, before he could offer to accompany her. She needed a respite, otherwise, she felt, she might explode in a way which would destroy this evening completely. Ritzi must have had an intimation of this, because he sat down again after having already half-risen from his seat. 'It's over there,' he said and pointed with his finger.

'Thanks,' said Fanny, almost gratefully. She took her shawl from the back of her chair, then realized she had no use for it where she was going and replaced it and picked up her small evening bag, which was what she had in mind in the first place. Fanny had been brought up not to rely on public toilets, and she always carried some toilet paper in her bag, just in case.

She turned and left the table, somewhat unsteadily. The few sips she had taken from her drink had already gone to her head. You should get into the habit of drinking, she said to herself without quite grasping what it was that she was saying, so you don't lose your balance after every little glass. Altogether you should get yourself into the habit, she said to herself, but didn't quite know which.

These thoughts carried her as far as the end of the corridor, where she stood confused for a moment, blinking in the strong light of the vestibule. Now she noticed for the first time that at the other end of the room, opposite the entrance to the corridor, there jutted out a small lit alcove. This must have once been the club's cloakroom, where the guests' coats and umbrellas were kept. Now it served a completely different purpose. The sill of the window which opened on the vestibule had been turned into an improvised counter, and behind it sat a saleswoman. On the counter were piled disposable white plastic plates, which contained three kinds of salted nuts: pistachio, salted almonds and a mixed plate of sunflower seeds and watermelon seeds and peanuts. Due to the lack of room, plates of the same kind were laid one on top of the other.

The woman, who had felt Fanny's gaze, retaliated with a sharp look. All at once Fanny realized, with great embarrass-ment, that she'd been standing there staring at her for several minutes already. Her face grew hot. It was all the plastic plates' fault. She couldn't take her eyes off them. These disposable plates, with the thin layer of peanuts on their bottom, embodied the absurdity of her dream of the beginning of the evening with unshakeable concreteness, and a fierce resent-ment rose in her towards the city which had glimmered at her from afar during the drive, beckoning, beguiling, constructed on scaffolds of illusion. From the peanuts her eyes climbed up to the woman's face, which was heavily made up, the hair so blonde as to be unreal, the face puffed, pale with the waxy unwholesome pallor of someone who rarely went out in daylight and spent her nights, or were they her days, in the light of an electric bulb. The light inside the alcove flattened everything around it, turned everything, especially the wom-an's face, uniform, harsh, one-dimensional.

'Can you tell me where the toilets are?' Fanny suddenly asked with desperate courage, sensing that she must snap the chains of the strange attraction which riveted her eyes to the illuminated alcove and to the woman inside it.

The woman gestured slightly with her chin. 'There,' she said. Her eyes expressed contempt and then nothing. Fanny turned around. She looked confusedly at the corridor she had just left and only then she noticed the small sign, barely illuminated by a dusty bulb, 'Ladies'. With burning ears she re-entered the corridor. Only in the toilets did the scorching sensation of the woman's eyes on her back let go of her, and she closed the door behind her and leaned against the wall. For a moment she felt a great relief, like one who had found for herself, if only for a brief moment, a place of refuge. But when she opened her eyes the murky reality of the place forced itself upon her, the oily, dirty walls, the thick smell which came from the stalls. She peed into the toilet bowl, taking care not to touch its rim, and used the paper in her bag. Then she rinsed her face and stayed bent over the sink in front of the mirror for a long moment, without looking at it. Finally she wiped her face with what was left of the paper and went out.

When she came back the big hall seemed quite different. At first she couldn't put her finger on the nature of the change, until she realized that the loud music had stopped and the dancing couples had cleared the stage and sat down at their tables. On the stage now stood a man of about fifty, wearing gabardine trousers and a shirt with pushed-up sleeves, who was holding a microphone. A red keyholder peeped out of the back pocket of his trousers. It seemed that she had missed the beginning of his speech. '. . . needs no introduction,' he was saying now. 'I give you – Gina! Straight from Rome,' he concluded in complete contradiction to what he had just said. Then he got off the stage, his bunch of keys swinging on his hips. A beam of light appeared on the opposite wall, felt its way across it like a dazzled animal, and focused. Ritzi leaned towards Fanny across the table. 'I've seen her before,' he whispered, crowding closer, and Fanny drew back. 'Real hot stuff.' He was about to add something, but at that moment a gap opened between the two halves of the curtain at the back of the stage and into it stepped a woman, a very big woman. She was wearing an extremely short black leather skirt and a tight leopard-skin top with the deepest neckline Fanny had ever seen. She had magnificent, astounding breasts, each one brimming almost fully over the leopard skin. Black leather boots reached up to her thighs and were laced there. Her eyes were covered by big black sunglasses, which indeed reminded Fanny of Gina Lollobrigida.

Suddenly a band – after a second Fanny realized that the music was coming from the big loudspeakers at the corners of the stage – broke into a number that Fanny recognized. They had played it once at that Purim party she'd gone to with Margie, and it had been cut off before reaching the end, and actually very quickly, due to some adamant protestations from the dancers. 'Who does he think we are?' Margie had said. 'Students?' Now the tune returned with a vengeance and while the woman in the leopard top was undulating her leather-swaddled legs, Fanny thought about the party. There really was something embarrassing about all that heavy breathing for people who were, after all, no longer twenty, and to be honest no longer thirty either, and at the Technion's Single Staff Residence Hall to boot; but here this song was quite in place and Fanny recalled its name, 'Macchina d'Amore'. That's what the singer whispered at the beginning of the song, and for some reason the name had stuck in her memory: Love Machine.

The woman peeled off her leather skirt with a single motion and remained in her black leather boots and in a tiny triangular slip, also black. Then she eddied – there was no other word for it – out of her top. To Fanny's surprise some sort of bra was revealed under it, but she immediately understood that it was vital, for it was its support which lifted the breasts and created the towering, glorious bosom which had astounded her on her entrance. The woman stretched her arms backwards and undid an invisible hook, and immediately flung the liberated bra aside. The heavy breathing in the background intensified. The singer's voice became intimate and entreating. The music whirled Fanny's head and muddled her senses. A veil of mist seemed to stretch before her eyes, blurring the big stripper, the stage, the audience. Through the mist she saw the woman tossing aside her slip and sprawling on a low velvet-covered sofa. Her sunglasses were still on her eyes like some kind of improbable proclamation. She spread her legs apart and started moving them with rhythmic motions, which at moments changed into the bicycle exercises Fanny did every morning to keep fit, and Fanny shook her head wearily to drive out the inopportune image. The woman continued with her rhythmic motions, raising and lowering her thighs. Through her veil of mist Fanny reflected that she was indeed a love machine, a big efficient machine working at a steady pace, driven by an excellent engine, a machine that could be trusted not to fail and to go the whole way until it arrived, before the crowd's eyes, at the finishing line.

And then, accidentally, the stripper turned sideways and for a moment her face looked straight at the audience. It was turned upwards, fixed in its mask of seduction, but this mask was crumbling at the edges, great cracks had opened up in it and widened and through them Fanny could see the other face, strained to the edge of endurance in its fixity, horribly weary, fixed on the ceiling as if there lay its only chance of salvation, as if striving to pierce through it and break out, but at the same time knowing there was no way out, and that it had to go through the entire show, up to the end.

The singer gave a great moan and fell silent. The body of the woman stretched in a convulsive arc to the ceiling and sank. Through the arc Fanny could see the back of the stage, greyish-black, faded, and the MC's silhouette as he passed through the gap in the curtain. The audience began to applaud, loudly but deliberately. The stripper stood up and bowed. Her great breasts dropped as she bent, almost touching the floor, and Fanny felt an unreasonable fear that they might fall off and hit the ground, but they didn't, remaining instead well attached to her ribs, and she straightened up, nodded again as though to thank them for the remainder of the applause, and turned and left. The curtain closed. The light dispersed and faded. A thin Arab youth with the hint of a moustache emerged, shadow-like, on to the stage and gathered the scattered articles of clothing, and like a shadow he disappeared. A nearby throat-clearing reminded her of Ritzi's presence. 'Good, huh?' he asked proudly, as if he had some claim over the stripper. Fanny nodded. He bent closer to her. 'Would you like to go now?' he breathed. His whisper steamed in her ear thick and urgent. 'We could see the rest some other time,' he whispered. His face took on an expression of obstinate expectancy. 'Don't worry, we can come whenever you like. I don't have to pay here,' he said in a louder voice and pushed her elbow lightly as if to urge her on, the way you urge a stubborn animal, and this touch infuriated her and returned to her the new Fanny, the one she'd already thought she had lost. She moved her arm away. 'No. I like it here,' she said firmly, and turned her face to the stage. Ritzi leaned towards her again, his expression like that of a man trying to coax a recalcitrant child, but a distant roll of drums silenced him. The MC came out on stage and announced,

'Thank you, Gina. And now something really special – straight from Spain – Nino and Mackie!'

With a sharp stride a very tall thin man in tight shiny black pants crossed the room. He was slightly bent to one side, the one further from Fanny, and at first she could only see the hands that were stretched out to him as he passed, octopuses of hands, extended and immediately retracted, touching and then promptly snatched back. Only later she noticed the monkey, a small creature with a mask-like face, or so it seemed to her, a Purim-mask face, so that she couldn't tell at first if it was a real monkey or a child in disguise. The monkey was dragged by its master in a protruding diagonal gait, swinging a little from side to side, sucking its free paw. The people on either side were constantly trying to touch it and the monkey extended its paw to them but didn't manage to touch any of them, perhaps its master didn't want it to and perhaps he had a good reason for this, perhaps the monkey bit, Fanny didn't know, but it was dragged quickly in a straight unrelenting line to the stage and there at a fast bewildering pace was required to do many different things one after the other and sometimes all at once, to go through hoops, to leap over obstacles, to catch things, and he failed in almost all of them. His clumsiness was touching, almost inevitable in view of the number of tasks that were hurled at him and the dizzying pace at which they changed. No sooner had he managed to complete one of them and already a new object had appeared which he had to catch, to leap through, to overcome, and the more the tasks multiplied the more awkward he became and the more he failed, and maybe that was what his master wanted, and maybe that was what the audience wanted, for they cheered loudly and even cried out with excitement, 'Look at him!' or 'What a sweetie!' or 'Poor thing!' in both feminine and masculine voices. The man in the black pants turned on a small phonograph which stood on the stage and the monkey mechanically began to clap his paws, obeying the pull of an invisible string. His paws were very large and there was something strange about the way he clapped them, something unwieldy and uncoordinated, not quite human and yet not completely not so, and perhaps that was what inspired the people's great sympathy, thought Fanny wildly, to see someone who was almost like them, and who strove to be completely like them, and couldn't be. And perhaps it was the other way around. Perhaps deep in their hearts they identified with him because they too had never succeeded in fulfilling what was required of them, they too stumbled when they tried to jump over the hurdles which were put in their way, just like him, and that was the reason why this poor imitation, touching precisely because of its rawness, aroused in them an outburst of generosity and love.

But the applause had not yet died down when the thin man started on a line of action which was altogether incomprehensible: he started dragging the monkey to and fro on the stage at great speed, dwarfing it with his height, pulling it by the hand forcibly, almost violently, from one end to the other and back again. Each time they reached the edge of the stage the monkey stretched out his hand to the audience, and again Fanny wondered if he did that in obedience to his trainer's command or out of some real need to touch, to touch, some foredoomed desire to to cancel the distance which separated it from them. Ritzi placed his hand on hers. 'What a moron, huh?' he asked, and without waiting for an answer added, 'Two years ago they brought over someone who did an act with monkeys. You've never seen anything like it.' He leaned towards her again, his face putting on the same wheedling expression, but Fanny averted her face and fixed it determinedly on the stage.

At that moment the music stopped. A curly blonde suddenly climbed on stage from the direction of the audience, placed on the floor a Coca-Cola bottle with a straw and walked on, but before she had the time to straighten up the monkey, suddenly quick as lightning, put out its hand and pulled her strapless black dress down to her waist, exposing a brilliantly white bosom. Just for the blink of an eye, for the woman immediately drew her dress back up and vanished behind the curtain. Only then Fanny understood that the whole scene was a habitual routine, and by the time she she realized that the gipsy had caught the monkey by the paw and tugged, or rather hauled it behind him down the stairs, again crossed through the audience, as fast and impervious as before, and he too disappeared from sight.

The familiar drum roll did not accompany him on his way out. The MC announced a short interval. And before Fanny's eyes, unfocused like the eyes of someone awakening from a dream, floated up, one by one, the table, the half-empty glasses and Ritzi sitting opposite her and nervously rubbing his palm on the elbow of his jacket. All this seemed to her completely unreal. She had been wholly captivated by the world inside the yellow circle of light, so much so that the thick layer of make-up on the stripper's face, shining towards the end of the show on her forehead and at the corners of her nose, the gipsy's tight pants, his hand powerfully gripping the monkey's large brown paw, all these became reality, all the more true for its concreteness, while the tables around them, the hum of the crowd, the waiters hurrying by holding plates of chips above their heads, and especially Ritzi's face, all these seemed a particularly insipid and disappointing invention. Ritzi said something which she didn't hear, though a minute later she realized that his lips were moving and that he was staring at her with an expectant look, and she tried to focus her eyes on his face. At that moment the MC came back on stage and announced a slight delay in the second half of the programme: '. . . and in the meantime you can listen to our favourite singer.' The spotlights went out and the stage again sank into darkness. The buzzing of the crowd intensified. Ritzi straightened up and stretched himself. 'So, have you have enough?' he asked. 'From now on it's less interesting. It's always less interesting after the break.' Fanny said, 'I want another gin and tonic,' and Ritzi gave her an astonished look. His face altered; he must have begun to realize that he'd made a bad bargain, but he shrugged and signalled to the waitress.

From the loudspeakers rose the voice of the invisible singer in a nostalgic song about good old Israel, which he couldn't possibly have known, reflected Fanny, for by his voice he wasn't yet born in those days he was singing about. 'Above, the blue sky/The mortar is dry/And you . . .' he sang, and Fanny's gaze wandered to the stage whose bareness was now exposed, faded and dusty, and from there to the couples sitting on the upper level. Right across from her sat a small, bald, somnolent old man. He seemed to Fanny quite indifferent to what was happening on the stage, and she pictured him to herself coming there every week to sit at the same table in the upper gallery, as far from the stage as possible, and dozing with his head sunk on his chest all through the show while his wife, in the same incredibly green dress, peers at the spectacle through the thick lenses of her glasses. The singer completed the refrain, 'Come back to me, come back, my love,' and suddenly Fanny noticed that the old man's sparse moustache was moving faintly, almost imperceptibly: he was mouthing the words. When the song ended he clapped enthusiastically, and smiled at his wife. It was a genuine smile, the simple smile of a man who's enjoying himself, and Fanny's heart suddenly contracted with pain. 'Give me your lips, give me some consolation . . .' sang the crooner, and the old man sat looking down, a sweet, slightly bashful smile slumbering on his face. But then the hidden drums thundered again; and Robert Richardson, straight from Las Vegas, appeared on the stage, materializing out of the white beam of the spotlights.

He was very tall, as long and as thin as a beanstalk, and when he appeared before the audience he was already juggling three little white balls which he alternately threw up and caught with amazing speed. Isn't it strange, thought Miss Fanny – to go around the world throwing three tennis balls up in the air? Robert Richardson evidently didn't think so. He tossed them up, three, four, five in a row, slipped them along his arm, bounced them on his elbow, his head, the little balls skipped merrily and suddenly, without her being able to tell when or how, they changed into silver rods, like baseball bats but surely much lighter; silver rods flying gracefully, shimmering in the air as they fell like a silvery waterfall – it's beautiful, Fanny thought with surprise, and before she could complete the thought the rods changed into round red sticks. Little by little Fanny was captivated by the charm of these objects flying around so freely and weightlessly, throwing behind their back the rigid laws which had imposed themselves on the universe; her heart went out to their easy, flowing flight, as though carried upon streams of air; she longed to fly together with them. But wait, something was wrong, the smooth flow was broken – a ball had fallen! Miss Fanny held her breath. Please don't let him fail, she begged soundlessly, don't let him fail. Let him go on. But her prayer was quite unnecessary, the entire audience was clapping sympathetically, the audience forgives anything to those it loves. And it loves the beanstalky juggler, who looks so young, it loves the beautiful smile on his lips, almost the smile of a child; and Robert Richardson, with the same smile which is half propitiating, half-saying: 'I love them! Those birds I'm throwing up in the air,' does not get confused. His momentary blunder is smoothed over, forgotten, and now the air is full of discs in all colours. They fly with redoubled energy, with redoubled speed, as though to make up for the previous mishap, changing shape, changing colours, they're multicoloured flying saucers, so graceful, orange, green, white, and they multiply, they multiply the faster they fly, like butterflies they fill up the stage, hovering above the people's heads, and they'll go on hovering there until the whole club is filled with them, and the whole of Jaffa, and Tel Aviv and the entire country will be filled with beautiful feather-light little rings, soaring and circling and whirling and trembling in the air –

183

Until they fall, one after the other, strung one by one on the tall American juggler's neck.

And then he takes out of his pocket spinning tops, colourful little skeins just like the ones Fanny remembers from her childhood, and turns them free at the end of their string – almost independent, it would seem, almost unbound – and gradually, whirl by whirl, Fanny too sheds the need to be bound to the earth, to obey the rules, and bears allegiance only to the long, sensitive hands which flutter up and down with inutterable speed. She's with them even when he finally lets them fly – hop! upwards, very high, and together with them she lands with great precision right in the pocket of his jacket.

He bows, smiles, takes his leave. The audience applauds some more, though again somewhat lazily, the thing's already behind them, but not behind Fanny, who goes on clapping vigorously long after everyone else has stopped, until she feels a tingling in her palms and she realizes that her eyes are full of tears.

After Robert Richardson a pair of roller-skate artists from France came on stage, a man and a woman. Connected to each other at the forehead by a narrow strap they flew around each other lithe and dangerous, the muscles in their backs contracting into dimples, glittering up and down in the spotlights each in turn to the thundering applause of the audience, who had finally, surprisingly, come back to life. And still, thought Miss Fanny, again clapping till her hands hurt, still she preferred that stringy young man who had made the objects fly. There there was no occasion for fear, not really, there was no need to hold your breath lest all their experience and skill, all the thousands of hours of training behind them, would not be enough. A ball was just a ball. And the objects flew around so effortlessly, you didn't have to watch their muscles contracting, the drops of sweat on their foreheads, the gradually darkening elastic band. And although she was riveted, entranced by the intensity of the spectacle, she couldn't bear the thought that people were risking their lives, the wholeness of their limbs, their ability to walk and move as other people did, all the beautiful sunlit days on the beach, for a ticket bought in that insignificant vestibule with the stucco-covered walls. And she longed to see again, even if only for a few minutes, the thin young man with his wonderful smile begging for love, flying his myriad birds in the air and looking straight ahead at the audience, while around him the rings soared, whirled, sparkled, bewitched the eye.

The loudspeakers went silent and the murmur of conversation grew louder and took over the hall. One could discern in it single voices and one could also perceive it all as one indistinct din, a texture of words woven into each other. The lights dimmed, grew murky. Cigarettes had been smoked here for long hours. The air was thick and greyish. For the first time the feel of the place came close to what Fanny had thought it would be. Even its proportions, it seemed, had shrunk in the hazy light and the space became smaller, denser. Somewhere in the back a piano began to play. Fanny hadn't noticed it before, but there was no mistaking the sound, the excessive sharpness of the high keys, the slight hesitation at the passages: the house pianist.

With deliberate slowness a young woman dressed in the style of the thirties descended the stairs, holding a microphone. Her lips were smeared a bold red, her lids sank beneath the weight of blue on them. Fanny hadn't seen her crossing the stage; she seemed to have materialized out of nowhere on one of the stairs leading down to the audience. Her thighs, rustling with silk, moved with calculated sensuality. Ritzi stopped talking. His eyes gradually lowered their gaze, and Fanny cautiously drew her legs back under the table and leaned back in her chair, concentrating on the figure within the circle of light. The pianist finished the introduction with a long trill. The girl started to sing. Amazed, Fanny recognized 'Lily Marlene'.

But not the 'Lily Marlene' she knew. Lily Marlene was here

in disguise, a kind of too-glittering evening dress she had been forced into, extravagantly strewn with gilded paillettes. Too low at the cleavage. Too highly at the thighs. Everything was somehow exaggerated, exceeding the right measure. It was evident that the singer had not grown up in Dietrich country. She pulled too much at the ends of the phrases, stretched the song this way and that as if it were a garment she was trying to lengthen, distorted its shape beyond all recognition. She has no right to do it, Fanny said to herself. But apparently she was the only one to object. The audience, especially the men in it, expressed its appreciation with whistles and calls of encouragement, or was it lust? It was hard to tell. The singer undulated, snake-like, among the tables. The microphone was very close to her lips and she whispered into it, alternately pushing it away and drawing it near, as though she were making love to it and it was resisting, just so as to yield to her a moment later.

At one of the tables sat a man and a woman of about forty. The man was applauding unceasingly. The muscles in his face were tense with concentration and his lips were pursed, as if in an effort to invert them from the direction they craved. His eyes glistened. The woman next to him drew back in an unconscious gesture, and when the singer went past, passing her free hand in a kind of a lingering caress on her husband's head, she put her hand to her mouth in a mixture of horror and pride. The singer proceeded to the next table without heeding her. Her twisting progress was strewn with men on whose foreheads she brushed a lingering, taunting hand. The women, captive in their festive dresses, giggled uneasily. The singer's voice sank to a hoarse whisper. Gathering up the microphone cable she sat for a brief, fluttering moment on the knee of a man with greying hair, put her cheek against his and sang from there, as if from his mouth, wide open with embarrassment and delight, for a moment that was long enough for him to extract a money note from his pocket and thrust it up her black net stocking, just below the beginning of the slit in her dress. Her voice became louder, rounder. The direction was now clear, the door open and beckoning. 'Wie Einst, Liebling'. Her smile, as she stroked her admirer's balding dome, was half-encouraging, half-derisory. She sailed on among the tables, her amorous, contemptuous mouth beckoning to the men in the audience and travelling over their wives as if they didn't exist. Towards the final line her voice grew louder, shrieking where it should have fallen away. Dietrich's broken whisper was hissed, discordant. I could have done it much better, Fanny said to herself and listened, astonished, to the reverberation the words had left behind them. Ever since she had given up her great dream, to be a second Elisabeth Schumann, she had not dared utter even in her thoughts such words as she had just now said.

The singer finished off with a great crescendo. Without a moment's pause the piano launched on a new tune, and again it was only after the woman began to sing that Fanny identified it: it was 'Milord', Edith Piaf's familiar beloved 'Milord'. But in the mouth of the young singer, with her well-rehearsed gestures quite unlike her age, the song had turned into a plaster mask of itself. The port girl's invitation, simple, direct and full of compassion, had turned into seductive coyness. And yet she knows that his heart is broken, Fanny said to herself. The singer was not listening. Her hand stretched out to the pates of middle-aged men in unbuttoned jackets, who raised to her covetous, shamed eyes, shamed before their wives, before their colleagues sitting beside them, before themselves. 'Dieu, qu'elle était belle', crooned the singer, but the iciness did not grip Fanny's heart as it did when Edith Piaf sang those words. This girl was incapable of giving the song its heartbreak, the shattered dreams it contained, the desperate proud smile of the street girl. She did not touch even the edge of its true power. Love makes you cry, as sometimes life does, sang Edith in Fanny's head, and Fanny said to her, true, especially life, and then she suddenly saw before her face a large, round, net-like object and identified it with horror. It was the microphone. She had been singing aloud to herself without realizing it.

Only now the previous moments returned to her clearly, the singer approaching their table and stopping by it, the longer-than-usual toying with the sweating, laughing Ritzi, fearful and attracted both but unable to stop himself, clinging to the proffered cheek and laughing foolishly when it was pulled away from him. His mouth hung open, his eyes fastened on to the singer's cleavage with bare, yearning hunger. He could not tear his eyes away from that cleavage. 'Allez, milord', the seductive, scornful voice undulated over him even before the singer herself slid on to his knees, crossing her legs, her face turned up to his stunned face, her lips pouting at him as at an invisible wedding photographer. Ritzi moved slowly towards the wide cleavage, obeying its call. Large drops of perspiration dotted the back of his neck under his collar. His face flushed a deep, alarming brick red. He might still have remembered vaguely the role he was required to play, but in the void he was flapping in, a doomed carp in the empty bathtub of her smile, there was no room for thought; any move was beyond him. The singer made a motion of disgust and turned to the other end of the table, rising with the smooth, dreamy slowness of a large lizard. Her head revolved until it encountered Fanny. She, too, Fanny realized now as if in an old dream that had already once been deciphered, she too had not behaved properly, she had not giggled and had not clapped her hand to her mouth and had not even looked at her when she sat on Ritzi's lap, *chéri*, and she could expect no quarter now. The singer would never let such an opportunity pass.

The song was perhaps Edith Piaf's most famous song. Padam, padam. *Padam*, the singer stressed again with drawn-out scorn. Padam. Padam. Come now, madam, you've begun so nicely, we're not going to wait all night for you now. And only at the last minute, when the microphone had already receded and was about to be taken away from her to the sound of the singer's amused, deriding voice, Fanny snatched it back, almost by force, and started to sing.

She started at the beginning, and the pianist, who had been

confused for a moment, immediately caught up and began
following her.

> *Cet air qui m'obsède jour et nuit*
> *Cet air n'est pas né d'aujourd'hui*
> *Il vient d'aussi loin que je viens . . .*

sang Fanny, her eyes staring at some spot beyond the stage,
beyond the lights, and her voice emanating from her without
her hearing it. The hisses and the giggles and the murmurs of
protest which had come from the audience when she had
begun to sing gradually died down, silenced one by one. A
great stillness ensued, and only Fanny's voice rose out of it.
Ritzi's face, which had reddened again when Fanny took up
the microphone, faded back to its original hue, and the
involuntary impulse which had moved his hand as if to grab
the microphone away from her, to stop her making a laughing
stock of herself and of him in front of all these people, was
checked. He looked at her with wide-open eyes, afraid to
believe his ears, and turned this way and that as if seeking
affirmation on the faces of the others, trying to understand this
new silence, the direction in which the wind was now
blowing in the room, but he found nothing to hold on to and
finally returned his gaze to her, as to a last point of reference.
But Fanny did not see him and only sang. She sang Edith's
song and her own, because even though she knew she was not
Edith and never would be, it was about her that the great Piaf
had sung, to her, to ordinary unremarkable women like
herself, and that was why she did not feel she was wronging
her by daring to sing her song. Perhaps no other song was as
right for her, for Fanny, whom this melody, and all the other
melodies, had kept pursuing across the years, across the
distances, not letting go of her even in her new home, in this
new country, not allowing her to listen to the music that came
from the radio in the office, not letting her love the singers
with the guttural voices who sang on it and their bold,

beautiful songs, but rather drawing her backwards all the time, to what no longer existed, with a hidden subterranean force she had never been able to resist for more than a short time, for more than one afternoon. Already on the street when she walked home from the office in the fast-failing twilight, or on the bus, on winter evenings, already then she could feel the new melodies growing more and more distant, fading away, and those old, deep-rooted ones, connected to her with an umbilical cord she could not sever, gaining in strength until they flooded her completely, and again she was left with them alone, just them. And without noticing she moved on to the song she loved the most, that of the woman robbed of her lover by the crowd, and was not even aware of the fact, surprising in itself, that the pianist had also immediately begun to play the song with her, but just sang, with her eyes closed, that woman's loss and her own, their shared pain, hers and Edith's, Edith of the songs, at least, who was always being loved and left, and she abandoned herself to it and followed it to the last, to the very edge of that woman's despair, and only the audience's applause wakened her from it.

The girl next to her bit her lips. With a scornful gesture, but it was a scorn with its sting removed, she seized the microphone and began to sing, in a high voice, 'La Vie en Rose'. But now the audience, that cruel, change-craving animal, had turned about. Or it may have been the women's revenge for the forced giggling, for the hand they had clapped to their mouth instead of using it to slap the face of the woman who had made love to their husbands so openly and so contemptuously, as if exposing their shabbiness for holding on to such a measly catch – whatever the reason, the crowd had now turned about completely and hurled at her a volley of catcalls. Her singing has now been revealed to them in all its nakedness, paltry and false behind its screen of dimmed lights and smoke, fake merchandise, and nobody wants to be sold fake merchandise, not them, the audience has grown fastidious now, and the first pistachio shell lands on her nose of all places, a ludicrous shot which shatters the remainder of the pretence she had so far managed to keep up. Peanut shells fly out from a few other tables, even from those which had had the privilege of her pausing beside them, perhaps especially from those, even from those where they've just stuck a hundred lira note to her thigh, and on the front of her dress now lands the peel of a mandarin someone had brought from home, and suddenly, all at once, the crust of the fake *femme fatale* falls off, and again she's a girl of twenty-something whose vanity has been hurt, tears well up at the corners of her eyes, her face twists in a grimace, and before she completely loses her self-control she mutters a curse and escapes backstage.

A tumult broke out among the tables, intensified and died down. Once everyone had voiced their opinion they lost interest in what had happened and turned back to one another. Fanny was left stranded on her chair as on a desert island, soaked with sweat, Ritzi's smirking face floating across from her on a heaving sea of smoke. '. . . Have another drink?' Ritzi asked with a new solicitude. Fanny nodded. As long as she could be alone for a few minutes. 'Half a second, I'll go over to the bar. Otherwise we'll have to wait here all night . . . disgraceful service.' He said something else but Fanny no longer heard him. All the noises merged in her ears into a single din, a monotonous hum rising and ebbing, and when she raised her head in alarm, finally realizing that the masculine voice which was addressing her from close range was not Ritzi's voice, she also realized, from its patient tone, that this wasn't the first time it was repeating the words.

'You wouldn't mind my joining you for a minute?' the man asked, and after a moment her vague glance recognized in him, by his gabardine trousers and the keyholder peeping out of his back pocket, the MC from the beginning of the evening. Without waiting for an answer he drew up a vacant chair from the next table and sat down. Fanny nodded superfluously.

'Allow me to get straight to the point,' the man said with an

odd mixture of old-style European gallantry and local rudeness. 'I'm the manager here. We've just found out that we've
made a rotten deal. This girl stinks. She's worthless. I came to
ask you . . . that is, the owner wanted me to ask you if you'd
be interested in replacing her.

'It's not big money,' he hastened to add, quite unnecessarily,
for Fanny was too stunned to open her mouth. 'It's not part of
the show, you see. Just a kind of filler, so people won't feel
cheated, you know, sometimes it seems to them that the show
is too short, and then it's always good to have something after
the show that doesn't cost much, not anybody famous, you
know, but with a pianist alone the audience is never satisfied.
The best thing's a female singer. After all it's a woman, it's
something.' He hesitated for a minute and then leaned over
towards her, so close she could smell his breath, peanuts and
stale Cognac. 'Usually he prefers someone younger. Because of
that, you see. I can tell you that you've made a great
impression on him.'

Fanny forced the muscles of her mouth to move. The voice
which came out was hoarse, a sort of cackle which frightened
her and probably her interlocutor as well. She said, with a great
effort, 'No, of course not. I wouldn't dream of taking . . .' This
was as far as she managed to bring herself.

The man sitting opposite interrupted her and said impatiently, 'Don't even think of that other girl. She hasn't got a
chance, she'll be out of here anyway. Albaz doesn't want her
here for even one more evening. The question is, do you want
to or not? The boss's really interested, it's the first time I've
seen him so hot for someone who's not a real star, some big
name from abroad, you can play on that. Between us I'll tell
you,' again he leaned towards her and again the stale smell hit
her nostrils, 'he said that for once he wanted some class. That if
this place got a touch of class by mistake, he wants it to stay.
Not that class is always good for a place like this, you know.
Too much class would ruin the business. But just a little, you

know, and after the show . . .' He fell silent and looked at Fanny expectantly.

Fanny looked at him and wanted to speak, but couldn't utter a word. Her heart beat so strongly it frightened her. It was a totally absurd idea, she, Fanny Fischer, and this club, a wildly improbable combination. Though actually, why not? What did she have to lose? The events of the evening, Nino and Mackie, the roller-skate artists, the big woman in the tiger-striped top, all of them were whirling in her mind one after another like the balls in red and green and white of the tall juggling artist, and suddenly, as if in a dream, she saw him standing before her, but apparently in the flesh and not in her spinning mind, for he smiled at her his wonderful, disarming smile and said in English with a distinct American accent, 'I'd be very glad if the lady agrees to join us. I found her singing marvellous,' and smiled again. The room started turning before her eyes, cartwheels upon cartwheels of smoke, tables and people and greying cigarette tips, with only the juggler's thin face steady in their midst like a pivot, and from out of the dizziness she heard herself say, 'Yes. I will.' In English, as though it was him she was giving her consent to, not to the proper person, the manager or his deputy; but whatever the language, the words had been said, she had agreed, she was taken on in this place, this third-rate nightclub, and she hadn't even asked about her wages.

Out of the smoke Ritzi's figure suddenly materialized – flushed, perspiring, carrying above his head, to keep them away from people's elbows, two glasses filled with some liquid which shook and spilled with every step he took. His image seemed at this moment quite illogical, completely unjustified, like the stubborn tail end of a dream which had succeeded in tresspassing into reality. What is he doing here? she thought with the same feeling of detachment, and immediately asked the more correct question: What am I doing here? And suddenly it was quite clear, she was here because she belonged here, this was where she sang, it was her workplace. And in a manner which was in itself arbitrary and illogical she raised her head and looked again at the tall juggler, straight in his eyes, as though it was with him that she had just sealed that contract, and with him alone.

All through the ride home Fanny sat inside a dim bubble. The road, the cars ahead, Jaffa's lights behind them and Ritzi on the seat beside her, all moved outside the bubble, existing somewhere in the distance but not felt. She didn't remember how she had taken her leave from Ritzi and whether she had done so at all, she supposed that she had, but what she had said and what he had said and how exactly she had left the car and climbed the stairs and opened the door to her flat, of all that she had no recollection whatsoever. All the other things she usually did before going to bed were also gone through with the same vague, stunned feeling, akin to losing consciousness. It was only after she had lain in bed and turned off the light, and darkness had flooded the room, that her eyes seemed to open. Her eyes looked at the ceiling, wide open and very lucid, and she saw with great clarity the flaws in the paint-work caused by the irregularity of the plastering, and the light falling from the neighbours' balcony, and the dark rectangle of the picture frame on the wall, it was already very late, and in her head the words repeated over and over again. 'Cet air qui m'obsède jour et nuit', and it was true, again she was struck, as the light strikes your eyes when you pass from darkness into a lit room, by the truth these words held for her, dazzlingly bright on the rough white ceiling, for this melody refused to let go, always insisting on speaking before she did and preventing her from answering, or listening, always coming up first and playing so strongly and with such seductive sweetness that she couldn't help listening to it, to this melody rather than to anything else which was taking place here and now, for nothing was beautiful enough to hold its own against it, or dear enough, and nothing else could make all her strings vibrate with the sweet, pleasuring pain of memory, against which reality stands no chance.

She lay thus for a long time, her eyes wide open, and looked at the ceiling, watching the car lights travelling across it and moving to the opposite wall and disappearing, the words playing themselves over and over in her mind, until she couldn't stand it any more and she started to shake her head on the pillow from side to side, trying to shake the melody out of it, trying to recall some other melody that would make her forget this one, but to no avail, because even if a few odd notes did manage to filter through, they only struggled for a moment and immediately the old melody grew stronger again and drowned them, nothing was of any use, and she began to be really afraid because it had never happened to her before that she couldn't get rid of a melody however hard she tried, until finally she decided to start going over the events of that evening one by one, from the ring at her door to the drive home, and as she had known, probably, in advance, in some hidden place, the song's relentless soundtrack stopped at exactly that point where her eyes met those of the tall American juggler, shipwrecked on the rock of his smile and refused to budge from there even one note further, and before his thin face outlined in strokes of light on the white plaster Fanny finally dozed off, and sank into a soft, kind sleep, inside which everything dissipated, and the song too.

27

The next morning she woke from a dream she couldn't remember, but which left her with a vague sense of alarm. The sun was dazzlingly bright in the room, and as soon as the memory of the previous night came back to her this hazy misgiving was translated into an urge – almost a panic – to call the club and cancel the preposterous contract she had made the night before. But while her spirit ran, panic-stricken, to the telephone in the entrance, her body remained lying in bed, watching the newly green branches of the tree outside the window swaying to and fro in the morning breeze, and another thought, a thought at the back of thought, dull and obstinate, unemotionally enumerated the reasons why she should accept the offer, preposterous though it might be. The reasons were three: first, that she was forty-two years old. Second, that every day that went by in the kitchen's south window was whiter and longer. And the third reason, and perhaps the main one, was that she didn't know what to do, and there were moments, during those long, white days, when she was overcome by such terror that she feared she might jump up all of a sudden and run out into the sunlight and tear screaming through the streets among the shops and the benches and the bus stops and the passers-by. In truth these three reasons were but one, and even that one wasn't a real reason, clear-cut and definite. Suddenly she understood that she had already made the decision two weeks earlier, when the blow of warm damp air struck her face as she came out of the Ritz, and only the offer hadn't come yet.

So she didn't go to the telephone and she did not cancel her contract. She got up late, unlike the last few days when she had woken far earlier than she used to for work; she got up at nine and prepared herself a leisurely breakfast, gazing over her cup of coffee at the white flutter of the curtains at the south window, and at the shafts of sunshine stretching across the kitchen, the wheels in her mind turning and turning without catching hold of anything, watching the day go by minute by minute, watching the spots of sun on the kitchen floor, until it was one o'clock and time to get into the bath. The rehearsal with the pianist had been set for three. She had meant to go over the songs at home before meeting him, but had been completely unable to stop the empty white spinning of her mind, or to tear herself away from the curtains' pale flutter, the coffee grounds on the bottom of her cup, the little insect crawling on the window sill; and so she shoved the Piaf album into her shoulderbag as well, in the improbable chance that she could play it there.

During the long ride on the no. 10 bus to Jaffa, looking out at the sea, Fanny reflected again on the old issue of her belonging or not belonging to this place, which she loved with the pain of unrequited love, and sometimes almost hated, with the rancour of a rejected lover, but had never allowed herself to fully feel either of these two emotions; and she wondered whether this ride in the old wobbly bus was, perhaps, finally bringing her to some sort of belonging, now that the only one she had had, that to Bruck & Sons, was taken from her, an illusion though it might have been. Her thoughts wandered over the sea gleaming with the cruel sheen of mercury, hurting her eyes, beautiful but not hers, belonging only to the teenagers who crowded its beaches, bare-bodied and tanned, or not only to them but also to paunchy middle-aged men and old women whose flesh sagged in their one-piece black swimsuits, just not to her. Perhaps now, she told herself, she'd reach something which would be really hers, or at least hers as well. But the image of the bare, dusty stage which flashed through her mind extinguished that hope too, and she let her eyes stray over the shining, mercurial surface and thought no more.

The streets, steaming in the three o'clock heat, gave way under her step like a large dusty beast. They bore no resemblance to the dark starry alleys of last night. At the club, after walking – without anyone addressing her or asking what she was doing there – up the stairs and through the vestibule, she met only the Arab janitor, the same youth with the apprehensive face and the vestiges of a moustache, and to her surprise he said that yes, there was an old phonograph which was sometimes used when there was no pianist and the tape player was broken, and dragged over to the stage from some corner a large, faded, dusty box and raised its lid. Fanny sat down next to it and began singing in a low voice along with Piaf.

Only half-way through the second record she felt the touch of a hand on her shoulder. She turned around and saw the pianist. 'Sorry,' he apologized with no special effort to sound convincing, 'I got held up. Shall we start?' And without waiting for an answer he went up to the piano and started playing fast, nervous scales. Fanny carefully lifted the arm of the phonograph and took off the record. She had identified the opening chords of 'La Vie en Rose', but for some reason she didn't feel like singing this song, not now, and she said, 'I'd rather start with "Milord", if you don't mind.' The pianist switched tunes without comment. She began to sing.

At about the middle of the rehearsal a young man with a dark unshaven face appeared and positioned himself at the entrance to the hall. The pianist, who all this time had been casting brief, nervous glances at the door over the piano top, muttered, 'Just a minute' and went up to him. They exchanged a few sentences in a low voice, then the pianist said aloud 'Not here' and they both went out into the corridor, where Fanny couldn't see them. When the pianist came back his face had an even more remote, unfocused look, as if he weren't there, but he played exactly as he had before, quite accurately and without any feeling, and whatever songs he didn't know he picked up from the album quickly, without showing any effort, and without waking up for that purpose from the dream he seemed immersed in the whole time.

At five o'clock he said, 'OK, I think that's enough for today,' and got up and closed the lid of the piano. He stretched his fingers back, making the knuckles crack one by one, and turned to go with a feeble 'See you'. Fanny, who had already understood that whatever she wanted to get out of him she had to insist on firmly and explicitly, called after him, 'Same time tomorrow?' The pianist turned around, his face evincing a faint dissatisfaction, and murmured, 'OK. All right,' on a note of faded surprise, as if it hadn't been agreed on already the day before. Fanny shrugged and decided to ignore this, before it began to get her down.

Once the sound of his shoes, tapping with surprising agility on the stairs, had died down, the place sank into a heavy silence. Fanny's eyes wandered over the dusty boards of the stage and from there turned to the depths of the hall. The mass of empty tables and chairs made her stomach flutter. Unaccountably she always felt like that in places intended for large crowds which stood empty for some reason, public libraries, for example, or museums. A ray of sun slanted down from a tall window on to the stage at the oblique angle of five o'clock, and she could see all the little grains of dust dancing in it. Fanny shook her head and went back to the phonograph. She felt she hadn't rehearsed enough, and in truth the record was just as good for this purpose as the pianist. She placed the needle on 'One More Day' and started to sing. Little by little she forgot where she was, forgot the frightened Arab boy who was standing at the door watching her, and abandoned the humming she had forced on herself to begin with, and her voice began to fill out and soar alongside the voice of the great Edith, like two kites flying over a single slope in a strong westerly wind.

Then the record ended and only the low scratching of the

needle was heard, circling in the grooves beyond the last song. A voice behind her said in English with a distinct American accent, 'And now without the record.'

Fanny didn't turn around. She said, her eyes on the old phonograph, 'I have to practise.'

'That's true,' said the juggler and came closer until he was standing in front of her, leaning on the piano. 'That's true, but I think that this way you'll practise better.'

'Why?' asked Fanny, still without looking at him.

'Because you're not Piaf,' said the juggler, and suddenly a certain resolution was revealed in his voice which hadn't been there before, or which she hadn't noticed before, 'and you'll never be.

'Nor should you be,' he continued, drumming his fingers on the piano lid as though in contradiction of his decisive statement. 'There was something very beautiful in the way you sang that song, yesterday. Even though it wasn't at all similar to the way Piaf sang it. Or do you think you were singing it like she did?'

'Not like her,' said Fanny. 'In her manner.'

The tall man shook his head. 'No,' he said. 'I know the song well. There was no resemblance.' He smiled again, as though to avoid any possible offence. 'There was something completely different about the songs when you sang them,' he said, and she felt his eyes on her face, 'and I don't think you should imitate her. Even if she's wonderful,' he said, and again his fingers drummed a little song on the piano, quite contrary to his words. There was always some little song humming inside him which turned his words upside down, thought Fanny, and immediately realized the absurdity of this generalizing thought, as if she'd known him for months, years even, a whole lifetime, when she'd only met him for the first time last night.

In the middle of 'Sous le Ciel de Paris' she raised her eyes and saw that he had gone, and she was all alone in the big empty room with its smell of old boards and with the peanut shells and the dust.

28

On her way back home on the slow, sweaty bus, jolted back and forth against the hard wooden benches, Fanny thought of Aunt Leda, whom she hadn't seen since that day in Maskit. Today was the day of her weekly visit, but somehow the thought of Aunt Leda's apartment, hermetically shuttered from December till March and from May till October, was intolerable to her, and on a sudden impulse she put out her hand and rang the bell. The bus stopped almost immediately. Nobody but her got off at this stop, which stood in a kind of nowhere across from a sand dune midway between Jaffa and Tel Aviv, and so Fanny had no choice but to descend. The sand trickled into her shoes and accumulated between the sole and the arch of her foot in a small heap which made walking difficult, but she ignored it as best she could and went on walking, limping slightly, up the dune, until she saw the sea.

The first time Fanny had ever seen the sea was on the day she arrived in Israel. It was strange because most of the people she knew had come to Israel by boat. Fanny had arrived by plane. She'd had exceptional luck: she had received the ticket as a gift from the Jewish community of some American town whose name she couldn't remember. Minneapolis, perhaps. Something with a Greek sound to it, of this she was certain. Maybe Delphi? Was there such a town, Delphi, Indiana, for example? Fanny wasn't sure of the existence of Delphi. On the other hand, she wasn't sure of the existence of the United States either. She had never been there, anyhow, and there was something almost too mythological in the ring of these words. The United States of America, in the electric smell of the synthetic wigs Aunt Leda used to get from her cousin in

Chicago, in the smooth, firm, athletic necks stretching backwards in the cinema advertisements, without a crease or a vein showing in them, to drink from a Coca-Cola bottle which was far more erotic than the girl and always gave Fanny a brief internal shiver. In short, she didn't always believe in the existence of the United States. At times she thought it was nothing but a fiction accepted by all, which allowed certain people, during the fifties, to get concentrated milk in tubes and thick chocolate bars which broke into such big pieces that your heart ached for the waste, and blue white-dotted nylon dresses for little girls, like Mrs Nussbaum's daughter, who nowadays wore only clothes made from pure dyolene in African designs.

But the sea, the sea was something that from the moment Fanny saw it for the first time she knew there could be no doubt about its existence, and that it had always been there, even before she herself had been there to see it, and yet she too had always been there, in it, in some form or another, a tiny particle of plankton, perhaps, or a foam bubble, or a glint of sunlight or an alga; because from the moment she saw it she knew that she belonged to this great smooth swelling creature in a way which couldn't be deciphered and couldn't be disassembled into parts each one of which could be separately explained, like you could an engine or a recipe, and sometimes, when she was in that special mood in which we can believe, for a moment, in the fictions that we ourselves create, she allowed herself to believe that in a different way, perhaps less justified, and very partial, it belonged to her too. But this she dared to believe only very rarely, and then just for a minute, for in many ways the sea had demonstrated to her that it did not love her. That first summer, when she had not yet learned to be wary of it, she went to the beach one morning to get a tan, and she so enjoyed the clear air and the toddlers' cries and the warmth of the sun on her body, that she was tempted to stay on and on, until the sun had crossed its zenith and started to descend in the belly of the sky. When she returned home, burning hot and seized with shivering, her neighbour Mrs Zeltzer, who amongst other things in her varied past had once been a certified nurse, rubbed her skin with yoghurt and clucked her tongue. '*Meidaleh*, this is not for you,' she told her, and Fanny kept silent, painfully acknowledging the justice of the words. But still her feelings towards the sea did not change. Her sense of belonging to the sea was not based on logic, but on a felt truth. And even if someone had come and proven to her in a scientific manner that all this was nothing but vague and groundless mysticism, he couldn't have undermined this conviction, for it was too steadfast, like the pang in her heart which never failed to resound, like the vibration of a drum, whenever she saw before her the open sea.

The first time Fanny saw the sea, the blue, gleaming, scintillating expanses had swelled within her, filling her to the brim, until there was almost no room left for herself. She wanted to flee and at the same time never to budge from there again, to enter them and be absorbed by them until they were both one and the same thing. The old Yemenite who was standing in the water a few steps away, trying, as she later understood, to fish in the shallows with a torn sieve, turned to her a wrinkled look out of narrowed eyes and asked suspiciously, 'Y'goner faint, Miss?' – It took her a minute to understand what he had said, but even after that she did not reply, for an answer was quite beyond her and she might really have fainted. When she was in Switzerland she had prepared herself thoroughly for coming to Israel and had read many of the Hebrew poets, and a line from one of those poems now came back to her: 'And there was nothing between us but brilliance . . .'. How true, she thought, inundated both on the outside and on the inside by the blinding brilliance of this huge surface of water glittering in the sun like an enormous precious stone, and with dazzled eyes she dipped her hand in the water and took it out, liquid now as well, shedding diamond-like drops that burned with a transluscent, almost white light.

It was late in the afternoon. The plane had landed at one

o'clock but the guide from the Jewish Agency who should have been there to welcome them had not arrived, as he later explained with a great deal of impassioned irritation, due to 'Pesya's usual mix-up with the memos'. The bus, luckily, did arrive, and Fanny found herself, together with a large group of new immigrants from Algiers who had boarded the plane in Paris, travelling on a half-full but very lively bus along a rather monotonous plain, dotted with eucalyptus trees, on the road to Tel Aviv. At the Women Pioneers' Home the clerk, or was it the supervisor, pointed out to her a bed in a room with two other beds and the shelves allotted to her in the metal cabinet. Then she said, 'Well, you'll manage,' and already her back was receding in the doorframe, quickly blurring in the dim corridor against the white glare which flooded the room. Fanny remained in the room all by herself. For a moment she stood motionless, hesitating, between the sombre door and the window effaced by the fierce white light. Then she broke away and without touching the suitcases, which remained standing in the aisle between the beds, quickly left the room and almost ran down the stairs, ignoring the supervisor's astonished look. Out on the street she asked the first man she met how to get to the sea. She could remember how he looked as if it were yesterday, a small grey man wearing a cap, on a bicycle, and he answered her in high German although she had addressed him in Hebrew and instructed her to cross the street and go straight, straight ahead all the time, until she reached the sea.

The old Yemenite went away after a few minutes, mumbling angry words in a language that seemed to Fanny to be all flute. She gathered that her presence had disturbed him and even upset him in some way, but all of this could not touch her because not only her eyes but also her nose and her skin and her fingertips, the tips of her toes, her entire body was tuned to only one presence, which she felt with such acute clarity that all other things seemed besides it to be mere shadows, and she felt completely exposed before the flashing, rising, swelling blue which seemed to be surging towards her, until she felt a sharp pang of fear that she might be struck blind. But the fear lasted only for a brief moment, and it was a fear the like of which she was to know only a handful of times, the fear you feel when you look at a man and know that this is the man you will love for the rest of your life.

For a moment it seemed to Fanny that she could see herself there on the water, receding in the fierce mercurial light towards the horizon, Fanny-of-old with straight smooth brown hair gathered with a velvet ribbon on her back, waving to her hesitantly in her typical, slightly disjointed fashion before dissolving into the dazzling glare. Later, in her room, as she placed two cold-water compresses on her forehead and when that didn't help, swallowed two aspirins and lay on her bed, in the vain hope that the hammering in her head would subside and die down, she understood for the first time with a sinking heart the inevitability in that the thing she loved the most would hurt her the most, and that she herself, in some mysterious, incoherent way, was forcing it to hurt her by her very love for it.

Occasionally Fanny used to wonder how it came about that she, who had never won any raffle or game of chance or lottery, she of all people had won one of the three airline tickets donated by that anonymous Jewish-American community for the Agency raffle. In the end she came to the conclusion, for in this she was indeed a mystic, that all of this had come about for no other reason than to give her that white afternoon hour on Geula Beach next to the old Yemenite with the sieve, so that she could, in this precise combination, see the sea for the first time.

The afternoon hours filtered slowly, protracted and golden, through Fanny's fingers. She didn't take note of the passing time because she knew she still had many hours left after dark in which she wouldn't be able to sleep, and until the air had turned cool and nippy, and a few Arab youths, waiters in the nearby hotel who had finished their afternoon shift, began walking back and forth behind her with their huge transistor radios, she didn't move. Something about sitting like that by the sea – perhaps because it was so open, with no visible boundaries, perhaps because of the ceaseless monotonous breaking of the waves – released her from the tangle of tortuous thoughts about the events of the last few days and gave her a sense of calm, almost, even, of freedom. Briefly she wondered how it was that she had made her way to this particular place today, how she had known, and then she wondered how come she hadn't done this even once during all this difficult year, and then she remembered the playground and the child Uri, with a strange wrench of longing, the sort that you feel when you recall something you know you will never see again, and then she thought that from now on she would come here often, maybe every day, and then she didn't think any more and just sat there until it grew completely dark and the lights of the kiosk on the beach grew sharp and pierced the darkness beyond the pile of rocks of the breakwater, and she rose and tightened her dress around her, almost shivering with the cold which assailed her all of a sudden, her limbs aching from the protracted sitting on the sand, and walked up the dune in the direction of the road.

29

The next day Fanny slept late again. There was a certain freedom in knowing she had a commitment later in the day, which released her from the anxious early rising of the past few months and allowed her to linger in bed until nine and even nine thirty. She was incapable of staying in bed any later than nine thirty. Anything beyond that, she felt, would be tampering with the delicate boundaries which delineated the day, imbuing it with order and thus making it tolerable. But she got up at leisure and made an unhurried trip to the grocery store, and with the assurance of a salary in the not-so-distant future, she indulged herself and bought a carton of chocolate milk and some goat's cheese and smoked fish, and even a bar of imported chocolate. She prolonged her enjoyment of breakfast as much as she could, and after lingering for a long time over her cup of coffee she rose decisively and washed the dishes and gave the counter and sink a thorough cleaning. Then she called Aunt Leda and invited her for a walk along the Yarkon, but Aunt Leda refused, because she had to prepare for the weekly *Kaffee-Klatsch*, which was to be held in her flat this time, and Fanny spent the rest of the morning in unheard-of depravity, sprawled on an easy chair on the balcony, whose existence she'd noticed for the first time in many months, reading *David Copperfield* for the one-hundred-and-second, or one-hundred-and-third time.

At three o'clock she was already hopping impatiently up the nightclub stairs. This time the pianist had arrived on time and even before her, and he was already sitting on his stool by the piano, stringing colourful glittering rainbows of notes, stitching and unstitching them with a single motion of sophisticated nonchalance. He greeted her with a nod, and without breaking his stride launched into the tune of 'Je ne regrette rien'. Give me a chance to breathe, said Fanny silently, but out loud she said nothing and just put her bag down and stood next to the piano, and once her breathing had settled she waited for him to reach the beginning of a verse and joined in. This time there was a better rapport between her voice and the piano, unlike yesterday when she had felt dissociated from it, singing with it but not making contact, like two people who happen to be walking side by side along the same road. Today they touched each other, with however light, noncommittal a touch, but this very lightness suited her, from this shared path you could easily break away and just as easily return, and she circled around the melody, nearing and withdrawing, touching-not-touching, like a bird. It was a good rehearsal, so much so that it took her a while to notice another, alien presence in the room, and when she looked back she saw the fat man who had told Ritzi to come in, whom even then she guessed had the say-so in this place and who in fact owned the place.

The fat man clapped a few times, faintly, briefly. The clapping echoed feebly in the room and immediately died down. Then he started walking down the aisle towards them with small bird-like steps, surprising in such a big man, almost like dance steps in their lightness, though not in any other quality they possessed. 'It sounds really good,' he said when he reached the stage. There he stopped. 'It sounds like you can already start with the show.'

Fanny opened her mouth to protest. For a minute it seemed to her that the sound had been blocked in her throat and her heart choked with sudden fear, but after a minute the muscle loosened and she said, though with difficulty, 'This is only our second rehearsal. It's really not enough.'

'It sounds good,' the fat man repeated, as if she hadn't said anything. There was in this sentence, in the way he had said it, something incontrovertible.

All the same Fanny said, in a faint attempt to salvage not her pride but her performance, which it seemed was going to fail even before it started, 'I still don't feel confident enough with the songs. I haven't found the right approach yet.'

'I don't think you understand,' the man said and the sound of his voice, although it remained as soft as before, took on the quality of a steel string. 'That other girl we dumped the day before yesterday. We don't have a filler, get it? We don't have anyone to pad out the show after it's over, to let the audience feel that it's actually not over yet, that they're still getting something. D'you get me? You can't do without a filler. You'll start working tomorrow,' he said, and Fanny knew that any additional word from her would be useless, even harmful. She nodded silently. And then the pianist spoke. 'I can't make it to rehearsal tomorrow,' he said. His voice was hoarse, croaky even, as if he had to force it to come out.

The owner stared at him expressionlessly. Then he turned to Fanny. 'You need another rehearsal tomorrow?' he asked. Fanny opened her mouth to say yes, and halted. The pianist's face had grown pale and the light filtering through the half-drawn curtains gave it an unnatural, almost greenish hue. His mouth twisted. Without knowing why, she connected the expression on his face with the unshaven young man who had come to the club the day before. 'No,' she said, and her own voice also sounded to her suddenly unnatural, forced and husky. 'I'd rather practise at home tomorrow with the record.' The fat man's gaze lingered on for her a long moment, until he finally removed it and said with a shrug, 'Suit yourself. Be here tomorrow by one at the latest. You'll probably not go on before half-past, but you never know when someone might screw you up.'

Fanny nodded. There were a few questions she had meant to ask him, like how much he was going to pay her and whether each night or as a monthly salary, but the words stuck in her throat and she only looked in silence at his broad back receding, briefly seeming to jam in the doorway, then finally passing through and disappearing from view. The pianist's voice, still hoarse and forced, woke her from her hypnotized staring. 'Thanks,' he said. Fanny nodded again and said, 'Don't mention it.' Then she suggested they start again with 'Milord'.

In the morning she woke up early feeling a sharp anxiety. The light was very bright, almost white, and it washed into the room in waves from the east window. Fanny tried to turn to the other side and and go back to sleep, but knew that her sleep was irretrievably lost. Then she tried to read, this time she was re-reading the stories of Wilhelm Busch, but even the Devout Helena was unable to chase away the dread which pounded against the walls of her body from the inside. Finally she gave up and got out of bed and prepared herself some breakfast, which she ate listlessly, and when she had finished she went out on to the balcony and sat on the easy chair and looked straight ahead at the street until it became too hot. At five, as though switched on by an automatic device, she changed her clothes and went to the playground.

A breeze started blowing from the sea, not cool but still refreshing. Fanny turned her face to the wind and delayed for as long as she could before turning south, so as not to leave this street, which was open to the sea, for one that was blocked by a row of houses. Finally she no longer had any choice, unless she wanted to take the long way around, and she turned into Bin–Noon Street. Already at the corner she could hear the distant cries of children and her pace quickened. When she reached the park she went straight over to her usual bench by the cypresses, to make sure no one got there before her, and only after she had sat down and caught her breath she looked at the sandpit and saw that Uri wasn't there.

Today was a Thursday and there was no reason for him not to be there. No reason at all, he always comes on Thursdays, she told herself in protest, almost in defiance, why shouldn't he come today of all days. Today of all days, when I need him, she said to herself again, then suddenly understood that this, perhaps, was precisely why he hadn't come, shouldn't have come, that this thing was over. And it was time that she stopped hinging her day around him, that he ceased to be her only reference point in a white, empty expanse of time. It was time she stopped needing him.

Still she sat there until evening came, big and purple, and enfolded everything, the screaming children and the ladders peeling in green and blue and the sandpit without Uri and herself, in hazy twilight, till it was hard to distinguish between the small figures running around between the swings. She sat up very straight, the way she had been taught, and did not think of anything or look at anything in particular, and only from time to time glanced at the sandpit, hoping against hope that he might show up after all, and from time to time, but without urgency, she wondered whether he was sick, or his mother was, or whether the girl next door was studying for an exam or had started dating boys. But she did not linger on any of these possibilities, and they melted away just as they had come up, and still she went on looking, even though she knew that she was no longer allowed to do so.

30

The vestibule was empty as usual, with only the three men sitting hunched in their windcheaters at the corner like three watchdogs, an ostensibly indifferent presence but one liable to leap into instant, surprising alertness. Fanny nodded at Albaz and hurried into the little corridor, deliberately avoiding his eyes so she wouldn't have to go up to him. At the end of the murky, silent corridor, illuminated by the faint light of the toilets, the buzz of the great hall hit her like a scream. The crowded tables and the chairs and the people sitting on them punched her, fist-like, in the stomach, and she turned on her heels, defeated, and retreated into the depths of the corridor. She went into the toilets and quickly shut herself into one of the cubicles, but it was useless after this day which had convulsed her stomach in nervous spasms, and in the end she succeeded in restraining to some extent the wild turmoil within her and regained her self-control. There were some advantages, after all, to the rigid discipline which was the cornerstone of Fräulein Neuerbach's method and indeed of Fanny's education in general. She splashed some water on her forehead and pressed against it one of the paper tissues she had brought. Then she dropped the tissue into the bin, smoothed her hair, and stepped into the corridor. What kind of nightclub is this, where the only way to reach the dressings-rooms is through the audience? she thought indignantly, in an attempt to screen out the threatening murmur of the many-headed beast, but this was quite unnecessary, for no one noticed her as she passed, no eyes were raised from the tables to stare at her, and she crossed the hall safely and went through the low door at the side of the stage.

Backstage she was greeted by a gust of dark, stifling air. There was a strong smell of paint, dust, damp wood, the smells of a storeroom. The music sounded muffled here and the clamour of the crowd subsided into a kind of indistinct hum, rising and falling in waves like the sound of the sea. Fanny looked around her. How typical, she thought, that it had never even occurred to her to check out the arrangements earlier, in order to spare herself this last-minute confusion. Then her eyes grew accustomed to the gloom and she saw that she was standing in a room which was indeed a kind of storeroom, where the sets of the various shows were kept. Dimly she made out the stripper's couch. There was no point in dawdling there and she advanced towards the faint light coming from the crack of a slightly open door.

'Still haven't changed the light bulb, the bastards,' a voice, or rather a kind of grunt, greeted her, and to her astonishment she saw that it came from the mouth, stuffed with hairpins, of the big stripper, who was supposed to be Italian – Gina, if she remembered correctly – but whose broad jaw appeared on close inspection to be northern rather, Teutonic even.

'No,' she agreed hesitantly. She looked around her. The main source of illumination in the room, which was steeped in a kind of dim twilight, was provided by a row of little light bulbs surrounding a large mirror which stood on the floor. Opposite it, behind a little dressing table, sat the stripper, gathering her hair – which now, from close up, Fanny could see was frayed at the ends – into a tight bun.

'It's the dye,' said the stripper and in the same breath she added, 'they want to save on electricity, the sonsofbitches.' Running down the nightclub owners apparently afforded her great satisfaction.

'Ah,' said Fanny, who couldn't think of anything else to say, since it seemed to her that the big stripper had exhausted the subject.

At the sound of this 'Ah' the stripper turned her head and examined her more attentively. When she had done, she turned back to the mirror and said, jerking her head sideways with her mouth still full of pins, 'Your mirror's there.'

'Ah,' said Fanny again, for want of anything better. She felt completely wooden, like a marionette. She had noticed the second mirror even before the stripper had pointed it out, a smaller mirror standing on a table at the other end of the room, which looked a bit too small for comfort. On either side of it were two very small bulbs which didn't provide any light worth mentioning, but the division of the room was clear, and she went over and put her bag on the floor. When she sat in front of the mirror she discovered that in order to see her face in it she had to crouch down and pull her head as far as possible into her shoulders, since the mirror didn't come up to her forehead. The stripper glanced at her through the opposite mirror. 'You can take that other chair from over there, you'll be more comfortable,' she suggested in a tone which was noncommittal but not unfriendly, and Fanny at last succeeded in smiling at her. 'Thank you,' she said. 'This is my first time here.'

'You're telling me,' said the woman. 'You know what a row Albaz and Greenspan had over you? Greenspan yelled that you were totally green, that you'd never performed to an audience before, that last time was just a fluke and you'd screw things up in such a way it would ruin the club's reputation – as if it ever had one,' she added contemptuously. 'But Albaz wouldn't even listen to him. Albaz never hears anything he doesn't want to hear, and he doesn't give a shit for Greenspan anyway,' she concluded, stuck the last pin into her hair and stood up. 'I'm getting out of here. Have you got everything you need?'

Fanny hesitated. She had brought with her the words of the songs and also a make-up kit and her hairbrush, but she wasn't sure this was enough. Perhaps there was something she'd forgotten.

'A tranquillizer, maybe?'

Fanny laughed, forgetting for a moment to worry. 'I already took one.'

All of a sudden the woman smiled, as if she suddenly felt a sense of solidarity with Fanny, despite her being so green. 'OK, so good luck. Break a leg,' she said, and picking up a large fabric bag from the floor she turned to go. As she passed Fanny she gave her shoulder a light tap with her open hand. 'Break a leg,' she said again, and Fanny nodded, smiling at her until she disappeared into the dark passage and the door slammed behind her.

When she was left alone it seemed to her that the smell of mould had grown stronger, the space emptier and stiller. For a moment she sat there, looking at the few objects scattered about the room, and wondered whether she should go back to the vestibule and to the three bears, since there was another hour and a half to go before the show began and what was she to do here, in this hushed, empty place, and then there was a light knock at the door and the long figure of the juggler from Las Vegas bent down in the doorway.

'I thought you might want some company,' he said in the same heavy American accent which up till now she'd only heard in the movies.

A feeling of great relief swept over her. Without thinking she said, quite illogically, 'Are you really from Las Vegas?'

The juggler laughed. 'Never been there. On the other hand,' he added, smiling at her, 'I've been to San Francisco, Nairobi, Hong Kong and Manila.' At the end of the list he paused for a moment, amused, and concluded, 'I'm from Alaska, actually.'

'Alaska,' said Fanny helplessly. Alaska was a place she hadn't even thought about. From her childhood she had retained a vague idea of that country, derived mainly from the stories of Jack London: endless expanses of snow, with bearded men wrapped in furs and dog sleighs.

'Not only sleighs,' said the juggler, as if he was reading her thoughts. 'We also have one of the best acting schools in the US.'

'Ah,' said Fanny, slightly confused. This was an image of Alaska she didn't know what to do with. 'Did you study there?' she asked quickly.

'No,' said the juggler and smiled at her amiably. 'But it's there.'

'Ah,' said Fanny. The feeling of helplessness overwhelmed her again. Again she remembered the stage she was supposed to go on in an hour's time, and the certain knowledge of her failure washed over her once more. The whole thing was a mistake, an illusion of some sort, a mirage, and suddenly she was filled with anger against the juggler of all people, as if he was somehow to blame for it all, as if by some sleight of hand he had tricked her into consenting to this terrible fiasco.

'No,' said the juggler. The smile disappeared from his face and he bent closer, his body lengthening towards her from the shadows as he leaned his elbows on the stripper's dressing table. 'This is not the way to go about it.'

'I don't know what you're talking about,' said Fanny, even though she knew very well. A strange blankness came over her, a kind of resistance to this mind-reading, to this invasion of herself without her permission, to the very fact of her being there because of him.

'You know,' said the juggler. 'If you decide to fail, you'll fail. But it doesn't have to be so. On the contrary.'

'Of course it does,' said the Fanny of Berlin, the Fanny of sober logic and reasonableness, the Fanny of Aunt Leda before she had grown old and begun buying ceramic bowls at Maskit's. 'I don't know anything about this thing I'm supposed to be doing tonight. I don't know anything about nightclubs. Or about singing in nightclubs. I don't know anything about singing before an audience altogether.'

'You do know something about singing,' said the juggler. He looked at her obstinately. His hand on the table absent-mindedly threw up and caught a stick of white greasepaint with two fingers.

'I once thought I did,' said Fanny.

'Whoever did once always does. It's like knowing how to be born,' said the juggler and laughed.

'Nobody remembers what that was like,' said Fanny.

'But you remember what it was like when you sang,' attacked the juggler. 'Then, once, whenever it was.'

'So why did you give that example?' said Fanny, almost angrily.

'I don't know,' said the juggler. 'It just came into my head. If it doesn't suit you, you can rub it out,' he said and made a sweeping gesture with his hand from left to right, as if to erase everything that had been there before and leave the air blank and empty. He smiled at Fanny his wonderful, disarming smile, and this time Fanny could not resist it.

'OK,' she said. 'You're right. Once I knew how to sing. I think —'. She checked herself. 'I just knew.'

'It really isn't something you forget,' said the juggler. 'Like I'll never forget this,' he said, and threw two sticks of greasepaint and a little jar of rouge into the air and caught them one after the other between two consecutive fingers. 'Even if I don't do it for years. After a little practice it'll always come back to me. Things you've found the right place for, in yourself, the exact split second,' he said and flicked his fingers again as if he was throwing something up into the air, 'you can never lose.'

'I don't know if I've found that place,' said Fanny.

'If you hadn't reached it, even once, you wouldn't have sung the way you did the other night,' said the juggler.

Fanny hesitated. She wanted to say that it had been an accident, or that it might have been an accident, but she stopped herself before she said it, because deep down she did not believe in accidents. She believed, and the whole of her education lay behind this belief, that a person got wherever he got by virtue of the effort he invested in it. She didn't believe in the gifts of fate or chance, or, as people sometimes liked to call it, luck. She didn't believe it was possible to achieve things with the help of luck. Things were achieved by hard work, and by talent, which you either had or did not have.

'Try to remember.'

The sticks of greasepaint and the jar of rouge returned to their places. The juggler stood up. Fanny was overcome by a sudden and violent panic.

'Help me,' she begged.

'I can't,' said the juggler, and she couldn't hear any trace of sadness in his voice, only a statement of fact. 'I don't know what you have to do. All I know is the right movement,' he repeated, 'and how to wait for the ball so it will reach your hand at exactly the right moment.'

With an ungainly, crablike movement he turned away from her and began moving towards the door.

'But I think you know,' he said, without turning his head. 'If you let yourself remember.'

He bent down and disappeared into the gloom of the storeroom. The bulbs gave a brief, ironic flicker. What if the electricity fails? Fanny wondered, and turned mechanically to the mirror to make up her face. But before she had made the first movement she stopped, and covered her face with her hands, closing her eyes.

The light from the projectors was dazzling. Yellow and blinding, it stabbed Fanny's eyes like so many splinters of glass and refused to let go. She hadn't thought the light would be so strong. In the relative silence that fell she could clearly hear the shell of a pistachio nut cracking. She didn't know whether this silence fell at the beginning of every act, even a filler, or whether it stemmed from the curiosity of the habitués at the sight of a new face, or perhaps it was the story of what had happened there three nights ago that had made people curious. She opened her mouth, swallowing blinding light like a nocturnal fish trapped in lamplight, and closed it again. No sound emerged. With mounting anxiety she heard the pianist playing the opening bars of 'Milord' for the second time, then the third. At least he had the sense to introduce each time a slight variation, her mind registered automatically, so that the repetition sounded deliberate. From the side, in the wings, she saw Greenspan's white face staring at her and she remembered what the stripper had said. All at once she was flooded by a hot, liberating wave of anger. Her eyes filled with tears and the light blurred and cracked, and all the layers which had congealed inside her, horny layers of solidified dust, seemed to melt, everything melted in the blaze of the yellow light and the anger and she remembered, opposite the dazzling glare, under the feelers of the eyes she could not see, something which Fräulein Neuerbach had not taught her, but which she had learned by herself in the long afternoon hours she had spent alone while her mother was out paying her visits, or rather which had revealed itself to her one day of its own accord, she didn't even remember what day it was, because from the moment it became known to her it was as if she had always known it, and this knowledge now illuminated the void in front of her with a great light, altogether different from the blinding light of the projectors, the knowledge that if she sang from this particular point within her, which was the one and the only true point, if she succeeded in singing right from there and resisted all temptation to sing around it, or from some other point which was easier to find, she would sing to the utmost that she was capable of singing.

And suddenly she didn't care any more. She didn't care what the audience would think of her, or if they threw tangerine peels at her or not, and she didn't care about the opposite either: she no longer aspired to reach that moment she'd had three nights ago when she felt as if she was holding the audience by an invisible thread, compelling it to listen to her, compelling it to remain attached to her by this thread. For what did she have to lose, she asked herself as she opened her mouth and began to sing the first verse – nothing. She would never be a great singer. She did not have the unforgettable, unmistakable voice of a Piaf or a Ferrier or a Schumann. And even if she did, it was too late by now. She would never be granted more than these moments, more than they held right now, this very instant, the creaking boards of the stage, the too-bright lights and the rustling of peanuts, and all that was left for her to do was to sing what she knew, these moments, herself, even if nothing remained after them, even if nothing remained of her, as long as she sang truly.

When she woke up the hall was again half dark. The lights must have been dimmed during the last song without her noticing it. There were fewer people at the tables, and those who remained were sitting closer to each other, leaning their elbows on the table and conversing quietly. A woman's voice broke through the low hum: 'And I told her, that if she dared . . .' and was silenced. Then a loud male voice could be made out, and the rustle of a few remaining chips on a plate flourished to get the waiter's attention. Fanny took a deep breath. All at once she realized that she was still standing there, stupidly stuck on the stage, the microphone in her hand, when the pianist had already closed the piano and the waiters had begun sweeping the floor around the far tables, hinting to the remaining customers that it was time to go home. She quickly retreated to the small door at the back of the stage.

'Disappointed?' asked the juggler's voice. Fanny raised her eyes, startled. The juggler's head was floating towards her in a cloud of haze, bodiless, like Alice's Cheshire cat. Only after a minute did she discern below the head an ancient wardrobe, shoulder-high, which was covered in its entirety by a mirror – a huge piece of furniture with peeling gilded legs, that was probably used as part of a set. In the dim light Fanny's reflection in the big mirror also seemed spectral, transitory. How many mirrors does this place have, she reflected absent-mindedly. Mirrors upon mirrors upon mirrors. And she made a small gesture of helplessness.

'I don't know,' she said. 'Maybe.'

'I'm sorry,' said the juggler. 'I should have warned you.'

'About what?' she asked. 'About not being able to cross the same river twice?'

'First you have to know that there is a river,' said the juggler. 'And that you are standing on one side of it and they on the other. Whatever you set floating on the current, little stalks of straw, or a flower, or a cry, will not reach them as you sent it. You mustn't expect, in short,' he said impatiently, 'that they feel you, what you're feeling. Even if you have found that place, even if you did what you had to do in the truest way.'

'Why?' asked Fanny, and at the moment she did so a shiver went down her spine. Suddenly Aunt Leda was standing there in her place, erect in the large space of the store, her face turned upwards to the laden shelves, straining to understand.

'Because they're not you,' said the juggler. 'They don't come from where you come from, and I don't mean that you come from Berlin and they from Bat-Yam. What happened the other day was a miracle, and even that wouldn't have been if not for the girl who went on before you. Now she's gone, you're what they have, the audience, and they take it the way one takes what one's got, without undue excitement. You don't even take your clothes off or put your life at risk.'

Fanny laughed suddenly. 'That's true.'

'You have no right to expect anything more,' the juggler said with cruel precision. 'You must remember that.

'I thought maybe you'd like to come and have a drink with me, to celebrate your first night,' he added, and his voice was now very gentle, too gentle for Fanny who suddenly felt weak at the knees, as though from the moment the sharpness was taken from his voice some sort of support had been taken from her, some resistance which she needed to lean on. Now she only wanted to dissolve, like a mollusc, to turn slowly into soft liquid foam and sink, all the way down, until she found some rest.

Trailing after him with her unnecessary coat on her arm, her face stinging after the rinse in cold water, Fanny passed through the hall, which was now almost completely empty. There was only one handsome old man with a white lion's mane, whom she remembered from that first evening, who was chasing after one of the waiters all along the length of the room, giggling shrilly, while the two well-groomed women who came with him and another man sat by their table impassively, waiting. The other waiters were lifting the chairs without so much as glancing at them, absorbed in themselves and in the night which was finally coming to an end. The Arab boy with the wisp of a moustache was scrubbing the floor of the bar with a wet rag. Fanny crossed the vestibule without looking at the table in the back and went out.

'Albaz,' the juggler said in his strong American accent, 'Albaz doesn't care about anything except that you do your job properly. You did OK, so you don't have to worry whether he saw you. As far as he's concerned you could have left the place with Nino.'

For a moment Fanny couldn't remember whose name that was. Then she laughed. 'I thought Mackie was the monkey,' she said.

'No,' said the juggler. 'Mackie's the gipsy from Hulon.'

Fanny laughed again, this time more relaxedly. 'I couldn't decide whether he was really a gipsy from Spain or a National Insurance repossession man,' she admitted.

'Neither. There's something really weird about that man,' said the juggler, whom she privately tried to get herself used to calling Robert. 'Except for his suit and his lace shirt, which's always starched and shiny, I've never seen him look at anything, not even his wife.'

'His wife?' asked Fanny.

'The curly blonde who brought them the Coke.'

222

It was strange to think that this girl, who had crossed the stage for one moment only to strip and then vanish, was the wife of the monkey man, the man with the dark gaunt face. He really hadn't even glanced at her when she passed by him, not even when her beautiful body was exposed down to the belly. On the other hand, he was probably familiar with it. 'It wouldn't bother me, if he didn't hate that animal so. It makes me sick to see him,' the juggler said.

'Do you think he hates it? I had that feeling too, but there was also something else in it. Something confusing,' said Fanny, 'like someone who hates himself.'

'Yes,' said the juggler. 'The monkey is that part of himself which he hates the most. It resembles him too much, on the one hand, and on the other hand it ties him down to what he is. It forces him to be what he is —.' He touched her arm and Fanny halted. 'But he's incapable of leaving it and being something else. You have a good eye,' he said. Fanny flushed with embarrassment and pleasure. And immediately, out of some strange defiance, as though she wanted to pick a quarrel with herself, she felt the need to differ with this man, to oppose him in some way.

'How do you know all this?' she demanded. 'How come you know him so well?'

'We live in the same house,' said the juggler. 'Sometimes we meet in the evenings.'

The need to contradict abandoned Fanny just as it had come, taking along with it all the words which crowded in its wake. 'I thought you said he was from Hulon,' she protested weakly.

'He is,' said the juggler. 'At least that's what he told me. But they're renting out their flat. It's in quite a lousy neighbourhood, but this way they can save a few pennies. Albaz doesn't mind, as long as there's enough room for performers from abroad. And there always is.'

Fanny said nothing. By now she could no longer remember what had made her fly in his face before and she felt acutely

223

embarrassed. 'Here, this place is open,' he said. A red light glowed through the crack in the door. 'Some people want to keep going after the club closes. Here they're open all night.' Again he touched her arm and she went in.

The place was steeped in red light. The candles were covered with red cellophane, and the tablecloths were red. Mobiles of red aluminium paper leaves silently swayed in the faint wind that came from the sea. The room was almost empty, rows upon rows of tables with candles which emitted a dim red light. The owner hastened towards them from the kitchen door, a small man in dark clothes. In the weak light it was impossible to make out his features. Robert led her to a corner table, which enabled them both to lean against the wall. Only three other tables were taken, also along the wall, and on the tiny stage a man sat next to an electric organ and another held a beautiful string instrument, studded with mother of pearl and connected to an electric cable, carefully in his lap. A third man, younger than the other two, was standing with his back to Fanny, talking to them both. All three had very dark skin. The patron placed on their table small bowls of chick peas, pretzels and peanuts, and hurried back into the kitchen.

Fanny kept silent and looked around her. The wall opposite her was decorated with lanterns made of the same coloured aluminium paper, and underneath them hung the framed picture of an old man with a severe look whom she didn't recognize, perhaps the father of the owner, who now came back and placed some more bowls on their table. At that very moment the guy with his back to them turned around and there was a shriek from the PA, which was immediately drowned by the sharp electrical sound of the musical instruments. The young man, only now Fanny saw how young he was, a mere boy, smiled partly at them, partly at the empty room, with a certain delicacy, Fanny realized, so that they shouldn't feel obligated to respond, and started to sing.

Fanny had never heard such singing. It was very powerful

and full of emotion, a far more bare emotion than she would have dared to put into her own songs, uninhibited, free of reticence. His voice rose in sharp bursts, like the voice of an adolescent, a voice which comes straight from the Adam's apple, then plunged and became deep and caressing. In spite of the trills which usually made her uncomfortable, as did any excess, Fanny liked this boy's singing more than anything else she had heard in this country. There was about him something which was at once timid and confident, and his mannerisms were touching without arousing antagonism. He had a good voice, strong and true and and pleasing to the ear. And above all, he really loved singing. Not just being the centre of attention, commanding the room with the microphone in his hand, not just the confident passing of the mike from one hand to the other and the waiting with a lowered face for the string solo to end, but the actual thing, the very act of producing music out of himself, he simply loved to sing. There was something wonderful about it.

Fanny and Robert sat silently and listened to him until he reached the end of his programme. He sang for a long time, and you could see it was hard for him to relinquish the microphone and stop singing. Nevertheless, when he finished, he said wholeheartedly, with the same intense enthusiasm which had characterized his singing: 'And now I'd like to call to the stage a popular singer. A great singer, a singer I'm sure you all know – Benny Amar!'

A young man with a handsome face came on stage and with familiar confidence announced his opening song. His hair was slicked back with brilliantine and his full lips pouted in an expression of pampered beauty. Feeble clapping came from the few occupied tables. Only then Fanny realized that the boy they had just heard had been brought on only to warm up the audience before the better-known singer's show. The singer started with an up-tempo number that sounded familiar to Fanny. He sang well, but his singing was too much like him, sliding smoothly up the throat, without the focus and tension the boy's singing had. He reminded Fanny of a person scattering sugared almonds at a wedding. Before he launched into the second number of his programme, so as not to leave in the middle of a song, they stood up and left. It was only long afterwards that she thought how odd it was, their first evening together and they hadn't exchanged even one word.

The next day Fanny arrived at the club as if in a dream. Not one detail of the day had been preserved in her memory, as if nothing separated this evening from the previous one, the empty restaurant, Robert's face flickering between shadow and light, the boy's singing. Everything was fluid and vague, no sharp edges, and the dim light in the dressing room only enhanced the dreamy, unreal feeling. Cautiously, as though afraid to crash into something and wound the dream's fragile crust, or be wounded herself, Fanny entered the room and greeted the stripper who was sitting at her dressing table, taking off her make-up with a huge ball of cotton wool. When she reached her own table she laid her bag on the floor, slowly, as if it might break, and sat down. For a few minutes that was all she could do, just sit there and stare straight ahead, sensing the sidelong glance of the woman at the other side of the room directed at her through the mirror. The stripper's voice tore her abruptly from the rounded, edgeless dream.

'You want me to make you up?' she asked, apparently for the second time. 'I can see you don't know much about it.'

'I . . .' hesitated Fanny. She was grateful to the stripper for her offer, but wasn't quite free of apprehension as to the results.

'You'll disappear if you don't put on any make-up,' the stripper said authoritatively. 'The audience wants to see what it's paying for, *capito*?' She rubbed her fingertips in the pinkish contents of a little box, and started skilfuly applying the cream to Fanny's face. Fanny automatically recoiled, shrinking from the touch of the oily, sticky substance, but the stripper held her down firmly with her other hand and continued working.

There was something soothing about the repeated circular movement of the fingertips, which were surprisingly pleasant to the touch, not too soft but not rough or scratchy either. The fingers flowed over Fanny's face with their damp cargo, dissolving in her any wish to resist, and when the stripper was through, she discovered that Fanny was almost asleep.

'Hey! Don't you fall asleep on me,' she said mockingly, but her smile proved that she was pleased by Fanny's complete surrender to the touch of her hands. She added some advice, 'The most important thing is to be on your toes, but not to look that way.' She went over to her table. 'Now put this on,' she said and threw her another small, elongated case. It was a lipstick, not the regular kind but the sort you smear with your fingertips, a blaring red.

'Thanks,' Fanny said and tried to endow the word with the gratitude she really felt, 'I'll use mine.'

The stripper shrugged. 'As you like. Remember, without strong colours no one'll see you.'

She turned to her mirror and began rubbing another substance on to her cheeks. 'This is not for the stage, it's for life,' she explained. Her mirror, Fanny again saw enviously, was much more convenient to use than her own. The bulbs on either side illuminated it directly and enabled her to see exactly what she was doing. 'I squeezed it out of that sonofabitch Greenspan,' she said, as if in response to the unsaid words. 'In this stinking place you gotta stand up for yourself. Otherwise you don't get nothin'.'

Fanny nodded and turned slowly to her own mirror. The bulbs, in a way she could not explain, lit only the bottom part of the mirror, and she tried to apply the lipstick carefully, so as to stay within the line of the lips.

'And it's not like he's short of anything,' the stripper went on. 'The storeroom here's bursting at the seams with stuff and all the time Albaz keeps sticking more and more things into it. He buys 'em at the fleamarket for pennies and then makes stage sets out of them. And it really comes out special, not just plywood like they have in the other places, garbage. You have to hand it to him, he's got golden hands. Anything he touches turns to gold,' she said in a voice which mixed admiration and hatred.

Fanny looked at her in her mirror and thought of Midas. The stripper's face in the mirror stared back at her, dimmed and milky, very much blurred, as if floating in heavy liquid. Its hue grew deeper as her hands continued their confident motion.

'Is your name really Gina?' Fanny asked hesitantly.

'Would you believe it,' said the stripper and pressed her lips together tightly, until the colour was evenly spread. 'But it isn't Italian. It's Romanian.'

'You're from Romania,' said Fanny with surprise.

'Yes. You got anything against it?' the stripper flung at her with sudden aggression, all the more violent for being so unexpected.

'No,' said Fanny, astonished. 'Not at all. Why should I have?'

'Dunno,' said the stripper, calming down, and went back to stroking mascara on to her thick eyelashes. 'Lots of people do. They say Romanians are the pimple on this country's arse.'

Fanny burst into loud laughter, then hastened to stifle it, alarmed, but to her surprise she heard the stripper joining in with a roar. 'Can't help it, it's funny,' she gasped between bursts of laughter. 'Even though it's dirt.' All at once she sobered up and contorted her face in the mirror into a brutal, quite a frightening grimace. 'If I could lay my hands on the sonofobitch who wrote that on the wall at Bugrachov Beach —'. Fanny didn't envy the the fate of the anonymous graffiti artist if he were to fall into Gina's hands.

'Do you go there often?' she asked. 'Bugrachov Beach, I mean.'

'Every day,' said Gina. 'I get up at around eleven or twelve, a cup of coffee and straight to the beach. The only thing that can make me feel good. A day without it and I'm half a person.' She gave herself a last lookover, pushing her metallic hair so that it stood out around her face. 'And you?'

'Me too,' said Fanny. 'That is, I like going to the beach. But I go to Sheraton Beach. Close to home.'

'I live on Hayarkon,' said the stripper. 'Thirty-two Hayarkon Street. If you ever want to go to the beach with me, come by. Best beach in Tel Aviv.'

'Thanks,' said Fanny, a little embarrassed. 'I'll come sometime.'

'You're welcome,' said the stripper. At the door she turned around and looked at Fanny with a critical eye. 'Not enough colour.' She gave her final judgement and vanished.

The juggler came into the room a few minutes before she was supposed to go on. Seemingly she hadn't thought of him until then, seemingly she hadn't been thinking at all but only reacting mechanically to the tasks which presented themselves before her – making up, rehearsing the lyrics of the songs, which were not the same as yesterday's; in fact, she now realized she had been thinking of nothing but him. Behind the mechanical activity, behind the thoughts revolving in empty space, all the time there swam this thought which she hadn't allowed to float up to the surface. 'Seems to me we'd better meet tomorrow during the day,' he said, sticking his head above the wardrobe. 'Otherwise we'd have to keep silent again all evening. I'll call you tomorrow at around noon. Are you awake by then?'

Fanny thought of Bruck & Sons, and almost laughed. 'Even earlier is fine,' she said. Later, after he went, she thought how wonderful this thing was that had just happened. When she was young she had still allowed herself to dream, for example that Herr Weinert, her tennis instructor, would come up to her suddenly after a lesson and invite her to have coffee and whipped cream with him in Charlottenburg. Weinert never did ask her out, and the first time she had real coffee she became so dizzy that she had to ask Lily to take her home, and spoiled her first time at Kranzler Café. Neither had Alex asked her to dance at school parties, even though she had wanted it so much that she almost believed that by dint of wanting she'd make him come up and ask her. Nothing she wanted too much ever happened. Since then she had taught herself never to dream of anything unless there was a logical, evident reason for it to happen, for the heartache that followed a shattered dream was far worse than the usual pain, and it taught her the destructive subversiveness of hope.

Now, suddenly, for the first time in her life, that very thing had happened which she had so painstakingly trained herself not to believe in. And only now did she realize that she had actually not changed at all, that she had never let go of her dreams, but had simply learned to push them well behind other thoughts, the housework, or filing the electricity and water bills in neatly alphabetized folders. This discovery filled her with wonder and dread.

32

But over her morning cup of coffee these emotions blurred, turning into a thick dismal mush. She got up late, her head heavy and dull, the thoughts trapped inside it beating against its walls like the initial throbs of a strong headache. When she woke up she found herself sitting and staring at the wall into which, so it seemed, the juggler's face had just been swallowed, again detached from his body like that of the Cheshire cat, and felt Alice's puzzlement and confusion. She couldn't understand why the juggler kept appearing before her in this image, and for a moment she resented it, as if it were a trick he insisted on playing on her. Then she thought it must have something to do with his profession. And still there remained, in the fast-dissolving train of the dream, the feeling that there was something more to it than that, till finally this thought too lost its realness.

The harder she tried not to think of twelve o'clock, the deeper her dejection grew. Why her of all people? The question kept coming up and there was no way of silencing it. Maybe, she tried to convince herself, he felt a stranger in this place, and even someone like her was preferable to loneliness. But this explanation brought her no comfort and it did not suit the man. The juggler did not walk the streets of Jaffa like someone walking in a strange town. It might have been stupid to venture guesses about someone she did not really know, but some inner sense told her that he did not remain on his own in those places he came to, and that even when he was alone he did not feel lonely, like she, Fanny, did. Something about him gave one the feeling that he always chose the people whose company he desired and that they responded to him, and if so, if so, she said to herself with a dangerous joy she tried as hard as she could to keep in check, if so, then he had chosen her as well.

When the phone did not ring at twelve, she told herself he must still be asleep. The minutes crawled, long and ominous, like the thin black legs of a spider on the wall. At three o'clock she slammed the door of the apartment behind her and went to the playground.

The day was clear and lucid, one of those clear dry days of the beginning of summer. It was hot and the playground was empty, completely empty. Fanny sat on her usual red bench at the edge of the park and looked at the abandoned swings. It was the first time she could see the actual skeleton of the park, the park itself, its essence; like an abstract work of art not intended to represent anything concrete, so the park lay, its own self, stripped of any child or mother, or nanny, not trying to fulfill any role, not serving any purpose, purely itself. There was something about this austere bareness, about the straight stark lines, that suited Fanny's mood. The park did not try to cheer her with the laughter or the shouting of children, it was simply there, and thus she could also simply be there, in it, merely present, not observing or longing or trying to take part, and in this manner, however bare and partial, she felt as if she, too, had been granted some reprieve.

When she came back home she found him sitting on the stairs.

Startled, she asked him how he had known how to get there and he said, smiling, that he had the address written down together with the telephone number. She didn't remember giving him her address, in fact she didn't remember giving him her phone number either, and only seemed to dimly recall him scribbling something in the faint light of the taxi the other night before he got out, but all that had no meaning. When she started climbing the stairs he put out his hand and stopped her. 'I thought we might go to the beach,' he said. She nodded silently. His movement, as he rose, was supple and light, like

233

the flight of the silver rods, and he took her arm and held it close to his warm body as they walked down the avenue in the direction of the sea.

After a while it was twilight and the evening slowly descended on the beach, seeping into it, wrapping itself around them like a blanket. The horizon was pink and then violet and finally a deep true purple which gradually blackened. But right above them the sky was dark blue. 'It's beautiful out here,' the juggler said. He turned over and lay with his face up, putting his hands under his head. 'It's very beautiful here on the beach in the evening. I like being outside at this time,' he added, his eyes on the slowly thickening blue. 'Maybe because of my work. Always enclosed spaces.'

Not when you're in them, Fanny wanted to say, remembering that marvellous moment when the juggler's rings had flown over the stage like a flock of butterflies, unfurling all around him an open boundless space, but instead she said, 'I like the evening too. Even though it's sad. Even before I left my job I used to go to the park every day at dusk —' and suddenly she fell silent, because she realized that this story about her evenings in the park could not but sound as an admission of their loneliness. What sort of person is it who has nothing better to do with her evenings than spend them on a peeling bench at the edge of a city park?

The juggler looked at her face as if he were seeking something there, and then as if he had found it. He did not ask her to go on, but Fanny felt that this wasn't because what she had to say did not interest him, but because he had already read the rest on her face. 'This light becomes you,' he said. Fanny felt her cheeks burning, but only for a minute. In this light she felt safe, it softened and unified everything, coloured everything with the same purple hue. She thought to say 'Thank you', but didn't, and instead asked, 'Was it nice growing up in Alaska?'

'I suppose it's nice growing up anywhere, if you're that kind of child,' the juggler said, 'and not nice at all if you're the other kind. Unless, of course,' he added after reflection, 'you're born in Africa during a drought. Then it doesn't matter so much what kind of a child you are.'

'No,' said Fanny and felt how the words were slipping away from her. The juggler looked at her and added, 'We used to play at Scott and Amundsen. My brother and I. The polar explorers, you know. We were each Amundsen or Scott in turn. Neither of us ever tried to skip his turn and grab more Amundsen. There was a great solidarity between us, my brother and I.'

'My sister was older than me by so many years that we never played together,' Fanny said, 'though I loved her very much. But she was a sort of wondrous figure who came and went, you know, some beautiful fairytale princess, more than she was a sister. Later she married an opera singer and died in the war. I asked her not to marry him.'

'I suppose she would have died in the war in any case,' the juggler said and looked at Fanny's face.

'No,' Fanny said stubbornly. Then she caught on to the absurdity of this answer and added, 'If she hadn't married him she'd have come with me to Switzerland.'

'Ah,' said the juggler, and suddenly he smiled and put his hand on the back of Fanny's hand which lay on the sand. 'You're nice,' he said. 'I like the way you hear the world: all in a minor key.'

'Not true,' said Fanny. 'Listen to my singing sometime: all flat.' The juggler looked at her, briefly surprised, then laughed. Fanny laughed with him. Then she told him about Fräulein Neuerbach. When it grew dark they went to her flat and she changed, and from there they left for Jaffa.

33

'You look happy,' remarked the stripper after giving Fanny's face a penetrating look.

Fanny did not manage not to blush.

The stripper tore off a large piece of cotton wool from its pack and rolled it into a ball. Then she dipped it in the tin of cream in front of her. 'It's not good to be happy,' she added.

'Not good to be happy?' asked Fanny with amazement. It seemed to her that this statement contained an irreconcilable contradiction.

'You fall from too high up. This way you don't fly, you don't fall either,' said Gina and vigorously applied the enormous creamed-up cotton wool ball to her face. The ball slid all the way down to her chin, leaving a light strip on the dark face, like an inverted furrow.

Fanny shrugged, refusing to enter into this debate which seemed to her absurd and possibly dangerous, and turned to her own mirror. Now they were sitting side by side at the two ends of the room, shoulder to shoulder, like two mannequins in a store window.

'It's all right, honey,' said the stripper. 'You don't have to tell me anything. And don't tell anybody else either, because I at least keep my mouth shut when necessary, not like Mercedes and all the others.' She brought her face closer to the mirror and scrutinized a spot which could have been a blemish or a stubborn trace of make-up. Then she rubbed it forcefully with the anointed cotton wool. The blemish disappeared. 'In any case it's always the same thing,' she added philosophically.

Fanny contracted her eyebrows and concentrated on the mirror in front of her. She felt the anger rising in her and finally could not restrain herself any longer and said, 'People are not all the same.'

'If you mean to tell me that just because it's this way with me it doesn't have to be so with you,' the stripper said pleasantly, 'you're right, but you're also wrong. Don't bother to argue,' she said, lifting a huge hand with very red lacquer peeling from its fingertips. 'Believe me, what I haven't seen they haven't invented yet.'

'I don't know what you're talking about,' said Fanny with mounting anger.

'Yours is not Moroccan,' Gina said, 'but in the end they're all the same.'

'Ah,' said Fanny, with an unsuccessful attempt at irony.

'My husband was Moroccan,' the stripper said, as if stating a great fact of life. 'We've been separated for − *w'allah,* it's been thirteen years now. Men are shit, believe me, but you know what − the family's worth everything. His mother is to this day my best friend. Like a mother to me. 'Cause my mom,' she said and looked at Fanny mockingly as if answering her unspoken question, and Fanny reddened again, 'my mom's not dead, not at all, very much alive, she is, but you know − the further away the better. What can you do?' she concluded in a surprising and not altogether logical manner. 'I was born in the wrong place. Bucharest. That's life,' she concluded once more and her eye finally let go of Fanny and turned to a rigorous survey of herself. 'I'm going to lose all my hair with these performances,' she muttered and sprayed it with a generous amount of foam from a large red container. Fanny was left with mixed feelings of anger and disappointment, such as one's always left with in the face of unfinished business, even if one did not want it finished.

'Who's Mercedes anyway?' she asked and heard the false note in her voice. But the stripper chose to ignore it. She had a certain generosity, even though it was revealed at unexpected moments.

'The flamenco dancer,' she said. 'She lives with me. At

thirty-two Hayarkon. You haven't seen her because she's been sick at home with the flu for three days now. She hasn't come today either, but tomorrow she'll perform for sure, otherwise she'll perform on Hayarkon Street on her ass. No fooling around with Albaz,' she said and a note of grudging admiration seeped into her voice. 'He rents this house rent-protected. Albaz a protected tenant, what a joke, huh?' she asked and gave a crude laugh. 'You know that a protected tenant is supposed to live in his flat all the time?' She gave Fanny a sly look. 'What d'you think, Albaz hasn't lived there for even a day. Albaz doesn't live in such places. But you know what, they're afraid of him. He has clout. No one would dare try to get him out.

'Not just Mercedes, everyone lives there,' she added. 'Albaz rented the house for those from abroad, but a lot of the regulars live there. We switch between the two clubs, so the audience doesn't get tired of us.'

'The two clubs?' repeated Fanny, not comprehending.

'His two clubs. Didn't you know that Albaz has two clubs?' the stripper asked impatiently. 'You really don't know from nothin'. He has two places, this one and the one in Bat-Yam. I work one season here and one season there, and one season I go to Marseilles. I have family there.'

Fanny refrained from asking if this was her real or her adoptive family, and only wondered whether when she was there she lived with them, or whether there too she had a room on Marseilles' thirty-two Hayarkon Street.

'Every three seasons I dye my hair. I've already been black, blonde, red and Swede, like now. Maybe next year I'll go blue,' she said and suddenly laughed such a free, uproarious laughter that Fanny's anger evaporated, and again she was swept by a wave of affection, almost admiration, for the big stripper. There were moments when she would have given up almost everything she, Fanny, was, in order to be like her.

'The regulars have their own room,' continued Gina. It was obvious that despite her apparent contempt for Albaz and for the arrangements he had made for his workers, she had a strong sense of solidarity, almost of belonging, with the house on Hayarkon Street. 'Me and Mackie and Reena, we also have a kitchen. Those who come from abroad only have a room, but they always eat out anyway. Don't think they've ever cooked a meal in their entire life. What characters, spending their lives running from one end of the globe to the other, it's a wonder they don't fall off. I'm not going anywhere from here, except Marseilles. And that's just for work. I like it here,' she concluded. 'Where else would I find such a sea in November?'

'That's right,' said Fanny enthusiastically. It was pleasant to feel that she and the big stripper shared the same opinion, even if only on that subject.

Gina went back to Hayarkon Street. 'Those two with the roller-skates also live there,' she said with a sour face which testified to the fact that she wasn't at all happy to be reminded of the couple, who had stolen her show. 'Those two that Greenspan said were from Paris and are actually from Perpignan. You only have to hear them.'*Voulez vouz coucher avec moi.*' She imitated the thick accent of the south of France with surprising accuracy. 'The flamenco dancer is also really from Argentina.

'And also that American, the tall one,' she added in a different tone of voice and fixed her gaze directly on Fanny. 'The one who has his eye on you.'

'What are you talking about?' protested Fanny weakly. 'He's at least fifteen years younger than me.'

'Young, young,' said Gina and the milky white of her eye became even thicker and foggier. 'Have you seen Zorri?'

'No,' said Fanny.

'You will,' said the stripper mysteriously. 'You will. Maybe you'll learn something.'

Fanny nodded uncertainly, and the stripper patted her on the back. 'Right, gotta go,' she said in farewell. 'No good sticking around here. Every extra minute in this place is costing me my health. Break a leg,' she said and kissed the tips of her fingers and touched them briefly to Fanny's shoulder, and vanished.

When Robert came in before the show to wish her luck, she asked him, 'Who's Zorri?'

'Oh,' said the juggler and smiled, sending the make-up sticks flying between his fingers, 'Zorri is –

'Actually you'd better see for yourself,' he said. 'It's a pity to put people into a box.'

'Sounds very mysterious,' Fanny said.

'Not mysterious at all,' said the juggler. 'I just thought it would be more interesting for you if I didn't define him in advance.' He looked at Fanny's face. 'But if you like, Zorri is our friend Gina's attempt to attain eternity. Open, Sesame.'

'A huge box,' said Fanny. The juggler laughed.

'Knock 'em dead,' he said and leaned over and kissed her on the forehead.

Then he left the room, but Fanny didn't remember him leaving. A flower burned on her forehead and it continued burning there when she stood on the stage and sang Piaf's songs, and in the taxi as she drove home along the empty streets, and it was still burning there in exactly the same spot when she went to sleep, and only the morning brought back her old, familiar face, which had never been branded with flowers.

34

The days went by bright and short like the pages of a book turned quickly, almost too quickly. They were probably short because they started late. She usually met Robert in the afternoon and for the most part they went to the beach. They'd lie on their bellies and talk as they looked at the sand strewn with scraps of paper and lolly sticks, raking it up in handfuls and letting it stream in warm trickles between their fingers, or lie on their backs and look straight up at the light blue, or lean on their elbows, watching the sea. At times she wondered if there wasn't something wrong here, in the way the days went by, each day flowing into the next without any perceptible change, with no great leaps, but since they were as precious to her as they were she didn't want to think too much about it. Perhaps more than anything she loved the special quality that time took on. And indeed what had most changed for her was time. With Nathan, as much as she had loved him, and in fact the more she loved him, she had always felt an intense, feverish sense of haste, a need to hurry up and do things, lest the right moment for them, the good moment, would pass and time run out. With Robert she felt just the opposite and that was strange and illogical, for Nathan lived here in Tel Aviv and had never gone away for more than a two-week vacation to Cyprus, whereas Robert did not belong to this place at all and at some time in the future, in a month, two months, half a year, he'd go far away, as far away as the mind could conceive, Singapore, Montevideo, Algiers. And still with him she felt that she was allowed to use their time as she liked, all the time she needed.

On Sunday the club was closed and for the first time they

had the whole day, wide open, to themselves, to do with as they wished. Robert suggested they go for a walk. 'I'll show you the Tel Aviv I like,' he said, and she agreed with a smile not to ask any questions and just go along with him, although it was a bit absurd that he, the tourist, should be her tour guide after sixteen years of living in this town. By the time they went out the sun had already sunk down to the horizon. They took the no. 4 bus and got off on Allenby Street, at the corner of the *souk*. In the open-air market the lights had already been turned on, and people, two-dimensional in the electric light, like cardboard figures, ran hither and hither, loaded with shopping bags, pressing under their arms rolled-up newspapers with herbs peeping out of them. But they didn't walk into the market, turning instead into one of the streets climbing eastwards, away from the sea. Here there were far fewer people. Robert chose to take the side streets, the quieter ones, and soon Fanny didn't know where she was any more. This was a part of town she hardly ever visited. Only very rarely she went to the market itself, or to the shop of an old jeweller she first discovered when she was still living in the Women Pioneers' House, but even then she never strayed very far from Allenby Street.

The evening grew dark and the streetlamps came on. The old apartment buildings stood in their courtyards, behind thick old trees, with their solid but graceful architecture of clean straight lines. From time to time there emerged out of the half darkness a renovated building, beautiful, gleaming white, a large white whale laden with balconies and intricate cornices. Gradually, Fanny fell captive to the charm of this neighbourhood, so different from her own. In the north of town the side streets were entirely residential and the architecture was newer, more uniform. Here each house was different from its neighbours. The variety of signboards was endless: a musical instrument workshop, a lab for medical equipment, a geriatric hospital, shops for picture-framing, upholsterers, glaziers. Like a sudden blow there presented itself before her a signboard she had believed extinct, Dubrovsky Ltd, Umbrella Repairs. In one of the darkening streets, she didn't know which one, they both stopped by tacit agreement. From the large window of a building standing in the depths of a courtyard there came, in the bluish light which poured forth from the top floor, the sounds of a song sung by a man, in English, on the radio probably, a love song. But the song was not the only sound. Behind it, a sort of muffled incessant background, they could hear a steady ticking pulse, like the beating of a heart deep inside the house, the noise of a wheel turning and stopping at rhythmic intervals, a machine. What sort of machine it was impossible to tell, a printing press perhaps, or a lathe. There was in this deep beat, especially in the way it was woven into the song, something which enthralled them and did not let them go. Robert leaned back against the low stone wall, and Fanny, as if this were a familiar movement, as if it had been imprinted in her long ago and had only waited for this moment to come forth, leaned backwards, against him, and he wrapped his arms around her. In the stillness of the falling night they heard the man sing to his beloved that she didn't have to tell him anything, nor do anything, just be there, and behind him the machine rattled its steady muffled beat, click-click, click-click. Although they were standing in a city street with apartment buildings on both sides, and behind them more streets and more buildings, Fanny felt that she was standing in an open space, wide and limitless, like a field. This might have been because of the sky, which had by now almost completely darkened, and covered the city on all sides until it was more real than the city itself, instilling its rule over the houses and the streets, and Fanny let it spread over her too and lay on her its shadowy burden of tranquillity and pain.

Then the song was over and the spell broke. The new song was completely different, up-beat and loud, it didn't have its predecessor's subtle fleeting beauty. On the veranda of the house opposite there appeared a wild-haired figure in a dressing gown who shouted, 'Stop that noise!' and the music ceased at once. Two cars pulled into the street and the second one stopped right next to Fanny and Robert and started to reverse into a parking space, its engine roaring, and they moved away from the wall and walked on.

Sheinkin Street was lit up and empty. The white light of the streetlamps gleamed at fixed intervals, its glow reflected in the shop windows. At the corner of Ahad-Ha'am they stopped at the old ice-cream vendor's stall and bought pink and white ice cream, and then licked it all the way to the bus stop and continued to lick it, giggling, on the stairs of the bus. Robert put his hand into his pocket to pull out some money, but his sticky fingers got entangled in the fabric and and refused to come out, and they both burst into loud laughter in the face of the surprised and irritated scowls of the conductor and the passengers in the front of the bus. At the corner of Nordau Avenue they got off and went home.

After the dimness of the street the electric light in the house hit them harshly, flooding their faces and their bodies and bleaching the colour out of them. Fanny put her bag on the chair with a last gasp of laughter and felt how the gladness and the serene perfection of the walk were leaving her together with the exhaled air. She was overtaken by a heavy weariness: What can you expect, she told herself, after all this walking, but she knew very well that the heaviness she felt did not come from the walk and was not really weariness at all. 'Let's sit down,' she suggested uncertainly. The juggler sat on the sofa and said nothing. 'I'll bring some water,' she said, but did not move. The armchairs stood opposite each other like two stuffed animals, insufferably solid and massive. The curtains hung lifelessly, as if their fabric had become heavier and pulled them down in stiff motionless folds. The air itself was hanging in the yellow light thick and still, as if it too were a fabric and they had to rip it, or draw it aside, in order to see each other.

But only when she sat opposite him in the strong light and looked at him knowing that all the words had been drained out of her, did she understand where the bad feeling, which stuck in her throat, thick and stifling, came from. She saw herself sitting opposite him, frozen in the too-strong light, her arms straight and rigid and her throat parched and dry and not one word breaking out of the empty space within her, and there was nothing she could do about it, even though it was quite different now, she desperately tried to tell herself, completely different, nevertheless she sat there in that light in front of the furniture she had always loved and now did not love any more and even hated, at this moment which was gradually congealing around her, just as she had sat that other evening, when she hadn't thought of the furniture and hadn't even seen it and its arid stuffiness, just laughed and talked cascades of nonsense and empty words, on that evening when she had sat at exactly that same spot, in the same too-strong light, opposite Ritzi. And all the futility and humiliation of that evening came back and stood in her throat in the yellow light like a shrivelled, terrifying corpse, and she couldn't do anything or say anything, in the total paralysis of someone sunk in deep despair.

'I'll put the kettle on for coffee,' she said and almost stood up.

'No,' said the juggler. He said this word with great weight and emphasis and his voice stopped Fanny as if it were a gunshot.

'I'm not comfortable here,' he said more quietly. 'If you don't mind, I'd like to go and lie down on your bed.'

Fanny looked at him with the strange giddy feeling of someone walking on a thin wire at a great height. The words lifted her all at once above herself, far from the bubbling mess concocted by memory, but also left her stranded there, high above the ground, blindly inclining her head like the acrobat uncertain if he will carry on, or fall.

'With you, I mean,' he added, as if he thought he might not have made himself clear. And in this absurd clarification there was suddenly something so funny that Fanny burst into a rollicking laughter, which shot out of her, like a cork, all the heavy dullness, and and in its place, like hot air, there immediately rose a complete light-headedness. 'Yes,' she said. 'You're right. It's unbearable here. All the stuffed animals.' Decisively she rose from her armchair. 'The whole of Berlin is crowded into this room,' she said. 'No wonder there's no place in it for us. Let's go to the bedroom.' Her laughter, returning to her from the corridor walls, was loud, free. Almost like that of the stripper, Gina.

The bedroom was dark and open. The night streamed in, lamplit and slow, and with it came the reverberation of the cars from the nearby avenue. They lay on their backs, their hands under their heads, and looked out.

'When I was a child', the juggler said, 'and lay in my bed at night, I believed that all these things outside talked amongst themselves. The darkness, the trees, the neighbours' dog. For years I've tried to understand them, and I put a lot of effort into it, but I didn't succeed. I always knew that these words I imagine the dog is saying, or the rain, were not what they were really saying. Until at the age of ten I got fed up with it and I stopped.'

'Pity,' said Fanny. 'You might have succeeded in the end.'

'No,' the juggler said and fell silent.

'Tell me more about how it was when you were a child,' asked Fanny. She turned her face to him and looked at his profile.

'When I was a child,' the juggler said, 'I was the neighbourhood's marbles champion. I was in fact school champion, because when my neighbourhood took on the kids from John Marlow I beat them too, and if there'd been a city tournament I probably would have been champion of the whole town.'

'Was it important to you?' Fanny asked.

The juggler turned around and looked at her. 'Sure. Wasn't it to you?'

Fanny's cheeks grew hot in the darkness. 'Yes,' she said, 'but I wanted to be an opera singer.'

The juggler laughed. Then he put out his hand and ruffled her hair. 'I knew you'd tell the truth if I got you with your back to the wall,' he said. Fanny felt her face flaming and suddenly, without realizing what she was doing, she drew her whole body close to him and held him tight, as tight as she could. 'Tell me more,' she begged. 'Tell me everything you remember.'

'Why?' asked the juggler. 'Don't you have memories of your own?'

'No,' said Fanny. The word dropped out of her like a big stone and she said it without touching it, the way you say something you're ashamed of more than anything else in the world.

'You said you remembered your sister,' the juggler reminded her.

'Yes,' said Fanny. 'I remember her. And my mother. But myself I don't remember. I don't remember myself at all.'

'Oh,' said the juggler and looked at her face, which lay very near him. 'It's very hard to live that way.'

'Yes,' said Fanny, and felt the tears trickling warm on her face. 'I haven't realized how hard until now.'

The juggler's arms, hard and supple, held her, her whole body, and he kissed her face with soft, warm kisses into which her entire childhood was swallowed, everything she had been and could not remember and everything she did not want to remember and everything it would have been best not to remember, and she sank inside them like inside warm damp dark caves within which it was possible to accept the disappearance of childhood, the disappearance of everything.

35

In the morning when she woke up he wasn't there. On her
bedside table she found a note which said, in a tall laborious
handwriting, a bit like that of a diligent pupil, that he'd be back
in the afternoon. It had been years since she'd slept so late, not
just lying in bed, watching the bright light streaming through
the poinciana leaves, but really sleeping, and she hadn't even
woken up when he got out of bed. She remembered her sleep,
which was heavy and dreamless, a sleep so dense as to be
palpable, like a thick blanket. On the kitchen table she found
fresh rolls and a jar of blackberry jam. She wondered how he
had managed to get back in and finally concluded that he had
reversed the little latch on the door and left it open, as she used
to do whenever she went down to empty the rubbish bin or to
borrow something from a neighbour. She ate one of the rolls,
slowly, enjoying its crispness, and licked the blackberry jam off
the teaspoon until it shone. The day flowed past her, dreamy
and shapeless, in hazy wisps from which she emerged every
now and then only to look around her in puzzlement and sink
back again, until the sun had climbed past its zenith and began
descending over the other side of the street.

The afternoon was the colour of saffron. The sun flamed in the
dark glass windows of the new building at number four (Mrs
Nussbaum called them *nouveaux riches*). Miss Fanny stood in
the middle of her drawing room, hesitating. Strangely, things
were no easier and no more self-evident than they had been
before, and she stood there not knowing what to do next.
Robert looked at her. Then he asked, 'Would you like to go

out on the balcony?' And she gave a big nod and opened the sliding doors.

On the balcony it was very pleasant. A light breeze blew from the west and the laundry flapped on the roof across the street. Fanny was reminded of Mrs Shelly and her heart contracted at the thought of the girl in the orange sweater. Somehow she didn't think that she could win her battle with the neighbours, although she was strong. Perhaps she was too strong. Fanny felt that this girl did not know the meaning of compromise.

Robert opened the easy chair and placed it so that it faced the invisible sea. Then he turned to her. 'There's only one,' he said and with a single motion slipped into it and pulled her after him. It was very uncomfortable. The chair was narrow and his body very thin and his protruding bones jabbed at Fanny. But there were places where his body was soft so that she longed to nestle in it, especially the part beneath the shoulder, near the armpit. There she could also sense the whiff of a faint smell, pungent but very pleasant, which drew her to him, to the skin and the stiff black hairs which grew on it and to the softness underneath, and she yielded to it and buried her head in the soft hollow, digging herself in deeper and deeper, inhaling the sweet bitter smell, which was unlike any other smell she knew.

Robert laughed and ruffled her hair, the only part of her that remained visible, and drew back the light blouse she wore until the shoulder was exposed. He kissed her slowly and between kisses passed his hand over the smoothness of her skin, slowly, lightly, as if sunk in thoughts of a completely different kind. The door of the roof across the street opened with a creak. Mrs Nissany, the first-floor tenant, walked on to the roof. Fanny felt little ants crawling on her bare flesh. Mrs Nissany started to collect her laundry piece by piece into a plastic tub she had brought. She wasn't as methodical as Mrs Shelly and gathered her laundry hurriedly, every which way, pulling at it quickly without entering into the spirit of the

249

thing. It was evident that all she wanted was to get finished as soon as possible and return downstairs. Robert's fingers traced a spiral trail on Fanny's back, leaving behind them a faint electric current. 'Are you afraid?' he asked. His voice was very close to her ear, so much so that she didn't know if what she felt was the warm breath of his words or the flutter of his lips. On the roof opposite Mrs Nissany took down a particularly obdurate shirt whose sleeves had entangled themselves in the line, flung it rancorously into the tub and turned to the second line of laundry. And then her eyes happened to rest on Miss Fanny's balcony. She stopped in her tracks. The light wind swelled the clothes that remained on the line and caressed Fanny's shoulder.

'No,' said Fanny. She raised her face to him while she spoke, but immediately buried it again in his body, deep under his arm. In the brief instant before the darkness filled her eyes she saw Mrs Nissany turning her back to them and beginning to take down the new line of laundry.

Inside, the touch of the bedsheets offered a soft respite, and all she wanted was to sink into them along her entire body, just as she had wanted before to bury herself in Robert, but what she really sought was to submerge herself in the moment itself, in everything that surrounded her, in the ridiculous belief that if she became part of it, it could no longer slip from her hold. Robert's hands slowly took off her clothes, a strange superfluous skin, one by one, and she closed her eyes so that he wouldn't see her and only stretched out her arms to him blindly, to get herself back. His body was bony and very hard against hers and she felt her breasts, her belly, her thighs being washed against him, river water around a wooden beam in the current, but knew that all that was given her was to surround him for this moment, these fast-fleeting moments, because this long hard body was impossible to dissolve or to contain, but she could take his hand in hers and feel it slowly tightening, and that was enough.

36

When she went to the grocery in the morning she thought about the enormous difference there was between buying rolls for one and buying them for two. The blue sky was so light as to be almost white, open and endless, and she raised her face to wash it in the azure radiance. The street smelled of sun-drenched geraniums. It was hot but not yet too hot, and she quickened her step to be back in time before the heavy noon heat. There was always a long queue in the grocery at this time of day.

In the grocery there was indeed a queue and she put her shopping bag down on the floor, glad of the opportunity to rest in the cool gloom. Meanwhile she examined the shelves opposite the counter, where one was allowed to take the products oneself, unlike the cheeses and the eggs which were kept behind the counter and which Avram scrupulously distributed to his customers, as if they still lived under the rationing of the fifties. On the shelves there stood cans of peas and cucumbers, and also asparagus and pineapple, exotic items she had never permitted herself to buy because she felt they had no place on the menu of a woman who lived alone. This time she walked decisively up to the shelf and took down a can of pineapple. In the evening she'd make a tropical fruit salad, she decided. With bananas and raisins. She turned to the counter to put down the can, and only then did she hear the muttering which rose from the row of women waiting their turn. A minute later she noticed Mrs Nissany, who was standing almost at the head of the queue. Mrs Nissany whispered something in Mrs Shelly's ear, and the latter gave Fanny a surprised look, revealing a certain shock but also a sort of strange respect, and quickly lowered her eyes. Avram, who had finished slicing some Swiss cheese on to a piece of wax paper, asked for the second time, 'Anything else?'

Fanny looked at the row of women opposite her and her face reddened. For a minute she had the cowardly thought of giving up her turn and looking for another grocer's. And then she seemed to step out of herself and out of the whispering queue and miraculously return to the small quiet street at the heart of town, where she had listened to the song with Robert. 'If you haven't made up your mind yet, Mrs Shelly, perhaps you can let somebody else go ahead,' she heard herself saying aloud, and Mrs Shelly recoiled at once. 'What on earth d'you mean? I was just waiting for him to finish slicing,' she exclaimed. In a lower voice she muttered, 'What a nerve,' but she turned back to the counter and to the puzzled Avram, who was holding out the slices of cheese and said, 'give me also two hundred and fifty grams of pickles in brine,' as some sort of territorial stake. As he bent over the pickle bin she added, 'In brine, you hear, not in vinegar.' The women dispersed and went back to taking groceries from the shelves.

On her way home, her face flushed with the heat and her hair falling over her face, slightly bent under the weight of her shopping bag – for once she'd made the first step and bought the can of pineapple, she decided to prepare a full dinner and also stopped at the butcher's and the greengrocer's – she saw a familiar pair of shoes standing in front of her. After a moment she recognised the pair of summer sandals Aunt Leda had bought at Mykolinsky's last year, and after another moment she recognized Aunt Leda herself. She put the shopping bag down on the pavement, pushed her hair up with the back of her hand and looked at Aunt Leda with astonishment. Aunt Leda hadn't visited her more than twice in the last five years, and certainly never without phoning first, and certainly not at noon.

'I thought I'd pay you a visit,' Aunt Leda said, somewhat belatedly. Fanny was still too surprised to speak. 'I wanted to talk to you about something. But let's go in,' she said with her usual impatience. 'We can't stand here talking in the middle of the street like a couple of Levantines.'

Fanny almost asked her to come up and then remembered this was impossible and said, slightly stuttering, 'No, Aunt Leda, I can't. I have to go somewhere.'

'You have so much work that you don't have a minute to sit down and talk?' asked Aunt Leda with disappointed sarcasm.

'I have to run as soon as I've taken these up,' Fanny said. 'It's about work, in fact,' she hastened to add. 'I have an appointment, an interview, I've been offered a job with some firm.' She repeated herself three times and asked herself angrily why, for God's sake, she was so afraid to tell Aunt Leda the truth. But deep in her heart she knew why: because she was afraid that in some way, unique to her, Aunt Leda would spoil everything. How, she didn't know.

'Oh, really? What firm?' Aunt Leda asked with interest, and without waiting for an answer continued, 'Well, in that case I'll just tell you in a few words. If I'd known you were going out I'd have called you on the phone,' she said resentfully, as if it was unthinkable that Fanny should go out without reporting to her first. 'You remember Lydia Fruchtbaum? Lydia, the blonde, who I once told you would go on dyeing her hair even after she died?' Fanny nodded, perplexed. Lydia Fruchtbaum wasn't a fascinating enough subject to get Aunt Leda out of her house on a hot summer day. 'And Leon, Leon Fruchtbaum, you remember him?' continued Aunt Leda. Fanny strained her memory, trying to fish a Leon Fruchtbaum out of it, but did not succeed. 'Her son, *nu*. You remember she had a son, but he was always abroad, didn't even come to visit her once in ten years? Lydia used to quote his letters all the time, she could drive you crazy . . . Anyway, he's finally come to Israel.' She stopped for a moment, panting. 'And what do you know,' she added victoriously. 'He's a widower!'

She held her finger up in front of Fanny's face. 'A widower! Would you believe it? After all these years. Maybe he'll decide to make *Aliya*, and if not, what's wrong with Brussels, you tell me? Diamonds,' she said, her voice ringing like a trumpet in battle, 'he's in diamonds. A whole polishing factory he's got there, at least that's what Lydia says, but even if you take eighty per cent off that, he's certainly not starving. *Nu!*' She looked at Fanny, noticing her silence for the first time, 'Are you going to say anything or what? Just fifteen minutes ago Lydia rang me up. We've arranged everything. She's willing to host a special meeting at her house. Only you and me and none of those blabbermouths. What do you say?'

'I – '. Fanny started to speak, but Aunt Leda, her eyes narrowed, did not let her go on. 'Don't start turning up your nose at me now, Fanny,' she said sharply. 'This isn't the time for it. You've left your job, another job you don't have, a husband you don't have. Who are you waiting for? Clark Gable?'

Fanny took a deep breath. Out of the mists of helplessness something like rage was gradually crystallizing. 'No, Aunt Leda,' she said, 'but –'

At that moment she felt a light hand on her shoulder. 'Hi,' she heard Robert's voice through the haze which flickered, pale-bright, before her eyes, 'I saw you weren't coming back and I thought maybe something happened. Besides, I'm hungry,' said Robert. 'Shall I take the bag up?' And he stretched out his hand to take the blue plastic handle, and then noticed the dumbness that had taken hold of Fanny and his eyes turned to Aunt Leda.

'Let me introduce you. This is my Aunt Leda,' said Fanny. The haze had dissipated and she felt an odd and unpleasant lightness, such as one might feel upon suddenly finding oneself floating in mid-air.

'You never told me you had an aunt,' said Robert. He held out his hand with a direct and very American gesture to Aunt Leda, who shook it mechanically. 'I'm Robert. Pleased to meet you,' he said. 'Perhaps we could invite your aunt up for breakfast?' he said to Fanny. But Fanny looked at Aunt Leda and said nothing.

Aunt Leda turned to her, her sharp face quivering. 'Who's that?' she demanded. Her anger and amazement were such that her voice almost betrayed her.

'This is Robert,' said Fanny. She did not mean to evade the question, but couldn't muster the strength needed for an explanation. 'He works with me.'

'Works with you!' gasped Aunt Leda. 'Works with you where, if I may ask?'

'At the nightclub,' said Fanny.

Aunt Leda gave a short moan. Then she collected herself, and pulled at the edge of her blouse with a quick sharp motion. 'At least don't try to sell me any *bobbe meinses*,' she said bitterly, and Fanny was thunderstruck. This was the first time she had ever heard Aunt Leda use Yiddish, a language she loathed and had never allowed to be spoken in her presence. 'Works with you. Huh! How old is he?' she asked suddenly. Fanny was shaken, as if someone had just come and pushed her with all their force. 'He's . . . twenty-nine, I think,' she stammered.

'You think,' said Aunt Leda with bitter satisfaction. 'You think he's twenty-nine. Well, at least he's not married,' she said with the same strange and bitter satisfaction. 'That I can tell.' She looked up at the smiling Robert, who towered high above her in his faded jeans and looked, thought Fanny despairingly, even younger than usual. 'Are you keeping him?' she asked directly. Fanny's mouth opened. Red stars began circling before her eyes and she said, with difficulty, 'Aunt Leda, if you want me to go on talking to you, I . . .'

'Don't bother, don't bother,' Aunt Leda interrupted her. 'I understand everything. Now I understand why diamond merchants from Brussels are not good enough for you. But when you get into trouble don't come running to me, do you hear me? Don't come to me,' she repeated, as though to make the words more real to herself. 'I won't lift a finger for you.

He's going back to Brussels in a week,' she fired her last shot and fell silent.

'Don't worry, Aunt Leda,' said Fanny. The cold rage she had felt earlier had abated, and now she no longer felt anything but a great tiredness and a strange sorrow that seeped into her, flowing throughout her body. 'I won't come to you.' Aunt Leda looked at her once more, took a deep breath and again pulled at the hem of her blouse, less decisively this time. In a voice which was half warning, half oddly pleading, she said, 'We'll talk yet.'

'I'll phone you tomorrow,' said Fanny, and watched her back receding down the street, giving a sharp hop with every tap of her high heels. Among all her friends, Aunt Leda was the only one who insisted on wearing fashionable sandals with high heels. All the others bought clumsy, comfortable walking shoes, some according to orthopaedic prescription. Not only Lydia Fruchtbaum, but Aunt Leda as well had not given up, Fanny realized, and suddenly her heart went out to the small erect figure who now disappeared around the corner of the street.

37

The evening was a very deep blue and Fanny and Robert lay in bed and looked at the window opposite them. It was closed, and reflected the window behind them and the evening which entered through it, and thus the evening was multiplied and became twice as blue and bold, the blue of a distant fairytale land, of a warm sandy island on whose beaches palm trees waved their fronds in the evening breeze.

'Why do they want to cut down the palm tree? And the poinciana. I don't get it,' Robert muttered and gathered her hair in his hand and then let it fall back again.

'They don't like trees,' said Fanny.

'That's what I don't understand,' said Robert.

'They say that trees mess up the garden,' said Fanny. 'When the poinciana is in bloom, lots of flowers fall on the ground. And in the autumn the leaves fall. The palm tree sheds its fronds.'

'So why do they bother planting those bushes in the front garden?' said Robert, stretching, and he groped for his pack of cigarettes and the lighter.

'They are evergreens,' explained Fanny.

'Ah,' said Robert. His eyes narrowed, as always when he lit a cigarette, and the evening in them disappeared.

'They say that its branches have already grown up to the house and will cause it damage. At least to the shpritz,' said Fanny.

'What's shpritz?' asked Robert. 'At home they used to call some drink a shpritz.'

'Maybe you do have *Yekke* blood in you after all,' Fanny laughed.

'I do,' said Robert seriously. 'My parents are of German extraction. My great-grandfather, that is. They came over from Germany at the beginning of the century.'

Fanny reflected how strange it was that suddenly things came full circle, although you never knew where it started or ended, and you could never have guessed that it would be, for example, in an evening as blue as a distant tropical sea reflected in your bedroom window.

'Shpritz is this material you spray on the walls. It helps protect them from dampness and some people also think it's pretty,' she explained.

'Ah, stucco,' said Robert. 'Well, they can clip the branches.'

'They say that a tree can fall on someone and kill them,' said Fanny.

'Oh,' said Robert again, but this time in a different tone of voice, without the scepticism she'd heard in it before. Fanny thought that probably the last argument, which really sounded weighty and menacing even to her, must have convinced him, but nevertheless she felt a certain disappointment. She gave him a sidelong glance. His eyes were now wide open and she saw in them the evening in all its splendour, so blue it broke your heart, and the neighbours' drawing-room lamp glimmering in it like a lighthouse.

'So you think they're right?' she asked, the same faint disappointment rising in her against her will and clouding the evening's final blue beauty.

'No,' Robert said. He released a thin pale column of smoke, which drifted towards the window, where the evening was gradually darkening, losing itself to the lights which were coming on in the building opposite. 'But I understand them now.'

'How come so?' asked Fanny. She glanced at the wristwatch lying on her bedside table. It was already seven and she had promised Gina she'd come early that night to see her new show. Something altogether different, honey. Something you ain't never seen yet. In my case, thought Fanny, that won't be difficult.

'I've realized what's driving them. Once you figure that out, the rest is self-evident,' the juggler said.

'And what is it that drives them, then?' asked Fanny with real interest, for she herself did not always manage to understand the motives of the people she met and she found it especially hard to understand her neighbours, whose actions often seemed to her peculiar, and their reasons altogether obscure. Mrs Shelly, for example.

'Fear,' said the juggler. 'A tree is a living thing, unlike shpritz. You can't control it. And that's frightening for whoever needs to be in control. Threatening. You can never predict with absolute certainty how it will behave. What's manmade always seems to such people much safer, even though' – he leaned over Fanny to knock the ash from his cigarette – 'it's not always so. I remember in New York last year, there was a big power failure and I got stuck in an elevator with seven other people. Believe me, I'd have given anything at that moment to be at the top of some palm tree,' he said and laughed. In his eyes, which narrowed with the laughter, the evening again vanished, and the hair on his chest tickled Fanny's ear. She drew apart from him with a little sigh and lay again on her back and looked out at the blackness dotted with lampshades. It was really late now and time to get up and prepare some supper. And yet she didn't get up but remained lying in bed, looking out at the palm tree. If not for the man from the Forestry Department, and how funny it was, reflected Fanny, that there was a Forestry Department in the very heart of Tel Aviv, the tree wouldn't be standing now outside her window. She looked at it again and felt gratitude – she'd almost have said love, if she weren't ashamed to attach such a human emotion to a tree. But the night was already entirely black, very black, as it always is in the first few moments after darkness falls and before your eye gets used to it, and the tree was swallowed in the shadows and its branches could no longer be seen. Only the rustling of the birds who had come to sleep in the cracks of its trunk still testified to its existence.

Jaffa scattered its gems in the night with a royal munificence, with the lavish generosity of someone whose wealth had come to them by inheritance. 'You're crazy,' Fanny had told Robert when he suggested they walk to Jaffa, but now she realized there was no better way to get there, long enough gradually to take in the city's bold, oriental beauty without losing sight of it after a few minutes of driving. At the club they skipped up the wide concrete steps two by two, and Fanny imitated the brief 'Shalom' Robert flung in the direction of the three bears who sat in the vestibule without moving, heavy and massive, as always.

With a last swirl of her skirts the flamenco dancer finished her part of the programme and disappeared backstage. The shrill, wailing Spanish music stopped all at once and Fanny regretted having missed this number once again. Greenspan came on stage, his keyholder jutting out of his back pocket, and said, '. . . needs no introduction. Gino – straight from Rome!'

To the sound of feeble applause Gina came on stage, walking into the brightening circle of light. 'Come on,' Robert whispered and took Fanny's arm, directing her to one of the tables. To Fanny's surprise it wasn't a vacant table, but one already occupied by a young man, very young even, eighteen at the most. The man gave them a brief uninterested look, then recognized Robert and nodded at him, and immediately his eyes returned to the stage.

Only when the spotlight had settled and it was possible to see the figure on the stage clearly, did Fanny realize the significance of the slight change in the name the MC had announced. If she hadn't known it was Gina she might not have recognized her until the critical moment, the moment when Gina wanted to throw her identity in the audience's face. Her hair was short and slicked back. She was dressed in men's clothes, down to the last detail, clothes which seemed to be taken from the Paris of the thirties, as certain men used to dress then, a sailor's shirt over a thin black woollen sweater, loose black trousers, a small moustache. A walking stick. Gina's proportions were marvellously suited to this disguise, and for a minute it seemed to Fanny that this was the first time she was seeing Gina in her true guise, or at least the one in which her enormous height and width could assume their true dimensions without having to belittle themselves. Gina opened her hand and Fanny saw that the stick she was holding was in fact a whip, a whip with several straps like the ones she had seen as a child in illustrations to *Uncle Tom's Cabin* or in pirate storybooks. Gina straightened up. There was in her stance something electrifying, charged with power, even though she stood there fully dressed and did not move her body to the music. At that moment Fanny suddenly understood the secret of Gina's power, and why Albaz continued to employ her even though the customers should long ago have wearied of her show. Only after Gina started to move Fanny saw that on the couch, the stripper's usual couch with the faded velvet cover, there lay another female figure she hadn't noticed until then because she was half-covered with a different fabric, velvet of a deep wine hue, on which the stagelights danced like on dark waters. Gina strode to the couch with broad masculine steps and violently pulled the cover off the recumbent figure, and with a gasp of surprise Fanny saw, as did the rest of the audience, a second Gina lying there, the same Gina exactly, the same opulent proportions, the same height and shoulder-breadth, the same platinum-blonde hair, and only after a moment did she grasp that this was not a woman at all, but a doll. The young man who sat at their table was the only one who hadn't let out an exclamation of surprise. He looked at the two figures on the stage impassively, but his gaze was so intent that it seemed that everything but them had ceased to exist, even the distance separating him from them, as if he could touch them.

'Take one!' screamed the loudspeakers in the background and the whip lashed out, a shrill whistle in the air and a muffled one on the velvet cover. The fabric heaved in waves, undulated and wrapped itself around the whip. The doll moved with the slippery cloth and it seemed that she herself was sliding, reeling beneath the lashes. With her other hand Gina undid a hidden button and the sailor's shirt dropped to the floor. 'Take two!' The lash whistled through the air again and the cloth quivered. One of the doll's legs fell over the edge of the couch. 'And three!' With a confident gesture Gina unzipped her trousers and undulated out of them. The audience began to whistle and cheer. Fanny said to Robert; 'Excuse me, I'm not feeling well,' and pushed her chair back. She walked fast but unsteadily and almost collided with the wall as she came out into the corridor.

In an instant the nausea became unbearable and Fanny vomited into the sink. This was already the second time this year, she dimly remembered as she stood over the sink and tried to control the convulsive shivering which passed through her body. Maybe there was something wrong with her. But she knew this wasn't the reason, even though paradoxically there was something reassuring in that possibility.

When she finally came out, after having rinsed her mouth with water and liquid soap from the metal container above the sink, she decided not to watch any more of the show but go straight to the dressing room and rest there. But the only way to get backstage was through the hall, and Gina was still there, at the climax of her act, entirely naked with the whip, still grasped in her hand, raised over the doll, until in a sudden about-face she flung it away and threw herself on the sofa, covering the doll with her body as the lights slowly dimmed and the crowd stamped their its feet and roared and applauded.

Even in the small storeroom, where Fu'ad had wheeled the couch after the lights went out, she didn't get up. She remained half-sprawled over the doll and only now Fanny saw that she was hugging her close, the way you hug a real doll, a little girl's doll. Her face was buried in the doll's body and she rocked back and forth, back and forth with her, the way a little girl rocks when she soothes her doll after having dealt her a hard, bitter punishment.

'Why are you doing this, Gina?' Fanny asked, and the taste of vomit rose in her throat again, sour and revolting.

'That's what they want to see,' said the stripper dully into the doll's soft body, 'that's what they'll get.'

Acting on a violent urge which she didn't fully understand but couldn't restrain, Fanny went up to her and knelt beside her, hugging her the way she hugged the doll, tightly, burying her face in her shoulder. 'Don't do this, Gina,' she said. 'You mustn't, you mustn't' and without realizing what she was doing she too began rocking with Gina, back and forth, back and forth, exactly like Gina rocked with the doll, exactly like each of them had rocked with her doll when they were small.

But suddenly Gina pushed her away with a big bare arm and Fanny flew aside. 'Leave me alone. It's none of your business,' said Gina and walked heavily to their shared dressing room. 'Stay out of it.'

A moment later, wiping her face with the large ball of cotton wool dipped in cream, she said with a sort of pride, 'Zorri made the doll for me.' Then she added, her eye gazing stonily straight ahead at the mirror like the eye of a fish, 'He said the same thing. But I told him, shut up and do as you're told. I'm old enough to be your mother, it's not you who'll make up my mind for me. You don't want to do it, I'll go to somebody else. So of course he gave in in the end. What else could he do, poor thing,' she sighed, and her eye again became a human eye and floated slyly to the right to peek at Fanny.

But Fanny, although she had a real fear of the stripper's wrath, could only say once more, 'You've got to stop it, Gina. It's terrible.'

'You saw how they loved it,' said Gina.

And suddenly Fanny knew what she had to say. She never imagined that she could be so wily. 'I never thought that's what mattered to you, what they want,' she said. 'I never thought I'd see you trying so hard for them.'

The stripper looked at her, her mouth slightly gaping and her eye half-open inside its layer of cream.

'You always said they could kiss your ass, that you were doing what you wanted and couldn't care less about them,' continued Fanny in a sudden and astonishing burst of courage. 'Now I see it's not true. You're doing everything just to please them.'

'Watch out,' said the stripper in a thickened voice, and looked at Fanny without moving. 'Don't push it.'

'That's what you said,' insisted Fanny. 'I believed you.'

Gina suddenly turned to the mirror and went back to wiping her face with the wet cotton wool. 'We'll see,' she said in quite a different voice, as if she'd undergone some sort of invisible process and was already somewhere else. 'I'll think about it.'

Fanny took a deep breath and fell silent. It was clear she mustn't add anything to what she had already said. She also realized they were not alone, and this may have been, she understood with a certain disappointment, the reason for the change in the stripper's mood. Robert and the young man who had sat at their table were standing at the door.

'I didn't get a chance to introduce you earlier,' said Robert. 'This is Zorri.'

But Fanny knew that even before he spoke. She knew it by the intent look the young man gave to Gina, as if there was no one in the room but her, the look of a whipped dog, though at the same time imbued with a pride he could barely contain.

'Don't be fooled by him being here,' said Gina, wiping her face for the last time with a cloth that was as worn and soft as paper tissue. 'It's only because of me that they let him in. He's only seventeen.' It was hard to tell whether the last few words were said as a chastisement, or out of a kind of strange pride, identical to that which Fanny had seen in the young man's eyes.

The young man kept silent. Upon hearing the words which stated his age his face contorted momentarily, as to the lashing of an invisible whip, but the grimace of pain was immediately erased and only one thing remained, the proud dog-like look he gave Gina. And Fanny knew, without being told, that this was Gina's hold on eternity.

'We thought we'd go and have something to eat together', said Robert, 'after you finish.'

'Yes,' said Gina. With complete disregard for the other three people in the room she took off her dressing gown and put on her bra. Zorri took one step forward and stopped himself, a split second before the warning flash of the stripper's eye. Then she put on a shirt and a pair of trousers. 'And try to finish quickly. I'm dog hungry.'

'OK,' said Fanny. Her head was buzzing so with all that had happened in the last hour, that she didn't quite grasp what it was that she had agreed to.

'We'll go and have some shishkebab in the Tikva,' said the stripper and licked her lips as if already tasting paradise, and Zorri smiled.

On Yefet Street Robert stopped a cab and the four of them got in. It was a small cab, and after Gina had sat in the front seat the three of them, Zorri and Robert and Fanny, crowded into the back. Fanny sat in the middle. Next to her she could see Zorri's face illuminated in the lamplight, thin and as yet undefined despite the faint wisp of a moustache, looking motionlessly forward. There was in this defenceless stubbornness, unable to disguise itself, something which wrung Fanny's heart, and she turned her eyes away. At that moment she felt a warm hand groping for her own and closing around it, Robert's hand, and a great wave of warmth swelled up and flooded her. She pressed the familiar fingers with grateful relief and thought no more of Zorri's face in the pale electric light, nor of the face of the child Uri, looking up from the sandbox at his mother.

At the end of the long dark drive they reached a street which was intermittently lit by bare overhead lamps around which swarmed hundreds of little winged insects. Strips of neon illuminated a variety of curious signboards. Shalom, King of the Skewers, Nissim, King of the Neighbourhood.

'Shall we go to Shalom's?' asked Robert.

'No, Sammy,' ruled Gina. 'Believe me, Shalom is for tourists. People in the know go to Sammy.'

Robert laughed. 'I haven't seen many tourists around here,' he said.

'You know what I mean,' said Gina impatiently. 'Like her.' She gestured with her thumb in the direction of Fanny. 'Come on, let's go, I'm starving,' she said and shoved a note into the driver's hand. 'Let's go,' she said again commandingly and they all crossed the street after her and entered a large room lit with brilliant electric lights.

Immediately a plump dark-haired man in a tight pinstripe suit hurried towards them. *'Ahalan*, Gina,' he called loudly and grabbed Gina's hand as if never meaning to let go of it again. 'We haven't seen you here for ages. What's the matter, you've forgotten your old friends, you never show your face here in the neighbourhood, we're not good enough for you any more, huh, Gilla,' and as he spoke he led the four of them to a comfortable corner table and sat them down and clicked his fingers at a waiter in a white shirt who was hovering in the background. 'Put on the table cloth and bring some appetizers, Menasheh, a bit of everything, you hear, only the best for my friend Gina who never comes to see me any more. And get them some of that *s'hug* I keep in the corner of the fridge, you know which one, get on with it, don't just stand there rubbing your toes.'

And as quickly as he had pounced on them he left them to themselves.

'Menasheh will take care of you, don't worry, you'll be happy,' he said with his eyes already turned to the door, where three unshaven men with red eyes had just entered.

'*Ahalan* Rami, Shimon,' Fanny managed to hear. 'We never see you at Sammy's any more, what's the matter, you've found something better . . .'

'Quit fucking around,' said one of the men and dropped on to a chair by the door. 'We know your tricks already. Better send us three hummuses before we faint.'

'You like it,' said Gina, and only then did Fanny wake up with a start and see that she was watching her with a mocking look.

'Uh . . . yes,' she stammered. 'An interesting place.'

'Interesting, interesting,' mimicked Gina, and turned to Zorri. 'Look at her, Zorri, I'll bet you this is the first time she ever set foot here in the neighbourhood. I'll bet she didn't even know it existed.'

'That's not true,' said Fanny angrily.

'That you've never been here?'

'That I didn't know about this place.'

'You're a tourist,' said Gina, 'Like all the others. All those who come here from Tel Aviv.'

'I thought the neighbourhood was part of Tel Aviv,' said Fanny, trying to sound ironic.

'We thought so too, honey, before we came to live here,' said Gina.

Robert leaned forward. 'Hey, hey, Gina. Don't take it all out on Fanny,' he said. His voice said more than that and Gina fell silent.

Zorri gave Robert a strange look. 'I didn't know you understood Hebrew, Robert,' he said. Robert smiled. 'I understand everything,' he said in his distinct American English. 'I just can't speak it.'

'Where do you know it from?' asked Zorri.

'It's not my first time here,' said Robert.

Gina snickered. Her bad mood seemed to have disappeared.

'Make no mistake,' she said. 'Robert and me are old partners.' Her broad palm landed on Robert's shoulder and stayed there, and a brief wince flew, as quick as a lizard, over Zorri's face, and vanished.

The white-shirted Menasheh emerged from the kitchen carrying a large plate loaded with pitta breads and beer bottles and a heap of small plates filled with all kinds of appetizers. Fanny had never seen such variety, and didn't even know what half of them were. Gina tore off a large chunk of pitta and dipped it in one of the plates with a sweeping motion, then shoved it into her mouth and swallowed it in a single bite. She leaned back with a sigh of relief. 'I'm better now,' she said.

Robert laughed. 'Gina's always afraid someone'll steal the food from her plate,' he teased her. Gina chuckled without rancour. 'That's true,' she said. 'I'm never sure where the next meal is going to come from.' She turned to Fanny. 'Robert knows me.' Again the brief grimace passed over Zorri's face. Fanny smiled uncertainly and took a piece of one of the pittas, which was hot and steaming in her hand, and dipped in the hummus plate as she'd seen Gina do. 'A quick learner, that one,' Gina said to Robert, whether jokingly or in all seriousness. 'She'll be OK in the end.' Robert smiled and said nothing and began eating as well. Only then did Zorri reach for the pittas, but he ate little and unwillingly, his eyes on Gina.

The shishkebab was just as Gina had promised, soft and tasty and melting in the mouth, and after all that food, the stripper said, what more could a person want but a cigarette. She extracted an elegant leather case out of her purse and took one. 'Light it,' she told Zorri. This was only the second time she had addressed him directly during the entire evening. Zorri's face, the thin-skinned face of a seventeen-year-old, reddened. Without a word he took a gold-plated lighter out of his pocket and lit her cigarette, and Gina sat back in her chair and exhaled a puff of white smoke. Robert also lit a cigarette. Fanny, who didn't know what to do with her hands, looked around her.

The restaurant was all lit up, no dark corners, no special features, like a new Formica table on which the years haven't made even one scratch. 'Bring some arak, Sammy,' shouted Gina. 'And not that shit you give your guests. Bring the real thing, *zakhlawy*, like my father used to serve, damn it,' and in her voice, after three beers, you could hear a slight whimper. Menasheh slunk out of the room and immediately returned, carrying a tall clear bottle and a large jug of iced water and four glasses. He put everything on the table and disappeared.

'That guy always reminds me of a snake,' Gina grumbled. She opened the bottle and poured the clear liquid into the glasses with a heavy hand. Then she poured some water from the jug into her glass. All at once the liquid fogged over and turned milky, storms whirled up in it and died down. Fanny looked at it, fascinated. 'Don't tell me it's also the first time you've seen arak,' said Gina hostilely. Her face darkened, and she filled her glass again and emptied this glass too in one gulp. And then her face changed completely. Suddenly it had a streak of sweetness in it, as if, so Fanny imagined, she'd gone back many years and again become a little girl, Daddy's little girl, who'd served his guests the best arak and maybe let his little girl taste a bit too: What's the big deal, woman? It can't do her any harm. Her eyes grew moist and lost all expression, staring at the window opposite her, but she didn't see the people who were passing there. She started to sway back and forth, like before, humming to herself a song whose words Fanny could not make out and whose melody, an oriental one, she had never heard before. 'My father very quickly learned what's good here,' she suddenly said to Fanny. 'Very quickly he found the only thing that was good here and from that moment on he never left it. He only left us.' And just as she had started she left off talking, with the same suddenness, and resumed swaying back and forth, crooning her strange tune, and Zorri, whose eyes had not left her all that time, leaned over to her and said quietly, 'Gina. Gina. Stop it now. You shouldn't have too much, you know it, your ulcer —' and Gina abruptly sat up in her chair, almost leaping out of it, her elbow knocking the glass and spilling its contents on the table, and cried, 'You stupid punk kid. Don't tell me what to do, you dirty brat, the milk's not even dry on your . . .' and with a startling, unexpected movement she fell forward, on him, and miraculously he was there, ready to receive her, all of her vast body, and then she started crying, crying and rocking in his thin arms, until her crying subsided and the tune she had continued to hum between sobs subsided also, and Robert paid and they went out into the empty street, most of whose lights had already gone out.

Later, at home, after they'd gone to bed and she heard Robert's measured breathing beside her, hushed and tranquil like that of a small child, Fanny thought how much her life had changed since she started working at the club, a radical change with no interim stages, and how many and varied the ways that people found to each other were, some of which she had never even imagined. Then she fell asleep.

The next day, when she came to the club earlier than usual even though she had determined not to do that, she heard the familiar sounds of 'Love Machine' coming from the big hall, and continued to hum them absent-mindedly on her way to the dressing room.

38

In September it was Fanny's birthday, and for the first time since she had become an adult, certainly for the first time since Nathan left her, she felt like celebrating it. She had always been afraid that the celebration would only underscore the foreignness she felt. A birthday was such an intimate thing, and the sense of loneliness she remembered from her first birthday away from home was so acute, that she preferred to bury this day each year in specially strenuous work. At the most she'd take herself out to a concert after Aunt Leda's traditional presentation of crochet centrepieces.

'How old are you going to be?' asked Robert and Fanny told him, forty-two. 'But that's what you told me when we met,' he protested.

'I always say one birthday ahead, so that it won't be too terrible when it comes,' Fanny confessed. Robert laughed till the tears welled up in his eyes.

Fanny invited Aunt Leda and Margie, and then discovered that she had no one else to invite. She very much wanted to ask Gina and Zorri, but did not dare to have Gina and Aunt Leda together under the same roof. It was bad enough thinking about another meeting between Aunt Leda and Robert, after that unhappy encounter on the street. She had wanted to invite Batya and Raya as well, but when she called the office she was informed by the voice of a receptionist she didn't know that Batya had left three months earlier and that no, she didn't have her telephone number. So in the end she was left with only three guests: Robert, who could hardly be considered a guest, since he lived with her, and Margie and Aunt Leda. This by itself was a rather bizarre combination, she thought heavy-heartedly, and would willingly have given up on the whole affair, if it wasn't for Robert, who announced categorically that he wasn't going to let her back down.

'Think of it as a performance,' he said, but Fanny knew this was life. Even when she strained her imagination to the utmost, she couldn't see Aunt Leda sitting at a table in the club and munching peanuts.

One of the advantages of having so few guests was that it was easy to get everyone's consent to Sunday night, their free night, and on the preceding Thursday Fanny went to look for a new dress for herself. To her great surprise she found the dress she wanted quickly and easily, without the endless doubts and debates which had characterized most of her shopping expeditions and because of which she hadn't bought even one evening dress since the beautiful blue one more than ten years ago. 'You won't regret it,' said the shop assistant. 'It suits you to a T.' But Fanny didn't need her compliments. Her decision was clear and free of doubt, and she wondered whether this radical change in her had taken place under Robert's influence, the thought of whom, as she waited for the bus in the slowly darkening street, filled her with a soft gladness, a gladness which was hers only in the medley of people hurrying to and fro, carrying parcels in their hands.

On Sunday morning Fanny started to prepare the refreshments. Robert announced that he would take care of the drinks, and even though Fanny explained to him that Aunt Leda never drank as a matter of principle, and that Margie preferred Romanian Whisniak or 'Sabra' liqueur, he came back loaded with all kinds of bottles and said that if they didn't drink them today, they'd find a use for them in the future. Just in case, Fanny bought a few bottles of grapefruit juice and a large bottle of Tempo orangeade, and went especially to Aunt Leda's wholesaler and bought the Ceylon tea she liked. With that she completed her preparations and there was nothing left to do but wait till evening. But this was exactly what she found hard to do, and she paced around the house so much, moving the vases from once place to another, that Robert asked her if she had never met any of the guests, and started to introduce himself by throwing the wine glasses in the air and miraculously catching them at the last minute before they shattered on the floor. 'Maybe that's how I should introduce myself tonight,' he suggested. 'A great way to break the ice.' Fanny made him swear he wouldn't do any such thing, and when he went back to reading his newspaper she tried to understand why, in fact, she was so tense about this evening. In the end she concluded that it was the combination of these three people, whom until now she had only seen separately and had never even tried to imagine the three of them, or any two of them, together. However, it was already too late to change her mind, and she went to put her cheese casserole in the oven.

Margie uncharacteristically arrived five minutes early, her face flushed, carrying in front of her, like a torch, an enormous bouquet wrapped in aluminium foil, and dragging behind her – like a small tugboat dragging a man-o'-war – Yosef, solid, bespectacled and smiling through his beard. It was clear that her curiosity had got the better of her. Yosef growled from the depths of his beard an apology for having come early. Margie, he announced, had rushed forth like Alexander the Great storming the Bosphorus, and there was no stopping her. 'Stop talking nonsense, Yosef,' protested Margie. 'I just wanted to see the house before the rest of the guests arrived.' Fanny laughed, the use of the plural was certainly worthy of Aunt Leda, and hung Margie's large straw hat with the cherries in a place of honour in the entrance. Margie's eyes wandered around the room. 'You've hardly changed anything,' she said finally, disappointed. 'There was no need to,' said Fanny. 'There was enough room in the cupboard, and we only had to clear out this corner so that Robert could practise without breaking the glassware.'

'You're just the same, Fanny,' said Margie in a note of

reproach, which disappeared, however, as she continued without pausing for breath, 'I had the whole flat redone. I tore down the wall between the kitchen and the drawing room . . .' At that moment the doorbell rang. Aunt Leda had arrived at exactly the appointed hour. She looked with astonishment at the large hat hanging in the hall, but refrained, to Fanny's relief, from commenting on it.

Now that everyone had arrived it was time to start serving the refreshments. 'I just need to pop into the kitchen for a few minutes, I'll be right back,' Fanny mumbled, but her route was blocked by Robert's arm. 'First we'll raise a glass in Fanny's honour,' he announced. Everyone agreed and Robert filled their wine glasses. 'To Fanny!' he said and they all repeated after him, 'To Fanny!' Fanny's cheeks burned and she was afraid that in a moment she would burst out crying. Through the mist which blurred her vision she seemed to see a translucent rose-coloured bubble of enchantment taking shape, growing before her spellbound eyes, and she tore herself away from Robert's embrace and ran into the kitchen with a terrible fear that any minute now it would shatter in a sudden explosive bang.

When she returned, carrying a tray of pastries, Yosef had advanced as far as Alexander's voyage to Persia, and Margie was admiring Aunt Leda's batiste dress. Even Aunt Leda could not resist such compliments, which revealed a discerning eye, for this was material she had brought with her from home, a fine Swiss cloth the like of which she hadn't seen since, and no wonder, in this country whose taste in general tended towards the cheap and fleeting rather than the fine and lasting. The mood lightened and Fanny reflected with a smile, as she made her escape to the kitchen once more, that one could indeed have guessed that Margie would find her way to Aunt Leda's scant charitable side. But after the subject of the batiste had been exhausted, and English wool had also been discussed extensively, Margie turned to Yosef and with an offended air informed him that they were sick of hearing about generals who were long dead, and it was time he learned to talk about subjects that interested ordinary human beings as well. 'If you have to talk about generals, talk about Dayan,' she said. Yosef bit his beard and Aunt Leda leaned back on the sofa and gave Robert a scrutinizing look. Fanny bent forward to try and divert the oncoming attack, but she was too late.

'Where are you from?' Aunt Leda opened with a frontal assault. She did not believe in flanking tactics.

'Alaska,' said Robert and picked up the bottle of whisky. 'I see you don't like champagne. Maybe some of this?'

Fanny doubted whether Aunt Leda even remembered where Alaska was. To her surprise, a small satisfied smile appeared on Aunt Leda's lips.

'Ah, Jack London,' she said complacently. 'What's the matter?' She countered Fanny's amazed look, 'You thought I'd never read Jack London? I have, and long before you did.' And to Robert she said, 'I don't drink whisky. But a drop of that wouldn't hurt.' She pointed a regal finger at the bottle of Cointreau, and Fanny almost choked with astonishment.

'Fanny thinks that because I grew up in Berlin I only got as far as Goethe,' said Aunt Leda in English with a heavy German accent, 'but she's wrong. We read everything back then. I was exactly the right age. We read Romain Rolland, and Zweig, and André Gide . . . Yes, yes, my dear,' she said to Fanny who hadn't uttered a word, and her eyes took on a growing lustre. It must be the liqueur, thought Fanny, torn between amazement and despair, but then Robert asked Aunt Leda if it was true that she'd lived for a few years in Paris, and Fanny, to her relief, found herself out of the conversation again. 'Another glass?' she asked Margie with a vague feeling of not doing the right thing, but her hostess' instinct got the best of her and Margie said Yes, it warms up one's stomach. Fanny poured her another glass of the thick red liquid. 'Genuine Whisniak,' Margie said appreciatively. Fanny was reminded of Gina and hastened to chase her out of her thoughts. Vaguely she heard Aunt Leda say, 'Back then they knew how to live. Not like here.'

'Some people know how to live here too,' smiled Robert.

Aunt Leda rejected that possibility with a gesture of contempt. 'They don't live here,' she said. 'Here they skip the only period in life worth anything, and right after the army they start worrying about settling down. Settling down,' she said, and her voice had the fine cutting edge of exquisite scorn. A pneumatic hammer started pounding inside Fanny's head. This combination of Aunt Leda and the words she had just said was simply not possible.

Robert laughed.

'There's nothing to laugh about,' Aunt Leda said, almost angrily. 'What I said wasn't a joke. No one lives here. Hilde's son is not even out of the paratroopers yet and he's already running to fix himself a job at City Hall. That's the way it goes here. People don't live. Neither does Fanny.

'Fanny', continued Aunt Leda with cold compassion, 'got here before she had time to live a period such as I did.' She took another sip from her glass. Her cheeks reddened under the influence of the liqueur, or perhaps of the past.

'I had two lovers when I lived in Paris,' she said. 'At the same time. One in the third arrondissement and the other in the rue St Jacques. I would take the metro every morning to rue St Jacques and eat my morning croissant there, and at night I'd dance with Joseph in the third arrondissement. They didn't know, of course. They would have killed me. Each one of them separately,' she said and laughed, but her laughter sounded odd and she stopped.

'Fanny', she said with her head held high, 'hadn't tasted enough of life.' She emptied her glass in one gulp, and thrust it stiffly forward. 'Pour me a little more. That's it. That's enough.'

'Life is like an apple,' said Aunt Leda. 'You have to take big bites out of it. Otherwise you don't get the taste.'

Fanny sat there, utterly speechless. And suddenly she was

overcome by tremendous rage. She felt betrayed as she had never felt before in her life. So you've deceived me, Aunt Leda, she wanted to shout in her face, you've deceived me all these years over your teapot with its impossible blue jasmine and the velvet armchairs, you've deceived me with a ration of three biscuits and one Foreign Currency clerk with a squint –

'Fanny thinks I don't know what life is,' said Aunt Leda with a sly titter and gave a sudden hiccup into her glass. 'But I did. In Paris in 'thirty-two you learned fast, and well. I was exactly the right age,' she said, not remembering she'd already said that, 'not too young –' and all of a sudden, embarassingly, no, not embarrassingly, unbearably, she started to cry, big tears, a drunk's tears, which dropped into her glass and on to her knees covered in fine Swiss batiste. Even Margie fell silent. And then Robert did something astonishing. He wrapped his arm around Aunt Leda's shoulder and hugged her, and what was even more astonishing was that Aunt Leda clung to his shoulder, wiped her eyes on it, and said in her regular voice, '*Also*. That's enough,' and then straightened up and served herself some of the mushroom pie, as if nothing had happened. Fanny felt as if the Eiffel Tower had suddenly upped and flown in the air, then crashed to the ground, and she was the only one among the passers-by to hear the thud.

But from the cloud of dust which was dulling her senses she heard Robert say, 'And with regards to Fanny you're wrong, Aunt Leda.' Aunt Leda chewed on her mushroom pie with her mouth closed and looked straight ahead at the bottle of orangeade, as if to make it clear that as far as she was concerned the discussion was over and to go back to it was nothing but evidence of bad taste. But Robert wouldn't give up.

'Some people flower late,' he said, twisting a lock of Fanny's hair around his finger, 'but no less beautifully for all that. Think of orchids.'

'I don't know much about botany,' said Aunt Leda.

Robert sighed and stood up. 'You're a tough nut, Aunt

Leda,' he said. 'Oops, sorry. It's hard to get away from botany.'
Then he asked if everyone wanted coffee.

When he returned with a tray loaded with steaming cups he
said, 'It doesn't matter when things happen. It matters that
they do, at some point. I for one am very proud of Fanny,' and
he drew Fanny close to him and hugged her. The magic
bubble again appeared before Fanny's eyes, erupting in rose-
coloured sparks.

'That's exactly what I told Sylvia,' Margie burst out. 'She
told me,' here she mimicked a heavy Hungarian accent, 'I've
heard Fanny's really hit bottom, performing at a *night*club,
doing str*ee*ptease. I told her, I've known Fanny for seventeen
years now and no matter what you tell me about her, I know
Fanny would never do anything vulgar. Fanny's not vulgar.'

'You never know what a person might do,' said Robert
with an obscure smile and took a few peanuts. 'And striptease
is a profession. You make a living from it.'

Aunt Leda gave him a sharp glance but didn't say anything.
It was clear that she had already said what she had to say for
that evening and it would be impossible to get even one more
word out of her.

'For my part, I think you could do worse than striptease.
But,' Robert smiled at Fanny, 'we already have a stripper. And
to be honest, I'm afraid Fanny is not really suited for the part.'

'I'll have to make do with singing, then,' said Fanny with
what she hoped was ironic restraint. For the first time it
occurred to her that there might be people who were
interested in what she, Fanny, did, and they might even have
something to say about it. In fact it was the first time, she
thought with surprise, that what she did aroused any interest in
others. There was something strange about it. As long as she
did what was right and proper in the eyes of the world, then
Sylvia and her kind, and even Aunt Leda, hadn't shown any
interest in her doings. It was almost as if there was a conspiracy
of silence around her. But from the moment she did what they

obviously despised her for not doing up till now, they pounced on her and tore her reputation to pieces. You can't win this game, Fanny reflected sorrowfully, and then the old rebellious spirit again flared up in her. She would never make the same mistake again. From now on she would do only what she herself thought was right. In any case, she realized finally, she would never receive their blessing, and the more she sought it the further it would recede. She also realized, with the fear of a person who has lost a large sheltering wing, that there was nothing more dubious in the world than this blessing.

'Listen,' said Margie, her face aflame, almost the colour of the Whisniak. 'Why don't I go on stage too? I can ride roller-skates. When I was little I had a special scooter, really high, and I used to ride it wearing green socks, like this,' and she lifted her skirt and showed everyone how she used to ride her scooter when she was eight. Fanny saw Yosef's tortured face and said that scooters weren't on the club's programme, which wasn't necessarily true. Anything was on the club's pro-gramme, as long as the audience was fascinated by what it had to offer, risk or sex, usually, sleight of hand or a clever tongue or a golden ass, and as long as it didn't cost too much.

'Forget it,' said Robert, laughing. The whisky had began to affect him as well. 'You don't want to join a bunch of outcasts like us. Soon they'll hang bells around our necks and that's the only way they'll allow us on the streets, so the decent people will have enough time to steer away. You should warn Sylvia,' he said and laughed, tilting his head backwards, until there were tears in his eyes.

'I'll show Sylvia,' said Margie, incensed. 'I'll show her till she's got peanuts coming out of her ears.'

'Exactly,' Robert agreed. To encourage her he flung ten peanuts up in the air and caught them in his mouth one after the other. He laughed a big laugh, which came straight from the belly and made his whole body quiver. 'We're gonna get that Sylvia,' he declared.

39

Robert fell asleep right after they got into bed. Just before he dozed off he held out his hand to her, and she took it and felt his fingers, lax and warm, tightening around hers, until his grip slackened and he began breathing the breaths of sleep, regular and lost. His hand remained stretched out towards her, the fingers curled slightly inwards like a limp male organ, inspiring compassion and a strong, unreasonable wish to protect them.

Carefully, so as not to wake him up, Fanny lifted her legs over him and got out of bed. Her head was very light, almost dizzy, yet she didn't feel tiredness but a kind of strange lucidity, and she knew that she wouldn't be able to sleep.

As she stood by the sink in the kitchen, pouring herself some tea, she sensed she was holding the cup's handle too tightly and, with a wonderment which slowly turned into certainty, recognized in herself the urge to take this beautiful cup, her white porcelain cup with the golden rim, and dash it against the sink until it shattered into a thousand pieces. Watching herself from the outside with the same cruel lucidity, she saw how, in the preliminary rinsing of the cup in boiled water, in the cautious tilting of the kettle spout, she resembled Aunt Leda in the measured parsimony of her movements. And yet Aunt Leda hadn't always been like that either, she said to herself, as if she only just this minute had realized that, and indeed this was the first time she had willingly returned in her thoughts to that not distant enough past in which there were already only Aunt Leda and the Grunwalds and Switzerland, rather than to that very distant past in which she loved to immerse herself. But she really hadn't always been that way, said Fanny aloud, and the memories, once she allowed them to surface, started welling up in a great painful surge. She remembered the day Aunt Leda had arrived from Paris, and how she embraced her in a painfully tight hug which was quite unlike her, so strong that it hurt, and filled her pockets with dusty sweets she had saved up especially for her, for Fanny, but the sweets were already old and when she took off their silver wrapping they crumbled in her hand into countless little crumbs of dust. But she didn't say anything, she was so glad that Aunt Leda had arrived, because it was the first sign that her parents would soon arrive as well. But they never came. Only Aunt Leda, who had promised her that in a little while, very soon, she'd find a house and take her in, a house which would be big enough for Fanny's parents too, but for some reason had never left the rooms kept by Mrs Tüller, a born widow, and soon it was no longer necessary for Mrs Tüller to tell her what she had been obliged to tell her in the beginning, and she herself began to pack up the remains of the cake at the end of the meal and wrap them carefully in wax paper and lock them in the cupboard, so they wouldn't spoil, and to collect pieces of soap and press them together to make a new bar of soap out of them, and to count the biscuits. Whereas the strongest feeling Fanny remembered of home was one of abundance. Suddenly she didn't want to drink her tea any longer and she poured it into the sink and watched the yellow stain spreading on the white porcelain. And what was left, after all? The trailing aroma of fresh *apfelstrudel*, the faded, elusive traces of persons long lost. What she had brought along with her was Switzerland, she realized now, hated Switzerland, and a wave of bitter resentment rose up in her, but it was no longer aimed at Aunt Leda. At first, she reflected as she dumped the dark-brown tea leaves into the bin and unthinkingly began to put on another kettle to boil, at first it wasn't so bad. She'd known the Oppenheims ever since she was a child, and in any case this was only a transition period, a waiting period before her parents came. But they never did come, and the Oppenheim family couldn't keep her any longer and she moved, or rather was moved, to the Grunwalds, who weren't bad people either, after all, she told herself in wonder, and might have even liked her in their measured Calvinist way; but then everything became so measured, so economical, not just them, and not just Aunt Leda, everything, trickling into her hands drop by drop with the miserliness of a broken tap, and she as well.

When she came back to bed she realized that she still couldn't fall asleep. She curled up on her side of the bed, so as not to wake Robert with her tossing and turning, and looked at the wall. Aunt Leda's face, crinkled by a sobbing alien to it, again twisted in a grimace, then recollected itself and said cruelly, 'Fanny had not tasted enough.' Fanny pressed her eyelids together as hard as she could and erased the vision of Aunt Leda, but the minute she let go Aunt Leda reappeared. Finally Aunt Leda vanished of her own accord, a bit like the witch in childhood nightmares, and with great relief Fanny realized she was not coming back. But then that old Piaf song, the one she hoped had finally stopped haunting her, began playing itself in her ears with absolute clarity, padam, padam, as if it was playing on the phonograph in the next room. All night the song churned around and around inside her. Fanny with two long braids and a skirt flapping between skinny legs, Fanny horrifying Fräulein Neuerbach with the songs she had brought back from her visit to Aunt Leda in frivolous France. Suddenly she remembered that Fanny with painful acuity, the Fanny of the last year in Berlin, and for a moment there rose in her again the precise feeling she had in those days, when she wandered around the streets in the cold autumn air and considered herself so modern and rebellious, or as much so as a girl could have felt growing up in a house with Aunt Leda on the one hand and her mother on the other, two diametrically opposed poles.

'*Java* – at best it's a brand of coffee, Fanny. And we could do without that too. They have excellent coffee at Kloninger's.'

But the truth was that she too, in the end, had preferred to return to Elisabeth Schumann and to the lieder. After all, she had ambition.

When this ambition had run out, she couldn't say even now, with the long perspective of the twenty-odd years which had passed since then. She had never been able to pinpoint the exact moment. It had nothing to do with the war, at any rate. Even this miserable consolation, to blame it all on the war, she couldn't clutch at. Nor had she tried; she had hoped to find something else here, in this country, something that would be truly, unreservedly hers, but now she saw that she had only managed to create another Switzerland, hotter and without the Grunwalds. Perhaps she should have changed her surname, as quite a few people had suggested when she had first come here. Bar-Giora from the Agency had expressed his opinion most decisively about Diaspora names. But she had always refused. If her parents should arrive, or her sister, if anyone should arrive – but it was more than that. This name, Fanny Fischer, was her, and it was all she had. She couldn't give that up too. Each time she thought about the possibility of a different name she became dizzy, as if her very being, the innermost core of her identity, was about to be taken away from her. She always said: Thank you, I'll think about it. Politely but firmly. Or so she hoped. At least that quality she wanted to inherit from Aunt Leda.

Aunt Leda would have had a stroke if she'd told her that she was considering changing her name. '*Gal*? What's wrong with Fischer?' Fanny heard her ask. 'Fanny Gal? What kind of a name is that? And if you're hankering after a Hebrew name, why don't you call yourself Dayag, Fisherman? Fanny the Fisherwoman, ho, ho,' she heard her give her strident, humourless laugh. 'All right, Aunt Leda,' she retorted, 'leave me alone. I wasn't thinking of it seriously.' 'I won't leave you alone,' replied Aunt Leda in this unrelenting daydream, or perhaps it was already a real dream, 'You're capable of anything. I know. You're even capable of singing Java.' And Fanny had to hold her peace, for it was true.

It was even truer than Aunt Leda had suspected, she reflected half asleep while the other Fanny whirled before her eyes, the one Aunt Leda had not even imagined existed because she had only lived in her imagination and in other people's youth, Edith Piaf's for example, Fanny-who-might-have-been, her dress flying above her knees. And perhaps for Edith too all these things, the whirling, and the Java, and the accordionist's long fingers, had only existed in her longing, the would-be of the heart. No, for Edith they had to actually exist, in all reality, it couldn't be otherwise. Unless her desire had been so strong that it brought them to life, so strong that she created them when she sang, and that made all the difference. But now I too sing them, the thought flew dimly through her mind, like a soft, fluffy arrow, and the answer, also dimmed, too dull to hurt, came back like an echo: but you sing them second-hand. And was that really all. Even when she made the effort, however hard it was, to sing only from that one single place from where you could draw forth the true sound, even when she sang all that was in her, all that she knew, she was still singing second-hand. True, only a little of what she sang had she actually accumulated herself. Most was stolen from furtive glances through illuminated windows of cafés where others danced, from lights and curling smoke that weren't hers, but always others', from scraps of looks which were almost never meant for her, and only fell her way by accident, yet wrung her heart as if they were hers, and could she not somehow make them her own. Were not the poor to inherit the earth, that's what Felix Grunwald always said.

Robert sighed and turned in his sleep. His warm body touched hers in the darkness and this light touch was suddenly the brush of a different possibility, so tempting as to almost hurt, and she longed to embrace him but did not let herself do it. She moved to the edge of the bed and turned her face to the window. The branches of the palm tree swayed in the night breeze and she watched them for a long time, until she grew very tired. Perhaps there really was nothing but this, she said to herself finally, sensing her thought being swallowed in the soft, blurring ether of sleep, perhaps this was really all there was, but it was still better than nothing.

40

The next day Margie called to thank her for the pleasant evening. She praised the refreshments and the hospitality and the new dress, then turned to a thorough review of the evening's events and participants until she finally arrived at the heart of the matter, namely Robert. She dangled glittering hooks of praise, but Fanny firmly refused to be enticed from the realm of facts to the shadowy kingdom of the heart-to-heart. Margie did not conceal her disappointment. 'You've changed,' she said. And then she fell silent for a moment and said in a surprised voice, 'Well, maybe not.' She must have realized at that moment that up till then Fanny hadn't had anything to tell; it was her unreasonable insistence on adhering to her silence even now, when her situation had changed, that was frustrating, irritating even. Nevertheless she informed her that the end-of-summer sale was starting on Tuesday at the Shalom department store and that she must buy herself, at least now that she had someone to do it for, a decent everyday outfit instead of that old beige suit from Switzerland which it was really time to throw out. Fanny felt a sting of offence, such as you feel upon being told that your favourite doll is nothing but a rag with one eye missing and a dangling leg, but on second thoughts she decided that perhaps Margie was right, and that in any case a new outfit wouldn't hurt; and driven by the wind of change which had been blowing in her sails since the preparations for the party, she set forth around noon in the direction of Allenby Street.

The number of people, of women actually, stunned her. For a moment she wondered whether Margie had summoned them all. The women covered the floors of the large display rooms like a colourful, mutating work of kinetic art, but there was something about this enormous acrostic which infused in one, and in one's wish to buy oneself a new summer suit, a sense of insignificance. Fanny hesitantly asked one of the assistants at the cosmetics counter where to find the women's wear department, and was answered by 'Look at the sign, lady, can't you see we're busy.' For lack of any choice she began looking for the directions and after a few minutes finally spotted them above the stairwell. The sign announced that the women's wear department was on the second floor. With some hesitation she mounted the escalator, which always seemed to her an unbridled horse, you never knew at what moment it might chose to throw off its rider, but made it to the second floor unharmed.

There, however, the crush was even worse. Despite the size of the sales room it was hard to take two steps without bumping into one of the customers who were running about, sweaty and dishevelled, among the circular clothes stands, their arms piled with dresses, sarafans, swimsuits and even, surprisingly, see-through raincoats in shiny colours. The variety was dizzying. Like women possessed the customers scurried from one stand to another and from there to the fitting rooms and back again, snatching one more pair of slacks, one more dress. At the sight of this great mob Fanny was overcome by weakness and searched for somewhere to sit, but the few chairs were already taken, mainly by mothers. The latter weren't sitting idly either, but were giving orders to their daughters, who were busy with the actual work of loading and unloading, or trying things on in front of the mirrors. For a moment Fanny considered beating a shameful retreat. Perhaps, her old voice tried to persuade her new self, she should come back some other day, when it was less crowded. But immediately she reminded herself that on another day there wouldn't be any suits on sale either. Anyway, she told herself, you have to get used to living in reality as it is. The world is not going to adjust itself to your needs, and the sooner you get used to it, the better. You've already held off recognizing its existence for too long. And these words prodded Fanny to step forward and ask where the suits were with such forcefulness that the salesgirl actually stopped attaching labels to the dresses in her care and pointed her to the place, and even added a few words regarding summer versus autumn suits.

Encouraged, Fanny marched to that corner of the room. But again her intentions didn't go hand in hand with reality. All the will in the world to change couldn't bring her to throw safety to the winds and plunge into the swarm of customers teeming around the two stands of discounted summer suits. About thirty women were hovering around the stands, buzzing and bustling, calling each other over a laden shoulder: Hey, Ruthie, I've got the one you wanted in green, Look at this one, Hemda, No, not that one, this one. Again Fanny was seized by a powerful urge to flee back home, make herself a cup of tea and sink into the sofa, and again she harnessed her spirit with the iron reins of will. You're not going anywhere, she announced to herself, until you try on at least two suits and see if they fit or not. You're not getting out of here with less.

After standing for a while in her corner, which was a convenient observation point overlooking the suits, and patiently watching the tumultuous billows of her rivals, she took advantage of a passing moment at low tide and hastened to take her place near one of the clothes stands. The women on either side of her were turning it to and fro, so all she had to do was to examine the suits as they appeared before her. She didn't ask of herself more than that, for, so she told herself, there was no use in demanding more than she was capable of. Finally she chose two suits: one brown and warmer, more suitable for autumn, really, and one, surprisingly enough, red, with big lapels, the kind she wouldn't have even looked at three weeks earlier except to think how pretty it looked on somebody else. With these spoils she retreated to the fitting rooms and waited patiently until one of them became free, and then went in and pulled the curtain closed behind her.

The first suit she tried on fitted as if it was hers already. There was something pleasant about this suit, about its colour, a subdued but pretty earth brown with a tinge of green, and it flattered her figure but did not emphasize it too much. The second suit was a completely different affair. Not only was it red, a violent red which refused to disguise itself as any other, milder colour, a fire-engine red, but it was also, to Fanny's surprise, really short, so short as to end above the knee. It was the first time she had ever tried on such a length, although she had seen, of course, many young girls and even women her age in even shorter skirts, their tanned thighs flashing and disappearing as they zigzagged between the cars. But she, Fanny, doggedly went on wearing her just-below-the-knee dresses, and never felt tempted to adopt this fashion, which had conquered, so she read in the magazines which Batya and Raya left in the office, the world as well as the movies. All that seemed to have nothing to do with her at all, as if the world were a movie and she was walking through it in her long skirts, the only flesh-and-blood character. And here she finally found herself in a short skirt and even, she was forced to admit to herself, a very short one. At least half as short again as what she was used to. She blinked. The cubicle she was using suddenly seemed to her very narrow, too narrow for such a change, and she went out into the hall and stood in front of the large mirror. She surveyed herself uncertainly. It was as if there appeared before her a new and unfamiliar figure, which needed to be scrutinized more closely than one's regular one, for which a glance is enough to take it in and decide whether the garment suits it or not. She scanned her body with a long look, from top to bottom and then sideways. Not bad, she decided. The knee which was revealed wasn't at all ugly, a little round perhaps, perhaps more so than could be desired, but not too much more. The exposed stretch of thigh was compatible with the knee. All in all, Fanny said to herself, she could certainly afford to wear this suit. If she wanted to. But did she want to?

And then she heard a voice to her right, a nasal voice, slightly hoarse but very loud and embarrassing: 'Listen. You. Yes, you. You took this suit from the cubicle where I left it. What's the matter with you? Can't you find your own clothes instead of stealing them from other people?'

Fanny turned and looked at her, shocked. 'I didn't take it from any cubicle,' she protested. 'It was hanging over there with all the others.'

'*Y'allah y'allah y'allah*,' said the woman, who was red-nosed and had lacklustre fair hair. 'Go tell that to somebody else. I took this suit about – maybe an hour ago, right, Beena?' She turned to another woman, who until then had been hidden behind a pile of hangers and now straightened up to stand by her friend. Her face was still hidden by the pile of clothes, but that didn't prevent her from nodding vigorously. 'Sure,' she added for extra emphasis with the same nasal intonation as her friend.

The woman turned to Fanny with fresh courage. 'You see?' she said triumphantly. 'So if you please, take it off and give it back to me. It took me ages to make up my mind, and now she just comes along and grabs it,' she complained, partly to her friend, partly to the crowd of women who had started to gather around them.

Fanny's anger began to well. Come what may, she was not going to give in to this low trick.

'Listen,' she said with as such calm as she could muster, 'stop talking nonsense. I took this suit from the hanger, like I told you, and not from any fitting room, and if you keep saying I'm a thief I'll call the attendant and have you thrown out of here.'

'It's true,' a new voice was suddenly heard from the crowd. 'I saw her taking down this suit.'

'Maybe the woman in charge of the fitting rooms took it while you were trying on something else,' suggested a third voice. 'They do that if you have too many clothes in your cubicle.'

'What do you mean, too many? I never had too many,'

exploded the claimant to the suit, but her friend, who seemed more sensitive to public opinion, interrupted. All that time she had been looking at Fanny as if trying to remember something, and now her eyes lit up with the flame of recognition. 'Forget it,' she said. 'I know who she is. I saw her on Friday with Ramy. Performing at a nightclub. You don't want to argue with these people. Not your class.'

The first woman straightened up and looked at Fanny. The insistent lack in her eyes was filled, satisfied. 'Performing at a nightclub,' she said. 'I should have known. You don't waste your breath on this lot. Trash,' she said, and with her head held high she turned and started to walk away from the scene of the fight.

For a moment Fanny stood there paralysed. This was a direct blow, not one softened by the word of a third party. But immediately afterwards her vision was obscured by a blood-red surge, redder than the suit, and through it she could barely make out the head of the woman who was weaving her way through the throng of customers milling around the down-ward escalator. Propelled by a mighty strength she didn't know she had in her, she sprang after her and grabbed her by the hair — by the hair! — and forced her to turn around.

'Apologize,' said the new Fanny, so new that even she herself was thunderstruck to hear her, 'apologize or I'll slap you right here in front of everybody.'

'You wouldn't dare,' panted her rival. The friend also turned around and looked at Fanny and at her companion with an open mouth, but kept a safe distance.

'Try me,' said Fanny. And for the first time in her life she felt such violence in herself that she knew she wouldn't hesitate to slap her opponent's face and even knock her down to the floor, if need be. And she didn't care in the least how ridiculous or crazy she would look at that moment, or what would happen to her afterwards. Even if they threw her in jail.

There was in the utter madness which had taken hold of her such great determination that even the woman in front of her couldn't help but feel it, and she stepped back. 'All right, a'right,' she said half-heartedly. 'You're not trash. OK?' Fanny tightened her grip on the woman's hair and shook her more violently. 'You'll apologize properly', she said through tightly clenched teeth, 'or I'll do what I said.' Now the woman was really frightened. 'OK, OK, I apologize. I thought you were somebody else. All right?' she said, a slight whine creeping into her voice. 'No. You didn't think I was someone else,' said Fanny. 'I'm exactly the one you were thinking of.' 'All right. I lied. It wasn't true. I'm sorry,' said the woman finally in a kind of wail, and Fanny loosened her hold and let her go. When she was far enough out of reach the woman turned around and shouted, 'Bitch!' and started running in the direction of the stairs, her friend lagging two steps behind her with the pile of clothes still on her arm, but by then the red wave of violence had already receded, leaving Fanny drained. Shocked and confused, the shame washing over her in waves as regular as heartbeats, she walked back along her via dolorosa under the dozens of eyes fixed on her, and put her old dress back on and was about to leave the store and go home, home at last, when unexpectedly, on a sudden and unexplained impulse, she went back to the cubicle and took out the red suit and paid for it at the till.

At night, in bed, she told Robert what had happened, but telling him didn't bring her any relief and she was left with a dull, pent-up tension which beat with impotent fury against the walls of her body, demanding to be let out. Even in the morning, when she woke up to a new sun-drenched day, this feeling had not dissolved. Robert was sleeping beside her, his breathing light and regular, breaking every once in a while into a soft snore then returning to its steady rhythm. Fanny turned over and reflected on the events of the previous day. There must have been some way, she thought, of resolving the business without becoming embroiled in that disgraceful scene. But however much she thought about the matter she couldn't see how she could have avoided it, for she had tried as hard as she could to remain calm and not to be sucked into the hysteria of her opponents, until the moment when the insult was hurled at her. At that moment she had no choice but to react, or forgo both the suit and her dignity, and when she thought of this possibility the red bull again leaped in her blood and she was frightened by its hot hurtling might, which blinded her for a minute and made her clench her hand with such force that it stretched the sheet from underneath her and pulled at Robert, and he turned around, his face smooth and blind with sleep, and murmured something before he turned back to the other, shaded side. His voice loosened Fanny's clenched fist and she let go of the sheet. All of a sudden she was filled with a real fear of the violence which had suddenly arisen in her and woken in her a strange, unknown woman. She didn't know what that woman was capable of or what she might do. Where have you been hiding all these years? Fanny asked her, and knew the answer: in that very same place you've so carefully kept under lock and key. This frightened her beyond all measure. Had you been more authoritative, she told herself, none of this would have happened. But she knew, deep inside, that it all had to happen the way it had, and that she could not escape the furious red bellowing of the bull whose hooves were pounding inside her, because it was time for it to come out.

41

'Listen,' said Gina excitedly when she arrived at the club that night, 'I've already talked to Robert. Tonight when you finish we'll go see the show at Zanzibar. On Friday they have a late show. There's something there I want to see.' When she said these last words her lips tightened and it was clear that she had a special reason for wanting to see this show, but didn't want to reveal it. Fanny said nothing. One show a night was quite enough for her, but it seemed that the matter had already been settled.

'You see, she's agreed,' Gina immediately told Robert, who appeared that moment at the door. 'I told you she would. It's important to see other people's work, what they're up to.'

Robert studied Fanny's surprised face. 'OK, Gina,' he said. 'But on one condition. You know what.'

'All right, all right,' said Gina crossly. 'You can't seem to forget that business. I'm older now. I don't do stupid things like that any more.'

'We'll see,' said Robert. Then he looked at Fanny and smiled. 'I packed everything in fifteen minutes,' he said. That evening, before the show, he'd gone to pick up the rest of his belongings from the house on Hayarkon Street.

'What was there left for you to do in the last five minutes, that's what I'd like to know,' said Fanny jokingly, but she was seized by a heavy apprehension. What if in the end it all turned out to be one big mistake? What if he discovered within a few days that the house suffocated him, closed in on him, or, that terrible word she didn't even want to think about, bored him? Whatever people had said about her, Fanny, they never said she was interesting. If only I was an interesting person, she

thought with longing. Wild, capricious, ever-changing, like –
Gina? This was the only example she could think of, and she
could only laugh at herself. That cheered her up.

'You're beginning to laugh to yourself, you'll get far,' said
Gina. She looked more nervous than usual and was removing
her make-up with short, violent strokes.

Robert smiled at her. 'A good start, Gina,' he said.

Gina banged her cream tin shut. 'All right, all right I said!
Leave me alone, will you?' With a swift motion she put on her
black blouse and trousers – the only outfit Fanny had ever seen
her wear offstage – and left, slamming the door behind her.

'What's got into her?' asked Fanny, at a loss.

'She's going to see the competition. There's a rumour going
around that the strip show at Zanzibar is blowing people out.
Two Brazilians, red hot. Our audience has dropped by half.'

'Ah,' said Fanny. She turned to her mirror and began
putting on her make-up. She had about fifteen minutes. For
some reason she wasn't looking forward to the evening before
her.

'You don't have to come if you don't want to,' said Robert,
who was standing there, watching her.

'No, I'll come,' said Fanny.

Robert shrugged. 'OK,' he said. 'Just don't complain later
on.'

'I won't,' said Fanny.

After he left, she thought this had been their first almost-
fight.

By the time they arrived at Zanzibar the dancing was over and
the shiny machine with the jumping balls was already standing
at the centre of the stage. 'Strippers and bingo, what a
combination,' sighed Robert. He sank on the plastic seat and
leaned his head back. He had chosen a rear table, next to the
wall and concealed from the entrance. 'You have something
against strippers?' Gina asked sharply and Robert said, 'No,
against bingo. I loathe this game,' and shut his eyes.

'We're getting close,' the MC announced dramatically. He drew out a ball and declared, 'B-three.' In precisely that tone of voice, thought Fanny, they had once drawn lots for human lives. She had seen this in a film. 'A-twenty-eight,' the MC shouted and Robert said with his eyes closed, 'I'm going to throw up.'

'Maybe I should bring us all something to drink?' offered Fanny, and Robert roused himself and jumped up to his feet. 'I'll go,' he said, looked at her as if asking for her forgiveness and kissed her on the tip of her nose.

After he left Fanny glanced around. Slowly her eyes grew used to the dim light and she looked at the people next to them, a young couple who were absorbed in the bingo card they held up to the light. Their eyes narrowed in the effort to discern the toothpick perforations they had made in the numbers called out by the host.

Robert came back, holding two bottles of beer in each hand. 'They don't like to give out glasses,' he said and disappeared, and after another moment brought four glasses, one of them half-full with the vodka Gina had ordered, a bottle of juice and two plates of peanuts. 'Hey, presto,' he called and scattered them all one by one around the table with a conjuror's dexterity.

'Sit down,' said Gina impatiently. 'The magician isn't on yet. And when he is you'll pray for it to be over.'

'Can't even have a little fun,' protested Robert unconvincingly. Gina kept silent and took a large handful of peanuts and put them in her mouth. Zorri, who hadn't yet uttered one word, poured himself some of the beer and lifted the glass to his lips. Gina's hand landed on his with a thump. 'Where's your manners? What sort of a gentleman are you?' she said. 'Pour for the lady first.' Frothing beer spattered on Zorri's trousers. Fanny saw his lips tighten and grow pale, but he said nothing and put down his glass. Then he poured the orange juice into Gina's vodka, 'I don't understand why you have to spoil the taste of the vodka with that terrible stuff,' said

Robert. 'You could at least use real orange juice.' She had never seen them all so nervous, thought Fanny, but it was obvious there was nothing she could do to calm things down, and so she just held out her hand and closed it around Robert's, as he had done that evening which now seemed so far away, in the taxi. Robert pressed her hand and then let go of it and put his arm around her shoulder.

After a while Fanny stopped paying attention to what was happening on the stage and also stopped looking at the people. The strange light which flooded the place made the drink in her glass glow with an azure radiance, the phosphorous azure of an aquarium, and she slowly shook it from side to side and watched its pale, heavenly transluscence. A roll of drums woke her from her hypnotized staring. The loudspeaker announced the arrival of Zargo, the celebrated juggler from Zagreb, five continents, fifty countries, now in Israel. For the first time in this country – at Zanzibar! Fanny felt Robert tense next to her.

A short black-haired man ran up on stage, gave a deep bow and immediately started juggling red-and-yellow striped bats, which looked like bees buzzing in flight. Then he switched to multicoloured blocks and then to balls, but even Fanny soon saw that he wasn't very good at what he did: his work wasn't smooth, although he only juggled three balls at a time, and he missed balls too often. At the end of each routine the drums thundered and the juggler from Zagreb, his face shiny with sweat, gave a deep bow and raised his hands in the quick draw of a gunman. Now he threw two red balls up in the air and added a third yellow one, which he tried to capture in the hollow at the back of his knee. The ball slipped off his leg and he was forced to dribble it on the sole of his shoe in order to catch it. Robert made a gesture of disgust and gulped down the rest of the beer in his glass. 'I'm going to get some more,' he said and stood up. 'Anybody else?' But he was the only one who had finished his drink and Gina said, not without malice, 'Aren't we nervous, Robert? And I thought I was the one being watched here.' Robert flung at her, 'Wait for the

Brazilians,' and Gina's eyes flashed under her eyebrows, which tightened up immediately, as if he had slapped her face. 'Is that what they brought him all the way from Zagreb for?' muttered Zorri, the first words he had said all evening, and Gina said scornfully, 'What Zagreb? The bastard's never seen Zagreb in his life. He's from here, from downtown Jaffa,' and she took a sip from her glass, looking at it as if she'd seen a fly there. 'I've known him since he was this high.' She made a small, token gesture with her hand, which didn't indicate any particular height. Robert looked at her, his mouth open, and burst out laughing. 'Gina Lullubrigida, straight from Cine-Città,' he mimicked Greenspan's Romanian accent. 'Why am I even surprised?' But his laughter was different now, not derisory but free, friendly, as if this improbable revelation had somehow dissolved his tension, and Gina felt this and was not offended but returned his smile, revealing her large nicotine-stained teeth. And then came the hard part.

The drums rolled again with even greater intensity. The music swelled, crescendoed. It took Fanny a moment before she grasped what was now taking place on stage. Only when her brain had registered what her eyes saw, did she realize that the two small white ping-pong balls were being ejected from deep inside the juggler's throat, then swallowed and again shot out, like little cannon balls. She saw his throat alternately gulping and ejecting, gulping and ejecting, the tremendous straining of the neck muscles, his eyes staring at the ceiling, almost turning in their sockets. The juggler's mouth had become a predatory red flower sticking out its red tongue, a fleshy bloom gaping open with frightening sensuality to eject and to swallow. Fanny wanted to avert her face but couldn't. At first she thought her revulsion had to do with the strong sexual undertones of the spectacle. Then she realized that it wasn't sexual at all. Rather it resembled a sort of public defecating, as if the man was turning himself inside out in front of them, exposing before them his innermost organs, swallowing and excreting before their eyes like a huge anaconda snake.

But the audience obviously thought otherwise, for the applause was loud and enthusiastic, and the Yugoslavian juggler from Jaffa kept smiling and bowing even deeper, and his face shone even more, and then he disappeared and the roll of the drums ushered in the next performer.

The following performance was one of artistic gymnastics, so the MC announced, and it came to us straight from England – Tracy Putnam: direct from London. As far as the MCs of nightclubs were concerned, Fanny reflected, there existed nothing but capital cities: London, Rome, Buenos Aires, Paris. The main thing was all and outside it there was nothing. It never entered their minds, or they never thought it worthwhile that it should, that someone could come from a place like Anchorage, Alaska. Did the audience believe them? In fact this question was irrelevant, she suddenly understood. It was a kind of unspoken agreement between the host and the audience: they deserved only the best, and he made sure that they got it. It was only right that the big names be called out, like the resounding words of a magic spell: London, New York, Amsterdam. They belonged to the thick light, to the dresses worn only once a week, or month, to the very act of going out, to that magic word: entertainment. She looked at Robert, but he was bent over the table, sketching obscure figures with his finger in the water which had collected under his glass, absorbed in a world that she couldn't enter.

The sound of cymbals suddenly resounded and Fanny almost jumped out of her seat: a glittering figure leaped on to the stage and bowed. The gymnast's body was all muscle and above it stood, as if a thing apart, a strange face, painted like a mask, an Indian's face. The lips in particular were extraordinary, almost rectangular, smeared on the face like the warpaint of the Indians in films. They were lighter than rest of the face and stood out at its centre, not belonging and almost impossible, yet its very essence.

Fanny felt Robert stirring beside her. 'Christ, I can't believe she's still working,' he murmured. 'She's been on stage for maybe thirty years now.'

'You know her?' asked Fanny.

'Not exactly,' said Robert. 'I've heard a lot about her. She inaugurated many of the places I've performed in. A pioneer in the business. A character.'

'It must be a difficult profession, at her age,' whispered Fanny.

Robert shrugged. 'What would you have her do? Be a gym teacher in some boarding school for girls near Brighton?'

Fanny didn't say anything, and Robert turned and looked at her. 'Not that that's so bad,' he said.

'But you wouldn't want to do it,' said Fanny.

'No,' said Robert and fell silent.

For the finale the MC promised a special acrobatic routine. With a slow, ritual motion the gymnast lifted a long pointed sword. Her face hardened, became completely the Indian's face. All the desire to please that was in it vanished without a trace. The eyes grew sharp, assessing the distance. The face was again a mask, centred entirely around the mouth. And then the sword was lifted and hurled at the table and behind it soared the gymnast, as if both were cast into a single jet of white-hot metal. The sword quivered in the air and the muscles in the woman's torso quivered above it, but they both remained where they were, hovering in a straight line above the same spot on the table, as the host suddenly thundered: 'Tracy Putnam – Look at that! She's balancing on the tip of a sword!' Robert let the air out of his mouth with a whistle. 'Unbelievable,' he muttered. 'Simply unbelievable. What an idiot.' The crowd buzzed. Tracy Putnam's face kept flowing into her mouth, naked in the powerful spotlights. For a few more seconds she hovered there, frozen in the air, and suddenly she jumped to her feet, raised her hand with the sword, smiled. The hard light struck her straight in the face and Fanny watched her, hypnotized, as she bowed again and again to the roar of the audience's applause.

Unaware, her eyes turned again to Robert's profile, half-illuminated in the light which fell from the stage. The gymnast's body gleamed one last time in the spots and vanished. Robert's face seemed expressionless in the faint light, yet at that moment Fanny knew with utter clarity that he and Tracy Putnam and all the others had to keep on going, travelling around the world from Utah to Madagascar, from one provincial nightclub to another, circling and circling around the globe like nightmoths around a smoky lamp, and they would never stop, whatever they said to the Fannys they met along the way. Only Gina was perhaps untouched by all that. Gina was interested only in the money which came in regularly every month to her bank account, and in the future her savings were building brick by brick, the future of a small public-housing flat in Bat-Yam, not far from the sea, with no need to work anywhere or to strip before any stinking audience whatsoever. That's also why she was here tonight, because she couldn't afford to have a couple of shitty imported strippers threaten her living, threaten this future she was driving towards so tenaciously and unflaggingly. Gina's motives were purely pragmatic and Fanny, watching her large figure on the narrow plastic seat, yearned to move closer and sit next to her, in the shelter of her heavy shoulder.

The singer came on and sang to the sounds of a non-existent band. His voice was false, as were his movements, his frequent pauses as he waited for the audience to applaud. Even the applause, Fanny realized in astonishment, was pre-recorded. Gina pulled nervously at a lock of her hair and muttered mechanically, 'What a stinking place.' It seemed that her nervousness, which had subsided during the earlier acts, increased as the performance she was waiting for drew closer. Zorri kept silent. Robert took small but regular sips from the glass in front of him and kept silent as well. Fanny felt a certain nervousness rising in her too. She wanted to relieve the tension, but found nothing to say, and her attempt ended with a nervous clearing of her throat. Gina put out her cigarette and mumbled, 'Well, get on with it already. Everything's taking ages in this place.' Her long fingers with their square tips crushed the cigarette butt on the plastic bottom of the ashtray until it disintegrated into fibres of foul-smelling tobacco. And as if in response, the singer ended with a mighty crescendo, bowed deeply to thundering applause from the audience and from the tape, and vacated the stage to the sound of the loudspeakers announcing the magician. 'Oh, no,' groaned Gina. She covered her eyes with her hands. All of her heavy body seemed to spill forward into her palms. 'Not that shit. Zorri.' she raised her head and her eyes looked at him from above her still-open hands. 'Bring me a glass of arak from the bar.' Zorri looked at her, but did not budge. 'Zorri,' said Gina. Her eyes became very big, no longer human eyes but the eyes of a large beast spurred on by some terrible agony. There was something frightening about it because you felt that any minute now this large animal might lose its apparent calm and fall upon those surrounding it, like a bleeding bull in the ring. Zorri shuddered and got up. With forced steps he went up to the bar and returned with a glass of the same milky drink that Fanny remembered. 'Who told you to pour water in it?' mumbled Gina and stared at him with her gigantic insane eye, but once she took the first sip she relaxed. Her eye shrunk back to human size and she looked around her almost with favour.

The drums rolled. The spotlight came on and focused on the stage, and a young man wearing a frock coat and a white shirt hopped nimbly into the circle of light. Gina muttered again, 'God, what shit,' and took a large sip from her glass. Then she leaned back and shut her eyes, as if to make sure that nothing which happened from now on could touch her. Robert drank and watched the stage. Zorri drank and watched Gina.

The talk spilled over Fanny like an avalanche of gravel. The steady stream of words prevented any possibility of distinguishing between the sentences, and it was only possible to understand that the magician was promising to show them some conjuring tricks the like of which they had never seen before, not even in their dreams, tricks which would strike them dumb with amazement so that they wouldn't even be able to clap. At that Gina gave a great snort of contempt, which scattered the ash and the tobacco fibres all over the table and released Fanny from the state of hypnosis she had sunk into. Only then did she see that behind the magician there hung from a pole, horizontally, in a completely untenable position, the figure of a woman. Her legs were the legs of a doll, shiny pink plastic, but her torso and her face looked like those of a real woman, a flesh-and-blood woman. It was hard to tell, the more so since she remained hanging motionlessly upstage in her impossible position, like a piece of the stage set, throughout the magician's endless speech. Fanny leaned over to Robert. 'Is it a woman or a doll?' she whispered. 'Stockings,' answered Robert briefly and pointed at the doll's legs. Now Fanny saw that indeed the legs were covered by a special kind of stockings, pink and shiny like a doll's plastic thigh. The hue of the bare arms was natural.

The doll stepped down from the pole and bowed. A glittering smile appeared on her face, a perfect, symmetrical smile. With an extravagant motion she took up a pack of cards from a small table in the corner and handed it to the magician. The magician explained, volubly and tiresomely, that he intended to choose four volunteers at random, each of whom would pick a card and memorize it and put it back into the pack, that he would guess exactly what card each of them had picked . . . From a certain moment onward his words lost all meaning. The pack flew out to the audience and then back to the stage, people stood up and the magician announced, in the midst of his relentless flow of words, what card had been picked. What was most obvious was the way he abused his volunteers. It was clear that everything he said was meant to

303

ridicule them in order to win the audience's laughter. Fanny tried to raise a partition between her and the stage, to screen out the numbing flow of words which poured from the magician, who was now looking for a volunteer with a hundred dollars in his pocket. Suddenly she saw before her eyes the magic show she had seen in her childhood, the show at Claire's birthday party. That magician had been the complete opposite of the one who was now grilling his volunteer – a silver-templed man of about fifty – about his occupation. 'Women's wear,' said the smartly dressed volunteer and leaned emphatically, as if to bolster his self-confidence, on one leg. The magician moved his hands insinuatingly along the sides of his body. Skin-tight, eh? The other magician's face had been thin, almost ascetic, his cheeks sunken and their complexion dark. He too had been wearing a long black frock coat, but his body was much thinner than that of this magician, who was now brandishing an envelope in front of his victim's face and demanding that he seal it. Lick it, lick it all around, Moshe. What's the matter, you don't like licking? The other magician had lowered his black grape eyes to the audience of children and with dizzying speed pulled a red silk handkerchief out of his empty hand, pulled and pulled and pulled the handkerchief which seemed to have no end and suddenly its colour changed to purple, then blue, green, yellow, and finally there appeared in his hand a red toy locomotive, which he offered with a light bow to Claire. Not one of the children uttered a word. The magician did not smile. With deadly seriousness he drew rabbits out of a large black hat and fished coins out of his ear. When he changed, with a mysterious turn of his hand above a glass, water into thick purplish wine, Claire's father said in a loud voice, heavy with generations of moneyed importance, 'Don't be frightened, sweetheart. It's just trickery, you know. Simple sleight of hand,' and Fanny, like all the other children, looked at him with hatred.

The magician's hand tightened around the glass and let go.

'And now – I need a volunteer,' he said in his toneless voice. Claire's father rose to his feet and stolidly approached the little improvised stage. The magician bowed to him, his face impassive. The tails of his frock coat rose on both sides like a fin. Then he made the usual gesture with his hand, a gesture which never varied whatever the magic was, and suddenly the air was filled with fluttering green ten-mark notes and reddish bills of fifty and even a few brown hundred marks, like birds which had suddenly left their perch and were now circling around the tree, a flock of birds in the autumn wind. Claire's father, his face flushed, bent down and collected the notes, muttering that there was a limit to everything. The back of his neck was flushed as well as he crouched to gather the notes one by one from the floor.

For Claire's next birthday they didn't hire the magician. Instead there was a well-known singer of children's songs, who had already performed at a few parties to which Fanny had been invited that year. Then Claire moved to another town and Fanny wasn't asked to her birthday parties any more. But even then she knew that there had been no sleight of hand there. The sleight of hand was here, on the large, well-lit stage where the magician was now lighting a match and igniting, under the volunteer's nose, the brown envelope which contained or did not contain a hundred-dollar bill. Look at his eyes burning, he says mockingly. You Persians don't like to burn money, huh? The doll's teeth gleamed. The audience, like a well-trained dog, clapped their hands.

'I don't want to see any more,' said Fanny suddenly in a loud voice. Gina's lips curled scornfully. 'Honey,' she said and crushed another cigarette in the ashtray, 'This is just –' and at that moment the stage exploded in a whirl of colour and movement. Two dark-brown girls, wearing colourful feathers on their heads and very little else, burst on to the stage to the strains of a wild samba.

One of them was a beautiful mulatto, her eyes slanted and their look black and opaque. She undulated on the stage like

305

an eel, arousing a shudder of desire and revulsion. The other was very dark, tall, her long frizzy hair streaming down her back like a coil of snakes. The music was sensuous and wild, played on instruments Fanny had never heard before, and underneath it vibrated the incessant beat of drums. The two Brazilians smouldered on stage like black flames, shaking to the rhythm of the music until for one hair-raising moment it seemed as if the stage would collapse under the intensity of their heat. And then the music became slow, insinuating. The two girls approached the edge of the stage.

One after the other they kneeled down, the motion of their pelvises never ceasing. The small mulatto kissed the man at her feet on the top of his head and rose up again, flowing like thick mocha ice cream towards the next man, and this time she gestured to him to put his hand on her quivering thigh. But the man, of whom Fanny could see only his greying hair, was afraid. His hand couldn't make the movement required of him, this is not Brazil.

'This one's not gonna let his wife get any sleep tonight, that's for sure,' muttered Gina.

The Brazilian lost her patience and without further ado she pulled the man up to his feet and dragged him with surprising force towards her, on to the stage. The man was slim, fortyish, with meticulously combed hair. He was wearing a well-tailored suit, just like those young Mr Bruck used to wear to the office even on the hottest summer days, and after a minute Fanny realized to her amazement that she was watching Mr Bruck himself, him and no other.

Fanny felt intense discomfort. She turned her gaze away, and then something clenched up inside her and she forced herself to turn it back to the stage. Now it's your turn, she said to herself, but for some reason couldn't derive any pleasure from this thought. The stripper pushed Mr Bruck down to his knees and pressed his hands together in a gesture of prayer. Then she herself began wriggling downwards. Her legs slid around the raised hands and locked. Mr Bruck's face locked in astonishment. 'Move your hands!' yelled the loudspeaker. The dancer's body moved up and down, pounding against Mr Bruck's clutched hands in a piston-like movement, until slowly, as if compelled, Mr Bruck's hands also began moving between the stripper's thighs, up and down, up and down. A bland smile appeared on Mr Bruck's face, a smile of hypnotized rapture, mingled with embarrassment. His eyes peeked briefly downwards, towards the table he had left, and Fanny looked in that direction and recognized his fiancée, whom she knew from the few times she had come to visit him at the office. The woman's face was frozen in an expression she could not decipher. Fanny wondered if they visited nightclubs often.

Suddenly the music slowed down. The mulatto moaned one last time and dropped off Mr Bruck's hands, abandoning them for one agonizing moment alone in the field of battle. Immediately afterwards Mr Bruck himself let them fall, gazing at them with embarrassment, as if they weren't his own. Then the music swelled up again. The tempo of the drumming increased. The two Brazilians pounced on Mr Bruck and pulled off his jacket. They shoved a red piece of cloth into his hands and with gestures explained to him what was required of him. Mr Bruck nodded to indicate that he had understood. He started to wave the red rag, matador-like, and the tall mulatto stamped her feet, one, two, three, and leaped on him, her long legs clasping him in chocolate pincers. 'America, Special Delivery! Take her home,' bellowed the loudspeaker with unfounded generosity, and Fanny looked again at the dark-haired figure sitting motionlessly at the table with only her fingers moving, tearing golden chocolate wrapping paper into little shreds, and felt sorrow and a great weariness.

She returned her eyes to the stage. Mr Bruck was still standing there, planted in the same spot, although the Brazilians had turned their backs on him and again started undulating in front of the audience. So that was her audience, she thought. It was the first time that the audience she sang to took on a face when she looked at it, a face with a distinct identity, and suddenly, for one horrifying moment, she saw before her eyes the image of her own club as it looked from above, from the stage. The guests were sitting there as always, scattered in small groups around the tables, but the faces raised up to her were all identical, and they were all Mr Bruck's.

A burst of brass instruments came from the speakers, a bizarre cocktail of samba and march, and the two dancers began to descend to the floor in a winding trajectory. Mr Bruck put his jacket back on hurriedly, like someone who had just been wakened. 'Hey, Yossi! Don't forget to take your prize,' shouted one of the two other men who were sitting at his table, and Mr Bruck gave him a smile in which embarrassment and a sort of strange pride were inseparably mixed, but the smile quickly wore off and only the embarrassment remained. Fanny thought with surprise that this was the first time she had ever heard young Mr Bruck referred to by his first name. Of course she knew his name, which was printed on the letterhead that Mr Bruck had made up after his father's retirement, but none of the girls at the office had ever called him that. They always called him 'Bruck' or 'Young Bruck', and to his face 'Mr Bruck', and his father, she suddenly realized, had never addressed him directly at all.

The Brazilians got off the stage. To the sounds of a slow, sensuous samba they wove their way between the tables, and every few steps sat on the knees of one of the men and rubbed against his body. Sometimes, when the man was especially shy, they caught hold of his hand and forced him to pass it over their skin. Mr Bruck pushed through the audience without looking at them. He seemed like a man still in a dream. When he finally reached his table his two friends slapped him on the shoulder with a cheer, but he didn't respond and sat down in silence. Fanny saw his fiancée bending towards him; her body leaned over with the rigid movement of an iron bar, then straightened up again. For a moment Mr Bruck remained motionless, then he nodded, said a few words to his friends, picked up the handbag and scarf which his companion had left on the table and stood up and began making his way behind her towards the exit. A long table made up of several people grouped together blocked his way and forced him to return to the depth of the room, and he tightened his brow in an expression that Fanny knew well when he raised his eyes and his gaze fell on her.

For a brief instant their eyes met. He opened his mouth as if to say something, his face assuming, absurdly, the expression of formal politeness it always wore when an important guest had arrived at the office, but immediately and even more absurdly he closed it and continued on his way. His gait was strained, and as he receded towards the exit its pace grew faster, as if he was gradually disengaging himself from some grip which was holding him back, until he was out of the room.

Fanny saw Robert looking at her. 'My boss,' she said mechanically. The words didn't arouse in her any emotion. Robert nodded. 'You're lucky to be rid of him,' he suddenly said and smiled, the same wonderful smile he gave on stage when caught making a rare mistake, and all at once the dullness which had taken hold of her disappeared, and she smiled back at him. 'Yes,' she said and felt her body swelling towards him, and almost said, let's go home, but the tall Brazilian who had approached their table in dark-brown quivering ripples was already there. She sat on Robert's knees, writhing against his legs, and Robert smiled at her and touched her shoulder gently to signal her to get up, but then in a sudden volcanic eruption Gina leaped from her seat. Fanny felt her enormous body shuddering as if struck by a series of electric shocks. 'Whores!' she screamed. 'Fucking whores! Cheap frauds, give nothing and fool everyone, it's all a lie, all one big trick, fakers, let's see you giving a real show —' Her hand darted out and seized the glittering silver thread which tied the girdle around the dancer's loin, and pulled on it ferociously. 'Who do you think you're fooling?' she yelled. The dancer pulled out of Gina's grip with a twist of her thighs and jumped back, grimacing. A sturdy body in a grey windcheater moved towards their table with surprising speed. In its wake advanced two more windcheaters. But Robert and Zorri had already taken hold of Gina and made her sit down. Robert's hand covered her mouth, not letting her make a sound, even though she kept on shaking her head from side to side in an effort to free herself from his grip, glaring at him furiously. Robert shook his head at the grey windcheater in a kind of agreed-upon sign, and the latter hesitated, then nodded and walked away. The people who had turned on their table curious, scandal-hungry eyes returned to watching the Brazilians, who after a brief pause went back to their winding, heaving trajectory leading to the small door at the side of the stage.

All that time Fanny sat frozen in her seat. She couldn't utter a sound, as if it was her own mouth that Robert's hand was pressed against and not Gina's. She followed the retreating windcheaters with her gaze and then her eyes were drawn again, as if against her will, to Gina. Gina's glare slowly cooled down. The shivering still passed through her body every few minutes, but now it was a mere echo of the fierce shudders which had shaken her before. Finally she moved her head briefly. Her eyes still stared at Robert, but now their expression was cold, postponing the settlement of her account until another time, a more convenient date. Robert lifted his hand, again as if by an agreed signal. 'You're gonna pay for this, you son of a bitch,' Gina said without emotion. Robert shrugged. 'With all due respect to your professional sensibilities, I won't have my face smashed on their account.' 'He's right,' said Zorri surprisingly. His voice sounded hoarse, as if it had been held in for too long under high pressure. Gina turned to him. 'And you —' she started, but immediately checked herself, as if he wasn't worth the trouble. She made a gesture of contempt and stood up and left. Zorri remained there, stooped. His hands dangled loose at the sides of his body but seemed clenched. Automatically he started after her, as if driven by a hidden mechanism, but Robert touched him and he stopped. 'Don't do it, Zorri,' said Robert. 'Tomorrow.' Zorri nodded and remained where he was, but his eyes followed Gina as she walked out of the club, and kept following her as she walked through the alley lit by the bright artificial light, giving off short, sharp rapping sounds as she kicked her high heels against the gravel.

When they got back home they lay in bed for a long time without falling asleep and without touching each other. The poinciana tree groaned in the wind. Mrs Nussbaum turned on the tap in her bathroom and the pipes gurgled and creaked. Finally Fanny said, 'It always seems to me Gina's holding on to something that Zorri needs. Something for the sake of which he always has to chase after her, so she'll give it to him, or at least let him touch it. Maybe even just look at it.'

'It's true,' said Robert. 'This thing's called life.' Then he gave a short laugh. 'Of a certain sort.'

'Why did you say that?' asked Fanny. Inexplicably she felt offended, as if it was her that Robert had insulted and not Gina.

'I don't know,' said Robert. 'Maybe because I also found it there once.'

Fanny felt as if she'd been struck by a punch, straight in the chest. She tried to say something but didn't have enough breath and all that came out was a kind of a brief exhalation. After a minute she said lamely, 'Is that what Gina meant when she said you were old partners?'

'Maybe,' said Robert. 'And maybe just that we've known each other for a long time. You never know with her. I thought she didn't have that feminine quality at all, of hurt and run, but you never know.'

I don't hurt and run, thought Fanny. Why is that a feminine quality? But instead of saying that she said, swallowing her pride, 'Does Zorri know?' She despised herself for not being able not to ask this question, again, apparently, like a woman.

Or what they say about her. It must be true, she thought and felt degraded.

'I think so,' Robert said. 'Gina is not the type to try and spare anybody anything. She doesn't believe it's possible to spare oneself pain, maybe because she's seen you can't escape it. Whichever way you turn, you're gonna get what's coming to you, one way or the other. So why bother?'

After another moment of stilled darkness he said, as if in answer to Fanny's silence, 'I don't think I'd have said this if I hadn't been so tired. Sorry. Goodnight,' and turned over. The long arch of his back seemed to Fanny to make a complete circle, closing her out.

Fanny lay in the dark for a long time without talking and without thinking and without feeling anything, except for the sharp pain in her chest where she knew her heart was supposed to be, and wondered whether she felt it there because she knew that was where the heart was, or whether the ancient poets located the source of pain there because that was where they had felt it in the first place. After a while the pain started to fade and lost the sharpness which had focused everything around it, and she was able to think. First she thought about Robert and Gina and then she realized with surprise that she felt no anger towards Gina, even if she had said what she'd said that night on purpose. She also realized that this revelation in itself no longer hurt her at all, and that the pain she was feeling now did not come from there, but from something else, which Robert and Gina's relationship only served to obscure; for it wasn't because of Gina that Robert did not belong to her, nor would ever be hers, and that wasn't why she had always felt as if she were standing outside some invisible circle, drawn by whose hand she didn't know, but it was because of a completely different reason, which had nothing to do with Gina. She thought back to the first time she had come to the club, which now seemed far away, although it was only a few weeks ago. Images from that show and from the show she had seen tonight flashed intermittently before her eyes, as if someone was screening two films for her at the same time, and in the middle of the screening she suddenly understood, and wondered how was it that she hadn't understood this right away, while they were still at the club, that in a certain sense the first show had opened a door before her, which tonight's show had closed.

The first time, she reflected and turned over on her other side, to escape this screening which hurt her eyes, the first time she had been captivated by the deceiving, elusive magic of the place, and the second time she had wakened from it, or more precisely, it had slipped away from her and did not allow her to be captivated any more. Now, without the tiny sliver of glass which had caught in her eye and distorted her vision, as with little Kay, she understood at last that she herself could never take a real part in this world, not even a dispassionate part like Gina's, for whom it was a source of livelihood and nothing else, for Gina did essentially, even if in a chameleon-like way, belong to that place, to its nocturnal colours, to the smell of pitta breads being baked in Abulafia's blazing ovens and to the red light of the restaurant next door, to the odours of cumin and sesame and roasted honey, and she did not. From the very beginning she had been an alien in it, and she would belong to it less and less, after Robert left, in a little while, and Mercedes and Annette and Pierre left too, and she would be left alone with Gina. Until they sacked her as well. Because the audience would not want to hear the same thing over and over again, this she knew. Novelty was the essence of the place, the axis around which everything revolved, and only Gina's ability to take on each time a new guise, a new persona, a different eroticism, had kept her there for so long. She, Fanny, only knew how to sing the way she did. She couldn't sing differently, not even in order to survive in that world which she so wanted to hold on to, to its smell of wooden boards and the particles of dust rising from the faded black cloth of the curtain and the two crooked light bulbs on either side of the mirror.

And she knew, as she lay there in the dark beside Robert's sleeping back, that she did not belong in this world, the world of the nightclub and of Albaz and Annette and Pierre, any more than she had belonged to the office of Bruck & Sons and to Batya and Raya, perhaps because she had arrived there too late, or perhaps because she was incapable of it in her very essence, and probably, she realized, but the pain wasn't sharp any more but rather dispersed, as though it existed in every single point of her body, in the very cells themselves, probably she wouldn't be able to belong to anything in the future either, and nothing would belong to her, except for a short time and on a strictly limited basis, like a bank loan. The only world she could perhaps have have been a part of was that of Elisabeth Schumann, the world of the lieder and the arias, and the notes which were free of any meaning one wanted to attach to them. And perhaps not even that.

And yet, she insisted, it wasn't the same. Fanny at the club, with Gina and Albaz and Mercedes, Fanny on stage singing Piaf, was no longer the same Fanny of the grey, metal cabinets, the files labelled with coloured markers, the Fanny listening to conversations in which she had no part. Here at least she wasn't only a spectator. She went on stage too. And there was Robert. Who was with her, now, even if not for ever, even if as a short-term loan. And she held on to that difference and tried to direct her whole being towards it, all the strength she had in her, in order to climb, like someone straining to climb a rope, a certain vital stretch, and not fall. Life, of a certain sort, she heard Robert's voice say from afar before she dozed off, and sleep muffled it completely.

42

In the morning the balcony was flooded with bright sunlight
and the air was pleasant and not too hot. It was eight o'clock,
and the walls of the houses across the street were almost white
in the pale light. Fanny reflected that it had been a long time
since she got up so early in the morning. She decided to go to
her favourite bakery and buy some pastries, which would still
be warm at this hour, and perhaps a loaf of fresh rye bread, and
prepare a good breakfast. The remnants of last night, which
were the cause for her waking so early even though she had
fallen asleep at such a late hour, had blurred and sunk to the
bottom of her thoughts, become a distant, hushed backdrop,
like the sound of the sea you can sometimes hear through the
noise of a busy street; something which was already behind
her. She felt that today was the beginning of a different era, in
what way she didn't know, but different, and she didn't want
just to let it pass. Along the way she went by the playground,
and when she reached it she stopped and leaned on the fence.
At this time of the morning there were only a few children,
toddlers who didn't even go to nursery school yet. There were
also mothers, or nannies, with babies in prams. These sat on
the edge of the sandpit and rocked the prams back and forth
with a slow motion, which stopped every now and then when
their attention was distracted. They talked amongst themselves,
a slow, hushed conversation that Fanny couldn't hear. Their
quiet chatter, the baby prams, the entire garden were
enveloped in the bright, benevolent light of the early morning,
which gave a golden hue to the handles of the prams and the
young mothers' ankles, and scattered golden or reddish glints
even in the darkest hair. Fanny leaned against the fence and

watched, but something in her remained detached, as if she couldn't remember what it was that had drawn her here in the first place, and after a moment she broke away from the fence and walked on. This park, this tranquil early-morning park, wasn't hers, and she too, so it seemed, was no longer the park's. This did not arouse any sorrow in her but only a flitting, curious puzzlement, which did not insist on an answer. One of the children shouted in his shrill bright voice, 'Uri!' and she started and looked back, but the child they had called for had red hair and a grimy spade and was a complete stranger to her, and she turned her back on him and walked briskly on to the bakery.

43

Now that she and Robert lived together, they didn't go out as much as they had in the early days. The days had become very hot too. At noon the beach was ablaze and the sand reflected the light like a molten mirror. And in the mornings they never managed to get up in time to catch the good hours, when the air was still fresh. They lay for a long time in bed, somnolent and lazy, slowly floating about in the warm pool of the sheets. Even after awakening they would sometimes be carried off by short, sudden slumbers, which sucked them in with a power they couldn't resist. They would read a little, talk, drink coffee in bed. Sometimes they made love in the mornings, drowsy, slow, lazy, optional love. Sometimes they would stop in the middle, sinking into a deep slow sleep which pulled them down, into flickering mercurial depths that were the direct sequel of their lovemaking and had the same quality. But mostly they made love at night, when they came back from the club. The show would infuse them with a high tension, a nervousness of the mind and body, and this was one of the best ways to dissolve it, perhaps the best way. Fanny sometimes wondered if Gina and Zorri also turned to each other immediately after coming back home, to the room on Hayarkon Street, falling upon each other with a desperate determination to get rid of themselves, to discharge the tremendous tension built up in them. Fanny found it very hard to imagine Zorri making love, indeed she found it hard to imagine him doing almost anything. He was too vague, impalpable, too little himself and always Gina's shadow, trailing after her everywhere, the echo to her commands, a cushioning for the inevitable moment when she fell. Who he really was, this she could not even guess. He was very young, she thought, and perhaps there was no other answer.

In contrast to him Robert seemed to be sketched in strong clear lines. But when she tried to capture him, like on a lit drawing-board, and trace his features with the point of a pencil, his sudden, loud laughter would contradict his shy, disarming smile on stage, and the things he said had the extraordinary quality that at the moment they were said, in the course of conversation, they were completely clear and comprehensible, but within a day, an hour, a few minutes even, they could envelop themselves in a kind of hazy halo which extended their meaning too much, and you had to try and re-extract the sense out of them. At times she thought that his essence was not in his feelings towards her, and it wasn't there that she should look for it, but in the things he said, and not necessarily to her – although he may have said more to her than he said to others – but also to Gina, to Mercedes the flamenco dancer, to Zorri; and there was something not quite comfortable about this thought, something she found very hard to live with. At times she felt, with a bitterness she could not suppress, that since he was a guide more than he was a lover, a mentor more than a companion, he could only love her a little more than he loved all the others, Gina, Zorri, Mercedes. Whoever loves everyone cannot love one person, she thought and tasted the insipid banality of that thought, at least not for long, not in the long run. This kind of love would confine him. And sometimes, when she woke up from these thoughts, they suddenly seemed to her utterly absurd, without foundation or context, and then she would wonder how she could have even thought them about this man standing in the spotlights in front of the audience, his silver rods flying around him on the force of his wonderful, disarming smile, or the one sitting across from her at the table toying with a glass of whisky in his hand, his eyebrows contracted and his forehead furrowed and lost and strange, or that man in the warmth of whose arms she curled up at night, after their bodies had relaxed into the crumpled sheets.

In the late afternoons they sometimes went to the beach. Now they talked less, read more and sometimes just lay and stared at the luminous azure paling towards evening. They found a café that played old songs from the fifties, Bing Crosby and Harry Belafonte and Sinatra and the Golden Gate, and they sprawled on the warm sand next to it and hummed the lines they remembered. After they went a few times they grew familiar with the cassette, which was always the same one and when it ended it was played again from the beginning, but only till sundown. Immediately after the sun had set the music would stop and the waitress would bring the customers their bills, and by the time darkness fell the plastic chairs would be taken inside and arranged upside-down on the tables and the door would be locked. It took them a while to realize that it was always the same cassette because they never arrived at exactly the same hour, but after having heard it a few times they already knew it by heart and knew which song would come next once the previous one was over. But in this very repetition there was something Fanny loved, perhaps the sense of security one derives from something familiar and dear which never varies, and if they grew a little tired of the songs they'd go for a few days to another beach, and when they returned they were always glad to hear them again, like an old acquaintance you're always happy to see, even though he has nothing new to tell you.

The new days were not like the old days, the early days, and surely this was only natural, but the problem was that they so quickly changed and turned from old to new. One didn't have the time to live them and already they were replaced, already they were transformed into new, other days, with the longing gnawing at their core.

And perhaps the problem was this, that once what loomed on the horizon was no longer the thing itself, the wondrous,

319

too-immense-to-contain possibility: to be together; once what loomed on the horizon was in fact the end — even if distant, even if necessary and unavoidable — once it appeared there as a small speck, it began eating into it, into the horizon, like a tiny black patch of rot spreading inside an apple, and soon you could no longer distinguish between the flesh of the apple and the rot, between their belonging and the want.

It was his going away which changed the quality of their belonging and changed it in a way which was impossible to fight, except perhaps during those few moments in which you could close the eye which turned inwards and simply be together, laugh, drink your cup of coffee and eat your croissant, drive to Jaffa with your head out of the window in the hot night wind of the *hamseen*; but then after a minute, maybe two, the knowledge of the departure would surface again, forcibly stick its head out from under the whirl of happiness and spoil everything. Its arrival was always heralded by a kind of shiver which suddenly passed through her, and she would all at once become much heavier, very heavy, and helpless. Her body temperature as well seemed to change, falling steeply, and the ebullience she tried to hold on to required a great effort. And yet she so wanted to remain gay, gay and careless, so that she could go on laughing with him, drink her coffee, fly with him on the wind; but it was beyond her power. She was heavy, so heavy during these moments, as if she had weights tied to her ankles, and how could she soar up and fly in the air? Her very wanting, she told herself, the wishing, the yearning, foiled the attempt before it began. The moment you yearn for something, it's no longer within your reach. And therefore, at a certain moment, she gave up. She stopped yearning because that was the most painful of all, and made do with those days and hours and minutes which were hers by right, and could be relied upon to stay in their place and not fly off and vanish at the blink of an eye. And from that moment on she felt easier. The heavy weight seemed to have been lifted, and she could breathe again. Her laughter was no longer forced, even though it was rarer. Once she stopped craving what she could not have, she could at least live wholly with what she did have: those days and hours and minutes which lay between now, between the piece of horizon in which she dwelt with Robert, the messy living room and the silver rods and the red and white balls on the chest of drawers, and that other scrap of horizon, still distant, but just as certain.

But she didn't always succeed. Sometimes, when his gaze strayed, and she felt, whether rightly or not, that he was wandering in foreign, faraway places, places she would never be in, or vice versa, when he was completely absorbed in the present, laughing over a plate of hummus in a small café on Yefet Street, she would be filled with that same sudden red rage and say or do things she would have never believed she would do or say, even within the walls of her own home, let alone in public.

'She didn't mean anything,' said Robert, watching the girl in the tight black dress who was walking away from them, her back held wrathfully erect. On his lips hovered a small, indefinite smile.

'Oh yes she did,' said Fanny. Her mouth was tight and she emptied the rest of her drink in one gulp. Robert looked at her. She couldn't decide whether this look meant to assess her, or to confirm what he already knew. Finally he leaned over across the table and looked straight into her face. 'You've changed a lot, my little Fanny,' he said, whether on a note of irony or of surprise she couldn't tell. 'Yes,' she said and signalled the waiter to bring her another drink.

'And are you happy about it?'

Fanny reflected for a moment. The girl in the black dress, who worked in one of the bars near the club, had come over to them while they were having something to eat before the show. She knew Robert from his previous visits to Israel, so it turned out, and now she fell on him with cries of joy and excitement, completely ignoring his companion. The stools on which they sat were low straw affairs and the girl stood right over Fanny, dwarfing her with her long figure and her high heels. The hem of the tight black evening dress, which made her even taller, fluttered over Fanny's knees as if she wasn't there.

'Robert, darling,' she cried, 'I haven't seen you for ages. Where did you crawl out from?'

'The waves,' said Robert and grinned at her.

'I swear I've missed you. Jaffa's not the same without you,' the girl said.

'Jaffa's always the same,' Robert said. 'Every time I come back here I'm amazed to see how nothing has changed.'

'No, that's not true. It'll never be like in the good old days,' the girl said, and Fanny wondered whether the good old days were the same as the good old days with Gina, or whether, at least, he hadn't slept with this one. Then she realized how far she had gone with this thought and all at once the scorching red anger welled up in her again.

'Everyone thinks that when they came to Jaffa for the first time, or anywhere actually, then was the best of times. I'm sure Fanny too will think five years from now that these were the good old days which'll never return,' said Robert.

The girl gave Fanny a brief glance, as if noticing for the first time that someone was sitting on the stool below. 'Oh, her,' she said and immediately returned her gaze to Robert.

'Yes, her,' Fanny said, gritting her teeth. 'The one whose foot you're stepping on.'

The girl started and moved her foot. It seemed that the pent-up rage in Fanny's voice had managed to penetrate even her thick skin.

'You're with Albaz again?' she asked Robert, and he nodded. 'I'll come and see you. Maybe we can go and have a drink sometime, for old times' sake.'

With a sudden motion Fanny got up to her feet, forcing the girl to step back so as not to fall. 'Robert now has some new times', she said, 'as you've already heard, and he has no need to celebrate what used to be. Unlike what you think', she said and raised her voice, flinging her privacy and her manners to the devil, 'these are the good times for Robert and before it was barely even so-so.' She picked up her glass and took a long sip a few inches away from the face of the girl, who stood riveted to her place, staring in astonishment.

After a minute, when she had recovered, she said, '*W'allah*. I see you have a good watchdog, Robert. But its teeth are about to fall out, maybe you should look for something more stylish. You used to have good taste. Pity,' she said and thrust out her chin right in Fanny's face. She has nerve, Fanny admitted to herself, but then the wave of anger swept over her again and she snapped, 'My teeth are still good enough to take off some of your make-up. You'd better clear out, otherwise people might see what you've got underneath.' The girl gave her another astonished look, and when she saw in Fanny's face that she was quite capable of carrying out her threat, she straightened up contemptuously and turned away, muttering, 'What a screwball' in a loud enough voice so that the rest of the customers in the café could hear. Only then did Fanny sit down again in her chair.

Now she looked back at Robert again and said, 'Quite.'

'I think you're right,' said Robert thoughtfully, and smiled at her, but this time his smile had more admiration than amusement in it. 'Although I sometimes miss the Fanny who's melting away. I mean, the Fanny you were when I met you.'

'I don't,' said Fanny determinedly. But her answer was thrown out automatically, less upon reflection than in order to repulse an attack, and she immediately felt a reverberation of regret deep inside her, an echo of longing for the lost Fanny. 'In any case, there's no changing it now,' she said.

'No. There's no way back,' said Robert and bared a set of menacing teeth at her and she burst out laughing. Then they quickly asked for the bill and left because Robert was due on stage.

44

Despite Fanny's persistent refusal to respond in kind with the same candour with which Margie had laid before her her own relationship with Yosef, there had been a certain warming up on Margie's part since Fanny began living with Robert. She phoned more frequently, and every once in a while they would meet in a café in the afternoon when Yosef was at work. The pattern of these conversations was quite uniform: Margie would interrogate Fanny on the state of affairs between her and Robert, and Fanny would say what she could, and the rest of the time she kept silent. This silence of hers, however, did not particularly hinder the conversation, since in any case Margie at some point would abandon Fanny's business, which though most interesting was still Fanny's and not her own, and plunge into a brilliant, one-sided analysis of her own marriage. Nevertheless, she usually managed up to that point to tell Fanny quite a few things. She was especially perplexed and even angry at Fanny for not pressing Robert to marry her. This is your last chance, she once said to Fanny bluntly, when the latter's silence had finally got to her. This is your last chance and you won't have another one and you can't afford to miss it. I didn't miss it, said Fanny and blushed. Margie grew even angrier. That's not what I meant, dummy. You could have had that a long time ago if you weren't such a fool. I'm talking about a home, security, a good life . . . That wasn't what I meant either, said Fanny, and Margie waved her hand as if washing it of the whole affair and went on to talk about last Tuesday when Yosef stayed late at work again, although he had promised to come home early and although they had made plans to go and see some friends. The education of Yosef was not yet complete, but, so she told Fanny with tightly pressed lips against which Yosef stood no chance, he would learn, even if it took her an entire lifetime.

Another time she said to Fanny: Well, you talk so much about this Piaf of yours. Edith Piaf also got married at forty-six to a guy twenty-one years younger than her. You told me so yourself. Yes, said Fanny, but I'm not Piaf.

And that was the simple truth. It was so true that even Margie had nothing more to say, and she looked at her with a puzzled face, vacillating between condemnation and consent, and finally asked her if she could lend her her red suit for Friday night.

Fanny knew what Margie couldn't understand, whether because it was outside the realm of her experience or because it was outside the realm of those things she was willing to admit, and that was that no effort she made could sway Robert to stay even one day more than he would have stayed anyway. And not because he didn't love her, but because such was his love and you couldn't expect it to be other than it was or expect Robert not to be Robert. And after all she loved him precisely because he was Robert and not someone else. But in any case she wouldn't have tried to convince him to stay, not even if it broke her heart. The way she behaved was the only reasonable way as far as she was concerned, and the only way that enabled her to live without the pain taking over completely. But those things she couldn't say to Margie. She could hardly say them to herself.

Before they parted, Margie invited her to a house-warming party in her renovated flat for the following Friday, the first Friday in October. The party had been postponed for so long, she explained, because she had wanted the house to be perfect down to the very last detail, but now she was ready. Even if the queen of England decided to make an impromptu visit, she, Margie, would have nothing to be ashamed of.

'We finish late,' said Fanny. 'Especially on Fridays.'

'That doesn't matter,' said Margie. 'It's all right. No decent party in this town starts before midnight anyway.'

'Then we'll be there, sure,' said Fanny. 'Do you want me to help you with anything? Shall I bake a cake?'

But Margie rejected her offer with a wave of her hand. The era of the cheesecrumb cakes and home-made casseroles was over, she intended to get a cook and let someone else break their head over the food. The less she did now, she explained with a sly smile, the less she aspired to do. Margie had left her job at Frankfurter & Co. and hadn't looked for another. She had worked hard enough, so she said, for the rest of her life, and now she was certainly not going to clean house and cook, and work at some office on top of that. She wanted to be pretty for Yosef, she said, when he came home, to drag him to the theatre and to the cinema and to dances. That's what he married her for. And as always, Fanny realized on second thought, she was right.

Margie's flat had one-and-a-half bedrooms, but she managed, with clever and efficient design, to make it look much more spacious. At first she had thought of moving to a bigger place, she explained, her face flushed with enthusiasm and pride, still panting from the dance she had been in the middle of when Fanny and Robert arrived, but flats were so expensive now, and in the end she decided that actually hers was exactly what they needed; after all, they weren't going to have any children. At these last words Fanny thought she saw Yosef's large face fall behind the cover of his thick beard, but he turned his head and she was no longer sure of what she had seen. 'It's really beautiful, Margie,' she said sincerely. 'Well done. Did you plan the changes yourself?' She didn't just do the planning, said Yosef, she was everything – the architect, the contractor, the work manager and sometimes even the hired hand, he added jokingly and put his arm with clumsy pride around Margie's shoulder. Something caught in Fanny's throat and she turned away quickly and admired the new closet in the bedroom, which they now entered. It too was custom-built, to precise measurements, explained Margie, who had freed herself from Yosef's embrace in order to show her how efficiently she had divided the hangers and the shelves in the closet. Finally they returned to where the party was.

The large room was dim, except for a few standing lamps covered with red and orange lampshades which cast light in the corners. The music was, to Fanny's surprise, not modern pop, but rather music from the previous decade and even older tunes, tangos and waltzes and foxtrots, which had been popular when Margie and she were teenagers. Margie sensed Fanny's surprise and said in a slightly defiant tone, 'Beatles-shmeetles, that's good for singles' parties. Now we need music for married couples.' Then she realized that perhaps this wasn't the right thing to say and cut herself short, but Fanny said quickly, 'Quite right', and immediately asked where she got those lamps in the corners. 'You're not going to believe this,' said Margie. 'These are ours from home.' – 'From home?' asked Fanny, confused. 'From Bratislava. You're not going to believe this. We went on our honeymoon, Yosef and I –'. 'But you went to Italy,' interposed Fanny, who was growing quite dizzy. 'Yes. And after that we went to Vienna. And at the end of the trip I said to Yosef, let's take a train and cross the border to Bratislava. Who knows if a year from now it will still be possible to get in. I haven't been there since the war, I want to see what it's like today. Yosef didn't really want to, but', here she smiled and rubbed the back of Yosef's neck, the way you'd scratch the neck of some big good-natured beast, 'eventually he gave in. Anyway, when we arrived at Bratislava I said to Yosef, I have to get into our flat. But he absolutely refused to come with me. That's as far as I'm going, he told me. So I went on my own. Yosef went to the Technological Museum, and I', Margie gave a cheeky metallic laugh, 'went home. And what do you think was the first thing I saw? Our lamps. The lamp that stood in my dad's study, and my mom's lamp, which stood in the living room. They never sat under the other's lamp. Well, I turned really pale, all the blood must have drained out of my face, and this lady who let me in, not that she wanted to, she got really frightened, and I said to her: "Frau Klinger," I said to her, "Frau Klinger, these are my lamps." And what do you think she said? "Take them," she said. Anything to get me out of there. And just as I stood there, in my light beige suit with my suede handbag, I picked up these two lamps, one in each hand, and left. This woman was so glad to shut the door behind me, you've never seen anything like it. To cut a long story short,' continued Margie in the same breath, 'I arrived at the hotel with these two lamps, one in each hand, like I told you, and my suit was no longer what it had been in the morning, and the handbag also had a big black stain on it, this woman didn't even polish them, can you imagine, and when I think of how hard my mom and Dutzi used to work on these lamps – anyway, Yosef was shocked. He thought I'd bought them somewhere. He was sure I'd lost my mind, otherwise why would anybody go and buy a five-foot standard lamp on a trip abroad, and not just one lamp but two. When I told him the whole story he himself turned completely pale, you should have seen him. "They can arrest you for a thing like that," he told me, and I said to him, "Arrest me? Me? These are my lamps, mine from home, my mom bought them at Kohn & Michler's and I can even remember exactly when, when I was eight and we moved to the new flat. If they'd arrested anyone it would have been her! She's the one they'd have arrested, and she knew it perfectly well. She knew all I had to do was go to the police and say that woman was holding on to Jewish property, and she was glad to get out of it so cheaply, believe me." So that's it,' concluded Margie abruptly and pulled the embarrassed Yosef into the throng of dancing couples, 'that's how I have those lamps. To tell you the truth,' she threw over her shoulder before they started moving toward the balcony, 'I knew it would be no use going to the authorities. That woman would have probably produced some documents to show that she got the flat legally, and how can you prove otherwise? And the reparation payments I get anyway. So I knew that I really had nothing to complain about. But I wanted those lamps,' she called above the heads of the couple who were dancing between them and Fanny, 'and I got them.'

Fanny looked at Margie's blonde head whirling towards the balcony, glowing in the electric light of the flat across the yard. This wonderful power that Margie had, simply to stretch out her hand and take what she wanted and never let go, filled her with admiration. She, Fanny, would probably have never dared to ask to see her parents' apartment, and if she had it would have never entered her mind to demand the old furniture back, although just the thought of it had filled her with a dull pain ever since Margie had started telling her story. And perhaps not. Perhaps the new Fanny would have gone there, would have demanded what was hers. In any case, she reflected, she was glad she hadn't found herself in that situation. Nor did she have any desire to go back to Germany, even for a short trip, no desire at all.

The tango ended and was replaced by a cha-cha, the couples separated and started swaying opposite each other, and Fanny, executing the right movements and blessing the dance lessons she received when she was twelve, was again reminded of Herr Weinert, who had not only been the tennis instructor but the dancing teacher as well, and for a moment she wondered whether he had guessed at the reason for her clumsiness during the lessons, or whether he simply thought that she had been born without a sense of rhythm. Then she stopped thinking about the dancing lessons and furtively surveyed the other guests. You can't introduce people when it's dark and everybody's dancing, Margie had said when they came in, we'll do it next time, and Fanny nodded and felt relieved to be spared this embarrassing stage of the evening. The women were about Fanny's age and the men mostly a bit older, around fifty, she estimated. The women were probably Margie's friends and the men – appendices. Margie hadn't dragged into her married life even one of her former suitors. 'A rule of thumb, mind you,' she told Fanny after returning from her honeymoon, 'if you don't want to ruin your marriage even before it starts.' The cha-cha was replaced by a slow English waltz, and the couples embraced again. They all seemed well used to each other, as if they had held each other through kilometres of tangos, as if they had already bent the slow dance to their needs and adapted the rhythm of their movements to their partner's body, the hand already finding its right place, the foot moving with almost automatic certainty, knowing that it won't be stepped on, or nimbly circumventing the danger zones which it foresaw in advance. Everything was so habitual, familiar and expected, thought Fanny, and for some reason just as she thought of that word, habitual, warm tears welled up in her eyes and she couldn't stop them, a kind of sudden flood, and she let them flow and only hoped that her mascara wasn't running and that Robert wouldn't notice, for what could she tell him when she herself didn't know whether she was crying because of those damn lamps or because of the couples who moved next to them, dark double-headed figures, and especially Margie and Yosef, whom she could see circling in the corner of the room, Margie's blonde head resting on Yosef's shoulder in that uncomfortable way in which tall women rest their heads on the shoulders of men who are much shorter than they are.

45

'You're nothing but a stinking snob,' said Gina.

Fanny reddened and said nothing.

'Why not? Why would you refuse if Albaz asked you?' Gina attacked. 'You really think it's worse than what you're doing?'

'Yes,' said Fanny. The big stripper's wrath frightened her, but in this matter she found it hard to lie.

'How?' demanded Gina.

'I like what I sing,' said Fanny.

'And me?'

Fanny shrugged.

'No, go on, say it, don't be shy. What about me?'

'You're selling them what they want to see. Regardless of what you want. Or like.'

'And you don't.'

'No,' said Fanny, 'I give what I want to give.'

'You really think I mind showing them my arse?'

'No,' said Fanny, 'but your job is to make them think that you're just dying to show them your arse, or that you're really terribly ashamed to show it to them but can't resist the temptation, depending on the show. In any case it has nothing to do with what you really feel. Or don't feel.'

'You nitwit, if I stripped the way I felt they wouldn't even throw me a worn penny,' said the stripper.

'That's exactly what I mean,' said Fanny.

'You don't get it,' insisted the stripper, bending her body forward at a dangerous angle. 'It's their dream. Wet, not wet, what's the difference? They want to see it live before their eyes, to finally see this woman do exactly what they want her to do. Why should I mind selling it to them?'

'Because it's their dream not yours,' said Fanny and Gina puffed her lips dismissively and went back to looking in the mirror. Suddenly she turned to Fanny again.

'And if they told you to sing Arab music, would you?'

'There's some Arab music I really like,' said Fanny and thought of the boy in the red restaurant.

'And if they asked you to sing bad music, the shittiest you know?'

Fanny hesitated. Then she said determinedly, even though she wasn't quite sure of her answer, 'I wouldn't.'

Gina snorted with contempt. Spatterings of spit flew up, propelled by the mighty blast and landed on Fanny's dressing table. 'Bullshit. You talk like that because you don't need money. You have your nice little account in the bank and probably all kinds of savings plans and pension funds and God knows what else.'

'I didn't have anything in the bank when I came to work here,' said Fanny. 'I've eaten up all my compensation money. I only have the pension left.'

'Only the pension,' mimicked Gina with real rage, 'and that's what you think I'm talking about. No, honey. You've never really needed money in your life, so bad that you knew you'd swell up with hunger if you didn't work. So bad that you picked up cigarette butts on the street just so's to have something to smoke. If you knew what it's like to rummage through the rubbish bins near a school, to see maybe somebody's thrown a half-eaten sandwich there, you'd talk differently.'

'Maybe,' said Fanny.

Gina snorted again. 'No maybe about it,' she said. 'You don't know from nothin'. Let me ask you this: if Robert was lying sick and you had no money for food and medicine, wouldn't you sing trash songs in the lousiest bar in town and turn tricks on the side to boot?'

'I'd sing,' said Fanny.

Gina waved her hand in a gesture of scorn. 'Oh yes, you'd

332

sing,' she said. 'And you'd do more than that.' To Fanny's relief she finally fell silent, finished cleaning her neck and chest and with a violent motion flung the dirty cotton wool ball into the waste basket.

She's right, thought Fanny, but nonetheless knew that she herself was also right. She thought about the show at Zanzibar: cheats, Gina had called them. And it was true, they cheated, they made the men feel like they were getting something when they weren't, when in fact they were being made fools of and degraded. Gina did an honest job, she supplied the package of illusion paid for by the customer in full, but was it really so essentially different? Ultimately, the name of the game was the same –

'And what do you think all women do?' erupted Gina anew. Her face was smeared with cream, and only one eye peered, wide open and terrifying, out of the white sea of her face. 'You think I don't see all these women sitting in the audience? The only difference is that I take ten minutes to take off my clothes and they drag it out for a week, a month, a year – what do I know? – lead him by the nose step by step until he finds himself buying the ring. And it doesn't end there either.'

'That's just talk, Gina,' said Fanny. 'Who goes to bed only after the wedding nowadays? Not even me.'

'You,' said Gina and the contempt in her voice was lumpy and heavy. 'You're not an example of anything. You're weird. That's what you are.'

The pain reverberated inside Fanny's body like a bell in a closed space. This was a direct hit, even though for once she didn't even suspect Gina of aiming at the spot she'd struck. How could she have known. She certainly hadn't had the chance to talk to Fräulein Neuerbach, who for many years now wasn't among the living.

'And what do you think happens at home?' continued Gina, her voice thick with rancour. 'What do you think happens there? The man wants her to be Gilla in the kitchen, and in bed – Gina. It doesn't matter if that night in bed she's feeling

333

Gilla and tomorrow after the beach — Gina. You think anybody's asking her?' She raised her voice in a coy trill, a cruel imitation of Fanny's earlier tone, '"Who exactly do you feel like now, honey?" No one's asking her. *She* has to ask herself: Who d'you want me to be now, honey? And be that. She can't even ask him, for God's sake. She has to guess, otherwise it's not *sexy*.' That last word was uttered with such tremendous contempt that it bordered on hatred. 'Otherwise it's against the rules of the game. It's a guessing game, honey, and if you don't hit bull's eye you can only lose, take Gina's word for it.

'So I'm through with all that, honey. I only deal with this rubbish on stage, and when I get off — *finito*. I do exactly what I want. Exactly the way I feel, you hear me, I, not anybody else. And nobody tells me how to feel and what to do. Nobody, get it? And you're telling me that I'm not good enough.'

'I didn't say —' Fanny tried to cut in.

'You didn't say, but you thought so, honey. I can see right into your brain.' And Gina stuck her face into the mirror, dismissing with her broad back both Fanny's existence and anything else she had to say.

It's no use continuing this argument, thought Fanny as she spread the make-up on her face with automatic motions. After all, what did she know? Maybe Gina was right. At any rate, she was right about one thing: there was a game, a great game in which everyone participated, and the only one not to know of its existence was her, Fanny. That's why she always lost. And that's also why, sooner or later, she had always felt — with Nathan, with Ritzi, with all the others — that feeling she could never explain to herself, a feeling of helplessness and confusion, like an actress on stage who didn't know what part she was supposed to play. The only one who hadn't required it of her was Robert, but Robert worked behind the scenes of the open-dream market, and every night, night after night *ad nauseam,* he watched this game in its rawest, crudest version.

334

Behind the scenes the trees and the clouds were brush strokes on plywood, there wasn't enough distance for perspective to deceive you. Pay me and I'll play for you, that was the name of the game here, and was it a worse game than love me and I'll play for you.

She started at the sound of a sudden bang. Gina had slammed her table drawer shut. 'I'm off,' she said in a savage voice. 'And don't you fool yourself. Here everything's the same. Exactly the same. And you're not one bit better than I am.'

46

The next day Fanny realized that her period was three days
late. She always used to mark the expected day on the
illustrated calendar on the kitchen wall to avoid any unpleasantness, but this time she forgot even to look, and when she
glanced at it that morning, still only half-awake, her heart
missed a beat as she saw that the earmarked day had already
crawled three days back.

Her thoughts ran riot in all directions. One said right away:
This should be taken care of. It was the automatic reaction of
her strong practical side. The second one said: Don't even
think about it, it's all because of the excitement of the last few
days, it'll pass. The third was hazier, and that one she refused
even to touch. Finally she didn't know what to do with this
discovery and therefore, after that initial moment, she pushed
it aside. She was going to meet Gina at noon at the Karmel
open-air market, to buy cheap fruit and vegetables, and by
now she knew Gina well enough to know that yesterday's
argument would have no effect on today's outing, and would
probably not even be mentioned, as if it had never happened.

Before she met Gina, Fanny had hated going to the *souk*. Its
vividness could not disguise the only half-concealed climate of
violence which she always felt she was walking through, like
through highly compressed air. The cheapest stalls were the
ones at the rear of the market, and whenever she went there
she felt hemmed in by the barrage of cries, as if the stall owners
were actually pushing her, felt their insistent demands striking
at her with waves of unprocessed resentment which hung in
the air, muddying the light of summer, pulling on the hem of

her clothes like an importunate cur. She always felt guilty for not responding to the offers flung at her from all directions. At least take a look, lady, they shouted, why are you walking by without even looking? We have the best and cheapest merchandise, lady, look at her walking with her nose in the air. Even the exaggerated welcome she received at the regular stall where she used to do her shopping couldn't make up for the violence she had to submit to on her way there. On the contrary, in some strange way it only added to it, as if it were merely the same thing in reverse.

When she went there with Gina it was altogether different, as if Gina, through her own belonging, made a place there for her as well. It could be that all this was merely in her imagination, or perhaps the tension just eased naturally in Gina's company, but it seemed to her that not so many harpoons of resentment were hurled from the stalls when she walked beside her, and those that were, were no longer aimed at her, at Fanny–who–was–with–Gina, but at other people, even more out of place in that setting than she was.

Still for a moment she felt apprehensive as she got off the minibus at the entrance to the *souk* and looked at the crowd of people streaming back and forth, until she saw Gina standing in front of the spice shop on the corner, where they had arranged to meet. When Fanny touched her arm she turned from the window and said, 'I might buy a packet of henna. They have good henna here. I'm sick of this blonde.'

Fanny laughed. 'What about the blue?'

Gina grinned back at her. 'Next time.' She looked again at the shop window and then turned away and said, 'No, I'll wait a bit longer. In any case I have to stay like this till the end of the season. It's always better to buy it as fresh as possible.'

They started to walk between the stalls of merchandise, colourful panties piled in heaps and decorated combs and T-shirts with inscriptions printed on them in large letters, between the pyramids of avocados and trapezoids of water-melons and towers of sweets arranged vertically in straight unbroken lines, and Gina said, 'Ah, sesame biscuits. I've been looking for these for ages. They're great when you have people over,' and then she turned to Fanny and said, 'Listen, I just remembered. We thought, I mean the girls and me, all of us, of inviting you and Robert over on Sunday evening for a special dinner. A kind of farewell dinner.' Fanny looked at her uncomprehendingly. 'It's only two weeks before Robert leaves, and we didn't want to do it at the last minute. In any case I wanted to ask you first, maybe you don't even feel like it. Maybe there's something better you want to do on your free night.'

Fanny was still looking at her, although the incomprehension was already gone, and in its place came a kind of numbness which blurred the straight lines of the wooden stalls and the beautiful gaudy mosaic of the fruit piles. Gina gave her a sharp look. 'You knew he was leaving, right?' Fanny nodded with the same obtuse numbness. 'A long time ago,' she said. 'Do you think they have strawberries yet?'

Gina kept looking at her with the same piercing gaze. Then she shook her head and said, 'Are you nuts? Strawberries are only in the spring,' and continued to walk down the market, her tall figure standing out in the crowd like a knight in a shiny helmet, arrayed in an armour of flowery dyolene.

When she returned home she handed the bags to Robert, who scolded her for going to the market on her own again. 'I went with Gina,' she said absent-mindedly, and he glanced at her and lowered his eyes and then looked at her again and said, 'I'm sorry. I meant to tell you tonight.'

'Gina wants to invite us for a farewell dinner on Sunday night,' said Fanny. The fruit and vegetables sat at the bottom of the shopping bags in a kind of curious equilibrium, stiff and upright, irritating her eyes, and she wanted to go over and empty them, but did not move.

Robert kept silent for a moment. He started to say

something and then changed his mind and said instead, 'Do you want to go?'

'Why not?' said Fanny. Something came undone in her and she could finally go over to the bags and begin taking out the avocados and peaches and arrange the fruit on the table. With two steps Robert overtook her and caught her by the shoulders and shook her. 'Stop that,' he said. Fanny had never heard him speak like that, his voice flat and without its characteristic clear ring, almost the voice of a stranger. She turned to him and said, trying to look him in the face, 'It's all right. I knew you were going.'

'It's not all right, damn it,' said Robert. 'Stop it.'

Only then was she able to look straight at him, but only for a moment, and even then she could only see him as a blur, the way the people had looked to her when she was a small child and played at squinting at the world through the green glass of a bottle.

47

On Sunday afternoon the first rain fell. It came early this year, and Fanny looked at it, fascinated, through the kitchen window. For some reason the first rain was always unexpected, always aroused wonder, as if each year anew she grew used to the thought that nothing else was possible but this summer, the dust rising from the vacant lot at the end of the street, the lolly wrappings strewn along the pavement. The sound of the large drops drumming on the ground came each year as a kind of renewed surprise, something impossible which took shape again every year, a miracle you didn't know whether to be glad about or not.

Robert raised his head like a horse sniffing water. 'Rain,' he said.

'Yes,' said Fanny. Stupidly, any such thing, any change, immediately seemed to her a sign, if not a pretext, a reminder to him that he had to go, as if the date was not already set and known.

'What do you do here on rainy days?' asked Robert. 'I've never been here in winter. For me it's a country where there's only summer. Sun and dust.'

Fanny smiled with an effort. In the last few days her system had started to crumble, too many holes had worn through it, moments in which the decision to give up in advance anything outside the realm of the possible didn't work, or wasn't enough, or wasn't even relevant any more. Only the pain held fast.

'You light the stove. You drink a lot of tea, or cocoa. Aunt Leda bakes an apple cake.' She looked outside. The big drops – the first rain always had large, heavy drops, spread wide apart –

hit the pavement with a cushioned sound, raising light, almost invisible clouds of dust. 'But winter is still far off.'

'How can you tell?' asked Robert. 'I mean, when do you decide that it's actually winter and you have to drink cocoa?'

'By the poinciana,' said Fanny. 'Every year at the beginning of December, no matter if it's a cold year or an especially warm one, even if it's still hot outside and everybody's going to the beach, it begins to shed its leaves, and around the middle of December it's already completely naked. Then I know that winter has begun. By the bare branches of the poinciana against the grey concrete of the house across the street, when I wake up in the morning.

'There's something amazing about it,' she added, looking at the tree's foliage, delicate and finely drawn like the lines on one's palm. 'It has its own seasons, a sort of inner rhythm which is completely its own, and whatever goes on outside doesn't matter to it at all. Year after year, always at the same time, if I checked I'd probably find it was on the same date exactly, sometime between the middle and the end of December.'

'Is that why you sit so much on the balcony?' asked Robert.

'I like looking at it,' said Fanny. Then she thought this might not be much of an explanation and added, 'It's reassuring, somehow. Even when it looks quite dead, when it's completely bare and grey, you know that in May it'll start growing new leaves at a dizzying speed, in two, three weeks the tree will be covered with a pale green foliage, as soft as fluff, and a fortnight later it'll erupt in a wild flowering the colour of flame. And it's even more strange, because the other poincianas on the street don't bloom at the same time at all. The tree on Shimon Hatarsy Street, for example, I always see it when I come from that direction, remains in bloom weeks after mine has already shed its flowers. Whenever I pass by there in July I'm filled with envy, but that's because its flowering comes much later. Each tree has its own private rhythm, and that's the only thing it obeys. What happens with the other trees, or with the weather, doesn't interest it at all.'

'And that's why you sit and look at the poinciana,' said Robert and looked at her face.

'Yes,' said Fanny. 'I'd like to be like it.'

Robert leaned forward and took both her hands in his.

'You are like it,' he said, 'you know. Without even trying.'

Fanny shrugged. 'I don't feel that way,' she said. Otherwise I wouldn't mind so much that you're going away, she wanted to add, but knew it was pointless and gave up in advance, as usual.

Robert leaned closer. 'Don't worry,' he said. The tone of his voice was different than usual, strained. 'You'll pull through. I know you.' And your kind, she wanted to fling back, but there was no use in bringing up that sort of accusation, and it wasn't fair either. And so she kept silent.

'Don't worry,' repeated Robert, his voice even more strained, as if he was trying to appease her about something that had not even been said, but around which in fact this whole conversation revolved, even though it always remained concealed behind the words. 'The audience will continue to love you. You sing very beautifully. Really. Almost like Piaf.'

This was the first time he had ever said to her something that wasn't true and she felt almost as if he was trying to deceive her. She couldn't bear it, not that he would try to deceive her, or even smooth things over, disguise them, pretend that they were different from what they really were, because you only do that when things are not good enough as they are, and that was why she said in anger, almost in hatred, 'No one can sing like Piaf. No one.'

Robert recoiled as if her anger was a hand striking his face. 'All right,' he said. His voice was toneless. He stood up and went into the apartment, and Fanny was left alone on the balcony.

The leaves of the poinciana rustled in the wind, long, crinkly hands. The rain stopped, but it hadn't lasted long enough to wash the air thoroughly, and had left behind it only a faint smell of plants mixed with dust, which floated up from the street to the balcony. The poinciana leaves reached out to Fanny as if to take her hand, or at least caress it, brush it with their soft rustling touch, and she stretched out her hand and stroked one thin branch that grew into the balcony in absent-minded gratitude, the way you'd stroke an animal, or a child.

48

By evening the air still hadn't cleared. A halo of haze hovered around the streetlamps, and the same halo swathed and dimmed the moon. Fanny and Robert turned from Trumpeldor Street into Hayarkon. Fanny's high heels made walking difficult and every few steps she stumbled clumsily, almost twisting her ankle, and felt a stab of anxiety and anger. Robert held out his hand but she didn't take it. All this anger won't get you anywhere, she told herself, and remembered what her mother used to say on her rare fits of anger as a child: It will end in tears, Fanny. But although she recognized the distorted wish in herself to be hurt so she could hurt back, she could not control this desire, which was stronger than she was.

When Robert stopped in front of one of the buildings she paused for a moment, breathing in the night air, asking herself if it was possible for air to be too damp and too dry at the same time. With the deep breath her bad feelings dissolved, and she looked at Robert who was standing on the edge of the footpath, tall and thin as a streetlamp, his head flooded by the white light of a bulb on the ground-floor balcony, and remembered the night he had come into her dressing room after her first performance, and she smiled at him and took his hand. Then they turned on to the footpath and walked towards the entrance of the building.

Most of the paving stones on the path were broken and laid down at odd angles, and Fanny walked slowly, placing her feet with care. The building was one in a row of identical edifices built in grey concrete, the plaster on their walls irreparably cracked by the sea wind. Fanny knew these faded peeling buildings from the daytime, when she sometimes passed there on her way to the beach, but at night, in the electric light, their shabbiness was magnified until it became menacing, the holes gaping blackly and the embroidery of cracks spreading over the walls like a malignant disease.

The stairwell suffered the stamp of the same disease. An acrid smell of piss stood in it and the walls were stained and greasy-looking. Fanny hurried up the stairs behind Robert. She enjoyed watching his hips move inside his jeans, his slim back in the white shirt. She enjoyed thinking he was hers, even if only as a short-term loan, even if there were only eight days left of it. On the second floor Robert stopped and waited for her to reach him, then rang the bell. The door opened right away, almost as the bell sounded: they must have heard their steps on the stairs.

In contrast to the stairwell, the entrance and the living room behind it were clean and polished till the tiles shone, although the walls were bare and had almost no decoration. Fanny looked at the row of grinning faces before her and said, 'Hi, Gina. Zorri. Mercedes. Mackie, Reena. You too, Nino,' she said and pressed the monkey's soft paw and felt the strange rubbery touch sinking under her hand. 'Hello, Annette. Where's Jean-Pierre?'

'He'll be right out,' said Annette, giving Fanny a powerful handshake with her strong arm, which always had a sweatband wrapped around the wrist, to protect it from the cold. 'He's in the kitchen. Preparing his masterpiece. Don't go in there, he's got a huge knife.'

'What's she saying about me?' asked Jean-Pierre, peeping out of the kitchen with a massive butcher's knife in his hand.

'That you're as gentle as a lamb,' said Robert and shook Jean-Pierre's damp hand.

Jean-Pierre laughed. 'It's true,' he said, 'except in the kitchen. There I turn into a wild beast,' and he leaned over and gallantly kissed Fanny's hand, a whiff of spices and herbs drifting from his sleeves.

'Let's sit in the living room until Jean-Pierre's ready,' said Gina. 'You don't want to mess with him when he's cooking.'

Everyone crowded into the narrow corridor and Fanny and Robert remained last. After Mackie had also gone in and they were left alone, Robert held back and pressed her briefly, tightly, against his body. For another moment they remained like that, motionless, looking at each other as if struck by a sudden light, until finally Fanny said, 'We'd better go in. They're probably asking themselves what's happened to us.' Robert laughed. 'Don't worry, they know,' he said. His laughter had something very young, almost boyish about it, like a teenager caught with his girlfriend in the gym after class.

'The flat is so different from the outside,' said Fanny.

'Oh, yes,' said Robert. 'Gina is holding everyone on a very tight leash. She's kind of the Flat Elder here. A reign of terror.'

'Somehow I didn't think she'd care,' said Fanny.

'You're wrong,' said Robert. 'Gina hates dirt and disorder. She can't stand it. Everything has to be exactly in its place and arranged at right angles. She scrubs her room twice a week and makes the others work just as hard. The fact that her sweater and trousers are black doesn't mean she doesn't wash them every day.'

'You're right,' said Fanny. 'Gina at home is not the Gina at the club. When she gets her own flat, the one she's always dreaming of, she probably won't let anyone in without first taking off their shoes.' She hesitated. 'Shall we go in?'

'Yes,' said Robert and took her hand.

Most of the living room was filled by a massive, heavy wooden table covered by a white tablecloth. 'It can be extended on both sides,' said Gina proudly.

'It's huge,' said Fanny.

'When it's closed this table takes up less than half the space. I bought it at the flea market, for pennies,' said Gina. 'You learn something from Albaz, after eight years.' She bared her large nicotine-stained teeth.

346

All the chairs in the room, even the armchairs, were placed around the table.

'There's nowhere else to sit,' said Gina, 'so let's already take our places at the table. Maybe it'll make Pierre shake a leg.'

After they sat down an oppressive silence fell. Nino also sat on a chair, between Mackie and Reena, his back slightly bent and his long arms dangling loose at both sides of the chair, like a small child obliged to behave politely in the company of grown-ups. Fanny, listening to the silence, suddenly realized that this was the first time she'd been together with the club people on a social occasion, and from the others' silence she gathered that the situation was as strange to them as it was to her.

'So when's your flight, Robert?' Mackie asked in his rough voice, the voice of a man not used to talking. Everyone glanced furtively at Fanny, and after Robert answered, 'A week from Monday,' the silence grew even heavier. Fortunately, at that moment Jean-Pierre appeared, carrying high above his head, like a clown, a tray of hors-d'oeuvres, and his arrival broke the uncomfortable quiet.

'Enough with your games, let's get down to business,' cried Gina.

'This is a work of art, I demand some respect,' protested Jean-Pierre, but he lowered the tray and put it down on the table. A wonderful smell rose from the plates. 'Livers in Cognac and black pepper,' he announced, and nimbly began to distribute the plates around the table. Everyone bent over their food, and Jean-Pierre smiled at Fanny and signalled to her to start eating as well. The wrinkles in the corners of his eyes deepened, and for the first time Fanny realized that he was much older than he looked on stage. She lowered her gaze to her plate and began to eat.

Everyone took this activity very seriously. Therefore, until the plates were emptied, no one spoke a word and silence reigned around the table, but a different silence, one of concentrated animation. When they had all finished, Gina

347

heaved a big sigh. 'What can I tell you, Pierre?' she said. 'You have a big mouth, but you're a great cook.'

Annette flared up. 'Instead of saying thank you for such a meal, you have something bad to say,' she said. 'You yourself have a big mouth.'

Gina shrugged. 'I've never denied it,' she said without excitement. Annette, her eyes still flashing, was about to go on, but then Robert interfered. 'I have a big mouth too,' he announced. 'Look,' and he opened it to an inordinate size and stuffed in a whole slice of bread without folding it. His face, Fanny discovered to her surprise, was marvellously flexible, a rubber face, and he could stretch it in almost any direction he wanted.

'*W'allah*, it's been years since I saw you do that,' said Gina, and her voice resonated with nostalgic affection. 'I already forgot. I swear, you should've been in the circus.'

'Isn't there one little liver more to throw inside?' asked Robert entreatingly and everyone laughed. The tension had dissolved and Jean-Pierre collected the plates and plunged back into the kitchen.

After the second course, a fine roast of veal in red wine accompanied by numerous glasses of Carmel Hock, faces were flushed and tempers inflamed. Everyone talked at the same time, loudly and enthusiastically, without listening to each other. Only the monkey sat in his place at the centre of the table, quietly excited, like a child who knows that he is only allowed there on sufferance, and that if he doesn't behave himself the grown-ups will slap his hand and send him away. He ate with short, urgent movements, each time snatching with his long nervous fingers one of the wedges of meat which Reena had sliced for him and immediately bringing it to his mouth and closing his lips over it. Then he chewed on it for a long time, thoroughly, his mouth tightly shut and his eyes darting around the room. His soft pink paw, furrowed in thin wrinkles, quivered with excitement, and every once in a while he couldn't restrain himself and tapped with his knife on the glass in front of him, drawing bright, clear, glassy sounds, which no one paid any attention to. Everyone leaned back in their seats. Gina opened the two top buttons of her blouse and let her enormous chest emerge. Mackie undid the button of his trousers, hastening to conceal the opening with his belt, a black leather belt resembling a snake.

'Why so shy, Mackie?' said Gina loudly. 'You've nothing to be ashamed of in front of us. We know the whole truth about you.'

'I certainly have nothing to be ashamed of in front of you,' Mackie shot back. His face was fiery from the wine and the heat that filled the room, and his hand, lying on the table, broad and pale and as if separate from his body at the end of his long thin arm, trembled. Reena looked at him worriedly. 'Don't start again,' she said in a low voice. Mackie's face ignited and his mouth opened to deliver an angry rejoinder, which would have probably put an end to the conversation if Zorri hadn't intervened this time. 'Tell me, Mackie, are you going back to Hulon when the season's over?' he asked. Mackie's face slowly regained its old colour. 'Sure,' he said curtly. 'What choice do we have? Not like this one,' he gestured towards Gina, who was watching him with a mocking smile. 'We're nobody's lackey.'

The old lightning struck again in Gina's eyes, the same one that Fanny had first seen at the restaurant in Hatikva. She leaned forward towards Mackie. 'It's not that you don't kiss ass,' she said with deceptive calm. 'You're just not very good. That's all. You're simply not good enough.'

Mackie's face flamed again. 'Look who's talking,' he flung at her. 'The big star. Gina Lulubrigida,' he imitated Greenspan's oily voice, just as Robert had done that night at Zanzibar but on a different, opposite note, 'direct from Rome.'

Gina still kept the same dangerous calm. 'At least I do my job properly,' she retaliated. 'You, you work with that monkey,' she pointed at Nino, 'so that everyone sees that you hate it. Dragging it from one end of the stage to the other as if you wanted to pull its arm out. Why don't you teach it to do something real?'

'Like what?' asked Mackie brutally. 'Strip?'

Gina's face was flooded all at once by a deep, frightening red, as if all the blood vessels in it had burst at the same moment. 'You — you shit,' she muttered in a low voice, looking straight into his eyes, 'you're the lowest thing I know.' Her voice caught and it was clear she could barely get the words out. Then, suddenly, as if to make up for the voice which refused to come, she shoved the table forward and up, hurtling in Mackie's direction everything it contained, the half-full plates, the glasses, all the dirty tableware. The remains of the veal flew up in a great arc. Mackie rose in his seat. His eyes blazed with a strange fire. 'Whore!' He gave a strange, hoarse cry and his long arms stretched out to take hold of her throat, but in an instant Robert and Jean-Pierre were at his side, and Zorri was holding Gina who thrashed against him, restraining her with suddenly powerful arms. The monkey chattered rapidly, emitting a series of high staccato clicks, and shrank in his chair as if he sensed the impending storm. He looked at the contracted, menacing faces, first at Mackie and then at Gina and then at Robert and Fanny and all the others, as if asking for help, and when it did not come he shrank even further into his seat and finally stretched his legs out and jumped from the chair and ran to the corner and crouched there, jabbering to himself with his face to the wall. Fanny wanted to go over to him and put her hand on his shoulder and soothe him, tell him that everything would be all right and they'd all soon calm down, but that would have been a ridiculous thing to do, and the ominous quiet that hung around the table numbed her as well. Nor did she believe the things she wanted to say to him. Gina was still thrashing in Zorri's arms. She butted her head into his chest and shoulders again and again until she finally dropped, like a large rag doll, against his body. Mackie had taken control of himself the moment he felt Robert and Jean-Pierre beside him. He pushed

Robert's hand aside and stood still and only his eyes continued to blaze, fixed on Gina.

In the stillness Jean-Pierre's voice could be heard lamenting, 'And I haven't even served the last course yet,' like a second theme played by the oboe, trailing, comic and absurd, after the main motif.

Fanny's eyes strayed around the room. Spatterings of wine sauce stained the chairs and walls, and even the white serviette Gina had spread over the radio. Shards of wine glasses littered the floor. The remains of the veal from the serving tray had landed on Robert's shirt, and he looked like someone returning from a bloodstained battlefield. Annette's mouth was open in a voiceless scream and only Jean-Pierre's face, covered as it was in sauce, seemed amused, a little aloof, as if untouched by all this mayhem which in a week he was going to leave behind.

Robert left Mackie's side and went into the bathroom. When he returned his white shirt was wet and semi-transparent, but it still showed some pinkish stains which, Fanny ascertained at a glance, would be impossible to remove. He came up to her. 'We'd better go,' he said in a low voice, and Fanny nodded mechanically. Suddenly Gina turned towards them. 'Running away, huh?' she flung at Robert, as if he alone was to blame for everything that had happened. 'Running away. We're not good enough for you, right – Mackie and me,' she said, as though the two of them had never been anything but the best of comrades, loyal allies in their campaign against him. 'We're not good enough for you. That's why you had to go and find her.' She gestured towards Fanny, 'This, this . . . *Fanny*,' she said, and the way she pronounced the word gave it a whole new meaning. 'I know what a Fanny is. A lady. In Polish. Or Panny, what's the difference,' she waved her hand without even glancing at Reena, who was trying to interject, 'I know that from the time I worked cleaning house. Before I got smart. Six years I did floors, you hear me?' she shot at Fanny. 'Six years. Since I was fifteen. For one Polish Fanny who used to tell me all the time in that sweet voice of hers,' Gina's voice suddenly became nauseatingly high and sweet, 'Not like that, Gilla. Gilla,' again her voice changed and was filled with fatuous despair, 'when will you finally learn how to work properly. I'll never make a proper person out of you, Gilla.' Her voice thickened into solid fury. 'But I learned. Oh yes I learned. I became a proper person. Gina,' she threw the name at Fanny's face in her new, full voice, resonating like a big copper bell.

Robert took a step forward, as if to shield Fanny. 'Stop it, Gina,' he said. 'Fanny's not to blame for all of this.'

'No?' countered Gina. 'What do I know? Maybe she is. Maybe it was her aunt. And if not, so what, they're all alike. All those Fannys,' she flung at her with loathing and Fanny shuddered at the hostility in her voice, which for the first time she heard aimed at her, straight at her.

'Stop it,' said Robert again and a note of impatience, or was it warning, crept into his voice. 'Fanny hasn't done anything to you, and don't lay it all on her. You're just looking for someone on whom to dump what's eating you up inside. All your life you've been looking.'

Gina stared at him. Her eyes bulged in their sockets, and for a moment it seemed that she was going to run amok again, but all at once, with her characteristic suddenness, her face changed. 'Maybe you're right,' she said in her regular voice. 'Sorry, Fanny,' she added casually, as if she had just happened to step on her foot. Fanny wanted to say that it was all right, that she understood, but couldn't utter a word and remained standing there, looking at her in silence. Robert gently pulled on her arm. 'Come on, let's go,' he said and turned her towards the door and they went out, into the smell of mildew and old trash hanging in the stairwell.

49

They walked for a long time before they found a cab. Fanny
sat in the corner of the seat, leaning back, and tried not to look
at the peeling façades of the houses they passed on the way. On
the radio the announcer was reading the news, but her voice
was too faint to be intelligible, and the driver, a big man
huddled inside his coat, whistled to himself softly. All the lights
were green and they drove without stopping until they
reached the corner of Kakal Avenue. There the lights changed
and they stood and waited. Suddenly Robert said, 'Actually,
take a right here. We've changed our minds, we have to go
somewhere else.' Fanny felt a momentary surprise, but it came
as if from a very distant place, from behind a screen, and did
not really touch her. She thought of Gina. Then she resolutely
shut her mind against the memory of Gina's face and no longer
thought of anything. The streets went past, large and gleaming
in the dark, and the streetlamps illuminated the black asphalt
and mainly themselves, casting no shadows. Soon she didn't
know where they were any more, but that too, strangely, was
unreal. Then the taxi turned into a side street and Robert
leaned forward and told the driver, 'Stop here.' He took
Fanny's hand and they climbed out.

For a moment they stood where they were without
moving, watching the shiny blot growing smaller down the
street, black on black. A cool wind blew, carrying the smell of
damp leaves and earth. The night was dark and very empty,
like a large wardrobe, and it had already left summer behind.
Sometimes you just can't stand this constant flow onward,
thought Fanny with the resentment of a child deprived of the
thing he most craves, always winter chasing summer and back

again, why can't you for once, only once, get what you want. 'You haven't told me yet what's here,' she said.

'You'll see in a minute,' said Robert. He started walking up the road. Only then Fanny saw that they were at the foot of a hill, quite a tall hill, whose outlines blurred into the darkness. She caught up with Robert and they walked side by side up the hill, their shoes making clear, separate raps on the empty road.

'Strange,' said Fanny, 'I didn't know there was such an elevation in Tel Aviv.'

'There isn't,' said Robert. 'This is already Ramat-Gan.'

They went on walking, silent now, along the road which climbed up the hill. It was a quiet residential street, with low houses on both sides. The hour was late and all the lights in the houses were out, except for those above the entrances, small bulbs whose weak yellow light only served to emphasize the darkness. It was strange to walk on an unfamiliar street at such an hour, almost like trespassing. On her own street she never felt that way, she always had in mind the house she would reach in a short while, in another few steps. Here she felt intensely the people sleeping, the darkened windows, the warm obscurity inside the houses, the sleepers' breaths. And for a moment it seemed that the night was a place one mustn't walk in, one was only allowed to stay in one's own home behind the pale shadow cast on the walls and sleep, pull the blanket up over one's head to be as sheltered as possible, and sleep. All of a sudden she was jealous of all these people sleeping in their beds protected by walls, blankets, the touch of another's flesh. And yet there was something sharp and invigorating about this climb up the hill. The wind sent a light, not unpleasant shiver along the exposed parts of the body, and everything on the bare nocturnal street was very distinct, despite the blackness: the contours of the houses, the little bulbs above the entrances, a tree standing upright in a garden, a swing.

'Wait,' said Robert. He stepped close to her and put both

his palms over her eyes. 'Walk carefully,' he said. 'We're very near now.'

Fanny said nothing and kept walking, letting Robert's warm palms lead the way. The sensation was very strange, as if she was being guided by the beam of a lighthouse, but instead of a shaft of cold white light, two warm, yellow, slightly chapped circles walked before her. The wind swelled up and beat against her face, keen and cold. 'Careful,' said Robert. 'There's a step here. And then there's no more road.' Fanny nodded and felt the touch of the hands slip up on her face, then return.

The ground under her feet changed and became soft and shifty, under her heel it crumbled into sand and her shoe bent sideways at a dangerous angle. You could hear leaves rustling in the wind and the smell of plants became more pungent. The slope inclined steeply now and the hands led her with slow patience step after step. Then the ground grew level and Robert stopped. 'One moment,' he said. 'Don't open your eyes.' His hands descended to her shoulders and began turning her around, first slowly and then faster and faster. The darkness spun around her in dim red flashes and then all at once the hands let go. 'Look,' she heard Robert's voice, and opened her eyes.

At first all she saw were veins of light, light streaming like a river and tributaries upon tributaries of light flowing into it, the arteries of a metropolis, and the lights flooded and blinded her after the prolonged darkness so that she had to close her eyes again, but she immediately re-opened them. The fine lattice of lights whirled in front of her until little by little the lines of brilliance trickled into place and settled, clear and piercing against the night, before her eyes. 'Look,' said Robert very close to her ear and she looked and saw the lights break away from the huge glittering mosaic one after the other, like shooting stars, and fall one by one into the palm of her hand.

50

'First thing in the morning,' said the grim-faced nurse. 'No solids, no liquids.'

Fanny stood there pressed to the table for another minute, her mouth half-open. There were some more questions she wanted to ask, but they all slipped her mind. The nurse said firmly, 'Yes, who's next?' with an air meant to signal to Fanny that with her lingering she was taking up other people's time, and Fanny pulled away from the table and made room for a couple of elderly men squabbling over who would be first for his insulin injection.

'Have you got your card, then?' asked the nurse, but Fanny, although she was walking away slowly, did not hear the old man's reply. This matter involved so much unpleasantness. First, the embarrassing request to her family practitioner, who had given her an amazed glance through the lenses of her glasses. She had been treating Fanny for fifteen years and it was obvious that she had not expected such an application. After a moment she realized that she was staring at Fanny, swallowed what was on the tip of her tongue and returned her gaze to Fanny's file, which lay open in front of her. 'Actually you should have got this referral from your gynaecologist,' she said, 'but I'll give it to you anyway.' She scribbled a few words on the form. You could see that the whole matter was causing her great discomfort, even, so it seemed to Fanny, some disappointment. Then, surprisingly, she raised her eyes from the paperwork and asked Fanny, 'And how's Egon Bruck? I know him from back home, you know. His brother was a well-known paediatrician in Berlin.' From back home, thought Fanny, she too. Suddenly she realized how numerous were the threads entangled around her, weaving her backwards, into the past, and that Dr Schuster was one of them. It was no accident that she had chosen her, when the other GP at the clinic had the reputation of being the better doctor. And suddenly she was very tired of it all and she said curtly, 'I don't know. I've left the firm.' Dr Schuster gave her an even more astonished look and Fanny stood up and took her referral note and said, 'Thank you very much, goodbye' and turned around and walked to the door, leaving Dr Schuster staring at her back. Before she had time to get out the doctor called after her, 'You know, Miss Fischer, as of next week I'm not going to be here any more. There's going to be a new GP, Dr Oren.' Fanny turned around, amazed in her turn. 'I'm retiring next week,' said Dr Schuster. 'Sixty-two is quite enough. As it is I already had all these young doctors breathing down my neck. I'm sick of hearing them whisper in the corridor when I pass by.' Fanny nodded, still too surprised to make a proper response. Dr Schuster was for her one of the fixtures of the health centre, even, she realized, of her life. But after a moment she recovered, went back and shook Dr Schuster's hand. 'I hope you enjoy your freedom, Doctor,' she said. 'Certainly,' said the doctor. 'Now I have a new job: babysitting for my daughter's children. Up till now I had an excuse, but not any more.' 'I'm sure you'll do it gladly,' said Fanny. The doctor smiled and suddenly she looked human and very tired. 'The truth is, that's what I want to do,' she admitted, 'but I can't tell this to my daughter. It should sound as if I'm coming with a certain reluctance, so she'll pressure me to help.' Fanny laughed. 'You too –' the doctor started to say and immediately checked herself. 'So goodbye. *Auf Wiedersehen*,' she said and shook Fanny's hand again and after a moment's pause added, 'and good luck,' and her voice, hoarse with cigarettes, expressed what she could not say before. 'Goodbye,' said Fanny, and she too did what she wouldn't have done a moment earlier, before she knew that Dr Schuster was retiring, and reverted to her mother tongue and said, '*Auf Wiedersehen*.' The door creaked to a close behind her and Bella, the clinic secretary who was passing by in the corridor, said to the clerk who was walking with her, 'We must oil the hinges of this door. We'd better do it before the new doctor arrives, or he might think we're all as creaky as Dr Schuster,' and the clerk burst into obedient laughter.

The old pain, the pain of parting, assaulted Fanny again at full strength, until she almost stopped in the middle of the stairs. Now she saw with great clarity why she had not until now torn the fine mesh of threads that tied her to her old world. This divorce was too painful, too frightening, like demanding of a foetus to tear the umbilical cord supplying it with food and oxygen. But now she had to do it. Now that she had another thread, free from the old tangle, even if it was still too thin for her to be sure of its existence. Now that she had something to lose. Perhaps.

When she walked out of the clinic the strong glare hurt her eyes, and she rummaged in her bag although she knew the sunglasses would not be there, and indeed they weren't. She leaned against the low stone wall of the building, waiting for her eyes to get used to the brightness. The creeper branches scratched her cheek lightly. People came and went on the footpath, and Fanny, in a sudden burst of panic, began searching for the scrap of paper with the address that the nurse had given her, and when she found it and calmed down she thought once more about Dr Schuster, and about the old melody that the doctor was a part of and that still trailed behind her everywhere, refusing to let go, and wondered whether the fact that she sang it every night on stage would help her uproot it, like some kind of exorcism, or whether it was the other way around, and so she stood for a few minutes leaning against the fence, humming absent-mindedly in a low voice, padam . . . padam . . . padam.

On her way back to the bus stop she remembered that Robert wouldn't be home when she returned. He'd gone to see Albaz at the club – squeezing your last pay cheque out of him was harder than extracting one of his teeth, he had said, laughing, and now she remembered that he also said he would be held up in Jaffa, because Albaz, as always when a contract was about to end, had invited him for lunch. 'If it's a Romanian grill he just wants to take a few days off your salary, because of the holidays or God knows what, but if it's a fish restaurant you can forget about the flight back,' he explained, the freckles dancing on his face, and suddenly, for one jolting moment, she thought that she was actually hearing him talk, that she was hearing his particular intonation right next to her ear, and she turned around quickly, but it wasn't him, but a middle-aged American who passed by her arm in arm with his companion, both of them in flowery Bermuda shorts and with cameras hanging from their necks. She slowly turned her head back and stared into the gaping jaws of the afternoon. There was nothing, not one single thing she could think of, that she wanted to do with the time. The heat became oppressive, and for a minute she felt unwell and wanted to lean back against the wall, but on this side of the street there was only the barbed-wire fence of a car park. She looked again at the receding backs of the American couple, at the florid Hawaiian holiday shirts, at the woman's hand, which pointed, laden with rings, at something across the street, and suddenly she didn't want to go back home, to the empty flat, suddenly she didn't want to move at all from where she stood, as if by remaining there, half-way between the clinic and the bus stop, she could make everything else stay where it was, everything would remain just as it was now, and both of them would be frozen in time in the exact position they held now, like in a fairytale, he leaning forward over the table at the club, his hand extended towards the ashtray and the cigarette burning between his fingers, and she standing on the street, her foot pointed forward in the direction of the bus stop she would never reach, everything would stay just as it was for ever and ever, captured in this picture which no one could break away from, and the foot would never complete the step it had begun, the cigarette ash would never never be knocked off, he would never go away.

51

It was two o'clock in the afternoon and the waiting room was crowded with dozens of women. So many women want to know if they're pregnant, Fanny thought, and then she told herself: Why not? It's a big city, what are you so surprised about? It was the hottest hour of the day and in the small crammed room the heat was irritating and exhausting. The mood of the women in the room did nothing to cool down the atmosphere. 'Why are they always late?' a young woman with frizzy red hair, vigorously chewing on a piece of gum, demanded to know. 'I don't see why they can't bring out the results the moment they're ready, instead of sticking us here for hours in this heat.' 'They always tell you to come at two and then let you wait till three,' a heavy, dark-haired woman seconded her, who to Fanny's joy looked even older than herself. The woman held by the hand a girl of about three, whose nose dripped unmolested. 'It's the Health Service, what do you expect?' a third woman joined the chorus, slender and very well groomed, with thin lips and the narrow beak of a bird of prey. 'Every time I swear I'll never be seen in this place again.' 'What do you want, lady, that's nature,' the large woman said and everybody burst out laughing, except for the well-groomed one, who twisted her mouth in a grimace of disgust, as if to indicate that this wasn't what she had meant, but she didn't say anything. Most of the women, so it seemed to Fanny, had visited this place before, and some of them seemed so familiar with it as to be indifferent both to the place and to the news it might bring them. Only two or three, the youngest ones, girls almost, leaned silently against the walls, almost as pale, and didn't take part in the general conversation. They didn't even seem to hear it.

'Don't you worry, honey,' the dark-haired woman, who was apparently a veteran of the place, suddenly turned to one of the wan girls next to the receptionist's desk. 'The committee will pass you in no time. Today there's no fooling around, whoever's not married gets approved automatically.' The girl didn't answer. Her hand on the counter tightened until it lost its natural colour. 'Look at her quaking,' the redhead said on a note somewhere betweeen commiseration and scorn. 'You know how many committees I've gone through? Five, sweetheart, five, believe it or not. Last time the doctor told me,' she launched into a mock imitation of an Anglo-Saxon accent, '"Is that you again, Ben-Chemo? Soon we'll have to build a special ward just to take care of your abortions." "Go on, build it, Dr Price," I told him, right to his face, "build it, it will do you good. Look how many *schwartzes* I'm saving you. A clear profit." He almost fainted, I'm telling you,' she concluded triumphantly. 'Didn't think I'd let him have it like that. And don't you worry either,' she remembered the pale girl again, 'they'll give you one look and they'll pass you just like that,' and she snapped her fingers to show how easily they'd pass her through. Suddenly the girl raised her head. 'Leave me alone,' she said in a low but clear voice. 'I didn't ask you for anything. Just leave me alone,' and her voice again faded and died down, so that the last words were barely audible.

'Did you see that?' the redhead turned to her audience. 'You try to help her and she spits right in your face. Go ahead and try to do somebody a favour . . .' The young girl's head rose again, and it was evident that she meant to give as good as she got even if she dropped in her tracks, but at that moment the nurse came in holding a stack of papers and the women's attention was diverted from the antagonists to the folded sheets of paper. Everyone pressed forward and tried to get as close as they could to the desk. Their eyes narrowed in an effort to read from afar and upside down the name written on the upper sheet. 'One minute, one minute, girls,' the nurse tried a bantering tone, 'there's no need to push, it won't do you any good, in any case I'm going to read them in order. You don't want to take someone else's result just to be first in line, do you?' 'Maybe I should, with me it's always yes for sure, dammit,' quipped the fat black-haired woman, who was apparently quite certain of her result and unimpressed by the whole process. The young girl next to the desk was pushed against the wooden surface by the women behind her and looked as if she was going to faint at any minute. Girls, the word had a familiar ring. When had she last heard it? thought Fanny and recalled the beauty instructress. It seemed that whenever more than three women were gathered together, they collectively regressed in age. No, that wasn't it, she said to herself while the nurse read out the names in a monotonous voice and hand after hand was extended to snatch its sheet of paper: Franko, Sofer, Goren, Biankoff. It wasn't the number that counted but the situation: whenever they needed something, whenever they were rounded up in a herd to await the grace of some power that be, then their status changed as well and from adult, mature women, independent in opinion and deed, they turned into a rabble of very young girls, obeying the authority of a strong hand. Did men crowding around a desk, at the Unemployment Office for example, undergo such a transformation? Fanny asked herself, and suddenly she heard her name, called out loudly and with a note of impatience which suggested that this wasn't the first time it had been announced: 'Fischer. Is there a Fischer here?' 'Yes, I am,' she replied in a louder-than-usual voice that betrayed the signs of hysteria. All at once she became one of the herd, and the only instinct which governed her was the wish to obey quickly so that her sheet of paper wouldn't be returned to the bottom of the stack and perhaps taken away from her as punishment for her inattention. 'This one's not too keen on getting her test back,' the redhead remarked, and surveyed

363

Fanny from top to bottom with an impudent gaze. She might perhaps have said something else, but the monotonous voice resumed reading out the names and she let Fanny go and again focused on the nurse's white uniform.

Fanny slipped through the door like a thief, tightly clutching the white sheet of paper folded in two. Interestingly enough, none of the women, not even those who behaved as if they couldn't care less about the result, had opened the paper inside the room. They all went out holding the printed sheet in their hand just as they had received it, folded and clumsily stapled. Like animals looking for a corner to be alone in, thought Fanny, and looked around to find a quiet place of her own. Further down the street she saw the tops of a few tall trees and remembered that when she had passed that way on the bus she had seen a small park. Although the park was quite far off and she would have to wait a few minutes before opening the paper, or perhaps for that very reason, she went there, and only after she had sat on a secluded bench at the edge of the park, which in any case was almost completely empty at this hot afternoon hour, and after she had taken a deep breath and looked at the treetops gilded by the fiercely orange three-o'clock sun, she had nowhere left to run to and she unfolded the sheet of paper. On the page, apart from her name and the official stamp of the Health Service, there was, hastily scribbled in large inky letters, only a single word – 'positive'.

Fanny leaned against the wooden back of the bench and looked straight ahead. The silhouettes of the trees with the sun behind them, like the paper silhouettes of a magic lantern, danced before her eyes, and she couldn't think of anything and just let the sun-flecks quiver before her and inhaled the warm, pleasant smell of grass and flowers which had absorbed the sun for almost an entire day. A light breeze stole into the park, caressed her face and vanished. When the wind died down, the smell of mowed grass smell filled her nostrils and she stretched her legs and laid her head on the back of the bench and closed her eyes. Everything was very quiet and only the hum of bees was heard, and the chirping of a few solitary birds who failed to keep silent during the noonday rest. She remained like that for a long time, immobile, letting the heavy heat sink down on her like a blanket and envelop her in the afternoon smells of the park and its sounds, until the press of the sun's rays became too strong and her cheeks began to burn. She slowly sat up on the bench.

'Mummy, look, the auntie's woken up,' she suddenly heard the voice of a child. When she looked in the direction of the voice she saw a small boy, about five years old, trying to escape the grip of his mother, who was trying to hush him. 'Look, she's woken up. Why is she sleeping here, doesn't she have a bed at home?' 'Quiet, Ido,' the embarrassed mother scolded the child. Her face was flushed and she endeavoured not to look in Fanny's direction. But Fanny was not offended at all. She smiled at the child. 'I do have one, but not as comfortable,' she told him. And then she remembered she had some sweets in her purse, which she had taken with her in the morning because she hadn't been able to eat anything and was afraid she might faint. 'Would you like some toffee?' she asked, and rummaged through her bag to find it, but then she saw the mother's face grow even redder, she was probably afraid of what might be found in the handbag of someone who slept on benches in public parks – diseases, maybe – and she murmured, 'Thank you, there's no need,' and snatched the child's arm and marched him quickly down the path towards the exit. 'How many times have I told you not to speak to strange people in the park,' Fanny heard her reprimand the child after they had disappeared behind the screen of bushes, and thought regretfully to herself that it was a pity children were forbidden to talk with strangers, and that she won't forbid hers to do so, only to go with them, and suddenly her breath was taken away when she realized what it was that she was thinking.

All that afternoon Fanny wandered about in complete abstraction. Part of the time she rode on the bus, staring at the windowpane with that focused look which is the sign of the totally confounded, and part of the time she wandered around on foot in different parts of the city – on Allenby, so it seemed to her, and near the fountain at Dizengoff Square, and along certain streets, familiar but unremembered, at the south end of town. All that time she tried to clutch at the tail end of some thought which throbbed somewhere inside her, but evaded her time and again just as she thought she was going to capture it. Finally she recognized that she did not really want to reach it, and at that moment her eye stumbled on something familiar and she pulled the bell and got off.

The evening fell grey on the playground. Miss Fanny sat on the edge of the sandbox and looked at the swings whose colours faded with the greying day. Her hand played absent-mindedly with the cool, damp sand, feeling its wet graininess, and she saw and didn't see the ground covered with a thin layer of earth and gravel, and the ladder bent in its middle as if seized with a sudden stomach-ache, a ladder that had paled in the sun from a leafy green to the yellowish hue of withered grass, stared with a kind of double vision at the merry-go-round whose colours had also faded until they became similar to each other, the yellow resembling the red which resembled the blue, and they were all peeling. In this double vision the merry-go-round was at the foreground of the picture, but the focus was not there, but further on, at some point behind it and behind the ladder and the swings and the slide, and the strange thing was that there, at that point precisely, it seemed to her that she could see herself sitting at the sandbox and looking at her.

52

Fanny walked alongside Robert in silence. She hated being in this big, crowded place which always gave her an empty feeling, perhaps because it was totally synthetic. A taste of plastic and glass filled her mouth every time she walked through the automatic doors and entered the huge airport lobby. She hated the tense efficiency of it, the purposeful step that always struck her as lost. She was always seized by a feeling of nervousness and alarm, always afraid that whomever she was accompanying would miss their flight, wouldn't find their ticket, would not be on the passenger list, would lose their luggage. And this time as well, absurdly, like some instinctive, irrepressible reaction, she was overtaken again by these same fears.

Robert put down his luggage at the end of one of the queues and they both waited silently till his turn came. The stewardess attached a green label to his suitcase and set it sailing on the black conveyor belt. Robert handed her his ticket and she reserved him a seat in the smoking section and attached his boarding pass, and that was all. So simple there was something insulting about it. They now had some time left before he had to go up to the departure lounge and they didn't know what to do with it, she didn't know how to excuse him from this moment, what to say, and a certain, very focused point in her hurt so much that she felt like a patient whose doctors had numbed a part of her body, but had forgotten to anaesthetise the main nerve. Suddenly, all at once, a large group of people invaded the area where they were standing, near the stairs leading to the departure lounge. It was a whole clan. The men wore clothes made of a strong, stiff fabric and dark caps, and the women had on flowery dresses they wore one on top of the other and colourful head scarves. Fanny guessed that they were Georgians or Kurds. They surrounded her and Robert on all sides, talking in loud guttural voices. The women made moaning sounds, apparently each time the coming flight was mentioned, and at a certain moment they all began to wail. 'Right,' said Robert. 'I'd better go upstairs. You shouldn't have come. There's nothing more depressing than airports. And you and I, that wasn't depressing, was it?' Because of the difference in their heights Fanny had to raise her face up to look at him, and this particular posture involved a great effort, which was required for her eyes not to be flooded by tears. 'Yes,' she said with difficulty. 'That is, no.' Robert laughed and the next moment he was receding up the stairs and his white shirt was blended into a multitude of others, and disappeared.

Mechanically she turned to go, and was already half-way to the exit when suddenly something in her broke free and she started to run, seized in sudden panic, through the crowd, struggling to get to the foot of the stairs from where she might still be able to make him out before he reached the second floor, suddenly she just had to see him, just one more time, simply had to find him at any cost, to identify among all those backs the back of the man she loved, but the crowd grew denser as the takeoff neared and it swept her along, spinning, whirling, gyrating in the farewell dance of the Georgian family, and by the time she reached the stairs there was no one to see but the old mother, for she, it turned out, was their passenger, climbing slowly, with difficulty, up the stairs, her legs quivering.

Outside it had begun to rain. The taxi driver was waiting for her by the entrance, Robert had insisted on paying him in advance for the trip back as well and for waiting at the airport. 'It won't take long,' he had told him, 'say what it's worth to you,' and insisted on paying the exorbitant price the man had quoted. Fanny hated his eyes fixed on her in the rear-view

368

mirror and the whoosh of the wipers on the front window, an incessant, monotonous hum that filled the interior of the car and reminded her that she was not alone, carried in this closed space through the gleaming rain-lashed streets with no refuge.

When they reached the corner of Ibn Gevirol and Arlozorov they got caught in the traffic and the cab began to crawl. Right in front of them a big blue rust-stained Ford Cortina slowly made its way, and Fanny felt that she couldn't look at it for even one more minute. The driver started grumbling under his moustache about the slow progress and about the hour, which was the worst time of day for driving in the city, and Fanny told him suddenly, 'You can let me off here.'

The driver gave her a surprised look in the mirror. 'It's all right, lady, I'll take you right to your door,' he said. His moustache had the same rusty hue as the stains on the Cortina. 'I want to get off here,' Fanny told him sharply and he shrugged and muttered, 'Whatever you say, lady,' and pulled over and stopped the car. She opened the door and got out, hearing him mumble behind her, Nuts, all these old Polish girls.

The rain came down incessantly, a uniform sheet of water. Mechanically she took out of her purse the headscarf she always kept there and covered her head. Within a few minutes the scarf was soaking wet, a useless rag. And the rain poured and poured. She walked with unseeing steps northwards in the direction of home, the rain lashing at her eyes. Her hair was soaked and its ends were dripping. She walked on and on. Water trickled over her face, her hands, her chest, water poured from her in rivers. Along the grey concrete wall of the new Shekem department store a row of impatient faces and umbrella tips looked out towards her, but did not see her. The street swallowed her, a woman in a wet dress, and she was swallowed in it, in the buildings, grey with rain, in the grey asphalt of the pavements, in the grey daylight. Even if they had stared at her she wouldn't have cared, but who looked at other people on a day like this, and at a woman of forty-two of all people, walking on the street crying, her head covered with a sodden scarf, and even as she walks and cries it seems she's only a part of this day, part of the air heavy with rain, of the slowly darkening evening.

53

When she rode to the club, at one o'clock in the morning, the streets were still damp, glistening with a black light. The lights of the houses passed by, clear and sparkling in the newly washed night air. In a strange way, which surprised her, she did not feel any sorrow or pain. Almost the opposite was true, as if a great weight had been lifted from her heart, and for the first time in a long while she could breathe freely.

It was only after she paid the driver and got out of the taxi, tripping with her usual clumsiness on the pavement while the driver poked out his head after her and muttered, 'Easy does it, lady. There's no rush,' and especially after she entered the club, that the heaviness descended on her again. It was a different kind of weight, but no less heavy. The vestibule blinded her with its barren neon light, and she hastened to cross it and walk past the hum of the audience and the tinkling of glasses and the waiters carrying their trays of potato chips to the small door of the dressing room. Still she managed, in spite of herself, to see on stage two new acrobats walking on one hand while tossing back and forth small phosphorescent balls. Their inverted faces were painted white and their lips smiled out of them in bright red. She had expected that, but nevertheless the sight was an additional blow, like a seal of finality. From the old gang no one was left but Gina and her and Mercedes, who had two days to go till the end of her contract. Annette and Jean-Pierre had left even before Robert, and Mackie and Reena had gone back to their flat in Hulon. Clearly nothing would be as it had been.

She slowly placed her bag on the table. The dressing room was empty, Gina wasn't there. It was the first time she hadn't found her in the room at this hour, removing her make-up with huge cotton wool balls, but she had neither the will nor the energy to wonder about it. She sat down heavily in front of the mirror and took the lipstick out of her bag and and placed it in a straight line with the other make-up she regularly kept in the room. Then, carefully, she bent over in the rickety chair and looked at herself in the mirror. Her face floated before her pale and insubstantial, like a fish in green aquarium water. She sighed and took up the tube of dark make-up and opened it. And then she heard steps and loud angry voices, and Albaz suddenly entered the room together with two unfamiliar men, whom because of the dim light it took her a minute to recognize as policemen.

'I'm telling you she doesn't know anything,' Albaz said in a loud, furious voice. This was the first time, Fanny realized, that she had ever heard him raise his voice, shout even, the first time she had seen him lose his temper. 'She didn't even know him. They only met here once or twice in the afternoon to practise.'

'And that's exactly what I want to ask her about,' said the shorter of the two officers, unruffled. Fanny saw the stripes on his shoulders but didn't know what they meant. 'I didn't say she had anything to do with it. I just want to ask her a few questions.'

'Questions, questions,' Albaz grumbled, 'I know you guys.' He spoke more quietly now. '*Y'allah*, ask her and have done with it. She has to be on stage in twenty minutes.'

The short policeman again turned to him and said calmly, 'We'll ask as many questions as we need to, my friend. The law doesn't go according to your show.'

Albaz's face flushed and for a moment Fanny was afraid he was going to blow his top, but he controlled himself. 'We'll settle accounts later,' he muttered, and the policeman answered him pleasantly, 'As you wish, my friend,' and turned to Fanny.

Now he looked at her attentively and his eyes widened with surprise. He had obviously expected something completely different. Or maybe it was Fanny's age which surprised him, for the tone of his voice changed when he addressed her.

'You're Fanny?' he asked, as if in doubt.

Fanny nodded.

'Do you know Albert Kuller?' he asked, and after a slight hesitation added, 'ma'am.'

Fanny tightened her eyebrows in an effort to remember whose name that was, for it did sound familiar to her, but she couldn't place it. 'The pianist, the pianist,' muttered Albaz impatiently. 'Ah,' said Fanny with relief and remembered where she knew the name from, from that afternoon when the pianist's friend had come to visit him and called to him in a whisper, Albert, Albert, from the door.

'Yes, of course,' she said. 'He plays with me. That is, he accompanies me when I sing,' she corrected herself.

'We know that,' the policeman said. 'I mean beyond that.'

'Beyond that?' asked Fanny, surprised. 'No, I've never met him outside the club.'

The policemen exchanged glances. Apparently they believed her because the first officer proceeded to ask, 'And at the club?'

'Look,' said Fanny, 'I don't even get the chance to talk to him when we're performing. I come straight here and change, and then I meet him on stage.'

The second policeman, the one who hadn't spoken up until then, stepped forward.

'And in the afternoon? Albaz already told us that you met a few times in the afternoon to rehearse?' he gestured backwards, to Albaz, as if to reinforce what he'd said.

Fanny hesitated. Then she thought there was no point in trying to conceal something she didn't even know the meaning of. 'Once somebody came to visit him here,' she said.

The man before her tensed, and tilted his head like a nervous bird. 'Well?' he demanded. 'Well, and then what?'

Fanny shrugged. 'I don't know,' she said apologetically. 'This man called him over and they went out into the corridor and talked for a few minutes. I couldn't hear what they were saying.'

Again the policemen exchanged glances. 'It must have been Zion, blast him,' the tall one mumbled uneasily and the short policeman smiled at him, the same expression of unassailable satisfaction on his round moon face.

The tall policeman looked like he had made a decision. 'Listen,' he said and bent even further towards her, 'this guy has got himself into serious trouble. Get me? Real trouble. If you're concealing even one detail, the smallest detail, you're getting into trouble with him. We're not joking here. Drugs are not a laughing matter. You understand?' Here he paused, as if waiting for an answer. Fanny, who didn't know what to say, nodded. 'So think carefully. Did anything else happen?' Fanny strained her memory, but the only thing she could recall was that the man had been unshaven, and she didn't think this detail could be of any use to the police, all the more so since they seemed to know the pianist's one-time visitor better than she did. She shook her head. 'No,' she said. 'Nothing that I can remember.'

'Think harder,' the policeman said and stared at her. 'Maybe you heard something else.' Fanny waited for a minute, since it was evident he expected her to do so, and then repeated, 'No. I couldn't hear anything. They left the room before they started talking.'

The two policemen looked at each other once more, apparently for the last time. 'All right,' the tall policeman said finally. 'That's all for now. But don't think that's the end of it,' he promised Albaz. 'We'll be back.' And he left the room, leaving the short policeman behind. The latter went over to Fanny and asked her for her personal details. 'It's only a formality, ma'am. We have to go by the law,' he said agreeably and opened his notebook and took down Fanny's full name, her ID number and her address. 'If we need you we'll call you,' he promised, closed his notebook, nodded to Albaz and left. Albaz was furious. 'Bastards,' he murmured. 'They're

374

gonna pay for this. It's not for nothing that I . . .' and then he cut himself short and fell silent. Suddenly he clutched his head with both hands. 'And the pianist. What do I do without a pianist?' he muttered. His eyes wandered around the room without focusing on anything in particular, the way a man looks whose real gaze is directed inwards, to the solution he's seeking, until they suddenly came to rest on Fanny. 'Can you play?' he demanded. 'Yes,' said Fanny with wonder, as if it had only just now occurred to her that she could. Albaz's shoulders relaxed in relief. 'So that's it. As of tonight you're also playing. You'll get more, of course,' he added hastily. Then he quickly looked her over and amended, 'not much more. I paid the pianist half of what I pay you,' and when he remembered the pianist his rage swelled up again and he added, 'the sonofa-bitch. Wasn't worth a penny,' and turned around and started walking quickly towards the door. Fanny remained planted in her tracks. 'But . . .' she called after him. She wanted to tell him that this wasn't a good idea, that in a performance like hers it wasn't right for her to be seated by the piano, that the way a singer stood on stage was crucial to the impression she made on her audience, but he didn't even turn to look at her. 'There's nothing to discuss. I need a pianist and that's it. And now that I think about it, there's no reason why I should pay two salaries when I can get both things from one person,' he declared without noticing the contradiction between what he said now and what he'd just said, and went out. Fanny was left alone. Shocked, her head whirling with this sudden unex-pected chain of events, she sat down, trying to make some sense out of them. After a while her thoughts grew calmer, and she remembered that she had to go on stage in a few minutes. Mechanically she turned to the mirror and saw her face looking at her, startlingly clear, and only then she realized that the room was flooded with a much stronger light than she was used to: during the conversation Albaz had turned on a switch unknown to her. And with this new clarity of her face her mind cleared up as well and she understood that Gina was right. She would sing in any kind of nightclub, and if they didn't let her sing she would accompany others on the piano, and when she could no longer play she would mop the floors. If things came to that, she, Fanny, would die standing up, like elephants and nightmoths, but she hoped that wouldn't be necessary. Yesterday, after Robert left, she felt like Adam in the story of creation: someone had come, given her life and gone away, leaving her all alone. But life remained in her. She understood that now. Gina was right. Life remained in her, in her body and within her body – in that tiny thing which did not even have a name yet. Life, of a certain sort, she heard Robert say and heard his short laugh, which was cut off by Albaz's nervous voice, 'Well come on, Fanny, get on with it, they're waiting for you.' She put on her lipstick with a few quick strokes and walked out.